The Language
of Spells

The Language of Spells

SARAH PAINTER

CARINA™

This edition is published by arrangement with Harlequin Books S.A. CARINA is a trademark of Harlequin Enterprises Limited, used under licence.

Published in Great Britain 2015
by CARINA, an imprint of Harlequin (UK) Limited,
Eton House, 18-24 Paradise Road,
Richmond, Surrey, TW9 1SR

© 2013 Sarah Painter

ISBN 978-0-263-91755-0

98-0515

Harlequin (UK) Limited's policy is to use papers that are natural, renewable and recyclable products and made from wood grown in sustainable forests. The logging and manufacturing processes conform to the legal environmental regulations of the country of origin.

Sarah Painter has worked as a freelance journalist, editor and blogger for the last thirteen years, while juggling amateur child-wrangling (aka motherhood) with her demanding internet-appreciation schedule (aka procrastination).

Born in Wales to a Scot and an Englishman (very nearly a 'three men walked into a bar' joke), she now lives in Scotland with her husband, two children and two cats. She loves the work of Joss Whedon, reading in bed, salt and vinegar crisps, and is the proud owner of a writing shed.

Sarah gives writing advice at www.novelicious.com and writes about craft, books and writing at www.sarah-painter.com.

For my mum and dad
for bringing me up with love, laughter and books.

For Holly and James for their all-round brilliance.

And for Dave. For everything.

PROLOGUE

The voices in the living room were getting louder. Suddenly the man's voice wasn't just loud, it was shouting. A big, frightening sound that sent Gwen out from under her quilt and into her sister's bed. Ruby was awake. Her eyes were shining in the light that came in under the door. 'It'll be over soon,' Ruby whispered.

'Who is it?' Gloria had at least two boyfriends at any time and an endless stream of people came to have their cards read. Gwen felt Ruby shrug.

Gloria's voice had risen. She sounded really angry. Gwen shrank down until the duvet covered most of her face.

There was a burst of noise as the shouting people moved into the hallway. 'Tell me a story,' Ruby said.

Gwen stretched her legs. She shut the angry voices out and thought for a moment. 'Once upon a time, there were two sisters, Rose Red and Snow White, and they were walking through a thick forest—'

'Not that one,' Ruby said. 'One with a prince. A really handsome prince. With loads of money.'

The front door slammed. 'My story does have a prince.' Annoyance broke through Gwen's fear. Ruby was always complaining.

'It has a bear,' Ruby said.

'That turns into a prince.'

The bedroom door opened. 'Girls?'

Gloria was framed in the doorway, her face hidden in shadow. 'You have to get up.'

'I'm tired,' Ruby said.

'I know, I'm sorry.' Gloria didn't sound sorry. She never did. 'We're moving on. Get your things together. Don't leave anything—'

'Because we don't look back,' Gwen and Ruby joined in. 'We know.'

CHAPTER 1

Gwen Harper had been brought up in the sure knowledge that everything in life came as a pair. Every coin had two sides, every person had an angel and a devil lurking inside, and every living thing was busy dying. Gwen couldn't imagine a good side to returning to Pendleford but, since she had no choice in the matter, she hoped that Gloria had been right about all that 'light and dark' business. She crested the hill and Pendleford spread out beneath her. The town was caught in a basin of land as if cupped by giant green hands, and the yellow stonework glowed softly in the winter sunshine. The dark river cutting through the centre was like a worm in an apple.

Gwen passed a sign that had 'Pendleford: Historic Market Town' in smart black lettering and then a smaller yellow one that said 'Britain in Bloom'. Slung in front of this was a collection of broken-looking dolls, their long hair tied together in a big knot. Gwen slowed down to take a closer look at the creepy faces with their dead eyes and pink Cupid's bow mouths.

She shuddered, trying not to think about broken things, dead things, or the icy water of the river. Her Nissan Vanette made a crunching engine noise which she decided to interpret as sympathetic nerves. She patted Nanette's dashboard reassuringly. 'Don't worry. We won't be staying.' Gwen glanced at the legal documents on the passenger seat that said otherwise but, before she could start worrying in earnest, her thoughts were derailed by the sight of Pendleford. The town looked eerily the same as it had when she'd left thirteen years ago.

Gwen took a couple of deep breaths and tried to calm her racing heart. There was no need to panic. Her mother was on the other side of the world and Pendleford was a full eight miles away from Bath and her exasperating sister. Not even Ruby could shout over that distance.

Navigating her way out of the town centre, past rows of Edwardian villas with tasteful 'bed and breakfast' signs, Gwen turned to logic. She was going to spend one night in her great-aunt Iris's house. Take a bath. Get one decent night's sleep before she headed to the solicitor's office in the morning and found a way around the stupid 'can't sell for six months' clause. Then she'd be out of Pendleford. Again.

Gwen carried on with the pep talk as she drove. She had a dodgy moment when she thought she saw Cam and nearly drove up onto the pavement. It was a tall man with messy dark hair, but as soon as she passed him and looked in the rear-view mirror, her heart in her mouth, she saw that it wasn't him at all. Cameron Laing was long gone. Probably in London. Or prison.

The big houses gave way to row upon row of traditional stone cottages and a town hall with a triangle of grass outside. A man in head-to-toe tweed was changing parish notices on the board outside. Pendleford's surface was as pretty and as tame as she remembered. If it hadn't been for the daily taunting at school and a very bad memory that began with the river and ended at the local police station, then perhaps she wouldn't have hated the place quite as much.

At the very edge of town, there was a row of box-type houses. Council – or more likely ex-council – houses, with neat gardens and freshly painted windows that did nothing to hide the brown pebbledash and the nineteen-sixties municipal architecture. Then the town petered out into farmland and Gwen almost missed the turning for Iris's road; the small wooden sign was weathered and only the word 'End' legible. After four hundred yards up a single track road, Gwen turned a corner and the house came into view. Stone-built, square and bigger than she expected. Gwen got out of the car and pulled on her fleece. The sky was pearl-grey and the weak November sun drooped in the east. It was quiet. 'Too quiet,' she said aloud, trying to make herself laugh. It didn't work.

Gwen hesitated at the front gate, her body rebelling against setting foot inside the boundary of the property. Which was ridiculous. She was homeless and she'd been given a house. It was crazy to be anything except insanely grateful. *Crazy.*

The front door had once been dark green, but was sorely in need of a paint job. To her left, fields stretched out to the horizon and a flock of black birds swooped down to the frozen earth.

Gwen spent five minutes attempting to unlock the door before realising it was already open. The porch was cleanly swept and a neat pile of mail sat on the windowsill.

The inner door opened and a woman wearing narrow black trousers and a yellow blouse looked at her in surprise. 'Yes?'

'Um, is this End House?'

'Yes.' The woman's pale blonde hair was cut in layers and she shook her head slightly to flick her fringe away from her eyes.

'This is my great-aunt's house. Um. That is, I think this might be my house.'

The woman's face changed and what could charitably be described as a smile appeared. It displayed a disturbing number of teeth. They were small and white, like baby teeth; alarming in an adult-sized mouth. 'You're Gwen Harper. I wasn't expecting you yet.' She took a step back. 'I'm not ready for you, but I suppose you'd better come in.'

'Thanks.' Gwen stepped over the threshold. The hall was large and square, floored in red quarry tiles. The walls were whitewashed, but patterned with tiny black cracks, like something dark was trying to break through.

'I'll show you around.' The woman turned to go, but Gwen stopped her.

'I'm sorry, but . . . Who are you?'

'Oh, bless you. I'm Lily Thomas. I've been helping out your poor auntie for years.'

'Helping?'

'Cleaning and cooking, that kind of thing.' Lily frowned at Gwen. 'She was very old, you know.'

Gwen looked at the woman's frosted-pink fingernails. They didn't look like they'd scrubbed anything in their lives.

The woman followed her gaze. 'Falsies.' She waggled them. 'Aren't they brilliant?'

The doors off the hallway were all shut, but the staircase of polished dark wood curved invitingly and Gwen took an involuntary step towards it.

'She needed help with all kinds of things towards the end, bless her.'

Lily's voice seemed to be coming from far away and Gwen could hear a rushing in her ears. I must be holding my breath, she thought. Good way to faint. She made herself take a lungful of air, but the rushing continued and the stairs seemed to be glowing just for her. She walked towards the bottom step, confused when yellow silk appeared in her vision, eclipsing the lovely warm wood. It was Lily, barring her way.

'The upstairs isn't ready. I've not had a chance to clean. I wasn't expecting you—' Lily hesitated. 'Not yet, I mean. I wasn't told—'

'That's okay.' Gwen stepped around Lily and took the stairs at a jog.

Weird, she decided, already on the landing. The door on her right was wide open, like someone had come out in a hurry. Through the gap she saw a double bed with a flowered wash bag lying on the quilt.

Lily appeared behind her, puffing slightly. 'It's a mess. I haven't had a chance—'

'Don't worry.' Gwen opened the other doors from the landing and discovered a small bedroom with a single bed and a desk underneath the window and another double with a brass bedstead suffocated by layers of blankets and a patchwork quilt.

'Let me show you the kitchen,' Lily said firmly.

Gwen allowed Lily to usher her back down the stairs and into a long room lined with 1950s cream cabinets with pale green trim and lemon Formica worktops. A red enamel coffee pot and an electric kettle were the only things visible on the spotlessly tidy work surface. A small table with two chairs tucked in was at the end and the small window above the stainless-steel sink was cracked.

'What's through there?' Gwen gestured to the door behind the table.

'That's the pantry. It's very small.' Lily smiled again. 'Go and take a look at the garden. I'll make us a nice cup of tea.'

'Right.' Gwen left Lily moving comfortably around the kitchen and walked into the cold, dead air. *Place must be well sheltered; there's no wind at all.* The garden was separated from the fields by a stone wall on one side and a line of trees at the bottom. Gwen identified rhododendrons in the corner, a giant spreading conifer thick with cones, holly, ash and hornbeam. A few fruit trees were dotted about the lawn. A lot of work, she found herself thinking. Around the corner was an untended vegetable plot. It had been cared for at one time, though, that was easy to see. Stone paths led along rows and the edges were defined with old red bricks. There were willow wigwams for peas or beans and fruit canes, but one was half pulled down by a mutant rhubarb that had clearly got ideas above its station.

The front garden offered more grass, many bushes, and wide borders filled with the seed heads and brown plants of a dead summer.

The crisp evening air cleared Gwen's mind. What was Lily Thomas doing in her aunt's house? The way she seemed so at home wasn't that odd – especially if she'd been working for Iris for years – but why on earth was she here now? She hesitated, wondering whether she was overreacting, when some bundles of greenery caught her eye. Half-tucked behind the water butt, three tied-together collections of foliage. She recognised branches of ash and broom, and remembered her mother fixing something similar above the door to their flat; to ward off malignant forces, she'd said. Gwen dropped the bundle as if it were hot, and went back inside.

Lily was squeezing a tea bag against the side of a mug as if it had personally offended her.

Gwen sat down at the table, feeling slightly dazed.

'I've made you a casserole but it's down at my house. I'll bring it up later.'

'That's very kind,' Gwen said, 'but I'm not sure—'

'No need to thank me. Least I can do for Iris's niece.'

'Great-niece.'

'Right.' Lily popped open the lid on a plastic tub and arranged slices of fruitcake on a plate. 'So, are you from the area?'

'Not really.' It was true. They'd lived in Pendleford for three years, but had moved around a lot before that. Gwen had never really felt like she was 'from' anywhere.

Lily frowned. 'Somerset?'

Gwen shook her head.

'Where do you live?' Lily pressed on.

'I've been in Leeds for the last six months.' Gwen had a rule for dealing with people: Never give away more than strictly necessary.

'But where do you come from? Originally.' Lily's inquisitive tone reminded Gwen of every bitchy queen bee at every new school she'd ever had to start. 'We moved around quite a bit.'

'Oh you poor thing,' Lily pulled a face. 'I wouldn't have liked that.'

'It was fine,' Gwen said automatically.

'I didn't see you at the funeral,' Lily said. 'Were you close to Iris?'

'No.' Gwen didn't feel like explaining that she'd barely known her great-aunt and had no idea why on earth she'd been given her house. She tried to gain control of the conversation. 'Do you live in Pendleford?'

Lily nodded. 'Just on the corner. I'm your nearest neighbour.'

Gwen opened her mouth to say that she wouldn't be staying, but Lily was still talking, listing names of neighbours that Gwen knew she would instantly forget even if she were paying proper attention.

Lily stopped listing and said, 'You look tired out, if you don't mind my saying.'

Gwen felt a yawn coming on. She put a hand to her mouth and then apologised. 'This is all quite sudden.'

Lily shook her head. 'I wouldn't say that. She'd been poorly for ages.' She took a generous bite of cake before adding, 'Bless her,' through a mouthful of crumbs.

'Why are you...?' Gwen stopped. 'I mean, did you have some sort of contract with my aunt? For this, I mean.' She waved a hand, taking in the freshly cleaned kitchen, the tea, her presence.

'A contract?' Lily laughed, a bizarre high-pitched laugh. 'We didn't need anything like that. She was more like a sister – well...' she wrinkled her nose '...a mother – to me than an employer. I know she'd want me to keep an eye on the place. Welcome you properly.' She paused, giving Gwen an appraising look. 'I'd be very happy to stay on and clean for you, too.'

So she was angling for a job. Fair enough. 'I'm terribly sorry, but I'm not sure what I'm doing about the house yet. And even if I did stay, I wouldn't be able to afford to pay for cleaning.'

Lily shrugged. 'No problem. Just offering.' She pushed back her chair. 'I'll let you get settled in and pop back later with that casserole.'

'Well. . .' Gwen thought about navigating the winding road back to the nearest shop and realised how tired she felt. Plus, she'd been surviving on cheap takeaways and supermarket sandwiches; a home-cooked meal sounded wonderful. 'That would be lovely, thank you very much. If it's not too much trouble.'

'We're neighbours now. That's what it's like around here.'

Gwen opened her mouth to say she wouldn't be staying, but yawned instead.

After Lily left, Gwen took her tea and wandered through the house, opening doors and getting her bearings. There were two large front rooms, both with big bay windows. One was a living room, complete with overstuffed brocade sofa and a riotous carpet of flowers, vines and leaves. The vast dining room looked forlorn and unloved by comparison. An oak dining table with twisted spindle legs and six chairs was marooned in an otherwise bare room and covered in a thick layer of dust.

Behind the kitchen there was a downstairs bathroom, tiled in black and white and with what was probably the original washbasin and tub. A small back bedroom completed the downstairs, with three bedrooms upstairs.

Big house, she thought, looking around at the triple wardrobe, dressing table and chest of drawers that fitted comfortably in the master bedroom. Something was missing, though. The flowered wash bag. Either she was imagining things or Lily Thomas had swiped it while she was in the garden. Odd.

Gwen got her suitcase from the van and lugged it upstairs. She was bone-tired. She wanted to run a bath and get clean. She'd been making do all week – taking her toothbrush and flannel into public bathrooms and splashing out for a shower at a motorway service station just the once. But she was so tired. So tired that she actually felt sick.

Although that could be nerves. Being in the house felt so wrong. Illicit. Growing up with her free-spirited mother, Gloria, there had only been one rule: stay away from Great-Aunt Iris. Her mother had described Iris as 'evil', and since she herself was known around town as 'Crazy Gloria', Gwen had seen no reason to disobey her. She'd always figured that Iris didn't want to know them, either. The thought gave her a jolt of guilt.

Gwen yawned again and lay on the bed, meaning to test it for just a moment. It was gloriously comfortable and after five nights on a camping mat it felt like heaven. She pulled the quilt over herself and closed her eyes. *Just for five minutes.*

Gwen woke up disorientated and very hot. She executed an ungainly quilt-wrestle and went downstairs. The curtains had been drawn and a casserole dish sat warming in the oven. Lily had clearly been and gone. Gwen ignored the creepy feeling that gave her. She was being a suspicious modern urbanite; things were different in the country. People obviously still looked out for each other. Gwen still felt disorientated from her nap. The week of sleeping badly and the weirdness of the situation had caught up with her and she couldn't summon up enthusiasm for food. Gwen turned off the oven and went back to bed. Tomorrow she would visit the legal people and straighten out the will. If she could sell the place straight away, she'd have the deposit to rent a flat and could get her business back on its feet. The money would save her life and she'd be duly grateful to Iris. She just wasn't going to live in Pendleford. Not even for six months.

She dragged herself back up the stairs, every step an effort, and by the time she'd unpacked her overnight bag, she was yawning so long and so hard it was difficult to brush her teeth.

Some time later, she sat bolt upright. The room was pitch-black and her eyes strained with the effort of trying to see. Her heart was thudding as she struggled to work out what had woken her. A scratching noise almost made her cry out until it happened again and she realised it was the sound of a tree branch against glass. She forced herself to breathe deeply, to snuggle back down into the bed. Silence. No traffic, no sirens, no late-night revellers vomiting or fighting outside her window. It was probably the quiet that had spooked her. And the scratching. She clicked on the bedside lamp and climbed out of bed. The window was open and a brisk stream of night air flowed inside. Gwen swallowed. She had closed that window earlier. She had definitely closed it. Forcing herself forward, Gwen approached the window, feeling the cool air on her bare arms. She pushed the window open further and leaned out. The moon was riding high in the clear sky. She couldn't see the offending branch, but there was plenty of greenery along the side of the house. She shut the window and latched it before getting back into bed and falling instantly asleep.

The next day, Gwen awoke to the sound of hammering on wood. She stumbled downstairs, trying to shake off the fug of sleep.

Her sister's voice cut through two doors like a razor blade through trifle. 'Gwen? I can see your van!'

Gwen opened the door and stepped smartly back into the hall, the full force of Ruby being too much to take in a confined space.

'Oh for goodness' sake. You were still in bed.' Ruby shrugged off her jacket and put down her leather handbag. 'You can't open the door like that. I could've been anyone.'

'Not really.' Gwen turned and headed back up the stairs. 'Put the kettle on.' She had to be dressed to deal with Ruby.

After hastily pulling on jeans, a shirt and hoodie, she found Ruby in the kitchen.

'This place is a museum.' Ruby frowned at the painted walls. 'It's not even tiled.'

'I like it,' Gwen surprised herself by saying.

'Really?' Ruby raised her eyebrows. She looked around. 'I suppose you could knock through and make a proper family kitchen.' She wandered through to the dining room next door, then hastily returned. 'Did you know the ceiling's sagging in there? It looks like it's about to come down.'

Gwen concentrated on pouring hot water onto tea bags.

Ruby opened some cabinets, ran a finger along the shelves. 'She was very clean, anyway.'

'She's got a cleaner. Or a housekeeper. I'm not sure of the difference.'

'Fancy.'

'I think she needed someone at the end. I wish we'd known.'

'It's not our fault,' Ruby said robustly. 'She could've called.'

'She might not have known you lived in Bath.' *What an awful thought. Iris all alone out here, her great-niece just down the road.*

Ruby shrugged. Then she said, 'It's weird that she left you the house, though.'

'I know.' Gwen said, feeling awkward.

'She always liked you the best.'

'I don't know about that,' Gwen said. 'I actually can't remember her at all. It's a bit odd.' Which was an understatement. Ever since getting the letter from Laing & Sons, she'd been thinking about Iris and finding a strange blank, like typed words snowed over with Tippex.

'God, do you remember that chicken she had?' Ruby paused, hand on hip and a faraway expression on her face.

Gwen shook her head.

'Oh, you do. It was like her pet or something. You nearly stood on it, remember? Iris went mental, but it wasn't your fault. I mean, who keeps a chicken in the house? Bloody disgusting.'

'I don't remember.' Gwen closed her eyes. A wave of nausea, like she was riding a roller coaster, swooped through her stomach and she opened her eyes again.

'You must,' Ruby was saying. 'You cried all the way home and Gloria took us for ice cream. She never did that. You must remember.'

Gwen's mouth filled with saliva. She tasted strawberry at the back of her throat and almost gagged. 'I remember the ice cream. Just not Iris. Not the house.' She gestured around. 'I don't remember any of this. Not at all.' *And that couldn't be right.*

'Well, we only came here once or twice. And you were young.'

'Not that young. Thirteen, maybe?' Gwen had a horrible feeling she knew why there was a blank in her memory. She'd probably asked too many questions and Gloria had solved the problem with a memory charm. Charms and hexes and simple casting were the kinds of thing Gloria had taught Gwen while other mothers were showing their kids how to bake fairy cakes.

Ruby shrugged. 'Well, you're not missing much. Apart from the chicken, it was pretty boring. Gloria and Iris talking and pretending they weren't arguing.'

'I don't remember,' Gwen said again, hating that she sounded so forlorn, hating that being back in Pendleford was reminding her of all the things she'd tried so hard to forget.

'I don't care,' Ruby said robustly. 'It's all in the past. Gloria's escaped to Oz and Great-Aunt Iris is dead; what does any of it matter?'

Gwen pulled a face. 'I just feel guilty. I don't deserve this place. I hardly knew the woman.'

'Well, according to Gloria, we were better off without her.'

'I guess.' Gwen handed her a mug, then sat down at the table to sip from her own.

'It's not our fault,' Ruby said. 'Gloria's the one who cut contact. We were just kids.'

They had been forbidden from having anything to do with Iris. In fact, sitting in her house was probably still a capital offence. Whether she had passed on or not. Gwen was just going to ask Ruby if she had any idea what had caused the schism between Gloria and Iris, when Ruby said, 'Look, she was a grown woman with her own friends and family and life. We weren't part of it, through no fault of our own, but that doesn't mean we missed out or that she missed out.' She looked around the kitchen again. 'It doesn't mean anything.'

'Then why leave me her house?'

Ruby frowned. 'How the hell should I know? Dementia?'

'That's not funny,' Gwen said. After a moment, she added, 'She sent me birthday cards.'

'Did she? When?'

'Every year after I turned thirteen. After we stopped visiting.'

Ruby opened her eyes wide. 'That's weird. What did she write?'

'Nothing. Just her name. Just her initial, actually. I used to hide them from Gloria. Did she—'

'No. Nothing.' Ruby shook her head. 'She never sent me anything. Didn't give me a house, either. It's not fair.'

Gwen thought that Ruby was only half-joking. 'Good thing you married rich.'

Ruby looked around. 'Can you imagine what David would do to this place?'

Gwen shuddered. David was a good man, but he was an architect and didn't seem able to appreciate a house unless it had weirdly big windows or a glass atrium in the middle or a roof made out of turf.

'Well…' Ruby had stopped assessing the house and focused on Gwen. It was disconcerting. 'I see you're still dressing like an art student. People will think you're mad.'

'I look fine,' Gwen said. 'For my job, this is normal.'

Ruby pulled a face. 'If you say so.'

Gwen thought about telling Ruby about the people she knew from the art fair circuit. Next to Bonkers Brenda, who crocheted bikinis and embroidered them with little faces, and often wore her creations on the outside of her clothes, she was positively conformist.

After a moment of silence, Ruby said, 'Are we going to pretend the last year didn't happen?'

Gwen realised that she didn't have the energy for a showdown with Ruby. The stress of the last few weeks and the oddness of being back in Pendleford crowded everything else out. 'I really don't want to argue. I'm too freaked out by all this.'

'Fine with me,' Ruby said. She pursed her lips. 'It's unseemly.'

Gwen laughed. 'Unseemly?'

'And it's bad for my chi.'

Gwen stopped laughing.

'I've had a course of colonics and I don't want to retox.' Ruby spoke as if expecting a medal of some kind.

'You had what now?'

Ruby gave her a withering look. 'You know perfectly well what it is.'

'And you paid for that?'

'Mock away. I feel lighter.'

'I bet you do.'

'In my soul,' Ruby said and the shock of hearing Ruby saying a word as loaded and mumbo-jumbo as 'soul' shut Gwen up.

'I'm doing yoga now, too,' Ruby said.

Gwen looked at Ruby in disbelief. 'Yoga?'

'It's transformed my life,' Ruby said. Her expression was a mix of anxiety and defiance, exactly the same as when she'd brought home a copy of *Smash Hits* magazine, aged ten. 'Marcus says I'm a natural. He says I'd be able to take the teaching course if I wanted, set up my own classes.'

'Marcus?' Gwen instantly pictured a bendy-limbed Lothario leaning towards her sister, his long fingers reaching for her golden hair. She suppressed a shudder.

'He's been brilliant,' Ruby said. 'And the yoga really helps with stress.'

Gwen refrained from snorting at the idea of Ruby being stressed. Ruby led a charmed life straight from the pages of a John Lewis catalogue while she'd been living like . . . Well. If she was being kind to herself, she'd say a free-spirited artist. If not, she'd have to go with hobo.

'You wouldn't understand,' Ruby said, as if reaching into Gwen's mind and plucking her thoughts clean out. 'You've never faced up to responsibility. As a mother—'

'Here we go,' Gwen said, irritation leaping to the surface. 'I'm not a mother so I don't understand.'

'Well, you're not. And you don't.'

This was why she shouldn't spend time with her sister, Gwen thought. At a distance she felt almost fond, at close quarters she could happily strangle her. 'Do you meditate?'

Ruby looked startled. 'Of course. The mind–body connection is fundamental to—'

Gwen shook her head and then found she couldn't quite stop. She clenched her fists, digging her nails into the palms. A tight ball of anger lodged in her stomach and, all at once, she realised why. 'Let me get this straight,' she said, surprised at the venom in her own voice. 'All this time, I've been keeping away from you, not wanting to infect your precious life, your precious family with my "alternative" ways and you've been doing bloody yoga.'

'You make it sound like a bad thing. I thought you, of all people, would be pleased.'

Gwen closed her mouth. There was nothing she could say to fill a pit of ignorance that deep. The unfairness of it burned bright and Gwen was surprised that Ruby couldn't see the raw energy sizzling under her skin. She counted to ten to stop herself from saying something she would regret later and then settled on, 'You must've had quite the epiphany.'

'It's not the same as your . . . stuff,' Ruby said. 'Yoga has been around for hundreds of years; it's a spiritual thing, it's not dangerous, it doesn't ruin people's lives,' she counted the points off on her fingers, finishing with, 'and it doesn't mark you out as a weirdo. Not these days. I mean, you can buy yoga pants at The White Company.'

'Well, if that's what's most important to you. The look of things—'

Ruby shrugged. 'It's a factor. Especially for Katie. You remember what school was like.'

Gwen repressed a shudder. Millbank Comp had not been a friendly place. Not for either of them. 'I haven't seen you in ages. I don't want to argue with you,' Gwen said. She pushed the anger and hurt back down and forced out, 'If yoga makes you happy, I'm happy for you.'

Gwen couldn't look Ruby in the eye, though. Instead she began to explore. She opened the door to the larder.

Old newspapers were stacked neatly in a cardboard box on the floor, a broom hung from a nail on the back of the door and there were empty glass jars filling the top shelf. A spider ran across the floor.

Ruby called across from the living room. 'It's got the original fireplace.'

Gwen joined her, trying not to shiver. The living room was misnamed. The walls were painted in oppressive purple which, combined with the patterned carpet and sofa, made Gwen's eyes itch. She sniffed. There was the shut-in house smell, but with something else underneath. A herb of some kind?

'Good cornicing.' Ruby pointed upwards.

Gwen pulled the curtains back, revealing big sash windows. 'These are nice.'

'Original?' Ruby said.

'I think so. I don't think Iris got around to doing a modernist makeover.'

Ruby prodded the sill. 'Probably rotten. Nightmare to look after, but people lap up this kind of thing. Very saleable.'

'Mmm,' Gwen said non-committally. She showed Ruby the upstairs, pausing underneath the loft hatch. 'I suppose I should look up there.'

'I'm not doing it. That's what a man is for.'

'How very 1950s of you.'

'Oh please. Spiders, itchy insulation, low ceiling. Why keep a dog and bark yourself?'

'True romance indeed. How is David?' Gwen asked, smiling as she pictured her brother-in-law. He was married to his work somewhat, but a good guy nonetheless.

'Busy. As usual,' Ruby said.

'But still utterly besotted.'

Ruby grinned. 'Of course.'

He and Ruby had met at the same time Gwen was putting in regular time in the back seat of Cam's car. When Ruby found out she was pregnant, David didn't hesitate to drop to one knee and, this was the part that would endear him to Gwen for ever; he made it look like he'd been planning to propose for months. Ruby had believed him and so she'd said yes and then he'd worked like a dog to finish his architecture degree while supporting his new wife and baby. Nobody could resent the beautiful house they now lived in, their Audi and healthy bank balance. Well, Gwen corrected herself, someone would. Someone always did.

The third bedroom at the end of the corridor was filled with cardboard boxes and black bags. 'What a mess.' Ruby wrinkled her nose. 'I don't envy you this.'

Gwen barely heard her. Ruby's voice had retreated, become thin and insubstantial, leaving space for the all-too familiar sensation of Finding. *Not now. Not in front of Ruby. Not when she was being so friendly and yoga-calmed.*

It was no good. She couldn't fight it. The tunnel vision had arrived, the edges of the room filled in with black shadows and she knew that the only way to get things back to normal was to obey the impulse. One of the bin bags was calling to her. Inside there was a tangle of old handbags, shawls, scarves and gloves. Gwen's hand plunged in and her fingers closed around something slippery and cool. A Liberty-print silk scarf with the peacock design it was almost impossible to find these days. She stared at the scarf and saw it on the stall, knew it wouldn't stay there long. Then her hand itched again and she reached back into the bag. A matching clutch purse. Barely able to breathe, Gwen clicked open the clasp and checked the lining. Immaculate.

Gwen didn't believe in signs. She knew she had an uncanny knack for finding lost things, but she didn't believe it meant anything. Not like Gloria reading palms and tarot cards and – on one memorable occasion – an oil leak from a red Volvo. She turned the purse over in her hands and tried to ignore the feeling that the house was trying to tell her something.

'Gwen? Gwen?' Ruby was frowning at her. Then understanding dawned across her face and her scowl deepened. 'Oh God. You're not—'

'No! It's nothing. I just found this—'

'I don't want to hear it.' Ruby put her fingers in her ears, just like when they were kids.

Gwen felt sick. She didn't want to think about it, either. She pushed aside memories of Gloria parading her like a performing monkey. People's gratitude for their lost car keys overlaid with a shrinking back, a look of fear and horror and, above all, disbelief. '*How did you do that?*' Like she was conducting an elaborate and pointless scam.

Ruby's lip was curled. 'I hoped you'd grown out of that.'

She marched down the stairs and Gwen stayed back for a moment, trying to calm herself. She didn't want to fight with Ruby. It wasn't Ruby's fault that Gwen had inherited the Harper family curse while she'd got to be normal. She headed downstairs, trying to think of a neutral subject. 'How's Katie?' People loved to talk about their kids.

Ruby shrugged. 'Fourteen. My days of being God-like are over.'

'That must be a relief.'

Ruby gave her an odd look. 'You wouldn't understand.'

'That's right,' Gwen said, in familiar territory. 'I don't understand true exhaustion, responsibility or *In the Night Garden*. Thank God.'

Ruby gave a grudging smile. She reached into her handbag and pulled out a BlackBerry. 'I'll give you the number of a good estate agent. David's used him before.'

'I'm not selling,' Gwen said. *Yet.*

Ruby frowned. 'What do you mean? You can't stay here.'

Gwen had been about to explain that, barring some kind of financial miracle, she might be stuck in Pendleford for the foreseeable future. Ruby's response pissed her off, though, so she said, 'I like it. It's *homely.*'

'You can't,' Ruby said, her face suddenly pale.

At once, her joke didn't seem so funny. Ruby looked genuinely horrified. *Nice.*

'What? You think I'll embarrass you? You live in Bath. You don't have to have anything to do with me,' Gwen said. 'Don't worry, I won't bother you.'

'I can't believe you're thinking about staying here. You hated this town, don't you remember?'

Of course I remember, I'm not an idiot. 'I didn't hate it,' Gwen lied. 'And maybe I feel like settling down.' She wasn't going to give Ruby the satisfaction of knowing her business was in trouble.

'I really don't think it's a good idea,' Ruby said, still looking thoroughly spooked. 'I mean, we're only just speaking again. It might be too much, too soon, you know?'

And there it was. Her typically selfish sister. 'This isn't about you, Ruby. I can't make every decision in my life based on you, or the horrible things you think and say about me.'

'I was just being honest,' Ruby said.

Gwen felt her eyes prickling with tears and she willed herself not to think about their argument. A year and a half of avoiding Ruby hadn't soothed the raw emotion one tiny bit. She still felt like a gigantic bruise. This was why she kept her distance, Gwen remembered with painful clarity.

'You only ever think of yourself. What about Katie? What about me? David's business?' Ruby said.

A part of Gwen wanted to placate Ruby, to make nice. A larger part was almost blind with fury at Ruby's unfairness. *This. Shit. Again.* Gwen stared at Ruby and realised something: nothing had changed. Yoga or not, Ruby still thought she was the anti-Christ in tracksuit bottoms. She didn't trust her and didn't want her near her precious life. It hurt. She blinked. This was why you didn't get close to people. They turned their backs on you. Better not to give a damn in the first place. She straightened her shoulders. 'Go away, Ruby.'

'We're in the middle of a discussion,' Ruby said. 'We need to sort this out.'

'I didn't ask you to come round today, you volunteered. Now I'm asking you to leave.'

Ruby took a step back. Her eyebrows drew inwards as she processed the words.

'You don't want to be around me, you don't trust me or whatever the bloody hell this lovely conversation is about, but I'm not going anywhere. This is my house and I'm telling you to get out.'

Ruby plucked her coat from the rack and slung it around her shoulders. 'Gladly.'

Well, that went well. Gwen leaned her head against the glass panel in the front door and willed her heart to stop hammering.

To calm herself, Gwen looked at the Liberty purse again. An item like that would sell quickly, she knew, and if Iris had a few more gems like that scattered around the place, she might be able to scrape together enough cash for a deposit on a flat. Not back in Leeds, but somewhere different, somewhere new. Her heart lifted as it always did when she contemplated a flit. There was always the wild hope that this next place would be the one, her forever home.

She clicked the catch on the purse and caught her breath. Nestled against the silk lining was a tiny cylinder of rolled paper and a key. She swallowed. They must've been there before. She'd been distracted by Ruby. *Nothing weird to see here. Move along.*

Gwen smiled grimly. She'd spent thirteen years quashing magic nonsense like this, and she wasn't about to lose control now. The paper would be an old receipt. The key was a dull silver and had simply been hidden against the grey of the lining.

Still, she couldn't help herself. She unrolled the paper, which was soft with age, and felt vomit rise in the back of her throat. It said:

For Gwen. When you are ready, seek, and you shall find. It is your gift.

'Sod that,' Gwen said and went to brush her teeth.

CHAPTER 2

Gwen had taken a long bath and eaten the bread that Lily had left with the casserole and, by the time she headed into town, she felt almost human again. All she had to do was remain focused. The next time she felt the Finding, she'd just ignore it. Simple as that. Just because she'd inherited one of the Harper family powers, didn't mean she had to use it. She'd managed to stand up to Gloria all those years ago and refuse any more training, and she'd kept magic out of her life for the last thirteen years. Being back in Pendleford for one night wasn't going to undo that. No matter how many creepy little notes Great-Aunt Iris had left for her.

The solicitor's office occupied an imposing Georgian townhouse on the main street. Of course, all of the buildings were impressive, so that diluted its effect somewhat. Gwen hesitated outside the building. It was ridiculous. She had no connection to the Laings, not any more, and she'd never met Mr Laing Senior. There was nothing to worry about. Gwen found the reception and was directed straight into Mr Laing's office.

'He's waiting for you,' the secretary said, her rose-pink lips pursed.

Gwen opened her mouth to explain that the parking in this undeniably quaint and picturesque town was satanic and the unexpected twenty-minute fast walk had made her late, and then closed it when she caught sight of Mr Laing. The man didn't look like he had much time left on this earth and probably didn't want to waste it listening to excuses or parking zone rants.

'Ms Harper. You'll forgive me if I don't get up.' Mr Laing gestured to his wheelchair. 'Please sit.'

Gwen sat and tried not to stare at the ancient being opposite. He must have been at least ninety. Well preserved, for sure, his nails freshly manicured and eyes bright, but surely someone who had earned retirement. What kind of firm was this? The kind you could only leave in a box?

Mr Laing picked up a sheet of heavy-weight cream paper and held it out. 'This is the original of the document that we sent to you. Your great-aunt's will. I understand there is some confusion on your part.'

Gwen kept her hands in her lap, refusing to touch the paper. 'Not confusion exactly.'

'How can I help?' Mr Laing steepled his fingers.

'I wanted to know if I could sell the house straight away.'

'The terms of the will state that the property cannot be placed on the market for six months. After that, you can sell as quickly as you like.'

'Right. I read that.'

Mr Laing waited.

'I was wondering, though.' Gwen swallowed. 'Is there a way around it?'

'I'm not sure I understand.'

'Can I put it up for auction, or something?' Gwen wasn't going to embarrass herself by explaining that she needed cash right now. Or that she couldn't stay in the house because Iris appeared to be talking to her from beyond the grave.

'Ms Harper was very clear in her instructions. She updated her will six weeks prior to her passing and instructed us to send it to you.'

'But how? How could she do that?'

Mr Laing's white eyebrows crept upwards again. 'She was an exceptionally organised woman.'

'I mean...we weren't in contact. How did she know my address?'

'She was your great-aunt. Isn't it possible that she spoke to another family member?'

Gwen shook her head. That was most definitely *not* possible.

'Is there no way to release equity from the house or something? Immediately?' Gwen realised that her voice was getting louder and she snapped her mouth shut again. Shouting at a defenceless old man was not cool. It wasn't his fault he worked in a soulless leather-and-oak hell and looked like an extra from *The Godfather*.

Mr Laing looked back at her calmly. 'I see.'

Gwen sank back.

'If you will excuse me, I will get my grandson in here.'

'Sorry?' Gwen sat forward.

'He prepared this file but...' Laing paused '...became overscheduled and passed the baton to me, as it were.'

'Okay. Fine.' Gwen remained perched on the edge of the padded leather chair and waited. She thought of her beloved minivan. It was stuffed full of her possessions and business stock and she barely fitted amongst the boxes. She didn't want to stay at End House, but she didn't want to sleep in the van again. Then she processed the word 'grandson'. It couldn't be—

The door opened behind her and Gwen turned.

The man in the charcoal-grey suit was both older and taller than she remembered. His face was tense, though, and that sadly fitted her last memory of him to a tee. She gaped, then, realising that she probably looked like a village idiot, closed her mouth.

'Hello, Gwen.'

'Cam.' The word felt odd in her mouth. Wrong.

'Don't get up.'

Gwen realised she was suspended, half out of the chair like she was poised to run a race.

'Is there a problem?' Cameron Laing had been twenty-three when she'd last seen him and thirteen years was a long time. Which would explain the blank and professional expression he was levelling in her direction.

'You're a lawyer,' she said stupidly.

'So it would appear,' Cam said.

'Ms Harper wishes to contest the Harper will,' Mr Laing senior said.

'No. I'm not saying that,' Gwen said, suddenly desperate to appear reasonable. She had a good idea that 'reasonable' was probably not the first word that Cam would use to describe her. She wanted to show him she'd changed. Not that she needed to. There wasn't going to be any antagonism after thirteen years. Probably no emotion at all. 'I was just wondering if there was a way to convert the house into cash. Quickly.'

It hardly seemed possible, but Cam's expression became more rigid. 'Let me see.' Cam ran over the same details, then plucked the paper from Laing's desk and put it into Gwen's hands. She took it to stop it sliding off her lap onto the floor and, despite her intentions, glanced down. Iris's signature was there at the bottom of the sheet. The same looping writing that was on the note in the purse. There was no mistake: Iris wanted her to have the house. She really wanted her to stay in Pendleford and had even put an instruction not to sell into a legal document. A part of Gwen felt flattered. It was nice to be wanted, even if it was by a woman she'd been taught to avoid like the plague.

Cam was frowning as he flipped through the file. 'Where are the title deeds? They should be here.'

Mr Laing senior shrugged.

'Great. Iris must've left them at the house.' He looked at Gwen. 'You'll need that when you come to sell. In May.'

Gwen looked into Cam's brown eyes and felt something thud inside her chest. 'Six months. Right.'

'You'll need to find it,' he said. 'It's pretty important.'

'Right. I'm just not sure if I can—'

'What? You're too busy?' Cam shook his head as he handed her the file. 'This isn't the usual way people react when they find out someone has given them a house.'

'Oh?' Gwen couldn't stop looking at Iris's handwriting. She felt as if the walls had shrunk, and when she looked up at Cam, the room swooped to the left.

'They usually say "hooray".'

'Cameron!' Mr Laing was shocked. 'Ms Harper has lost her aunt.'

'It's okay. I didn't know her,' Gwen said.

Just as Cam said, 'It takes more than that to shake Gwen.'

'Hey!' Gwen said. *So, a little hostility still.*

'Spare keys.' Cam plucked a brown envelope from the desk and tipped it upside down.

'Thank you.'

'Well, if that concludes our business?'

Cam's face was older, harder. Gwen didn't think it was possible, but she actually found him even more attractive than the Cam of her memory. Which was inconvenient.

'I don't want to keep you,' Gwen managed.

Cam bowed his head slightly and left the room.

'Well…' Laing senior looked baffled. 'What was that about?'

Gwen shook her head. She felt sick. It shouldn't have been a surprise that Cam's grandfather didn't know about them; not many people talked in-depth to their grandparents about their relationships but, still, it hurt.

She shook Mr Laing's hand and thanked him for his time. It wasn't his fault that she couldn't convert the house into money and go rent a flat in Leeds or London or on Mars. *Six months. How bad could it be?*

Back at End House, Gwen closed the door, then leaned her head lightly against it. Perhaps the country air was getting to her, but it felt as if the house was breathing with her. She closed her eyes and saw Cam. Frowning at her.

She went to the kitchen and flicked through the file that Cam had given her. There was a white envelope with her name on it, written in Iris's handwriting. Inside, there was a small key and a single folded sheet of paper:

My dearest Gwen. I'm sorry I never got to know you. I hope you are all that I believe you to be. With power comes responsibility. I want you to accept all that I bequeath you but, by doing so, you accept all that it brings. Yours in haste, Iris.

Nicely cryptic, Iris. *Thanks for that.*

The back door swung open. 'Knock, knock.' Lily appeared, her spike heels gouging chunks out of the worn lino. 'Only me.'

'What can I do for you?' Gwen asked, pushing the letter back into the file and flipping over the brown cardboard cover.

'It's what I can do for you. I have such happy memories of helping your auntie, I'm willing to offer you a discount.'

'Sorry?'

'To help you out.' Lily looked pointedly at the mess of papers, used coffee mugs and plates on the table. 'Looks like you could do with a hand.'

Gwen felt pressure around her temples. 'I don't need any help, thank you.' She stood up and tipped crumbs from the cake plates into the bin. 'And I couldn't afford it if I did.'

'If I clean, it will free up your time for—' Lily paused '…well, whatever it is you do.'

'I'm fine, really.' Lily didn't appear to be listening and was unpacking her bag on the table. A flask appeared. And a brown paper bag that smelled of yeasty goodness.

'I brought you some soup and bread.'

'You don't have to—'

'Just while you settle in. Bless you, I'm sure you haven't been shopping yet.' She gave Gwen a disconcertingly direct look. 'Don't worry. I'm not staying. I'm not one of those nosy neighbours. Always popping in. Some people like to be social and some people don't. We respect that round here.'

'Right—'

Lily gave a little tinkling laugh that lifted the hairs on the back of Gwen's neck. 'Watch out for Janet, though. She runs the Honey Pot and is the town gossip.'

There was a pause as Gwen wondered how to get rid of Lily. 'I was thinking about sorting through things today.'

'Don't forget to check the list.'

'The list?'

'The list of contents. Everything is in its place. I don't want you thinking I have light fingers. You have to sign to say everything is as it should be.'

Understanding dawned and Gwen blushed. 'I didn't mean I was checking. I didn't—'

'That's all right. You don't know me, after all. You aren't local. You don't know what a good friend I've been.'

'I'm sure you've been wonderful.' Gwen wanted Lily to leave. She hadn't sat down, which was a good sign, but good manners overtook her mouth. 'Would you like a cup of tea?' *Idiot.*

'I won't take up any more of your time. You've got your work cut out for you here.'

Gwen smiled. Relief made her giddy. 'I'm quite looking forward to it. I've never had my own house before.'

Lily looked at her curiously. 'You've never bought a house?'

'No. Just rented. Usually just a room in a shared house, actually.'

'Oh?' Lily pursed her lips. 'Isn't that a bit cramped?'

'A bit. I've always moved around so much – for my work – my domestic arrangements haven't mattered much.' Gwen had always felt safest moving around. Pendleford had been the last place she'd called home and that hadn't ended well.

'You're not working now, though.'

'Not right at this second. No.' Gwen didn't feel the need to explain Curious Notions to Lily. She seemed like the type who would turn her nose up at second-hand, let alone 'craft'.

'You're going to stay, then?'

'Yes.' *For now.*

Lily made a face. 'Make sure you find that list. I don't want any trouble.' She picked up her bag and headed out of the door at a clip. 'And make sure you have that soup tonight. It's chicken.'

Okay, Gwen thought. So Lily was a bit odd. A bit intense. She opened the file again and plucked out the sheaf of stapled A4 paper with 'End House, Contents' typed on the top sheet. It was handily split into rooms, but after a minute of reading: one candlestick, pewter, broken base; one wool rug, red; three fountain pens; one wastepaper basket, her will to live fled. She was sure Lily hadn't taken anything, anyway. She flipped to the last page and signed the declaration at the bottom. She made another mug of tea and drank it at the kitchen table. Why would she be so anxious for Gwen to check the list if she had? Unless she was looking for something. Gwen shook her head to release the ridiculous thought, but instead found herself staring at the small grey key.

A key for a locked door. Gwen didn't have to pause; the knowledge jumped to the front of her mind; an extrovert piece of information that couldn't wait for its turn in the spotlight. She ventured outside to the small outbuilding beyond the vegetable patch and tried the whitewashed door. It was locked. The key turned smoothly and the door swung inwards. The room wasn't big, but it was obviously well used. A scrubbed wooden bench sat against one wall, a chair pushed neatly underneath. Another wall was filled by shelves and these were crowded with jam jars, neatly labelled. Gwen picked one up and read 'Wolfsbane'. *Okay.*

There were bunches of herbs hanging from the ceiling and a butler's sink in the corner with a wooden draining board to the side. There was a tartan-print cat bed in the corner. Gwen sighed with relief. That explained the noises in the night. The poor thing could be shut in somewhere or was hiding out of fear. Odd that Lily hadn't mentioned a pet. Her heart clenched as she imagined it hungry and afraid, clenching harder when she realised that she was now responsible for it.

Her eye was caught by a notebook. It was spiral-bound and had a plain cover. She flipped it open and was confronted with tightly packed writing in black Biro. Iris's writing sloped violently to the right and she seemed to have little regard for the spaces between words. Gwen pulled out the chair and read a page at random.

M D came again today. I knew she would've been drinking to get up the courage and by the smell of her it was sweet German wine. Not surprising that she has the palate of an illiterate eight-year-old. I gave her the usual prep (2 x WB, 1 x F, 1 x LLB).

Okay. So Great-Aunt Iris had an acerbic streak. She flipped to another page.

That bloody woman was sniffing around again. There's nothing worse than a frustrated witch.

Witch. Gwen felt sick. If the cat's black, she thought, I'm out of here.

That night, Gwen didn't even pretend to consider sleeping in Nanette. Yes, she didn't want to be in Pendleford or inside End House, but it was forecast minus six and too late to drive very far. Gwen knew she could be irrational, but she wasn't about to sleep in her van when she owned a perfectly good, warm bed. And food. She poured the soup from the flask into a pan to heat it. Rich smells of leek, garlic and chicken rose up. Gwen got down a bowl and cut a thick slice of the fresh bread. She managed a couple of mouthfuls, but tiredness mugged her and she put the spoon down. She trailed upstairs to the master bedroom and the enormous bed. Her mind and heart were trying to reconcile the coldness from Cam. Coldness that she'd expected. It was exactly what had stopped her from picking up the phone so many times over the last thirteen years. She'd heard that the anticipation of pain was usually worse than the pain itself. Well, not in this case. Gwen couldn't believe how much it hurt to look into Cam's face and see nothing. Nothing but a chilly disdain. She closed her eyes and a spiral of colour twisted in the darkness. She watched it turn and writhe until sleep took her.

Gwen opened her eyes. The darkness pressed against them as she struggled to wake up. She'd been dreaming about the river. Black water, icy-cold. Stephen Knight's pale face emerging from the thick depths as if he were floating in oil, not water. His eyes open and accusing. His mouth opening, filling with the black liquid.

Scritch, scratch. There it was again, the sound that had woken her up. Gwen forced herself properly awake. She ignored the window that had inexplicably opened and tiptoed onto the landing. She peered over the banister and there, sitting squarely in a patch of moonlight on the hall floor, was the skinniest cat she had ever seen. She crept down the first couple of stairs, watching carefully to see if the cat would bolt. It stayed motionless, watching her with unblinking eyes that were nothing more than reflections in the half light. Gwen looked casually away and then back, showing that she wasn't a threat. The cat hadn't moved and it looked reasonably relaxed. In fact, it looked like it was waiting for her, so she tried a couple more stairs. Then it meowed. Instinctively, Gwen put her hands over her ears. The noise that split the air wasn't feline. It was like a rusty saw being dragged over corrugated iron. 'Jesus!'

The cat regarded her with disgust. Perhaps it didn't like blasphemy. 'Sorry,' she said. 'You startled me.'

The cat got up and walked into the kitchen, its bottle brush tail high in the air.

Gwen followed obediently and then realised there wasn't any cat food in the house. She took down a tin of tuna and mashed up a little on a plate, while the cat wound its wiry body round and round her legs. 'You're going to trip me over,' she said.

The cat screeched.

'All right, all right.' Gwen put the plate down in front of it.

While the cat made short work of the tuna, she filled a saucer with some watered-down milk. 'You shouldn't really have dairy, but you look like you need the extra calories.' *I'm talking to a cat. God help me.*

The cat sniffed the liquid, then lapped. Gwen felt a ridiculous sense of achievement.

She fetched one of the sad-looking cushions from the living room and put it on the floor of the kitchen. 'You can sleep in here tonight.' Then, shutting the kitchen door, she went upstairs. She went to the bathroom and washed her hands. There was no knowing what the animal had. Worms or fleas or, quite possibly, scurvy. She would need a litter tray, food, a new cat bed, and to get it checked by a vet.

Gwen paused on the landing, looking at the moonlight on the hallway tiles and listening to the night-time sounds of the house.

The cat was curled up on the foot of the bed. Gwen looked at it for a long moment. The cat looked steadily back at her. Then she got into bed.

Gwen opened her eyes. Two yellow ones hovered about an inch from her nose. She stifled a scream and blinked. The cat stretched lazily and jumped off the bed, landing with a thud. 'I thought cats were light-footed.' The cat paused, looking at her with expression of disgust. In the daylight, Gwen could see that it was most definitely not a black cat. It had a mix of markings, not tortoiseshell or black and white or marmalade, but all of them. Like several cats had been put in a blender. Which was a horrible image and one Gwen instantly tried to whitewash over. The cat regarded her sternly as if mind-reading. 'Sorry,' she said, and then felt ridiculous.

She fed the cat some more tuna, bulked out with bread soaked in water. Then she remembered the leftover soup. She took it out of the fridge and sniffed it. Chicken. The cat started to wind around her legs, crying out and purring. 'Smells good, huh?' She poured a tiny bit into a saucer and put it on the floor. The cat dived for the dish, then stopped. His hackles rose and his fur stood on end. He hissed at the dish, then disappeared through the door, a streak of fur and fury.

Gwen picked up the saucer and sniffed it again. Maybe the cat objected to herbs. She began clearing up.

The back door, that Gwen would've sworn blind was locked, swung open. 'Knock, knock. Only me.'

Lily Thomas smiled, her tiny teeth sparkling. 'Soup for breakfast?'

Gwen realised she was still holding the Thermos in one hand. 'Just washing up.' She plunged it into the sink full of soapy water. 'What can I do for you?'

'Just come to pick up my dishes.'

'Of course.' Gwen finished rinsing the flask and dried it on a checked tea towel. Then she fetched the ceramic casserole and handed them over. 'Do you know the name of Iris's cat?'

Lily frowned. 'Iris didn't have a cat.'

Gwen decided not to mention the cat bed in the outbuilding. It would be like directly calling Lily a liar, which probably wasn't the way to be a friendly neighbour. Besides, there was something snake-like about Lily's eyes. She kept her voice mild: 'Well, I've got one now. He seems pretty at home.'

'Must be a stray. Don't feed it or you'll never get rid of it.' Lily paused. 'Have you had a chance to check that list yet?'

'Kind of. Yes.'

'Did it mention a notebook?' Everything about Lily was casual – her stance, leaning against the kitchen counter, her voice, her open expression – but Gwen could feel the tension thrumming in the air.

She shook her head. 'Sorry.'

'It's completely fine. Just a little thing. Silly, really, but I was so fond of Iris and it would be something to remember her by.' Lily wiped delicately at her dry eyes.

'A notebook?'

'With recipes,' Lily said quickly. 'I always admired Iris's tomato chutney and she promised to leave me the secret.'

Gwen frowned. 'Why didn't she just give it to you?'

Lily laughed. 'I keep forgetting that you didn't know your auntie at all, did you? She was very protective of her recipes. Adamant that they should be passed down through family —' She broke off, perhaps realising what she'd said, then continued smoothly, 'And she always said I was her closest family, that I was like a granddaughter to her.'

'Well, as soon as I find the recipe I'll pass it on.'

Lily smiled properly, her face lighting up and becoming pretty. 'Thank you. I'd appreciate it.'

Gwen drove to the big supermarket on the outskirts of town and stocked up; she couldn't rely on handouts from the neighbours for ever. She picked up cat food and a red velvet collar and put the receipt into her bag without looking at it. She was close to the limit on her emergency credit card and hoped, fervently, that the cat didn't eat very much.

Back at End House, she set up her iPod dock and put on Johnny Cash at full volume. She stacked tins and packets and jars, filling the kitchen cupboards, then cleaned through the house, swiping away dust and cobwebs and muddy paw prints.

The cat appeared and pronounced the cat food a success. 'Don't get too used to that stuff. It'll be value tins next time.'

The cat tilted his head and regarded her disdainfully.

'And then I'll have to re-home you, I suppose.'

The cat blinked slowly.

'Unless I stay here. And adopt you.'

The cat began licking itself.

'Great,' Gwen said. 'Is that supposed to be a sign?'

The sun had disappeared by four o'clock, making Gwen think about an early dinner. She pulled out pans and knives and started cooking. It was such a treat to have a kitchen again. And no annoying housemates to share it with. A spark of happiness flared as she followed the ritual of making pasta sauce. The movements were soothing. They calmed the feelings stirred up by the shock of seeing Cameron Laing.

Gwen chopped a handful of fresh basil, almost cutting off the tip of her pinky in the process. 'Damn it.' She ran her finger under the cold tap and told herself off for thinking about Cam while in possession of a sharp object. She threw the basil into the tomato sauce simmering on the stove and tried not to think about him in his dark suit. Cam in a suit was weird. When they'd been together, she would've sworn his Ramones T-shirt was surgically attached to his body. Except when he was peeling it over his head that time on the beach. She shivered, remembering the way his eyes had turned black, holding her like he was a drowning man. It had always been like that. Something wild and desperate and, with hindsight, probably not all that skilful. She closed her eyes and imagined what Cam might've learned in thirteen years. She leaned against the worktop, breathing in garlic-and-wine-scented steam and feeling the pressure against her suddenly thrumming and alive body. Her eyes flew open. Someone was knocking on the back door.

Gwen knew her face was flushed, but figured she could blame it on cooking. She wrenched open the door, ready to tell Lily Thomas politely but firmly to sod off, only to find a woman she didn't recognise peering at her anxiously in the dusk. She was wearing a navy trouser suit and carrying a matching handbag, but she still looked a little ragged around the edges. Her skin was pale and there were dark circles around her eyes.

'You've got to help me,' the woman said and pushed past Gwen into the kitchen and sat in the biggest chair.

'I'm sorry?' Gwen managed.

'You're Gwen Harper, aren't you?'

'Yes.' Gwen tried to smooth out her frown. Manners cost nothing, after all. 'Do you live next door?'

'Of course not. I'm Marilyn Dixon.'

'Right,' Gwen said. It was official; the people in this town were insane. She gestured to the stove. 'I was just about to eat. Are you hungry?'

Marilyn opened her eyes wide. 'Will that help?'

Gwen gave up on reason and took the chair opposite. 'Can we back up a bit? Speak slowly; I feel like I missed a memo or something.'

Marilyn's fingers gripped her handbag on her lap, her knuckles bright white. 'You are Iris Harper's granddaughter, aren't you?'

'I'm her great-niece.'

'Oh.' Marilyn looked ridiculously disappointed. Her bottom lip stuck out like a toddler. There was a short silence, broken only by the soft popping of the simmering sauce.

'Did you know my great-aunt well?' Gwen tried for some polite chit-chat.

'Not really. She kept herself private. Not a mixer.'

'Right.'

'But she always helped.' Marilyn sniffed. 'Wasn't very nice about it, but she helped.'

'I thought she was quite infirm herself.' Gwen couldn't imagine what Iris had been doing for Marilyn Dixon. Marilyn was no spring chicken, but she was easily thirty years younger than Iris.

'Ha!' Marilyn said and Gwen jumped a little. 'She was as strong as a horse. Healthy as anything. Never got ill. Well…' Marilyn paused and Gwen could almost hear her thinking '…until she died, of course.' Another pause. 'God rest her soul.'

Gwen frowned.

'I'm sorry. Should it be goddess rest her soul? I was never really sure on that,' Marilyn said.

'I'm still confused.' Gwen shook her head to clear the fog. It didn't help. 'Can we start with the basics? Who are you and why are you here?'

Colour flushed up Marilyn's neck. 'Your great-aunt was known for helping people. She said you were going to move in after she was gone.'

Gwen frowned. That made no sense. 'The last time I saw my great-aunt I was thirteen and she said no such thing.'

'Don't shoot the messenger,' Marilyn snapped. 'And besides, I would've thought you'd be a little more grateful.' She waved a hand. 'She left you her *house*.'

'Does everybody know my business?'

Marilyn looked at her in surprise. 'In Pendleford? Of course.'

'God help me.' Gwen raised her eyes skyward.

'Well, I can see I'm not wanted.' Marilyn began to rise.

'Don't go. I'm sorry if I was rude. I'm just a little confused.' *And frightened.* Gwen took a deep breath. 'Can you talk me through the kind of help my great-aunt dished out?'

Marilyn sat back down. Her face softened in sympathy. 'You really don't know?'

'I really don't know,' Gwen said, although she was starting to suspect. The secret room full of jars. The weird noises. The cat. Great-Aunt Iris had been a bit eccentric. And it seemed that the Harper family reputation for 'weird' was alive and kicking.

'She was magic.'

'I'm sorry?' Gwen hoped she'd misheard.

'She could help with stuff.' Marilyn shrugged. 'Like if your hens stop laying or you've got a cold that won't go away. She's got a brilliant medicine for that.'

'Like homeopathy?' *Please let it be homeopathy. No flipping tarot cards.*

Marilyn's face brightened. 'Exactly. People are always using homeopathy or reflexology or having someone stick needles in your sore bits. Seeing Iris was no different.'

'And you paid her?'

Marilyn's face fell. 'It wasn't like I didn't try. She wouldn't take it.'

Well, that was different. Gloria had had a price list printed up. Gwen got up and stirred the sauce. The motion was soothing and so was not having to look at Marilyn Dixon, who had popping blue eyes and a determined set to her mouth.

'I always knew I owed her a favour, though. She didn't take money, but you knew she'd ask you for something, some time.'

Okay. Enough nonsense. Gwen stirred the sauce faster. She couldn't help this woman. She didn't make potions or cast spells or even give good advice. *And she wasn't about to start.*

Gwen turned to face Marilyn. 'I'm sorry. I'm just not sure how I could help you. I'm not Iris.'

By the door, Marilyn gave her a long sweeping look, up and down. 'No.' And then she left.

CHAPTER 3

Gwen ate her pasta and drank a glass of red wine, but she didn't feel any better. Marilyn Dixon. The name seemed oddly familiar. Against her better judgement, Gwen fetched Iris's notebook and opened it at random. It was disturbing how easily she found an entry about Marilyn. Almost as if the book was being deliberately helpful.

Marilyn Dixon was here again about dry patches on her cheeks. That woman sees problems where there are none. I gave her tincture of rose for her nerves and told her it would give her the skin of a fourteen-year-old.

Gwen flipped the book shut and put it in the bread bin so that she couldn't see it any more. If she couldn't see it, she wouldn't be tempted to read it. She needed to stay strong. *Don't get sucked in.*

She also needed to repay Lily for the casserole and the soup, and something told her that a packet of HobNobs wouldn't cut it in Pendleford. She baked a couple of fruit cakes, steadfastly ignoring the siren song of the notebook. She vacuumed the living room and plumped the thin cushions on the sofa. It just looked sadder and quieter, and the cat wouldn't settle. He kept crying to be let out and, sixty seconds later, crying to be let back in. By the tenth round, Gwen was losing her patience.

'For the love of—' Gwen flung open the back door, ready to sit the cat down for a serious heart-to-heart vis-à-vis the wisdom of pissing off his source of food and shelter. 'Oh.'

'Don't leave me out in this cold; I'll catch my death. And you're letting all your heating out.' The man was at least a hundred years old, his face scrunched-up like a used Kleenex.

Gwen stepped back and he made his way up the step and into the warmth of the kitchen.

'I need Iris,' he said, taking the comfy chair.

'Course you do,' Gwen said. She flicked the switch on the kettle. 'Tea?'

'This isn't a social visit.'

'Fine.' Gwen sat opposite him. 'You are aware that I'm not Iris?'

'I'm not senile.' The man glowered at her. 'I went to her funeral. You don't get up after one of those.'

'Not usually, no. What can I do for you?'

The man looked down, his face abruptly red. He didn't answer.

'The thing is, as we've already established, I'm not Iris, so I probably can't help you anyway. You're better off going to the chemist. Or the doctor. Or A&E.' *Not my bloody kitchen.*

He looked up. 'You're turning me away?'

'No. It's not like that. But I can see it's something you're embarrassed about and if you do tell me, I'm not sure it'll be worth it as I don't know how I could help. I run a crafts and antiques stall and I barely knew my great-aunt and I've just moved in and people keep turning up and won't leave me alone.'

The man chewed his lip. 'Iris mixed me a cream. It soothed my chilblains.'

'Chilblains?' What was embarrassing about poor circulation?

He nodded defiantly.

'The problem is, I don't know how to make the cream. And there wasn't anything left in her work room. It was cleaned out as far as I could tell. I don't even know what's in it. I don't know where to start.'

The man got creakily to his feet saying, 'I won't bother you again.'

Gwen felt like hell. 'Won't you stay for a cup of tea, at least?'

'I won't bother you,' he said again, his mouth set into a stubborn line.

'I really am sorry.' Then Gwen spotted the fruit cakes she'd just taken out of the oven. She got one of the tins down from the cupboard.

'Take this.'

'What is it?'

'Fruit cake. Drop the tin back to me when you've finished.'

'Will it help my chilblains?'

'No, no. I just feel bad about you coming out in this cold and—'

The man had the tin and was tucking it noisily into a carrier bag that had appeared from his coat pocket.

He stuck out his hand and they shook awkwardly. 'I'm Fred Byres. Number six Meadowmead.'

'Nice to meet you,' Gwen said.

He raised a hand and disappeared down the path at a surprisingly fast clip, rustling.

Gwen took a deep breath and then dialled the number on the solicitor's letterhead and asked for Cam. When she heard his voice, she sagged against the wall.

'It's Gwen. Harper.'

His voice changed, went tight. She couldn't blame him. He'd made it quite clear that he was still angry with her for the way she'd left things all those years ago. *Time heals* was a big fat lie. 'I was wondering if I could talk to you about my aunt.' She looked around the hallway; the doors leading off were like eyes watching her. 'I feel a bit weird living in her house when I didn't know her. I've been sorting through her stuff and it just feels wrong. I feel like an intruder.'

'So go home.' Cam's voice was flat.

'I don't want to,' she said carefully. No need to explain that she didn't have one. Or, rather, End House was it. 'I'm going to stay.'

Cam didn't say anything and Gwen could almost hear his sneer down the line.

'At least for the time being,' she added, wishing with all her being that he wasn't so hostile. Or that it didn't bother her so much.

'Why don't you ask your family? What about your mum?'

'They didn't get on. Something happened when I was a kid and we weren't allowed to see her any more. We weren't allowed to use her name, actually.' Gwen forced a laugh to show she knew it sounded overblown and ridiculous. Not the kind of way that she, rational, normal, Gwen Harper would ever behave.

'I didn't know her very well,' Cam said. 'Just in a professional capacity.'

'Please. Anything at all would help.'

'Didn't you say you live next door to her old carer? She'd know more than me.'

'Cleaner. And I'd rather get a different viewpoint. I know it's an imposition, but I won't take up much of your time. I'll come into town and we could have coffee. Or lunch. I'll buy you lunch.'

'Bribery is illegal, you know.'

Gwen smiled, relieved at the lightening in his tone. 'Whatever it takes.'

There was a sudden loaded silence. Then she heard him sigh. 'Tomorrow. One drink after work.'

'That's brilliant, thanks so much—'

He cut across her. 'And you're buying.'

The next day, Gwen parked Nanette as close as possible to the town centre, realising too late that she would've been better off just walking from the house. She ended up in a small pay and display car park, and trekked the mile to Cam's office. Irritatingly, he was waiting inside his Lexus at the kerb. She pulled open the passenger door and he jumped slightly. 'Hello.'

'Is the pub far, because my car is practically back at End House, closest I could get.'

'Oh, yes. Sorry. Parking is a pain.'

'It's fine,' Gwen said, and got into the car. She needed to dial down the hostility, get things with Cam onto a polite, grown-up footing. He wasn't looking at her, though, which was annoying. Then he spoke to the steering wheel. 'I was just about to call you and cancel, actually.'

'Oh?'

A high-pitched chiming noise interrupted them. Gwen winced and looked around for the source of the awful sound.

'Yeah.' He frowned. 'That's the seat belt warning.'

'But we're not moving.'

'We could get rear-ended and you'd fly through the windscreen.'

Gwen put the belt on.

'Anyway,' he said, in what could only be a deliberately casual tone, 'it's been a mad day and I'm knackered.'

'But this is the time we're meeting. You couldn't call to cancel at the exact time of the appointment. That's not cancelling, that's cutting the meeting short.'

'Okay. Then I'm cutting our meeting short.'

Gwen made a show of looking at her watch. 'One minute. That's very, very short.'

'I'm exhausted. We can do it another time.'

'Fine,' Gwen said tightly.

His shoulders sagged slightly. 'I'll give you a lift back to your car.'

'Thank you.'

Cam drove carefully and in silence, keeping his eyes on the road. Gwen looked at him once, clocked the set of his jaw, the faint brush of stubble and the dark shadows under his eyes. He did look tired and he didn't owe her a thing. He looked so familiar, she had to stop herself from reaching out and brushing a stray hair from his jacket. It was as if she'd been carrying around his image, tucked safely in a corner of herself, without even knowing it.

She looked out of the window instead. The tail end of the shopping crowd was straggling home and they passed a bus queue so full it was spilling into the street.

'I don't remember there being so many people.'

'We kept different hours.'

That was true, she thought. She'd been half-halfheartedly completing her A levels while Cam was doing whatever mysterious things he got up to in the hours they were apart. She'd been out with a couple of friends, going from pub to pub, waiting for the clubs to open, and everywhere was packed. She'd gone to the beer garden in the Pig and Fiddle to see if she could find a seat and there he was. Sat on top of a bench, reading a paperback copy of *Fear and Loathing in Las Vegas*. If he'd looked like a student from the university on the hill she'd have thought he was a pathetic poser. But he didn't. He had scuffed black boots and narrow jeans that looked genuinely old and not 'artfully distressed' by some designer. He was wearing a faded black band T-shirt and his dark hair was falling into his face. He was completely absorbed in the book and didn't look up when his companion spoke. His friend nudged him and he finally glanced up and Gwen realised that she had been standing still and gawping like a lovesick teenager. Which, she'd abruptly realised, was exactly what she had become.

It would always be something that Gwen would be grateful for. No agonised waiting, no sleepless nights, no wondering. One moment she was staring at Cam with the full knowledge that her world had tipped forwards, propelling her towards the man on the bench, and the next moment she was so close she was touching him and his hands were on her face, holding her gently while he kissed her, the paperback discarded on the bench next to them. At least, that was how she remembered it.

'We did,' she managed. 'I don't remember a lot of shopping trips.'

'No,' he said, his voice clipped, and she wondered if he was having a memory-fest, too. Probably not.

'I need a drink,' he said.

'I would love a drink,' Gwen said.

'I have alcohol.'

That was more like it. 'Is your place far?'

'You know it: Widcombe Street.'

Gwen looked at him in horror. 'You live with your mother?'

'No!' Cam said. 'I have a flat. It's self-contained. Separate entrance.' He collected himself. 'I have the top floor.'

'Oh.'

'Those houses are too big.'

'Okay.'

'And I needed somewhere to live while I was getting qualified.'

'Right.'

'And then I got the job at the firm and it seemed easier to stay.'

'It's really none of my business.' Gwen paused. 'How is your mother?'

He gave a wry smile. 'The same.'

'Super.' She looked at her watch. 'You know, I've just remembered I've got to be up early in the morning. I think I'll just head home.'

'Coward.' Cam was smiling.

Gwen pulled a prim face. 'I'm a very busy woman.'

'You made this date.'

'And you broke it. We're even.'

There was a pause. 'So, you're really not coming for a drink? I have Southern Comfort.'

'So do I and mine doesn't come with a chaser of abject terror. Sorry.'

'That's okay,' Cam said. 'I'd forgotten how much you disliked her.'

Gwen sucked her breath in. 'That's it. Stop the car.'

'What? No. We're nearly there.' And he was right; the entrance to the car park appeared. Cam flicked the indicator and slowed down.

'Pull over. We need to talk.'

'We're already talking,' Cam said, but he steered the car into the nearest available space.

By the time he cranked the handbrake and half-turned in his seat, an expression of patient confusion on his face, Gwen was furious. The words came out distinct and calm, though; she enunciated each one carefully. 'It isn't a question of my disliking your mother. She hates me.'

Cam smiled and shook his head slightly. 'Come on now. She's not a very warm person, but that's a bit over-the-top.'

Gwen bit her tongue to keep the words *She told me I was no good for you* inside. She tasted blood. These things only worked if you did them for real.

Cam fidgeted, reaching into his pocket before withdrawing his hand empty.

'You gave up, then,' Gwen said. 'Smoking.'

'As soon as I realised I wasn't actually immortal,' Cam said, the corners of his mouth turning down in a sardonic smile.

Why did he have to look so good? 'Yeah, that's always a tough one,' Gwen managed, after a pause.

There was silence again. Then Cam said, 'It's really weird to see you again.'

Weird. Nice.

'It's going to take a bit of adjustment.'

Gwen felt angry again. Something about his sensible phrasing pissed her off. 'I didn't ask to come back here. And I didn't do it to mess with you or anything.'

Cam raised his eyebrows. 'I didn't say that you did.'

And there was that tone again. Gwen felt words building up, but she knew she wasn't going to voice any of them. He was a stranger to her now. The silence stretched on. Gwen realised that she was physically incapable of looking at him. Incapable of speaking. And that if she stayed in that car for one second longer, she was going to start crying.

Across town, it was lunch break at Millbank Comprehensive and Katie was getting the third degree.

'Does she turn people into frogs?'

'Shut up.'

'I heard she dances naked when it's full moon.'

'Seriously. Shut up.'

Katie stretched her long pale legs, inched her navy school skirt a little further up her thighs. She was sitting with her back against the gym and Imogen was lying flat out, face down, her head cradled in her hands.

'Are they turning brown yet?' Imogen asked.

Katie squinted at the backs of her friend's calves; they were goose-pimpled in the cold air. 'Not really.' She didn't know why they were attempting to tan in November. Imogen had said something about classy people getting brown in the winter.

'It's so hard to get the backs to turn, I wonder why.' Imogen lifted her head and squinted at Katie. 'You should start on them now.'

'The fronts of mine haven't changed yet. I don't think I've got the kind of skin that goes brown.' Katie looked at the smooth golden skin on Imogen's wrists, then closed her eyes and leaned her head back against the wall.

'We need baby oil. That's what Leila uses,' Imogen said. 'Speeds up the tanning process.' Leila was Imogen's older sister. At sixteen, she was the fount of all Katie and Imogen's knowledge regarding beauty tips, boys and sex.

'Like basting a chicken,' Katie offered.

'Yuck. You're gross.' Imogen sat up cross-legged and began re-tying the sparkly black scarf around her neck. 'Don't you have Italian blood? You should tan in, like, two seconds.'

'I take after my dad.' Katie's father had strawberry-blond hair, wide shoulders and a goofy smile. She hoped her colouring was their only similarity. 'We shouldn't be doing this, anyway.' Katie said. 'Sunbathing gives you cancer.'

'Not in November. And we're too young to get cancer, anyway,' Imogen said, her voice full of certainty.

This was one of the things Katie liked best about Imogen. She was so pleasingly definite.

'If they don't turn in a week or so, I'd go for some fake tan, though. Otherwise you'll have milk bottle legs.'

'Can't afford any.' Katie said this automatically and felt a funny itch behind her left ear. She shook her head to dislodge the feeling. Truth was, she didn't want to use fake tan. It had become bound up in her mind with girls-who-should-know-better and cheap clothes. Probably from her mum, who had a less pleasing kind of certainty.

'You could get your aunt to magic you brown.'

This was something Katie liked less about Imogen. Her inability to leave a subject alone. She peered at Imogen's exposed knees. 'It might be the goose bumps, but that mole looks funny.'

'Shut up,' Imogen said, but she sat up and tugged her skirt a little lower. 'So. What's she like, anyway? My mum says she was a complete mental case at school.'

'Boy alert,' Katie said. She'd been trying to distract Imogen but, on second glance, she realised that the pack of boys crossing the yard contained the delicious form of Luke Taylor. Katie felt the familiar dipping sensation in her stomach.

Imogen followed her gaze. 'Yum,' she said. 'I usually prefer older men, but even I have to admit that Luke is a Class-A hottie.'

'I do have excellent taste,' Katie said. 'Now I just need him to realise I exist.'

'You will,' Imogen said. 'And then he'll fall for your extreme cuteness. And you and Luke can double-date with me and Gavin. It'll be perfect.'

Katie smiled. It was a nice fantasy.

CHAPTER 4

Having spent the previous two days cleaning and moving bin bags around End House, Gwen had a touch of cabin fever. She also had to face the horrifying truth: she couldn't ignore her business any longer. Gwen didn't want to parcel up the customer's order. She didn't want to look at the last shadow box that she'd made, and she certainly didn't want to remember how hopeful she'd been when she made it, before the final demands piled up and her eviction notice arrived like the Grim Reaper, but she didn't have a choice. Curious Notions might've been as-good-as bankrupt, but she wasn't going to let a customer down. The shadow box was a rare commission and the woman had wanted 'something about love' for a wedding anniversary. Gwen had created a miniature apothecary shop with rows of tiny bottles and jars. You needed a magnifying glass to read the labels, but there was 'tincture of true love' and 'heart's desire' in amongst the foot powder and cough mixture.

Gwen was filing off the back edge of the box, making sure it was perfectly smooth, when a familiar figure appeared at the back door.

'I'm going out,' Gwen said, standing up. 'Sorry.'

Lily stepped into the kitchen anyway, her smile as bright as ever. She ran one hand protectively over the Formica worktop as she looked around the room, seeming to take every detail in. 'Everything okay?'

'Fine.' Gwen put down her file.

'What's that?' Lily peered at the shadow box.

Gwen wanted to say 'my art', but didn't want to sound like a pretentious twat. 'It's kind of an assemblage thing,' she said. 'It's what I do. For money.' *Kind of.*

'What's it for?' Lily leaned over, her nose almost touching the Perspex front of the box.

'Nothing. It's just a decoration.'

'Oh.' Lily straightened up. 'How much do you charge?'

Gwen blinked. 'Sixty-five pounds. This one's more because it was commissioned.'

'Nice little earner.' Lily gave her an approving nod.

'Not really,' Gwen said. The apothecary shop had taken over sixteen hours to make and the miniature till was an antique that had cost ten pounds. Gwen had a sudden flash of fury at herself. No wonder she was broke. What was *wrong* with her? The new-yoga-obsessed Ruby would probably say that her chakras were unaligned or something.

She put tissue paper over the box, added a 'thank you for your purchase' card and began folding layers of bubble wrap.

Still Lily lingered.

'I'm going into town to post this,' Gwen tried.

'That's fine,' Lily said. 'I'll come with you. I can show you around.'

Gwen knew that she should explain that she used to live in the town and that she probably knew it as well as Lily did, but the words remained stuck in her throat.

She hoisted her bag onto her shoulder and locked up the house.

'Iris never locked her back door,' Lily observed.

'That was very silly of her,' Gwen said.

Lily laughed her unnatural tinkle. 'I keep forgetting you're a city type. You don't know what it's like in Pendleford; we all look out for one another here.'

Fed up, Gwen snapped, 'I suppose there's no crime at all, then? If I buy the paper, it'll be completely blank.'

Lily looked away, but she didn't say anything. They walked past the frost-touched hedgerows in silence, reaching the end of the track and joined what probably counted as a main road in Pendleford.

'You have a lovely garden,' Gwen said as they passed it. A peace offering.

'Not as big as yours.' Lily's voice had real bitterness in it, but a moment later she said brightly, 'Have you looked at the town bridge yet?'

'I've driven over it,' Gwen said, adding silently: *And, a lifetime ago, I snogged Cameron Laing underneath it.*

Lily slid her a sideways look. 'But have you really looked at it?'

'Why?'

'You'll see,' Lily said with satisfaction.

Gwen breathed in, enjoying the crisp autumnal air, the sunlight that lit the trees into beacons of flame. Within minutes, the roads narrowed and they entered the town centre. 'Some of the buildings are medieval – like the Tithe Barn,' Lily said, pointing down a side street. 'That's a big attraction.'

A queue of cars inched slowly down Silver Street, spoiling the olde worlde effect somewhat.

Lily saw Gwen looking and said, 'We weren't built for cars, that's for sure.' She spoke as if the town were alive.

'Mmm.' Having walked down the winding street, balancing on the cobbles and narrowly avoiding pitching into a silver sedan, Gwen stopped outside a small shop called The Crystal Cave. It was filled with crystal balls, decks of tarot cards, and a tabby cat. It was the kind of place Gloria loved to browse in for hours and she breathed in, half-expecting the scent of incense to permeate the street.

'It's for the tourists,' Lily sniffed. 'Wiltshire is known for its ancient stones, ley lines and mystical energy.'

Gwen didn't ask what a fake crystal ball had to do with a prehistoric stone circle.

'It's silly really,' Lily said.

Gwen hadn't been paying proper attention, but now she realised that Lily was watching her carefully. 'Silly,' she said, hoping that agreeing with Lily would make her stop staring at her in that unnerving way. She added, 'Harmless, though.'

'One woman's cupcake is another's shit sandwich,' Lily replied.

'Pardon?'

Lily gave her a calculating look. 'That's what your aunt always said. She said it was impossible to do no harm. One hungry family's roast dinner is the sad demise of a chicken.'

'Right.'

'She was full of them. Said everything was a war and that there could only be one winner.'

The cold air was making Gwen's nose run and she pulled out a tissue. She was getting the creeping sensation that she might not have liked her aunt very much. Question was: should that make her feel more or less guilty about inheriting from her?

'Look...' Lily pointed down the street. 'There's the roundhouse.'

At one end of the bridge was a round stone structure. Its shape was a cross between a minaret and a beehive and there was an ornately carved fish mounted on the roof.

'The bridge is thirteenth century, but the roundhouse was added in the eighteenth. It was used as a lock-up for drunkards and criminals.'

'There's a fish on the roof,' Gwen said. She was working on automatic pilot, her voice handling conversation while her brain concentrated on ignoring the river rushing under the bridge.

Lily nodded. 'A gudgeon. Round here we still say "over the water and under the fish" when we mean in jail.'

'That's colourful.'

'Oh yes. We've got colour coming out of our arses round here,' Lily said and walked onwards, her heels clicking on the pavement.

Gwen stamped down on her rising panic. She'd spent so long squashing all thoughts of Stephen Knight that she wasn't prepared for the assault of memories. He'd been a funny-looking boy. One of those awkward teens that look both younger and older than their age all at once. A baby face that somehow carried the gruff, sunburned features of his farming parents at the same time. Until they fished him out of the river, of course. Then he'd looked exactly, tragically, his sixteen years.

They reached the main shopping street. A steeply sloping affair, lined with self-consciously pretty painted wooden fronts and chichi window displays. It was all much more upmarket than Gwen remembered.

'What do you need to do?' Lily was showing no signs of leaving and Gwen couldn't think of a polite way to extricate herself.

'Um. Post office?'

'At the bottom of the road, turn left. It's next to the Co-op.'

Lily paused, a sly look flashed across her face and then disappeared. 'You should go and see the green. It's a little further along the river.'

'Okay.'

'And the Red Lion does bar meals if you fancy a bite.'

'Thanks.' Gwen shifted her weight, preparing to walk away.

'It's haunted, mind, but I'm sure that won't bother you.'

Gwen forced a laugh. 'I don't believe in ghosts.'

'Quite right. It's probably dreamed up as a lure for the tourists.'

Despite herself, Gwen asked, 'What is?'

'Ghost of Jane Morely. She was tried as a witch on the green outside the pub.'

Lily's stare had become disturbingly intense and Gwen decided the best policy was a polite smile.

'It's in the town records if you don't believe me. She was executed in 1675. They strangled her and burned her.'

'Better than the other way around, I suppose.'

Lily looked at her sharply. 'I would prefer neither, myself.'

'Well, yes,' Gwen stumbled. How did she end up in a conversation about preferred methods of execution? 'Obviously.' She stepped aside to let a woman laden with shopping bags pass. The woman stopped, turned, and retraced her steps. 'Excuse me? Aren't you Gwen Harper?'

'Um. Yes.'

'You've just moved into the big house, haven't you?'

'Sorry?' Gwen felt panicky, as if she were in the middle of an exam that she hadn't revised for.

'Off Bath Road? End House, is it?' The woman had a thoroughly freckled face topped with a teal beret.

'Yes.'

'I'm Amanda. I'm in number twelve on the main road. We're neighbours.' She shifted her clutch of carrier bags from one hand to the other. 'I'm so sorry we haven't been by to welcome you. We've all had the sickness bug that's going around.'

'Oh don't worry,' Gwen said. Then there was a pause, so she added, 'It's fine.'

After another, lengthening, silence, Gwen realised that Amanda was waiting for something. With a flash of understanding, Gwen dragged up the words, 'You're very welcome to pop by any time. Come for tea.'

Amanda smiled. People were too happy in this place. It was unnerving.

'You don't remember me, do you?'

Gwen stared at Amanda's wide grey eyes and freckled skin, something tickling the back of her mind, and then it came to her. 'Biology,' she said, just as Amanda said, 'We were in sixth form together.'

'God. I'm sorry. It's been ages. How are you?' Gwen was struggling to reconcile this slightly matronly-looking woman with the sullen teenager she only vaguely remembered. Biology, like most of her classes, was a bit of a blur. She'd been dreaming her way through her A levels, thinking only about Cam and when she was next seeing him. Your basic teenage cliché, she now realised.

Lily stood frozen, her face a mask.

'I'm sorry,' Gwen said, gesturing. 'Amanda, this is Lily.'

'Oh, we know each other,' Amanda said dismissively. She put down her shopping bags and stretched her fingers. She had purple gloves on with an extra pair of fingerless woollen ones over the top.

'You didn't tell me you used to live here,' Lily said, her voice tight.

'Yes.' Gwen turned to Lily. 'For a while. A long time ago.'

'How long?' Lily said, her gaze unnervingly intense. 'You went to school here?'

'We moved onto Newfield Road when I was ten. But I haven't been back for ages. Not since sixth form, actually.' She forced a laugh. 'It feels like a different life.'

'You let me go on like a fool, showing you around. Telling you things.' Bright spots of colour appeared on Lily's cheeks. 'You didn't say you knew Pendleford, that you used to *live* here.' Lily was almost stuttering in her horror. 'I feel like an idiot. You let me go on—'

'No, I liked it,' Gwen said, trying to make it better. 'It's all so different. It was useful. Really.'

Amanda laughed. 'Pendleford? Changed? Not likely.'

Gwen shot her a look that said: *not helping*.

'Well, I assume you can find your way from here,' Lily said, furious embarrassment clear on her face. 'I'll leave you in peace.'

Gwen watched her walk away, her back perfectly straight, her highlighted helmet of blonde hair hardly moving. 'Damn it,' she said under her breath. *Way to make nice with the neighbours, Gwen.*

'Are you renovating the house?' Amanda asked, oblivious. 'I know a great builder if you need one.' She looked self-conscious for a moment. 'I suppose I would say that. He's my husband, you see, but he's very good.'

'I'm sure.'

'Ask anyone.'

'I'm not really planning—'

'He can get references. Written ones.'

'I've only just moved in and I haven't worked out what I'm doing yet—'

'Reputation is everything round here, so you can rely on a local.'

Gwen gave up. 'I'll bear him in mind. Thanks.'

'Well, I'd best get on.' Amanda stooped to retrieve her bags.

'Right. Will do. I'm just—' Gwen waved in the general direction she was heading. 'I think I'll get some lunch and wait for the post office to open.'

'He won't be back till one.'

'Right. Thanks.'

'You want some advice?' Amanda leaned in. 'Avoid the Red Lion.'

'Bad food?'

Amanda sniffed. 'Bloody unfriendly.'

Gwen watched the bulky figure of Amanda retreat up the twisty street and then turned resolutely in the direction of the pub. Unfriendly sounded perfect. She could cope with the ghosts if nobody living spoke to her for the next half an hour.

Gwen finished a ploughman's lunch and half a lager and read the newspaper. She was feeling a great deal warmer towards the town. The pub was the kind she liked. It had traditional decor with a few old photographs and horse brasses on the walls, scarred wooden tables and benches and an open fire in the front room.

She'd even enjoyed the surly service from the barman; it made her feel more comfortable than anything else in Pendleford so far. It felt somehow more honest, which was probably a sad reflection on her life so far.

Gwen left her plate and glass on the bar on her way past. The barman rewarded her with an almost-smile. The front room had filled up in the time she'd been eating, but Gwen noticed Cam right away. He was eating alone, a paperback book splayed open next to his plate.

Gwen hesitated. She wanted to walk straight past, but if he looked up she didn't want to get caught ignoring him. So he hated her. So what? She swallowed, feeling sick. If she was serious about staying in this town, she was going to have to get used to seeing him. She straightened her shoulders and tried to arrange her face into a relaxed expression.

He looked up.

Gwen forced herself forward. *Breezy. Just breeze past. Breezily.*

'Hello.'

'I just had lunch.' Gwen motioned to the back room.

Cam nodded, his expression unreadable.

'I'm just going,' Gwen said.

'So I see.' Cam looked like a spectacularly bad day had just got worse. Well, she'd just walk on out of there and relieve his stress.

'Where are you running off to?' Cam said, his face perfectly still.

'I'm not running,' Gwen said with dignity. 'I'm leaving you in peace.' This cold politeness was unnerving. She hadn't expected much after their last meeting, but there wasn't so much as a flicker of warmth. Gwen blinked. Her insides suddenly felt hollow.

'Nice to see you,' he said. Then, as if they were perfect strangers, 'Welcome to Pendleford, again. Do call my office if you need anything.'

Gwen got the hell out before she pushed his cool, calm, collected face into his lunch.

On the way home, she called into the big chemist to stock up on essentials. She was filling her basket with three-for-two offers and trying to block out the Christmas music, when she spotted a familiar face. Marilyn Dixon. Lurking behind the perfume counter. There were dark circles under her eyes; purple shadows visible through the mask of pale beige make-up. Gwen felt a stab of guilt. She shouldn't have left things the way she did. She should've been nicer. More sympathetic.

Gwen waited for the queue to empty, then took her basket up to Marilyn's till.

For a moment she thought Marilyn wouldn't recognise her, but then she said, 'Iris used to make all her own stuff. Body lotion and toothpaste. She said you couldn't trust the chemicals.'

'Won't you get in trouble for saying that here?' Gwen was aiming for humour, but Marilyn didn't smile. 'Watch out for the botanical range. It brought me out in a rash.'

'Right. Thank you.'

There was a pause, punctuated by the beep of the scanner.

'I'm sorry if I was rude last night,' Gwen said.

'That's all right,' Marilyn said stiffly. 'It must've seemed very odd, my coming to you like that.'

'Well—'

'I don't know what I was thinking. I don't know what I'm doing any more.' Marilyn rammed a tube of hand cream deep into a carrier bag. 'It's not been an easy time for me.'

'I'm sorry.'

Marilyn added the cotton buds, lip balm and moisturiser to the bag.

'If you want to talk—' Gwen began awkwardly.

'I have friends,' Marilyn said defensively. A furtive look crossed her face. 'And I went to see your neighbour instead. *She* was very helpful.'

'Oh. Good,' Gwen said. 'My neighbour?'

'She said it'll make Brian come to his senses.'

'What will?'

Marilyn bagged the last item – a lipstick Gwen had picked up on impulse – and gave Gwen a sickly smile. 'Thank you for shopping with us today.'

Gwen braved the cold to spend some time sorting through her stock in the back of Nanette. She knew she ought to be making plans; working out what she was going to do about her business, money, her future. Instead, Cam's carefully polite expression and Marilyn-bloody-Dixon's voice kept popping into her mind. What did she mean by 'come to his senses'? And why had she looked so tired and sad? With fingers that were too numb to open any more boxes, Gwen headed into the house. She ate some bread and jam and drank a glass of wine. Perhaps it was her imagination, but the house seemed just as cold as the van. Trying not to think about Cam or the business or Marilyn or anything at all, Gwen retreated to bed. She pulled up all of the blankets and quilts and, within moments, fell asleep.

Gwen snapped awake. The room was freezing, but she knew a noise had woken her up. She listened, ears straining. There was a muffled thump and her heart damn near jumped out of her mouth. She pushed down the fear and forced herself to switch on the lamp. The cat stalked out from the end of the bed and picked his way to the door. Relief flooded her system. 'Bloody cat!' He paused at the door but didn't turn around. Gwen took a deep breath and willed her hammering heart to slow. She knew she wasn't going to fall back asleep any time soon, so she swung her legs out of bed. Her Sudoku book was downstairs. A few minutes struggling with the 'super-hard' level puzzles was usually enough to cure any insomnia. It was cold and she pulled on her dressing-gown and slippers. 'I'm on my way,' she said to the impatient cat, who stood by the door. She readied herself for him to squeeze past her, but instead he wound around her legs, like he was trying to imitate clothing. 'Not now, Cat.'

He kept up the furry ankle-socks impression all the way down the stairs until she said, 'You win. I'll feed you.' The words died in her throat as she saw a detail that was all wrong. The back door was ajar. She went cold all over and then liquid with fear as the door clicked shut. Someone had just left her house. At two o'clock in the morning.

CHAPTER 5

Gwen slipped back into the hallway, heart thudding, and dialled 999. An oddly rational part of her brain observed her doing this. *You've never rung the emergency services before*, the calm part of her brain said. *Apart from that one time*, an unhelpful section piped up. *Down by the river. A bloated white face. Black water weeds tangled around his neck.* Gwen squashed the memory back down, ignoring the sickness that came with it as best she could. *Don't think about that. No time. Look, now you're giving your address. Aren't you doing well?*

The woman on the line said that someone would be there very soon. Gwen went back upstairs and locked herself and Cat in the bathroom, her ear pressed to the door to listen and her mobile phone gripped in one hand. Six minutes later, the doorbell rang and she went back downstairs. Blue lights were strobing through the glass panel at the top of the door and she opened the door to a six-foot tall policewoman, her male partner dwarfed beside her.

Gwen gave a swift recap, showing the now-completely-shut back door and waiting while both PCs checked the garden, the gates, and down the road. She was proud of how calm she was being until the policeman – PC Davies – suggested that she sit down and put her head between her knees for a moment and she realised that her peripheral vision had entirely disappeared.

'Quiet up here,' PC Green said, tactfully ignoring the fact that Gwen had her head at floor level and was taking deep breaths.

Gwen sat up slowly and the kitchen tilted. She swallowed. 'Yes.'

'Nice.' Green looked around. She had brown hair in a high ponytail and discreetly chic make-up. She looked capable and grown up and, even if she hadn't been wearing a uniform, Gwen would've trusted her.

'Have you lived here long?'

Gwen explained about her aunt and the inheritance. 'It's all been quite strange.'

'So, you've been a bit disorientated?'

'Well…' Gwen said.

'And what are the neighbours like? This is usually a pretty friendly place.'

'Oh, very nice.' Gwen said quickly. 'Very friendly.'

'Do they pop by?'

'All the time.'

PC Green nodded. 'You lived in a city before, right?'

'Yes. Leeds.'

'Different place, I bet.'

'Well, obviously, but—'

Green called to PC Davies, not even attempting to hide her impatience. 'False alarm.'

Gwen decided she wasn't so trustworthy after all. What self-respecting police person wore a scrunchie, anyway?

'You probably left the door open and the wind blew it shut,' she said to Gwen.

'I definitely locked the door before I went to bed,' Gwen said, stamping down on her anger. 'City girl, remember? Paranoid.'

'Well, maybe someone popped by for a visit. One of your neighbours.'

'At two o'clock in the morning?' Gwen said tightly.

PC Green shrugged and walked to the front door. PC Davies was already there, holding it wide open and letting a wall of freezing air into the hall.

Gwen hugged herself to keep from shouting at an officer of the law. 'If a neighbour decided to visit, why didn't they speak to me? Call upstairs?' As she spoke, Gwen remembered Lily's stealth casserole.

PC Davies looked apologetic. 'We'll file a report. Let us know if you have any more problems.'

'I definitely locked that door,' Gwen said again, trying not to sound shaky and pathetic.

Green was already halfway to the panda car.

'I'm not crazy,' Gwen called to her. Green raised a hand without turning round.

Gwen shut the door and locked it. There was something tugging at her memory, too. A feeling. When she'd gone downstairs and seen the door closing, she'd had the strong sense it was a man on the other side of it. Gwen had been brought up to pay attention to her intuition, to believe in it. She closed her eyes and concentrated. A strong smell of aftershave filled her nostrils. She opened her eyes and it dissipated. Definitely a man then. She couldn't exactly call Green back and explain how she knew that and it seemed that the house was magnifying the Harper family intuition. Either that or she was going crazy. Cat wound around her ankles, purring like a jet engine. 'Bloody marvellous,' Gwen said, and went to find him some tuna fish.

The next morning, Gwen was reading in bed after a fitful night. She told herself that she was completely calm and fine, but for some irritating reason she still hadn't been able to sleep for more than half an hour at a time. Iris's notebook wasn't exactly comforting, either. Amongst the unknown initials of Iris's customers and acquaintances, her own name kept leaping out.

Gloria was here with her girls today. She didn't tell me, of course, but I could see it straight away: Gwen has the Finding. Poor child. There's a reason Finding Lost Things was banned by the charter of 1539. Some things aren't meant to be found.

Gwen closed her eyes. Iris wasn't wrong about that. Before Gwen had started to refuse to do her party piece on demand, Gloria was always pimping her out. Lost car keys, wallets, pets, wedding rings. When she was eleven, she'd had to tell a woman that her lost engagement ring was at an address that turned out to be a pawn shop. Rather than believe that her husband (who everyone knew had a teeny-tiny problem with gambling) had hawked it, she accused Gwen of nicking it and then trying to squeeze some more cash out of her by finding it. Being screamed at by a member of the school PTA wasn't the worst Gwen had experienced, but she still remembered the feeling of betrayal. Why had Gloria made her do it? She was supposed to be the grown-up, the protector. Sure, she'd hauled Gwen out of the woman's kitchen, taken her home and passed her tissues to wipe her face, but the experience didn't stop her asking Gwen to find something for a client later that same day. Gloria didn't let a little thing like her daughter's feelings get in the way of increasing revenue.

At half past eight, Cat stalked into the room and jumped onto the bed. He landed with a thud that made the bed springs creak. 'How are you so heavy?' she asked him. 'You defy the laws of physics.' Unless the cat was a black hole. That would make sense.

The doorbell rang. Gwen pulled on slippers and a dressing-gown and picked up the cricket bat. The man at the front door wasn't in uniform or a bad suit, but she could see he was police just the same.

'Detective Inspector Harry Collins. Please don't hit me.'

Gwen leaned the bat up against the wall and took a step back.

He walked into the hallway with a puff of icy winter air and the smell of frost.

Gwen held her hand out for his heavy jacket.

He shook his head. 'That's all right.'

'You have to take it off now or you won't feel the benefit when you go outside.'

The policeman grinned, instantly looking about ten years younger. 'That's what my gran always said.'

'Smart lady,' Gwen said, hand outstretched.

Harry shrugged off his coat obediently and handed it to Gwen.

In the kitchen, Gwen was confused to find the tea bag tin out of the cupboard where it lived and sitting on the counter. Lid off. Either the intruder had got halfway through making himself a cup of tea, or Iris was moving things around. Which was impossible. Gwen put the tin back and poured two strong coffees. She cut thick slices of fruit cake and pretended that her hands weren't shaking.

'Isn't it early for cake?' Harry said.

'Never too early for cake. Anyway, it's got fruit in it. It's practically a health food.'

'Well, then.' Harry took some cake and then said, 'Can you tell me about the disturbance last night?'

'I don't want to waste your time,' Gwen said stiffly, not in the mood for another round of 'laugh at the loony out-of-towner'. 'I got a case number last night.' Gwen turned to look for it.

'I read the report, but I'd like to hear it from you.' He gave a small smile. 'If you don't mind.'

Gwen frowned. 'You're a detective. Isn't this a bit below your pay grade?' She gave him a searching look. 'Quiet day at the office?'

He smiled that easy grin again and held up his hands. 'I have a confession to make.'

Gwen closed her eyes. 'Don't tell me you knew my great-aunt.'

'Don't think so. I do know Cameron Laing though.'

Gwen frowned, ignoring the flare of excitement that Cam's name ignited. 'I don't—'

'So, when I saw your call on the log, I recognised your name and address and thought I'd better deal with it personally.'

'Oh.' Gwen didn't have a follow-up for that.

'Don't want to give Cam a reason to fall out with me. He buys the drinks,' Harry supplied.

'Right.' Cameron Laing the lawyer. Cameron Laing, friend to the local detective inspector. Life was odd.

'So,' Harry said gently, 'can you talk me through it?'

Gwen took a sip of coffee, gathering her thoughts. 'I woke up. Something woke me up. I guess a noise, although I wasn't aware of anything clearly. I got up and went downstairs.'

'On your own? That wasn't sensible.'

Gwen glowered at him. 'There are a lot of creepy noises in this house. You want me to call the police every time the radiator burps?'

Harry waved a hand. 'Continue.'

'I went downstairs and when I walked into the kitchen, I saw the back door shut.' She paused, feeling the fear all over again. 'Someone had just left.'

'No forced entry, so we're looking at someone with access. How many people have a key to the house?'

'I have no idea.' Gwen said, feeling stupid. 'I doubt Iris was in the habit of giving them out, but—'

'Can you show me the keys?'

Gwen got up and fetched her key ring. It still felt bulky and awkward in her hand and it took her a while to locate the front and back door keys.

'Okay. The front door has a new Yale, but this one,' he held up the brass back door key, 'looks vintage.'

'I don't know who has the key. I know Lily Thomas – my great-aunt's cleaner – had one, but she left it here.' Gwen went through to the hallway and picked up the spare key.

Harry nodded, his phone at his ear. 'Michael? Got a job for you in Pendleford.' He paused. 'Nope. Got to be today. This morning for preference.' He looked at Gwen. 'Eleven o'clock okay with you?'

She nodded, dumbfounded by the way people kept taking charge, bringing her things, helping. It was unsettling.

Harry collected his jacket. 'Thank you for the cake. It was very nice to meet you.'

'What's going to happen about my intruder?'

'Well, we file a report.'

'And?' Gwen said. 'Don't you dust for fingerprints or something?'

'Sometimes,' Harry said. 'But it's not all that easy and, as your intruder had a key, technically we don't have much of a crime. Entering, but not so much with the breaking.'

'But you're here. The detective inspector.'

Harry smiled again. 'Like I said; you're a special case.'

I've been called that before, Gwen thought wryly, and she opened the front door for Harry. An icy blast blew straight through her clothes, making her feel suddenly naked. She wrapped her arms around her body. 'Goodbye then. Thank you for your help.'

'Anything for you, Gwen Harper,' Harry said with a grin and headed down the path.

Gwen shut the door, utterly bemused. 'They're all crazy around here,' she said, turning around and leaning against the door. She tried not to wonder what, exactly, Cam had said about her to Harry.

'Prrup?' the cat said, looking as innocent as the seven-year-old Ruby after she'd been left in charge of their joint haul of Easter chocolate.

'That goes for you, too, Cat,' she said, straightening up.

Later that day, the doorbell rang and somebody started pounding on the front door. Gwen rushed through, tightening her dressing-gown cord as she went.

Cameron Laing stood in front of her, arm raised from bashing seven shades out of the paintwork.

'Is something on fire?' Gwen said, stepping back to let him in.

'Why didn't you call me?' His face and voice were as neutral as they had been in the pub, but there was a tightness around his eyes.

'What?' Gwen closed the door against the howling gale.

'You were broken into,' Cam said. His forehead creased. 'You should've told me.'

'I called the police.' Gwen folded her arms. 'And I'm fine. Thanks for asking.'

'I know you're fine.' Cam sounded irritated. 'I spoke to Harry.'

'You two are like a pair of little old ladies.' Gwen was determined not to be pleased that he cared.

Cam frowned. 'What?'

'Gossiping. This whole place is filled with people talking about other people's business and turning up at all hours and talking and wanting . . . stuff.' Gwen realised she was babbling and forced herself to stop.

'Are you all right?' Cam dipped his head to look at her properly.

'I'm just tired.' Gwen tried a smile. 'Actually, I'm exhausted.'

He ran a hand through his hair, leaving the front standing up. 'Shit. Sorry. Did I wake you up?'

'No.' Gwen was momentarily confused, and then she remembered that she wasn't dressed. 'I was just going through Iris's papers. Trying to make sense of the open-door policy in this place.'

'It's your house, now. You can do whatever you want. Don't let people in.'

'That's easier said than done,' Gwen said. The temperature in the hallway suddenly dropped further, as if she hadn't just shut the door, and she shivered.

'Right,' Cam said, and pushed past her, heading for the back door.

'Help yourself,' Gwen said drily. He bent down to look at the door and Gwen found herself staring at his backside. She swallowed. It was just as appealing as the front view. Maybe even more so because she couldn't see him scowling at her from this angle.

'The locksmith is coming round. I thought you were him. He. Whichever.'

'You should replace the whole thing. This glass isn't safe. Someone can knock it out and reach through—' He stopped when he saw her expression and stuffed his hands into his pockets. 'It's fine. This is a very safe town. Our crime rate is really low.'

'I'm sure,' Gwen said politely.

'Well. I'm glad you're okay.'

'I'm fine.' She smiled to show that she was fine and that he didn't have to be politely concerned for her any longer.

'Good,' Cam said. 'I'll leave you to your reading.'

He paused at the door, looking like he might be about to say something.

Gwen dug her fingernails into her palm to stop herself from blurting out something stupid like: *stay*. Or from reaching out and grabbing the front of his shirt. 'See you later,' she said. After he'd gone, she ran upstairs and watched him get into his car from the bedroom window. She laid her head against the cool glass and marvelled at the heat in her skin.

The locksmith came as promised, but he kept his coat on while he worked. The house was freezing and Gwen couldn't get the pilot light on the boiler relit. By the afternoon, ice had formed on the inside of the windows and Gwen answered the door wearing thick socks, tartan flannel PJ bottoms and an enormous hooded sweatshirt that was rolled up several times on the sleeves.

Gwen was surprised to find Cam on the doorstep. He was looking serious, which wasn't so shocking. Gwen wondered if the frown was regulation issue, handed out after the bar exam.

'You look terrible,' Cam said.

'The words every woman longs to hear.' Gwen stepped aside to let him in.

'Sorry. I mean, you don't look well. Are you all right?' His face softened in concern and instantly he looked like a different man.

'The boiler's broken and the repair guy says he can't come out until tomorrow and I can't stop thinking about some stranger walking around in the house while I was asleep and touching all my stuff. Well, Iris's stuff. Apart from that, I'm fabulous.'

He held up a hammer and a piece of plywood. 'I come bearing gifts.'

Gwen brightened. 'Can you fix heating?'

'Sorry, probably not. I'm going to nail this over the glass in your back door.' He shrugged. 'I'll take a look at your heating, although I warn you not to get your hopes up.'

'Good enough.' The hallway suddenly seemed too small a space to share with Cam, so Gwen led the way to the kitchen.

She flipped the switch on the kettle and got a tin down from the cupboard while Cam examined the back door. She wondered if Cam, as executor of Iris's estate, had some legal obligation to look after the property. The thought that he might be bound to the house and, by extension, her for six months, was appealing. 'Is this part of the service?' *Or do you still care about me?*

Cam turned round. 'What do you mean?'

Gwen didn't know how to ask whether he was in her kitchen out of personal concern or professionalism. And suddenly she didn't want to know the answer. 'Nothing,' she said. 'Would you like tea or coffee?'

Cam pounded nails with a focus that Gwen found alarmingly attractive. He had taken off his suit jacket and hung it over the back of one of the kitchen chairs. His shoulders filled out his white shirt very nicely indeed and the way his hair curled over the nape of his neck did something odd to Gwen's insides. She leaned against the counter and contemplated his back. It was soothing to look at him when he wasn't frowning at her.

Then the doorbell rang and spoiled Gwen's moment of quiet enjoyment. Cam glanced over his shoulder. 'You expecting someone?'

'Not exactly.'

It was a tall man with a checked scarf tucked into a dark wool coat. His skin was suspiciously smooth and evenly toned. He had the well-kept look that went hand-in-hand with a disgustingly healthy bank balance. She would lay money that he didn't want chilblain ointment.

'Ms Harper?'

'Hello.' Gwen stuck out her hand. The man gripped it firmly and pumped her arm, while Gwen tried to work out if he was wearing foundation.

'I'm Patrick Allen,' the smooth man said. 'As head of the Rotary, 'I'd like to welcome you to our little town.' He gave a fake modest chuckle that made Gwen want to throw up. 'I heard about the unfortunate incident and I wanted to assure you that this is a very safe town.'

The cold air was streaming through the open door and Gwen saw a hard frost clinging to the lavender bushes that lined the path. Politeness said that she had to invite him into the house, but Gwen felt a stickiness in the air that was almost like a barrier. *Damn house making all the decisions*. She ignored the feeling and smiled as cheerily as she could manage. 'Would you like to come in?'

Cam appeared in the kitchen doorway, the hammer dangling carelessly from one hand.

'This is Patrick Allen,' Gwen said quickly, trying to ignore the way her heart had sped up. She was having a ridiculous throw-back reaction to Cam. Something to do with old memories.

'I know Patrick.' Cam smiled, but it didn't reach his eyes. 'Don't often see you on this side of the river.'

'I could say the same to you, Cameron.' Patrick inclined his head. 'I wanted to talk to you about something, actually.'

'You'll have to make an appointment at the office.'

Patrick ignored him. 'It's about this ridiculous folk festival.'

'I've told you before,' Cam said. 'Not something I can help you with.'

Patrick crossed his arms. He looked unaccustomed to hearing the word 'no'. 'What's the point in having laws, then?'

'A question I have asked myself many times,' Cam said with a tight smile. He turned to Gwen. 'Where will I find your boiler?'

'If you can't even use them to protect what's right . . .' Patrick was still talking and Gwen revised her initial impression from 'smooth' to 'irritating'.

'Upstairs. Back bedroom in the cupboard in the corner,' Gwen said.

Cam started to turn away, then stopped. 'The law isn't about what's right. It's about what's legal.'

'But this so-called festival will be an embarrassment,' Patrick said. 'It's an affront to the decent people,' he went on, his chest puffed up with importance, 'the decent businesses—'

'Are they having a craft market?' Gwen said.

'Pardon?' Patrick glanced at Gwen.

'At the festival. Are they planning to have a craft tent or something? These things often do.'

'I have no idea,' Patrick said, his expression sour. 'What I do know is that they will ruin the town's green.'

'Chippenham and Trowbridge have held them for years without any problem,' Cam said. 'And, as I understand it, the town council have made it clear that the green must be left in the state in which it was found.'

'We're not Chippenham,' Patrick said in a withering tone.

'Just, if there's going to be a craft market, I'd love to join in. I have a stall.' Gwen knew she was being childish, but she couldn't help it. Patrick reminded her of every authority figure she'd ever rebelled against. Old habits died hard.

Patrick looked momentarily at a loss for words. Then he rallied with another false laugh. 'Ah. I take it I won't be able to count on you to sign my petition, then?'

'As a local business owner, I welcome anything that brings in the punters,' Gwen said sweetly.

'Well. Yes. I suppose.' Patrick looked as if he dearly wanted to say something else.

'I've got to get my tools,' Cam said and went out of the front door. Gwen didn't blame him.

'Would you like a cup of coffee? Tea?' Gwen ushered Patrick to the dining room. She was damned if he was sitting in her lovely kitchen.

'I can't stop, really. Just wanted to welcome you and to see if there was anything . . .' Patrick trailed off as he took in the mausoleum chic of the dining room. He turned on his heel. 'Did you say your boiler wasn't working? Can I help with that?'

'I don't know. Can you?' Gwen was nonplussed. She had the feeling that Patrick wasn't the kind of person who offered favours out of the goodness of his heart.

'I have a man for that sort of thing.' Patrick took a business card from his wallet. 'Call me if you need anything. Anything at all.' He looked deeply into Gwen's eyes as he said this. Probably something he'd learned on a management training day.

Once Patrick was safely off the premises, Gwen fetched painting supplies from the shed. She felt itchy, like she needed to take some control back and show Iris who was boss in the house. Painting over the horrible purple walls seemed like a good place to start. She spread dustsheets over the furniture in the living room until the place looked like it was filled with snowy hillocks.

'What on earth are you doing?'

Gwen turned to find Cam standing in the doorway, a metal toolbox in one hand. 'This room is oppressively horrid, so I'm brightening it up.' She waved a paintbrush.

'It's November.'

'I know what month it is,' Gwen said. 'I need to keep busy.'

'But you'll freeze. You'll need the window open for ventilation.'

'I'm already freezing.' Gwen gestured at her layers of clothing. 'And I appear to be surviving. So.'

Cam crossed the room and forced the sash window open a couple of inches. 'I hope you enjoy frostbite.'

'Not at all; that's why I want you to focus all of your admirable energy on my boiler.'

She'd barely started rollering the first wall when Cam called out. She went upstairs and met Cam coming the other way, his expression grim.

Gwen stopped. 'What?'

'Come and see,' Cam said.

Cam had taken the white casing off the front of the boiler and leaned it up against the open door of the cupboard.

'What?' Gwen began, then took a closer look.

A small plate that housed the electrics was bent outwards, deep scrape marks gouged into the metal and a tangle of wires hung out drunkenly. The copper pipework had been smashed almost completely flat and a couple of dials were cracked.

'I think I can see why it wouldn't relight for you,' Cam said.

CHAPTER 6

Gwen went downstairs, trying to rub life back into her frozen hands. She stabbed the button on the kettle and got down a couple of mugs. Cam walked in a moment later, slipping his phone into his pocket.

'Tea?'

'No, thanks.'

His expression made her body temperature drop another couple of degrees. 'What is it?'

'Was the boiler working when you moved in?'

'Yes. I think so.'

'Someone's really gone to town on it. Probably with a hammer. Do you have a hammer?'

'You think I hit my own boiler?' Gwen's brain seemed to be as frozen as her hands.

'No.' Cam shook his head. 'Harry wanted to know. If you had left one lying about your bedroom—' he paused, stuck on the word, then carried on, 'that could be a spur of the moment crime. But if the person brought it with them it was planned.'

'Does that make a difference?'

'Very much so. In court—' He broke off. 'Sit down.'

'Okay.' Gwen felt her legs wobble and hastily sat in the chair Cam had jumped up to offer. Last thing she wanted to do was collapse in front of him like a needy, useless lump.

'I've rung around, but no one can come out before tomorrow.' Cam looked almost murderous.

'I know,' Gwen said. 'I told you that.'

'It's not good enough,' Cam said.

'Well, this early cold snap—'

'So you'll have to come and stay with me tonight.'

'No,' Gwen said. She might have no choice about staying in Pendleford for a few months, but she had not come back to her home town to play the damsel in distress. She was a grown-up, an independent woman and she did not need charity from anybody. Especially not Cameron Laing.

'I'll sleep on the sofa,' Cam continued, ignoring her. 'We should probably go now. I've told Harry we'll be there when he comes off shift. You can give him your house key and he'll swing by and take a look '

'I'm not leaving,' Gwen said.

Cam gave her a disgusted look. 'You're being ridiculous. What about your sister? Can't you go and stay with her for a couple of days?'

'No,' Gwen said. She didn't elaborate. Cam already thought she was unstable; there was no need to tell him that she was fighting with the only family she had left.

'I'm not deserting this house just because it's a bit chilly.' Gwen stood up to make her tea. She told herself that she felt strong. She was an independent woman. Self-reliant.

'It's freezing,' Cam said, his voice reasonable. 'And it's going to get worse. They forecast minus ten tonight.'

'Who's they?'

'Google.'

'Oh, well then, if Saint Google says so.' Gwen was hoping to make him smile, but nothing doing.

'It's not funny,' he said.

'There's an oil heater in the outbuilding, I'll bring that in. I've got hot water bottles and plenty of blankets. I'll go to bed early and keep warm. I'll be fine.

Honestly, you don't need to worry.' As she reassured him just how fine she was going to be, a place opened up inside Gwen, reminding her that someone had broken into the house last night. She tried not to think about the quiet road and the long, dark path that led to her house. She tried not to see the single light at her window, shining out in the night like an invitation. She'd put on more lights; that was all that was needed. Maybe make a couple of silhouettes of well-built men and move them around the house with her.

Cam had pulled out his phone and was fiddling with the buttons. He spoke without looking up. 'I'll stay with you then.'

'You don't have to do that,' Gwen said automatically, ignoring the tiny voice that said: *yes, please.*

'I'm not leaving you on your own.' The door to the living room banged open in a gust of wind. Cam frowned and went to close it. 'You'll probably start digging the garden or replacing the windows or something.'

'Very funny.' Gwen wrapped her hands around the mug and tried not to feel irritated. It would be nice to think that he cared. If only he could stop being so officious, she might even be able to convince herself that she was something other than another problem to solve.

Cam called Harry back while Gwen lugged the oil heater from the outhouse and set it up in her bedroom.

Cam appeared in the doorway, just as she was checking it worked.

He leaned against the door jamb and crossed his arms, staring at the bed. 'Sure you've got enough blankets there?'

'Ha ha,' Gwen said to stop herself from offering him a test run. 'And the heater works. I'll be completely fine.'

Cam hesitated.

'I've got new locks. I'll keep my mobile with me. You don't need to worry.'

He followed her downstairs and Gwen wondered whether he was going to leave right away.

'I need a drink,' Cam said, running a hand through his hair.

'I've got Southern Comfort.'

Cam pulled a face.

'Fussy boy. How about red wine?'

Gwen opened the bottle and poured two glasses. Nothing seemed real. Someone had got into her house and messed up her heating. Deliberately. She'd only been back in Pendleford for a week and someone already hated her that much. She took a gulp from her glass and handed the other to Cam.

'Shall we stay in here? I think it's the warmest room at the moment.'

Cam shrugged. He took a sip of his wine and pulled a face.

'Cheap stuff, I'm afraid,' Gwen said, then felt irritated for apologising. She fiddled with her thumb ring, twisting it round and round. 'Why do I get the feeling you're annoyed with me?'

'Well, you're the one insisting you stay in this house on your own. It would be much better—'

'Not just about that. You always seem as if you're angry, but you're trying not to show it.'

'Do I?' Cam's forehead creased. After a moment he said, 'I don't feel angry. Sorry.'

'Because if you are, I'd understand, but I'd much rather we had it out and you said whatever it is you're trying not to say.'

'I'm not hiding anything,' Cam said, but he didn't meet her eyes.

Gwen decided to just say it. Get it out there. 'I've told you I'm sorry about how I left things. Before.'

Cam's expression went blank. 'Ancient history,' he said.

'Water under the bridge,' Gwen said.

'And it's done.' Cam shrugged. 'No point crying over spilt milk.'

'Look before you leap.'

'What?'

'Sorry. I thought we were trading clichés.'

There was a short silence, then Cam said, 'How's the living room looking?'

Gwen shook her head. 'Not good.' She showed him the one wall she'd painted. The purple had turned the white grey and was seeping through in patches, giving it a scabrous look.

'I think you're going to need another coat.'

'Or a flamethrower,' Gwen said. 'At least it's not as bad as the dining room.'

'That's worse?'

'Look.' Gwen threw open the door and let Cam behold the hideous wallpaper, the cracked ceiling. 'Ruby says it's unsafe.'

'Nah. That's just cosmetic. It's fine.' He looked around. 'The wallpaper, however, is psychotic.'

He clinked his glass against hers and they drank. Nothing like alcohol to make everything seem more manageable. Of course, alcohol had always led to one thing with Cam, but then, back in the day, anything and everything had always led to one thing. She took another sip, the glow in her stomach spreading warmth and battling with the cool, damp misery of the dining room.

'I'm sorry I didn't say goodbye.' The words popped out before she could stop them.

Cam went still.

'I couldn't.' Gwen kept her gaze locked on the red liquid sloshing slightly in the glass. 'If I'd seen you. Or spoken to you even, I wouldn't have been able to go and I really thought I had to.'

She heard movement and then Cam was right next to her. Her skin was tingling and she could swear that there was electricity jumping across the tiny space between them. She kept completely still, willing him to move closer, to put his arm around her. To say 'hey, babe' in the way he'd used to.

He cleared his throat. 'I tried to find you. After you left. I spoke to your mother, but she wasn't any help.'

Gwen could imagine. She and Gloria had been arguing pretty much solidly at that time. Gloria was probably frightened that Cam would bring her home.

'Your sister said she didn't know where you were.'

'She was telling the truth.'

'How did you do that?' Cam still wasn't looking at her. 'Just leave everybody. Not just me: your whole family, your whole life. Didn't you miss it?'

'No,' Gwen lied.

They stood like that, almost touching, sipping their drinks and watching the flowers and vines writhing over each other.

After another couple of hits of her wine, Gwen was beginning to see figures in the pattern. The writhing was beginning to look distinctly suggestive. She stepped away from Cam and backed out of the room. 'Let's sit down.'

The kitchen would be better. The kitchen was bright and clean and didn't have pornographic wallpaper. They sat at the table and Gwen opened the cake tin.

Cam pulled a face. 'Not with booze.'

'It's dark fruit cake. Got enough brandy in it to sink a ship.'

She watched as he took a bite and then realised that she was just staring at his mouth. He swallowed and she had the impulse to lean over and smell his neck. *Oh, sweet Jesus.*

Cam put the cake down and took a long drink of his wine. He looked tense again. 'Why did you think you had to leave? I thought everything was fine—' He broke off. Shook his head slightly. 'Actually, forget I asked. I don't want to know. It's in the past now.'

Before Gwen could react, Cam said, 'So. Tell me what you've been up to for thirteen years.'

Gwen blinked at the change. *Okay.*

'Come on,' Cam said, leaning forwards and fixing her with a look of total focus, 'I'm interested. Really.'

The look seemed sincere and, for once, he wasn't scowling at her, so she did. She sipped her wine and told him about her work. She talked about Curious Notions and how she'd started out by selling her own creations and then, in the course of seeking out vintage miniatures for her shadow boxes, she'd started to pick up loads of other cool pieces and decided to put them on the stall too. 'I was just messing about, really. Killing time while I worked out what I was really going to do with my life and then, one day, I saw this silk scarf.'

Cam's eyes glazed over slightly.

'Stick with me. This was a thing of beauty.'

'Scarf. Beautiful. Got it.'

'This obnoxious guy had it on his stall in an antiques fair in Peterborough. He knew it was a Missoni and had it priced up accordingly, but as soon as I touched it I knew it was the last of its kind.'

'You knew it?' Cam frowned.

Gwen was too excited, reliving her moment of triumph, to care that she sounded crazy. 'It was such a rush. I bought it and put it on my stall. Sold it for ten

times what I paid for it.' It was one of the moments
when the Harper family intuition had seemed like a
blessing rather than a curse.

'Wow.' Cam straightened up. Suddenly interested.
'So there's money in this—' he paused '…stuff.'

'I know it probably looks like junk to you, but I love
it. Some people hate the idea of secondhand, but I love
the history, the hunt, the way everything is unique. It's
so much more interesting than the same boring mass-
produced crap that everyone else has bought from Argos.'

'I don't buy things in Argo,.' Cam said.

'Not you. You're rich. I mean normal people,' Gwen
said. 'Anyway, you just buy things in the expensive
version of Argos. It's still not individual or anything.'

'I see,' Cam said politely.

Gwen put her glass down carefully and said, 'What
about you?'

'Not much to tell. Paperwork. Court. Paperwork.
Court.'

'You don't like it?'

He shrugged. 'Actually, I kind of do. I like the
puzzles and I like the challenge. I like arguing and I like
winning.'

Gwen smiled. 'I still can't quite get used to the idea
of you as a lawyer. I mean, you were in a punk band.
Weren't you going to go to London?'

'I did,' Cam said, suddenly serious.

'What happened?'

Cam drained his glass and poured another. 'I'm
sorry about the other day. In the car. I just wasn't ready
to—' He broke off and ran a hand through his hair, 'I
don't know. Jesus. I just wasn't ready to talk to you, I
suppose. Do you still want to hear about your aunt?'

Gwen jerked back to the present.' Yes. I do. Yes,
please.'

Cam settled back in his chair and closed his eyes. After a moment he said, 'Don't take this the wrong way, but she was kind of odd.'

Gwen stiffened. *Odd*. That was one of the many words used to describe her family over the years.

Cam opened his eyes and looked right at her. 'She was a very strong person. She told the truth. If someone was in need, she always tried to help. Always.'

'Oh.' Gwen swallowed. That sounded better.

'She wasn't a tactful person. Didn't suffer fools gladly.'

'I've never understood that phrase,' Gwen broke in. She waved her glass. 'Who does suffer fools gladly? Some kind of fool-fancier?'

Cam ignored her. 'She put a lot of people's backs up. Didn't play the politics game. I heard that when the police chief's wife went to see her, Iris insulted her shoes.'

'I thought she helped people?'

'Oh she did,' Cam said. 'You just couldn't be too choosy about the kind of help you got.'

Gwen opened her mouth to say something about people in general being too choosy for their own good, when she heard knocking.

Cam raised his eyebrows. 'Expecting someone?'

Gwen sighed. 'Increasingly, yes.'

She opened the door with a sense of resignation.

The woman on her doorstep was clutching a blue dog bowl with a cartoon-style bone engraved on the side. 'Are you Gwen Harper?'

Gwen nodded.

'Oh, thank God. I'm Helen Brewer.' The woman tucked the bowl under one arm and stuck out her hand. She had brown hair pulled back in a ponytail and looked older than Gwen. Although Gwen always assumed people were older than her. Ruby would probably tell her it was down to her essential immaturity. Arrested development and all that.

Gwen shook it. 'Can I help you?'

'I hope so. Please.'

'I suppose you want to come in,' Gwen said, stepping back.

'I'm sorry to interrupt.' Helen peered at Cam curiously. 'Are you busy?'

'Yes,' Cam said.

'I'm always busy,' Gwen said. 'In fact, I might have that engraved on the back door.'

'Well,' Helen put the dog bowl on the table, 'this won't take long, I hope. If I don't find Archie before Christopher gets back, he's going to kill me. He loves that dog.'

'Christopher?'

'My son. He's coming home from university for the weekend. He's studying chemical engineering in Cardiff. It's a very difficult course.'

'I have no doubt.' Gwen tried to send a *sorry about this* look in Cam's direction but he was too busy sending death rays at Helen. She refocused on the woman. 'Did you say your dog is missing?'

'Yes, I haven't seen him since yesterday morning.' Helen pulled out a small rectangle and passed it to Gwen. It was a picture of a Highland Terrier taken in a photo booth, Helen Brewer's hands just visible holding him up.

'This is his bowl.'

'Not yours?' Cam asked.

'No.' Helen frowned at him, leaning to one side while she struggled to pull something out of her coat pocket. 'This is his favourite toy.' She put the object onto the table and Gwen stifled the urge to laugh. What had once been a reproduction *Spitting Image* Margaret Thatcher was now nose-less and ravaged.

'Archie has excellent taste,' Cam said, draining his glass.

'Why have you brought this stuff?'

Helen frowned. 'Don't you need them? I heard that Iris did something. Maybe set fire to them and the smoke forms an arrow and points to where Archie is hiding—' She caught sight of Gwen's expression and broke off. 'Or something.'

'You can't burn that,' Cam said. 'It'll give off toxic fumes.'

'Maybe you get a chemical burn in the shape of an arrow,' Gwen said. She was trying very hard to ignore the fact that she *could* help. Probably.

Helen narrowed her eyes. 'Are you going to help or not? I can pay you.'

Gwen took a breath and tried to formulate a nice way of saying *no* and *you are insane*. 'Have you asked your neighbours? Put up posters?'

'No one has seen him. I've been along the streets and asked people to check their garages and sheds, in case he got trapped.' Helen was fumbling in her pocket. She brought out a couple of twenty-pound notes.

Gwen tried not to think about how much she needed that money. 'I don't think I can,' she said. 'I'm sorry; perhaps—' Gwen reached out to poke the chew toy. The instant her finger connected with the rubber surface, images exploded behind her eyes. A pink carpet close to her nose, as if she were lying down, although she was moving very fast, her back legs straining to clear a height. Going up a step and another and another, the pink carpet sharp-smelling with a base note of wood and newspaper. She jerked her hand back and stared wide-eyed at Cam and Helen.

'All right there, Jumpy?' Cam said.

She focused on him. Solid, normal, legally trained Cam. He wasn't crazy. He wasn't asking her to cure chilblains or solve marital problems. He looked perplexed and mildly amused by Helen Brewer. He belonged to the normal world. The one she wanted to join.

'What's wrong?' Helen said. 'If you can't do this, I need to get back home and carry on looking. He's out there, all alone—'

'Pink carpet.' *Damn it.*

'What?'

Gwen reached out and touched Maggie's chin. She was more prepared this time and tried to concentrate, tried to interpret the images that flashed into her mind like a jerky film reel. More pink carpet, flat now, though, maybe the landing. A glossy white surface rising from the pink, a corner. Gwen saw a grey leg with a paw stretched out pulling at the corner of the door, heard the scratching noise. Then sickness hit. She launched herself away from the table, making it to the sink just in time. She lost her cake and her red wine with grim efficiency, then became aware of a hand on her lower back. Cam reached across and ran the cold tap, filling a glass of water and putting it into her hand.

'Sorry,' she said, hot with sickness and embarrassment. *Glamorous, Gwen. Really attractive.* She washed away the evidence and reached under the sink for some bleach, the clean smell turning her stomach over.

'Come and sit down,' Cam said. 'Do that later.'

'What's wrong?' Helen said. 'No one said anything about sick.'

'Do you have pink carpet on your stairs and landing?'

'Yes.' Helen looked astonished. 'How did you know?'

'Archie's in your house.'

'No.' Helen shook her head. 'Not possible. I've checked.'

'Go check again.' Cam said. 'Gwen's not well.'

'Don't fob me off,' Helen said. Then she began to cry.

'Christ's sake.' Cam said.

Gwen, deciding she wasn't going to be sick again after all, reached over and patted her on the shoulder. 'I'll come to your house and find Archie. He's definitely there. I promise.' Gwen hadn't felt a Finding as strong since she was a teenager. She hadn't been fond of the nausea then, and it hadn't improved with time.

'Thank you.' Helen gave her a thin smile, her tears drying. 'I'm sorry, I'm not usually a weeper.'

'I can see that,' Gwen said. 'Come on then. Let's get this over with.'

'I'll drive,' Cam said and picked up his coat and car keys.

Helen Brewer lived in a neat two-bed starter home on a new estate. As they walked up the front path, Gwen leading with Helen on her heels and Cam bringing up the rear and making smart comments, Gwen tried to ignore her discomfort. What was she doing in the middle of some woman's lost dog drama? It was insane. She didn't do things like this. Not any more. She didn't join in. She had a comfortable seat on the sidelines and that was how she liked it. Hell, even the sidelines were a little too close for comfort.

The front door opened onto a narrow hallway, made even narrower by the fussy console table with a dried flower arrangement on top. The laminate floor stopped at the stairs, taken over by a dusky rose carpet that Gwen recognised. She swallowed. She'd forgotten just how weird a strong Finding felt. The sane and sensible part of her brain was feebly trying to say it could be a coincidence. That small stubborn voice of rationality was wittering about wine drunk too quickly and dumb luck. She wasn't listening to the sane part, though, she was listening to the tiny voice that was telling her to climb the stairs.

She was vaguely aware of Helen and Cam's voices. 'Stay down here,' she said. 'Go and sit down.'

'Well I never,' Helen said.

Gwen ignored her and walked up the stairs. There was the short landing and there was the door. She didn't even glance at the others, knowing instantly which was the right one. She pushed it open, feeling herself acting as if in a trance, and walked into a bedroom. It looked as if Laura Ashley had thrown up over it: floral wallpaper, bedspread, rug, cushions, and a flounced pink valance. She knew even before she dropped to her knees and lifted the material that she would see Archie and, sure enough, there he was. Pressed into the far corner was a bundle of grey and white fur and a pair of black shining eyes.

'Hey, Archie,' Gwen said, keeping her voice low and soothing. 'That's a good boy.'

Archie tried to press himself further back into the corner while simultaneously wag his tail. What a sweetheart.

Gwen felt her neck stiffen up and shifted so that she was lying down. Archie's eyes rolled white and his paws pedalled as he panicked.

'It's okay, baby, I'm not moving.' She stayed still until Archie calmed a little.

'You're going to have to come out of there sooner or later, you know. You must be thirsty and hungry and there's good stuff to eat downstairs. It's probably served on a flowery mat, but it'll still taste good.' Gwen kept up the flow of words, using a gentle sing-song tone while moving her body forwards a centimetre at a time. Archie was still quivering, but he wasn't trying to push himself through the wall, so that was progress.

'It's okay, baby, come on out.' Gwen was half under the bed now and she thought if she reached out, she could probably grab the dog. It would be better if he came to her, of course, but she wasn't sure how long that was going to take. She inched her hand forwards and then, in one quick movement, reached out and hooked her fingers under his collar. Archie lurched forwards and she got a better hold of his body and hauled him out.

Archie was shuddering, his tiny body convulsing in her arms, but he wasn't struggling to get down. Gwen held him firmly and stroked his back, keeping up a stream of soothing words. Slowly the shaking lessened and he licked her hand. She felt a warmth flowing through her and thought: maybe I'll keep him. What was wrong with her? She didn't need any more responsibilities. A cat and a house were bad enough. Shaking her head at her insanity, she walked carefully downstairs.

'Archie!' Helen leaped off the sofa and rushed to pet the little dog. 'Where was he?'

'Under the bed,' Gwen said. 'You might want to clean up under there.'

Helen's eyes were shining and she held her arms out. 'Poor Archie.'

Gwen stepped forward, loosening her hold experimentally. Archie gave her a final lick and lurched towards Helen, who caught him and buried her face in his fur. 'What a silly boy, Archie. What were you doing? Why didn't you bark?' She looked up. 'I don't understand. Why didn't he come out? I've been calling him all around the house.'

Gwen put her hand out to scratch behind Archie's ears. As soon as her fingers connected, an image flashed into her mind, accompanied by an overwhelming sense of terror. Navy trainers. She looked at Helen, startled, then checked her feet. Black ankle boots with a little heel.

'Who wears blue trainers?'

Helen frowned. 'Christopher. But he's not here right now—'

'He's the reason Archie was hiding.'

'That's impossible. He hasn't even been here for days. And he dotes on Archie.'

Gwen shrugged. 'I'm just telling you what I saw.'

Helen's face hardened. 'What are you accusing my son of?'

'I'm just telling you what frightened Archie. Christopher's shoes.'

'Get out of my house.'

'I'd like my payment, please,' Gwen said, feeling hellish.

Helen thrust the notes at Gwen. 'Don't you dare repeat what you just said. Not to anyone.'

Cam put his hand on Gwen's arm. 'Come on.'

Back at the house, Cam stayed in the car while she walked up the path. That was what she got for using the Finding in front of him. Still, he waited until she had the door unlocked and was safely inside before driving away. *Because he's a decent human being, not because he feels anything.*

CHAPTER 7

16th June
Lily Thomas has moved into her father's old house
around the corner. There is something very hungry
about that girl. I was compelled to make her a gift of
one of my nicer lavender bushes. I don't know why, but
that's often the way.

At Lily's house, Gwen pushed the gate and walked
through a preternaturally neat garden. A square of raked
purple gravel gave way in places to allow subdued
shrubs. A large terracotta pot by the front door held a
neatly clipped topiary, the white care label still attached
to a branch. Compared to the house on the other side
– which sported a child's climbing frame on a scrubby
patch of lawn and some broken toys – Lily's garden
looked almost sterile.

Gwen pressed the doorbell and heard an ethereal
chime faintly inside.

Lily opened the door, her face falling the moment she
saw Gwen. The door began to close.

'I'm really sorry,' Gwen said quickly.

Lily was wearing a pale green silk blouse tucked into
smart grey trousers. She folded her arms protectively
across her chest and notched her frown up a gear.

'I should have told you straight away, and I don't
know why I didn't.' Suddenly it became desperately

important to Gwen to make things okay with her neighbour. Lily had been nothing but kind to her since she arrived back in Pendleford and, after her confrontation with Ruby, Gwen could see how valuable that was. Someone in this god-forsaken place who gave a damn. She held up a carrier bag. 'I come bearing gifts.'

'You'd better come in.' Lily turned and walked down the short hallway.

Gwen followed, closing the door behind her. She passed a gigantic painting of a white unicorn, its mane being brushed by a simpering blonde in a long white dress, inexplicably set against both a blazing orange sunset and a full rainbow. It should've prepared her for Lily's living room, but Gwen still nearly dropped her bag.

Shiny gold frames held more unicorn paintings, while every surface was covered in figurines. Winged unicorns, white unicorns, pink unicorns, unicorns with girls riding on their backs, china unicorns with real hair sprouting from their tails and heads and crystal unicorns that refracted the light. The etched-glass top of the coffee table was held proudly aloft by four carved wooden unicorns, their horns painted silver. Wherever Gwen looked, unfeasibly large unicorn eyes stared back.

Lily perched on the edge of an armchair. 'You may as well sit down.'

'Thanks.' There was a pale blue sofa that matched the chair, complete with three gold embroidered unicorn cushions. Gwen didn't think she'd be able to fit her backside onto the sofa without moving them, but wasn't sure if that constituted a social faux pas. She certainly didn't want Lily to interpret the action as a commentary on her décor. She chose one of the spindly metal dining chairs from around the glass-topped circular table in the dining nook and crossed her fingers that it was sturdier than it looked.

'What can I do for you?' Lily's excessively polite tone was more effective than a slap in the face. Gwen swallowed. 'I'm sorry if I hurt your feelings. I didn't mention that I'd lived here before because—'

'It's really none of my business,' Lily interrupted.

'I just wanted a fresh start. I know it sounds stupid. I didn't mean to embarrass you.'

'You didn't,' Lily said tightly. 'What's in the bag?'

Before Gwen could explain that she hadn't found Iris's recipe book yet, but that she'd made Lily a cake, a man wearing a towel and nothing else appeared in the doorway. He was blond and good-looking in a calculated kind of way. 'Oh,' he said, 'I didn't know we had company.'

Gwen realised that she'd stood up. 'Sorry. I didn't . . . I was just going.'

'Don't leave on my account.' The man lounged against the doorway and took a long, lazy look up and down Gwen's figure, as if she were the half-naked one.

'This is Ryan. He's a journalist, so watch anything you say,' Lily said.

'Hey,' Ryan said, mock-offended. 'You think I've got a Dictaphone hidden under here?' He gestured to his towel, grinning.

'Right. Well—'

'So, are you Lily's latest acolyte?'

'What?' Gwen wanted to leave. Lily was radiating hostility and Ryan was radiating pheromones. His pecs kept twitching as if he were unconsciously flexing them as he spoke to her.

'You've got the right look. Wild-haired. Nervous.' Ryan held up his hands as if he were a photographer framing a picture.

'This is Gwen Harper,' Lily said. 'She just moved into End House. Although she's not new to the town. Not that she wants anybody to know.'

Ryan dropped his hands. 'Oh.'

'I'm really sorry,' Gwen said again. She tried to look Lily in the eyes to convey her sincerity, but Lily stared resolutely past her shoulder.

'Perhaps she has a dark secret,' Lily said to Ryan, as if Gwen were not there. 'Perhaps you ought to investigate her. Get a scoop for the local rag.'

Ryan puffed up his chest. 'It's just a stepping stone, you know.'

'I'll let you get on,' Gwen said. She made to pass Ryan, but he didn't step back and she was forced to squeeze past him. Up close, he was older than he first appeared; his eyes were bloodshot and there was something unpleasant lurking inside them. Something mean-spirited.

Lily didn't get up or say goodbye. The last image Gwen had in her mind was of Lily staring viciously at Ryan and him grinning back at her with a determined lack of concern.

Gwen moved the oil heater downstairs and had it running on the highest setting. It was still freezing, though, and she wasn't in the best mood even before Ruby arrived.

'Yes?' Gwen opened the front door and pointedly didn't step back to let Ruby inside.

'Can we talk?' Ruby looked as immaculate and in control as she always did. It was irritating.

'Are you sure that's wise?' Gwen said. She felt sick with the anger and guilt Ruby inspired, but she didn't have the energy to deal with it. Not on top of everything else.

'Please. Katie wants to see you.'

Her niece's name did it. Like a magic word, Gwen felt her anger drain away. She turned on her heel and marched into the house. 'Shut the door behind you.' Well, most of it.

Ruby stopped in the hall, looking awkward. She made no move to remove her coat, which was probably for the best. Gwen was surprised their breath wasn't fogging in the frigid air.

'So?' Gwen said.

Ruby swallowed. 'Katie has been asking about you. She doesn't understand why you haven't been round to visit.'

'I hope you've explained,' Gwen said.

Ruby folded her arms. 'Not exactly. I just said we'd had a bit of a fight.'

'Eighteen months, Ruby. Not a "bit of" anything.'

'I don't want to talk about it,' Ruby said. 'I didn't come here to argue with you. I just wanted to see if you'd let Katie visit. Today, actually.'

'With you?' Gwen thought for a moment that her niece might be sat out in Ruby's car, waiting for the two responsible adults in the scenario to stop bickering.

'No.' Ruby's voice dripped sarcasm. 'She's fourteen. She has to do everything herself. She'd get the number nineteen bus.'

'Okay,' Gwen said. '*She's* very welcome.'

'Fine. If she isn't with you by eleven, call me.'

Ruby made to leave and Gwen was suddenly seized with uncertainty. It had been a while. 'Um. What am I supposed to do with her?'

'I have no idea. She's a mystery to me these days.' Ruby sounded properly upset and Gwen was surprised to find herself trying to reassure her. 'Hey,' she said, 'I'm sure it's not that bad.'

Ruby gave a short laugh. 'Have fun bonding and then tell me that.'

'Right. And—'

Ruby interrupted her, the words coming out in a rush. 'Don't talk about that stuff, okay?'

'What stuff?' Gwen said. 'The birds and the bees?'

'You know very well.' Ruby rubbed her gloved hands together. 'I don't want her exposed to all that—'

'I remember.' Gwen felt like crying. Why did Ruby always have to treat her like she was a loaded gun?

'Okay then. Thanks.' Ruby practically ran out of the house and down the path.

Gwen made herself a cup of tea to warm up and fed the cat. He stared at her with his strangely mismatched eyes. Gwen had a list of things to do that felt about a mile long. If she was going to live in this mausoleum of a house for six months, then she had a lot of cleaning to do. Not to mention sorting through Iris's junk, mending the ceiling in the dining room, and working out how to cope with the reappearance of Cameron Laing in her life. The cat looked pointedly from Gwen's face to the empty dish and back again. 'Yes, yes,' Gwen said. 'I know. I need to do something about you, too. Get in line.'

At ten to eleven, the doorbell rang. Gwen was dressed in cleaning clothes which weren't, she had to admit, very different to her normal clothes. Old jeans and a well-washed V-neck jumper that used to be navy. If the expression on her niece's face was anything to go by, she ought to add clothes shopping to her to-do list, too.

'Hello, Katie. Long time, no see.'

Katie slouched in, avoiding eye contact and glaring at the floor as if it had personally offended her.

'Do you want something to drink? I've got orange or apple juice.'

'Coffee,' Katie said.

'Um. Are you allowed to drink coffee?'

Katie shot her such a look of disgust. 'I'm *fourteen*.'

'No problem,' Gwen said. 'I'll just call your mum to check.'

'Oh for God's sake,' Katie said, tossing her hair over her shoulder in a practised move. 'I don't want anything anyway.'

Well, that was a good start, Gwen congratulated herself as Katie stood hunched in her green parka and showed no signs of taking it off or coming any further into the house.

'I was going to clear the dining room today. It's a junk room at the moment. Loads of boxes and stuff.'

No response.

'Do you want to give me a hand?'

A tiny shrug.

'I've acquired a cat, too. Do you want to meet him?'

Katie looked up for the first time. 'Yes, please.'

'Through here.' Gwen led the way into the kitchen, praying that the cat was still there.

'He's gorgeous,' Katie said, despite all evidence to the contrary. She dropped to the floor in front of him and held out her hand. To Gwen's surprise, the cat padded straight over and sniffed Katie, then began rubbing his head on her arm, begging to be stroked.

Katie looked back over her shoulder. 'What's his name? Do you have any cat treats? They love the ones with catnip.'

'I'm not naming him. I'll never get rid of him if I name him.'

Katie gave her an odd look. She turned back to the cat. 'Hello, Cat,' she said lovingly.

Gwen skirted past the happy couple and pulled a pair of rubber gloves and a roll of bin bags from under the sink.

'I'm going to get started.'

Katie rubbed the cat under the chin and didn't reply.

Gwen had re-stacked the boxes to allow for better access and was just opening the first one when Katie appeared in the doorway. She'd taken off her parka and looked about a third of the size without the bulky coat. She stood still and looked around. Then whistled. 'Craptastic.'

'Indeed.' Gwen hadn't fully appreciated the extent of the mess until she'd started lugging boxes. 'I'm wondering whether to just lock the door. I mean,' she looked around, 'it's not like I need a dining room.'

Katie was squinting at the ceiling. 'That's a big crack.'

'Your mum said it was going to fall down. Don't tell her I let you in here, okay?'

Katie smiled for the first time. 'Okay.'

'So, do you want to help me with this lot? I'll pay you.'

Katie's smile widened into a proper grin. She looked like the cheery twelve-year-old Gwen remembered.

Gwen plugged in her iPod dock and hit shuffle. As luck would have it, Katie's favourite Aretha Franklin song rang out. She looked sideways at the girl as she ripped open a cardboard box with more enthusiasm than precision. 'You used to dance to this song when you were little.'

Katie didn't react.

Okay.

Katie pulled out a handful of brown curtain material, then let it fall back in a heap. 'Do you have a system?'

'Um. Not really.'

'Well, we need one. Like on *Life Laundry*.'

'If you say so.'

Katie tipped the box she was holding upside down and shook it. Righting it, she said, 'I need a marker pen.'

'There's a pack in the kitchen,' Gwen said faintly.

Two hours later, they had several boxes marked up in block letters: charity, loft and house, and three black bags for the tip. There was also a plastic crate filled with old notebooks, scraps of paper with Iris's handwriting, and shop receipts with items highlighted with little stars.

'You should at least throw out the receipts. That's just rubbish.'

'I can't. Iris kept them and, until I know why, I can't throw them out.' Gwen didn't want to admit that she couldn't let go of anything that Iris had written on. It would make her sound unhinged.

'Maybe it was for her tax return. Dad keeps all of his.'

'Good thought.' Gwen frowned unintentionally at the dreaded words. She decided to focus on the day's achievements, gazing at the neatly labelled boxes with satisfaction. She found her purse and extracted a five-pound note.

Katie looked at the floor. 'You don't have to pay me. I enjoyed it.'

Gwen handed her the note. 'Just for that, I'll give you a lift home.'

Katie's face fell.

'Or into town,' Gwen continued smoothly. 'We could go for hot chocolate.'

Katie brightened. 'Can I come again another day? To see the cat.'

'Of course.' Gwen smiled at the whip-fast emotions of a teenager. She remembered what that had been like. Exhausting.

Katie bounced into the hallway and began dragging on her coat. 'I'll bring him treats.'

She kept up a stream of chatter all the way into Bath. Gwen tried to relax and enjoy her niece's company, but she felt a nagging guilt. Marilyn Dixon's tight features kept popping into her mind. It was annoying.

'What do you think?'

Gwen glanced at Katie, who was wearing an unnervingly intense expression.

'Um . . .'

'I know. You think I should stand up for myself more. That's what Mum says.'

'I—'

'But Imogen is so, like, intense, you know?' She scowled into her lap and Gwen stamped down on the sudden urge to laugh.

'She's cool, too. Much cooler than me. She's had a boyfriend since she was nine.'

'Well, that's—'

'And she always looks good. She's got the best hair.'

'Hair's good,' Gwen managed.

'I'm just not sure about the party.' Katie paused for breath. 'I might wait and see.'

Gwen parked the car and turned to Katie. She prepared to ask who the hell Imogen was and what they had been talking about, when Katie suddenly treated her to a big smile. 'Thanks so much, Auntie Gwen. You are so great to talk to.'

'You're entirely welcome,' Gwen said, sticking to safe ground.

Katie paused, quiet for the first time in the last half an hour. 'I want to ask you something.'

'Shoot.' Gwen felt uneasy.

'Mum said you used to help the police sometimes.'

'Did she?'

Katie looked disappointed. 'It isn't true?'

'It's kind of true. I helped out just the once. I'm just not supposed to talk about it.'

Katie's face lit up. 'Are you a spook?'

Gwen laughed. 'No. Nothing as cool as that.'

'What did you do?'

'Katie,' Gwen said as gently as she could. 'Your mum—'

'Oh, I know.' Katie waved a hand. 'She's all freaked out.'

Great. Gwen tried not to feel hurt.

'So is that what you've been doing? Is that why you went away?'

'It's complicated.'

Katie wasn't giving up. 'How?'

Gwen paused. She tried to think of a nice way of putting it. 'Finding isn't all that specific.'

'It doesn't always work?' Katie fiddled with the fringing on her scarf.

Gwen shook her head. 'You always find something. It's just not always what you thought you were looking for.' Gwen's left ear itched from the lie. There was no way she was telling her fresh-faced niece the truth, though. The one time she'd used the Finding to help the police, she'd ended up a suspect in a murder case. Only briefly, but that had been enough. She closed her eyes and tried not to see the boy's white body, bloated with river water and trailing weeds.

Katie opened her mouth, but Gwen held up a hand. 'Please,' she said. 'Your mum is only just speaking to me again.'

After two giant mugs of hot chocolate and Katie's treatise regarding marshmallows: 'they're like, completely pointless until you melt them', Gwen watched Katie get onto her bus home. Being near Bath had its perks, she thought, even if she had little idea what her niece was talking about for fifty per cent of the time.

That evening, Gwen was contemplating the necrotic walls of the living room and wondering whether Iris would have some really bright paint somewhere amongst the junk when the phone rang and she dived to the hallway floor to retrieve it. She added 'hall table' and, a moment later, 'cordless phone' onto her list of things to buy. It was Ruby.

'Thank you.' Ruby's voice was quiet. 'For today, I mean.'

Gwen straightened up in shock.

'Katie is glowing,' Ruby said. 'I haven't seen her this cheerful in weeks.'

'I took her for hot chocolate,' was all that popped into Gwen's mouth.

'Out? She was happy to be seen in public with you?'

Gwen was just about to be offended when she processed the hurt in Ruby's voice. 'I'm sure that won't last. I'm just a novelty.'

'Well, anyway,' Ruby said. 'Thank you for having her.'

'Any time,' Gwen said.

Ruby hesitated, then asked in a rush, 'She's already asking about visiting again.'

'Of course.'

'After school one day?'

'Sure.' Gwen couldn't stop herself adding, 'If you don't mind Katie spending time here?'

Ruby's voice was so quiet as to be almost non-existent. 'I said I was sorry.'

'You didn't actually,' Gwen said. *And then I left and you didn't even try to get in touch.*

'So, you want to talk about this now?'

Gwen was gripping the phone so tightly her fingers were hurting. She made herself relax them slightly. 'Good a time as any.'

'I didn't mean to say that you were "bad". It just popped out,' Ruby said. 'I was scared.'

'I believe the word you used was "evil".' Gwen didn't mean the words to come out so seriously, but the hurt bubbled up and soured her tone.

'Look, I said I'm sorry, but I can't help the way I feel,' Ruby said righteously.

'It was a card trick, Ruby. From a kids' magic set.'

'I know that. Now.'

'I was wearing a felt top hat. Katie had just pulled Mr Bun Bun out of it.'

There was a silence. Gwen gazed at the cracked paintwork of the hall and willed herself to go numb.

'I thought it was a real rabbit,' Ruby said finally. 'Bun Bun is very fluffy. I couldn't tell. I thought—'

'You thought that I was . . . What? Conducting a ritual sacrifice with a live rabbit in front of your eleven-year-old daughter? You actually thought I would do that?'

'Mum would.'

Gwen gritted her teeth for a moment. Then she said, 'I'm not Gloria.'

'I know. I know I overreacted a little.'

Gwen opened her mouth in shock.

'I think I may have been repressing certain feelings. My yoga teacher says I'm very repressed.'

Gwen closed her eyes. 'What feelings?'

'Like how Mum only cared about you and how she thought I was a waste of space.'

'That's not true.' Gwen shook her head. 'Mum was angry with me for not using my gift.' She put air quotes around the word even though Ruby couldn't see them.

'At least you had one,' Ruby said. 'She used to look at me like I was adopted. Like she was wondering who I was and how come I'd wandered into her house.'

Gwen remembered that look well. 'She did that to everyone, don't you remember?'

Ruby sighed. Then she said, 'Do you remember how she'd read someone's cards and as soon as she'd finished, she'd show them the door. Even if they were crying or whatever.'

'Oh God, yes. I'd forgotten about that. Do you remember Mr Barnes?'

They fell silent, remembering the shuffling form of their maths teacher as he'd struggled down the road, bowed with the weight of grief after Gloria had informed him that his wife had been cheating on him for the five years prior to her death.

'She didn't pull her punches.'

'Never,' Gwen said.

'Why?' Ruby exploded. 'Why did she have to be like that? The number of times we had to move after she pissed off one person too many—'

'Preaching to the choir, sister.'

'You should ask her,' Ruby said. 'Have you phoned her about the house yet?'

'What? And told her that I'm living on the forbidden planet? Uh, no.'

'You should. If she shouts, you can always hang up,' Ruby said. 'Anyway, it's not the same. Iris isn't there.'

'No,' Gwen said, looking around the living room at the remaining dark purple walls. They seemed to press in on her. 'I suppose not.'

CHAPTER 8

Helen B from number twenty-one has missed her third Sunday in a row. She usually calls in when she's walking that ridiculous dog of hers. Something is wrong, but I don't know what yet. It's probably that bitter little man she married. More fool her. I'm so tired today and I've been dreaming of the sea. I wish I could just stop. My mother used to tell me to 'mind my own beeswax' and I wish I could. I'm tired of all these people, all these lives. I didn't ask for any of this.

Still.

He is a nasty piece of work.

Gwen blinked. The light had gone out of the day while she'd been reading and she stood up and put a light on. She'd never felt so close to Iris; she was absolutely right. Helen B and her nasty husband had been none of Iris's business. And Marilyn Dixon was none of Gwen's business now. Gwen ignored the itch that started behind her left ear and travelled down her back, calling her a big, fat liar.

She flipped through the journal until she saw Marilyn's name.

Marilyn needs to learn to stand on her own two feet. She can't keep running to me for every little problem. She asked me to hex John from the corner shop today because he gave her the wrong change. That woman needs a hobby.

Gwen sipped her tea. Marilyn had wanted Gwen to do an Iris impression and had then backed off, saying she'd got help from a neighbour. Gwen was beginning to worry about exactly what kind of help. What if Marilyn had decided to stand on her own two feet, maybe with a bit of amateur hexing? That would be bad.

Cat stalked across the kitchen.

'Hello, baby, are you hungry?' Gwen reached for a tin and dish, but Cat carried on moving. He paused in the doorway and regarded her, the crazy fur above his eyes like raised eyebrows.

'What? You want some tuna?' She tapped the tin. *She wasn't going to get involved. She wasn't going to end up like Iris.*

Cat didn't move.

'Lovely, lovely tuna,' Gwen said. Marilyn's anguished face swam into view. *Buggeration.* 'You think I should do something, don't you?'

Cat sat back on his haunches and began licking himself in a pointed fashion.

'Oh hell,' Gwen said and got her keys.

Gwen arrived at the Hearty Baker just in time to see Harry slip into a seat opposite a familiar suit. Cam. *Marvellous.*

Gwen pretended she hadn't seen them and went to the counter. The woman behind it was either in her fifties and wearing expertly applied make-up, or in her forties and had lived life with enthusiasm.

'Mrs Conatello?'

'Who's asking?' The woman arched a shapely black eyebrow. Her hair was elaborately combed above a colourful headscarf and she wore a bright yellow top with a low neckline. Gwen felt a stab of sympathy for the sour-faced Marilyn.

'My name is Gwen Harper, I'm a friend of—'

'I know who you are.'

'Okay. Good. Can I see Mr Dixon, please?' There had been approximately two seconds between Gwen deciding she'd try to help Marilyn and the Hearty Baker's sign swooping in to perch in her mind. She filed it under 'worry about later'. Once she'd checked on Brian. It should be easy to see if he was under some kind of influence. Gloria had taught her the signs and – luckily enough – the cure.

The woman reared back as if slapped. 'And why would he be here?'

Gwen opened her mouth to say 'because you're having intimate relations on a regular basis', but was distracted by Harry waving enthusiastically. *Crap*.

'Come and join us,' Harry called. Cam glanced around, his expression neutral.

Gwen gave him a quick nod and turned back to Mrs Conatello, who was busying herself arranging pastries on a plate. Two red spots of colour had appeared in her cheeks.

'Mrs Conatello, please. I really need to speak to Brian—' Gwen began, but at that moment the door to the café was thrown open with such force that it rebounded off the wall. A man wearing a grey jacket with sweat patches and a red face stood panting in the doorway.

'Uh-oh,' Gwen said. She recognised the manic gleam in the man's eyes and moved out of the way just as he vaulted over the counter, knocking a plate of scones onto the floor.

'Brian!' Mrs Conatello said.

'Oh, hell,' Gwen said and retreated to Harry and Cam's table. Marilyn had definitely hexed her husband.

'That man just broke my afternoon snack,' Harry said dolefully.

Brian sank to the floor in front of Mrs Conatello, his bald spot disappearing from view behind the counter.

'Oh my God,' Harry said, 'that's gotta be unhygienic.'

'What?' Gwen tore her gaze away to glance at Harry.

'Is he . . . He's not going to *pleasure* her, is he?'

Cam snorted. 'Get your mind out of the gutter. He's just talking.' He squinted at the counter. 'I think.'

'I can't go on like this, Mary.' Brian might've been invisible, but his voice carried clear and true around the café. The mid-morning crowd had all stopped and turned in their seats to watch. A family of tourists got out their cameras, perhaps thinking it was some improvisational theatre.

'Get up, you idiot,' Mary hissed. 'My husband's here.' She jerked her head at the kitchen door.

'I love you, Mary Conatello.'

Mary looked less than delighted.

'Ahhhhh,' said a good many of the punters.

'He's behind you,' shouted out one of the tourists, really getting into the spirit of things.

'Oh Christ,' Mary said, turning round. Mr Conatello stood in the doorway to the kitchen, a metal spatula in one hand and a filthy towel in the other.

'This gentleman fell over,' Mary said hurriedly.

'Staff only behind the counter, mate,' Mr Conatello said, looking down with a bemused expression.

'I need to speak to Mary,' Brian said. 'Ouch.' He looked at Mary with confusion and adoration in equal measure. 'You kicked me!'

'My foot slipped,' Mary said. She waved her husband through the door. 'I'll deal with this. You see to your eggs.'

'Sod the eggs,' Mr Conatello said, but he disappeared back into the kitchen.

Brian gazed at Mary. 'Darling, I thought this was what you wanted – we've talked about it.'

'Not. Like. This.' Mrs Conatello bit off each word. 'Have you lost your mind?'

'No, Mary,' Brian said earnestly. 'I've come to my senses. Will you marry me?'

'Isn't he already married?' Harry asked, sotto voce.

'So's she,' Cam said.

'Say "yes, honey",' one of the tourists called out.

The kitchen door swung open again and Mary stepped neatly away from Brian. She lifted up the flap in the counter and said loudly, 'On you go, Mr Dixon. It was just an accident. Nothing to worry about.'

Mr Conatello glared at the mess of smashed scones and crockery and snapped at his wife, 'Get this cleaned up before someone trips and sues us blind.'

Brian, looking bewildered, stumbled over to an empty table.

Mr Conatello glared at the rest of the café for good measure and disappeared back into the kitchen.

Harry turned to Cam, his eyebrows raised. 'Well, that was interesting. I didn't think PDAs were Brian's style.'

'I don't think he's quite himself,' Gwen said.

'It's not usually so exciting in here,' Cam said. He stood up and pulled a seat out. 'Would you like to join us?'

Gwen couldn't stop looking at Brian, who was sitting at a corner table looking dazed. There was a part of her that couldn't help but be a little impressed. Who'd have thought mousey Marilyn had it in her? Of course, she probably wasn't going to be thrilled with Brian's reaction, but it was clearly a powerful spell.

Harry stood, too. 'I'm getting a custard slice before someone else decides to take a dive.'

'Gwen?' Cam said. He was still holding the back of the empty chair.

He was just being polite, Gwen knew, but she felt a bit wobbly from rushing to get to the café, so she sat down.

Cam glanced at Brian. 'He looks bamboozled. Wonder what got into him.'

Gwen stiffened. Cam wasn't suggesting Brian was possessed, but it was close enough to the truth to make her feel nervous. 'Do you know Brian well? Do you think he'd join us if we asked?'

'Christ no. He'll want free legal advice. Everyone always does.'

The bitterness in Cam's voice got her attention. 'That's a bit cynical.'

'You wouldn't understand.'

Harry appeared at the table carrying a paper bag and licking his fingers. 'I've got to go.'

Cam looked at his watch. 'But it's only half three.'

'Ah, the lightning wit of a keen legal mind.' Harry smiled cryptically. 'I'm on a secret mission.'

He turned to Gwen. 'Always a pleasure. Try to get our resident legal eagle to take some time off. He's grumpy when he's tired.'

'Nothing to do with me,' Gwen said, holding her hands up. At that moment, Brian rose and headed shakily towards the counter. He veered towards the staff-only door.

'Oh, no,' Cam said, standing. 'That's a bad idea.'

Gwen followed Brian, catching his arm just before he reached the door. 'Hello, Mr Dixon. Would you—'

Brian shook her arm off and carried on. Which was good in one way as Gwen had no idea how to finish that sentence. On the other hand, there was a good chance that Mr Conatello would be displeased to make his acquaintance.

'Brian!' Cam was next to her, and he grabbed Brian's arm but with considerably more success. Brian executed a balletic turn to face Gwen, Cam's other arm firmly across his shoulders. He blinked at Gwen and then at Cam. To the untrained eye, he probably looked drunk. To Gwen he looked enchanted.

'Let's take a walk!' Gwen said brightly.

'Come on, mate,' Cam said. 'I think you need some fresh air.'

Cam led Brian out of the café. One of the tourists leaned out of her seat and patted Brian as he passed. 'Don't you give up, honey.'

The drizzling rain had turned into hail and Brian was putting up some resistance. 'Got to go to her,' he mumbled.

'What now?' Cam said over Brian's head.

'He needs to sober up.' What he needed was to be disenchanted, but Gwen wasn't about to say that to Cam.

'I don't think this is just alcohol talking,' Cam said, peering into Brian's face.

Gwen hid her surprise. 'We need to get him away from here.'

'Should we take him to hospital to get checked out? What if he's having a breakdown?'

'He's upset,' Gwen said. 'And he's in love.' *And someone had been burning verbena.*

Brian's eyes flicked open. 'Love!'

'Uh-oh.' Cam renewed his Vulcan grip on Brian's shoulder. 'Come on, Brian, we're going for a walk.'

A few steps down the street, Gwen's hair was plastered to her face and Brian's grey jacket was black from the rain. Cam was soaked, too, and looked rumpled for the first time since she'd arrived back in town.

They made it as far as the toy shop at the end of the street, with Brian pulling against Cam all the way. The rain was mixed with stinging hail, and Gwen couldn't see how she was going to ditch Cam. Even if he agreed to leave, Gwen would lose Brian the moment she let go of him. She didn't know how she was going to get Brian to take his cure, or even if it was going to work. *Just do it.*

'Hold on,' Gwen said, and Cam stopped half-dragging Brian.

Gwen tugged them both to the shelter of the toy shop awning. 'Sorry about this,' she said to Brian and then licked his cheeks, the left and then the right. Brian didn't seem as surprised as he should've been.

'What on earth was that?' Cam looked horrified.

Gwen thought about lying, but couldn't think of anything convincing. Besides, she had messed things up with Cam thirteen years ago. What did it matter if he thought she was a lunatic?

'I'm just checking to see if he's under a spell.'

'What?'

Gwen reached up on her tiptoes and licked across Brian's forehead and up the middle. She tasted soap, which was something of a relief.

'Stop licking him!' Cam said, sounding annoyed.

'Salt,' Gwen said, wiping her mouth with a tissue. 'He's been hexed. Enchanted. Whatever you want to call it.'

'Maybe he's salty because he's been sweating, Gwen.' Cam was speaking in the slow voice of one speaking to a toddler with a hunting knife. Gwen ignored him.

'Okay, Brian. I need you to put this under your tongue. Let it dissolve, right?'

Brian gazed over Gwen's shoulder in the direction of the Hearty Baker. 'Let me go to her. I know what I have to do.' He looked beseechingly at Gwen. 'It's all so clear.'

'I'm sure it is. Open wide.'

Brian obediently opened his mouth and Gwen popped the slice of dried lemon inside.

His face twisted. 'Urgh.'

'Don't spit—' Gwen said, just as Brian spat the lemon onto the floor.

'Are you going to help?' Gwen said to Cam. 'Hold his jaw shut this time. Like when you're giving pills to a dog.'

'I don't have a dog,' Cam said. 'What is that, anyway?'

'Dried lemon slice covered in salt.' One of the more useful things she'd learned from her flaky mother was to always be prepared for the worst. She'd been carrying hex-removing lemon slices around with her since she was fifteen, along with the stub of a candle, some thread, and a feather. She was like a freaky Girl Guide.

'And that's supposed to do what exactly?'

'Lift the curse,' Gwen said.

'Of course.'

'Open up, Brian.'

Brian looked marginally more with it. 'I don't feel right,' he said.

'This will help,' Gwen said.

'You promise?' Brian said.

'I promise.' Gwen gave him the lemon slice and watched as Brian slipped it underneath his tongue. His shoulders convulsed and he pulled extraordinary faces, but the lemon stayed in.

'I hope he doesn't sue you,' Cam said.

'At least I know a lawyer,' Gwen said, avoiding Cam's eye.

After a moment, Brian swallowed and coughed. His eyes were watering, but they looked a little clearer. He wasn't pulling at Cam, either. He sank to the ground instead, and sat on the wet pavement.

Gwen crouched down beside him. 'Brian? Mr Dixon?'

Brian raised his head. He was crying. 'Holy Mother of God, what have I done?'

'It's all right.' Gwen patted him awkwardly on the arm. 'Go home and take a nap. You'll feel better in the morning.'

Brian blinked. 'I'm supposed to be at work. I just left the office. I didn't even tell anyone where I was going.'

'Probably for the best,' Cam said and Gwen shot him a *you're not helping* look.

'Marilyn. Oh Jesus. Marilyn is going to kill me.' Brian took out a handkerchief and blew his nose.

'You need to drink plenty of water,' Gwen said.

'Will that help?' Brian clambered to his feet.

'For the dehydration.' Gwen stood up too. She stuck out her hand and Brian took it automatically. 'You're fine now. Good luck.'

'But what am I going to tell Marilyn?' Brian wailed.

'Tell her you had a breakdown, but you were cured with a slice of lemon,' Cam said. 'Or, if you love your wife and you actually want a chance at making it work, tell her that you've been a complete and utter fool and that you're deeply sorry and you'll go to marriage counselling. If that doesn't work, try poetry.'

Gwen looked at Cam. 'You're good at this.'

Cam smiled tightly. 'Part of my job. Unfortunately.'

'Well.' Gwen stuck her hand out and shook Cam's hand. 'Thanks for your help.' His hand was warm and touching him sent every nerve-ending in Gwen's body into overdrive. *Bad idea.*

'Any time.' Cam was smiling a little less tightly, now, and time seemed suspended between their clasped hands. For a moment, Gwen could almost believe there was a connection between them still.

'So,' Brian gave a phlegmy cough. 'Is that it? Do you have any more of those lemon-thingummybobs?'

'You have to do the next bit on your own,' Gwen said. She was distracted by the intensity of Cam's gaze and the sudden awareness that her hair was probably plastered to her scalp by the rain.

She let go of Cam's hand and waited for him to leave. Something in the back of her brain told her it was important for him to walk away first. And then, with a final crooked smile, he did.

CHAPTER 9

I thought I would be so happy to have Gloria back in my life, but when I look at her I see the sixteen-year-old spitting bile and leaving without a backward glance. I know that I should rise above it, be a proper mother, forgiving and calm, but I can't. Truth was, I never was very maternal. Motherhood has changed Gloria, though. She's remaking everything, refusing to see the things she doesn't like, arranging the world until it suits her. She's like a biscuit-cutter. Everything that passes through her comes out heart-shaped and smelling of cinnamon. It can't end well.

Gwen blinked. She tried to fit this view of Gloria with the woman she knew. It was strange to think of Gloria back then. She'd left Pendleford – and Iris – back when she was just a kid: a pregnant kid. Frightened and angry. For a moment, Gwen felt sympathy for Gloria. A kinship that jolted her.

Gwen took a deep breath and dialled her mother's number. The most self-obsessed woman Gwen had ever known had chosen to relocate to a farm in Australia, complete with three hundred cattle and a new husband twenty years younger than her. It must've been true love after all. 'Gloria?'

'Sweetie! Lovely to hear you, but we're up to our eyeballs in newborns. Can I call you back?'

Gwen knew that Gloria's ability to phone a person back was minimal. 'Two minutes.'

'We need more than that. It's been an age. When are you coming over? The weather is to die for, did I tell you that?'

'You mentioned it, yeah.' Gwen looked through the frost-coated window. 'I've got some news. I don't know whether you've heard. I assumed you would've done and then I realised you might not have—'

'I know money is tight, honey, and I'd love to help you out but it's just too tricky right now. You can get some great deals, though. There was this flight for under three hundred. Of course, you have to stop in Kuala Lumpur for three days—'

'Iris is dead. She passed away.'

There was a silence. Gwen imagined she could hear crackling as the sound of her mother not speaking travelled around the world. Gwen filled the silence with, 'She left me her house.' Like ripping off a plaster.

Gloria didn't miss a beat. 'And what does she want in return?'

'Nothing.' Gwen considered adding: *she's dead*, but didn't want to sound callous.

'That doesn't seem likely. You stay away from that place, okay? Curiosity killed the cat.'

Gwen closed her eyes so that she wasn't looking at Iris's walls, her furniture, the open doorways. 'I just thought you should know. About Iris.' Gwen didn't know what she was expecting. Some kind of revelation. Or maybe a thunderbolt all the way from Australia for saying the forbidden name.

'You remember what I told you about that woman?' Gloria said.

'That she never let a truth out untwisted.'

'Good girl.'

'What should I do?' Gwen surprised herself by asking. She thought she'd given up looking to Gloria for advice a long time ago.

'Stay well, be happy, and don't let the bastards get you down.' Gloria's voice was back to cheerful. It didn't sound forced, just light. Gwen pictured her in the dry sunshine, red earth beneath her feet and a smile on her lips. 'And keep away from that house. It always had a bad feeling. Do you want me to check your cards?'

'No,' Gwen said quickly. 'Thank you.'

'Okay. I'm sorry, I've got to go, sweetie. It's calving time.'

Gwen stayed with the phone held to her ear for a moment, listening to dead air and looking around the hallway of the forbidden house.

Gwen stared in disbelief at the best-before date on the packet of flour. For two pounds fifty, she would expect five-hundred grams of self-raising to be made of gold or ground-up unicorn horn, not bog-standard wheat flour, best consumed before 1999. She put the packet back on the shelf and, as she did so, felt a prickling on her palms. A moment later, a wave of sickness swept up from her toes to the top of her head and her peripheral vision went black. She swallowed hard, but the nausea had already passed, leaving her with a clear image of a packet of in-date flour, its green and white paper bag intact and the yellow price sticker curling very slightly at one edge. The image was so stable, so clear, she felt as though she could zoom into it like with a digital camera. She blinked and the image disappeared, replaced with the real-life vista of the corner shop shelves and the looming face of John, the guy who ran the shop full-time because the owner – his mum – was eighty-four and no longer inclined to do so. 'All right, miss?' John's tone was dubious.

'Fine, thanks.' Gwen lied. She blinked because the shop lighting was suddenly too bright. She moved down the aisle, away from John and his questioning look. A woman in her fifties with a sleek ponytail and a navy velvet Alice band, padded gilet and dark green wellington boots was picking up apples from a basket, one by one, and studying them intently before putting them back. She glanced at Gwen and gave a tight smile. Gwen nodded and smiled back but, before she could add a friendly 'good morning', the woman put her hand up to cover her mouth and said in a loud, raspy whisper that carried clearly through the quiet shop, 'Check everything before you buy it; the man's a crook.'

'Um…' Gwen glanced at John-the-shopkeeper, who was rearranging the cigarette display with an air of studied unconcern.

Alice band tilted her head to one side, considering Gwen as if she were some interesting new breed of dog. 'You're the girl that's moved into End House, aren't you?'

Gwen agreed, happy to move off the subject of the shop's stock.

'Well, it'll be nice to have someone normal.'

'What do you mean?'

The woman leaned in, but didn't lower her voice. 'Let's just say, the previous owner was a little bit eccentric.'

'You didn't visit my great-aunt for help, then?' Gwen said, smiling sweetly.

The woman pulled back. 'Your great-aunt?'

'Yes. Iris Harper. Resident of Pendleford for over fifty years; you probably knew her. Seems like everybody did.'

The woman fiddled with her gold watch, twisting it to look at the face. 'Oh goodness, I must get on. It's coffee morning in the town hall. For the seniors. You're welcome to volunteer, of course . . .' And she put down her last apple and rushed out of the door as if pursued by hell's demons.

Irritated – both by the snotty woman and with herself for caring what the snotty woman thought – Gwen stuck out her hand to grab a tin of tomatoes. Her hand slipped through the line of cans and closed around a soft packet. She drew it out and stared: a green and white bag of flour. In date. Okay. She'd spent years resisting the Finding and now it was helping her with her grocery shopping.

After a slightly frosty exchange with John, Gwen stepped out onto the main street and wondered what to do next. She had plenty to do at the house, of course, the list of things that needed fixing, cleaning or throwing away unrolling in her mind like a serpent, but the air was pleasantly crisp and the pale November sun was high in an almost cloudless sky.

She walked along the roads at random, tracing a vague circle around the town. On a back road, the narrow pavement and green verge gave way to a small, flat green, speckled still with the remains of the morning's frost. Beyond the green stood a church.

She walked through the lychgate to the ancient graveyard, the stillness complete. At the back of the yard there was another gate and, beyond that, a much larger, newer graveyard. The rows of marble and stone were more regimented, their polished surfaces shining in the light.

Gwen felt drawn to the stones, drifting down the rows until she came to Iris's. It was a small, simple shape, made from speckled dark grey stone. The inscription read:

Iris Harper. 1924–2010. You get what you get.

Well, that was chirpy. 'Sorry I didn't bring anything,' Gwen said, suddenly feeling rude. The woman had given her a house, for goodness' sake. She slipped her rucksack from her shoulders and opened it. Flour, milk, carrots. She rummaged and her fingers touched a brown paper bag she didn't remember buying. Inside was a small aubergine. Gwen frowned; had there even been aubergines in the shop? Had she picked one up? She held it up, its perfect purple skin glowing as if lit from within. Oh Christ, she was having a religious experience over an aubergine. That was blasphemy at the very least.

She balanced the aubergine on Iris's grave, in the place where wilting flower arrangements sat on the others. It reflected in the surface of the stone, making the cold grey look warmer. More homely. Gwen felt a lump in her throat and her eyes pricked. Madness or not, she felt calmer than she had in months.

She hesitated, glancing around the graveyard before speaking out loud. 'Is there something special about your house?' Gwen's voice was thin, trailing off at the end of the sentence and she blushed even though there was nobody around to hear her talking to herself. She wanted to ask if End House was somehow amplifying her abilities. The Finding was happening more and more, and the lemon slice had de-hexed Brian Dixon right in front of her eyes. She felt breathless, overwhelmed, sick. What if Helen Brewer's dog and the packet of flour were just the beginning? What if she couldn't control it any more?

On the way home, she called into the corner shop again. John looked at her suspiciously and she bought a bag of apples as a mark of friendship. There was no way to ask the question without appearing unhinged, but Gwen swallowed her pride. 'Did I buy an aubergine earlier? I wasn't sure.'

John looked down at the counter, his cheeks reddening. 'I put that in. Free of charge.'

'Oh.'

'I used to order them just for Iris. Special, like. That was the last one and no one else will want it, so it seemed like the right thing to do . . .' He trailed off, his cheeks pink.

'It was,' Gwen injected as much warmth into her voice as possible and John smiled properly, showing nicotine-stained teeth.

Back at the house, Gwen was surprised to find Cam waiting for her in his car. Truth was, she found it difficult to deal with the actuality of Cameron Laing; she'd spent so many years coming to terms with him in the abstract. The living, breathing, frowning Cam still seemed like a creature from another planet which, Gwen supposed, he was.

'Would you like some tea? Coffee?' The saying 'you can never go back' was on a loop in Gwen's mind, which didn't help matters.

'Coffee, please,' Cam said, seemingly oblivious to the effect he had on her. He dug into his bag and produced a brown cardboard folder. 'I was supposed to give you this when you came to the office. I can't believe I forgot.'

'That's okay.' Gwen concentrated on unlocking the front door. 'It's nice of you to bring it round.'

'Not at all,' Cam said. 'It was my mistake.'

Gwen moved around the kitchen. Soon the smell of good coffee filled the air. She opened a tin and frowned at the contents. 'A neighbour left these on the front step as a house-warming. I think it's ginger cake.'

'It's a friendly town,' Cam said.

'Apparently.' Gwen sat opposite him and took a slice.

Cam was looking at her with an odd expression on his face.

'What?'

'It's funny seeing you being so domestic. It's not how I remember you.'

'I was eighteen,' Gwen said, irritated. 'And I think you mostly saw me horizontal and with my shirt unbuttoned.' As soon as the words were out, Gwen could've hit herself with her plate. She felt the redness rush up her face.

Cam nodded, as calm as ever. He took a slice of cake, then paused before eating it. 'No salty lemon in this?'

Gwen forced a smile. 'I told you, I didn't make it.'

'That was a weird day, wasn't it?'

Before Gwen could work out whether Cam actually wanted to have a conversation about the de-hexing of Brian Dixon, the back door swung open and Lily appeared.

'Hello.' Lily peered at Cam with interest. 'Are you the lawyer?'

'Cameron Laing.' Cam stood up and offered his hand.

'What can I do for you?' Gwen said, pointedly not standing. This open-door policy was beyond a joke.

'I'm Lily Thomas.' Lily took Cam's hand and stared up at him with a winsome expression. 'I looked after Iris.' She turned to Gwen, switching gears: 'I haven't been paid for the last month, either.'

'Oh God, I'm sorry,' Gwen said. 'Did Iris leave a chequebook or anything? I know I can't access her account for six months.'

'I don't remember seeing anything, but we can check again,' Cam said. 'There might be something in this lot.' He tapped the file on the table.

'Personal service,' Lily said. 'I'll have to remember that. If I ever need legal help.'

'Certainly,' Cam said. He offered her a business card.

'Or perhaps it's the irresistible charms of our lovely Gwen here.' Lily smiled without warmth. 'Has she bewitched you, Cameron?'

'Uh—' Cam managed.

Lily turned back to Gwen, suddenly all business. 'I'd appreciate my money as soon as possible. If you don't have it, then I'd happily take Iris's notebooks instead. I'm sure I'll be able to find that recipe, as you're too busy to look.'

'Recipe?' Cam said.

'Chutney,' Lily and Gwen spoke at the same time.

'Well, I won't impose.' Lily nodded to Cam. 'Nice to meet you.'

After Lily had left, Gwen turned to Cam. 'You said something about papers?'

He opened the file on the table. 'Just formalities. You've got to agree to the covenants on the house, sign that the house contents match the list, things like that.'

'What sort of covenants?'

'Old regulations that were made when the land was originally developed. Let's see.' He flicked through the papers. 'Okay. You're not allowed to farm sheep.'

'Damn it!' Gwen clicked her fingers.

Cam smiled and continued. 'You can't run a medical practice, barbershop or paint the gable end of the house a "gaudy colour".'

'It doesn't say that!' Gwen reached for the paper and her hand brushed his. A bolt of electricity shot up her arm and she felt the blushes coming on again. It was embarrassing.

'Well, what do you know?' she said, studying the paper. 'I wouldn't have thought "gaudy" was a technical term. Do you think blue counts? I've always liked blue.'

'Paint your walls whatever you like. I can argue it for you.' Cam was smiling in that capable way he had. The way that made Gwen want to jump him and push him over at the same time.

'Nothing for Lily,' Gwen said.

'There are no instructions from Ms Harper, so we can't action a withdrawal on her account. Legally, though, you're on safe ground. There is nothing in writing, no contract of work.'

'But she was helping Iris. Looking after her. She shouldn't be out of pocket. That's not right.'

Cam shook his head. 'If you haven't got the money, she's going to have to wait. Also, I couldn't find the title deeds for the property. I'm assuming you took them with you?'

'No,' Gwen said. She got up to fetch the papers she'd brought home from Laing & Sons. 'I don't think there was anything like that.'

Cam frowned. He held his hand out and she passed the stack of paper across. He flicked through quickly, then checked through the brown file that he'd brought. 'That's odd.'

'Odd doesn't sound good,' Gwen said.

'I'm sure it's nothing to worry about. Iris must've kept them in the house somewhere.'

Things went quiet. Gwen sipped her coffee. Cam took a mouthful of his own. His eyes closed as he swallowed and Gwen couldn't stop herself from staring at the movement of his throat, the exposed stretch of skin.

He opened his eyes and caught her staring. 'Good coffee,' he said.

'Thank you,' she said. Gwen was very glad of the solid wooden table between them. A cavernous space opened in the pit of her stomach. She wanted. That was it. Being near to Cam made her want very badly.

'I don't want to worry you, but you ought to find the house deeds,' Cam was saying, 'and I'd recommend keeping them in a fire-proof safe or lodging them with a bank. They charge a small fee, but it's worth it for the peace of mind.'

Gwen blinked. 'Okay.'

At the door, Cam seemed about to say something, but then he hesitated. Finally he raised his hand in a half-salute and thanked her for the coffee.

'Any time,' Gwen said and then wanted to slap herself. If she was going to get any kind of control and equilibrium back, proximity to Cameron Laing was not the way forward.

CHAPTER 10

I was shopping in town today and couldn't stop myself from buying a cat bed. I knew as soon as I touched it, that Gwen was going to need it. I'm getting more and more flashes like that; it's like nesting for a baby, I assume. It reminds me of the time after Annie died and I prepared for Gloria's arrival. I'm glad I'll be dead before she gets here. I couldn't go through the disappointment of another Gloria. I'm too old for all that again.

Gwen was going through the bedrooms. She told herself that the past was the past and that she didn't care, but still she found herself squinting at bare patches on the walls, the heavy oak furniture, the half-finished tube of toothpaste in the bathroom cabinet, looking for clues.

She stood in the doorway to the third bedroom. The window looked onto the garden and the fields beyond; a line of trees at the horizon stood out like charcoal scratchings against the pale sky. There was nothing in this room that said 'teenage girl', but Gwen would've laid money that it had been Gloria's room back when she'd lived with Iris. She lay on the narrow bed and looked at the cracks in the ceiling, the low bookcase, the bedside cabinet.

She slid open the drawers in the chest underneath the window. The first three were empty, lined with faded wallpaper offcuts. The bottom drawer was stuck and Gwen sat on the floor to pull it out. Loose photographs and a stash of unopened seed packets.

She sifted through the pictures until she found one of Gloria. Standing in front of a tall woman who must've been Iris. Gloria wasn't looking at the lens but to something out of the picture. Iris was staring so directly, Gwen felt she was looking right at her.

She rang Ruby. 'There are photos of Gloria here. Do you want me to bring them over?'

'No.'

'Okay.' Gwen was going to hang up, sibling duty done, when Ruby said, 'Has Katie been by today?'

'Nope. Not yet.'

'She keeps asking questions I can't answer. Like why you've been away for so long. Why you haven't been here for Christmas and stuff.'

'You can answer that. Just explain that you told me to stay away, that I wasn't allowed—'

'I can't believe you're still going on about that. I've said I was sorry.'

'You didn't actually, and it's not about a crappy soft toy rabbit from a kid's conjuring set. It's that you don't trust me. You've never trusted me.'

'That's because you don't respect my feelings. My therapist says—'

'You've got a therapist? Is that as well as the yogi, or are they the same lecherous guy?'

'Marcus isn't lecherous. That's a horrible thing to say,' Ruby snapped. 'You're so prejudiced.'

'Oh yes, I'm the one with the closed mind. Absolutely. Uh-huh,' Gwen said.

'Well, you do have some very set ideas. And you're unforgiving. I made one mistake and it was a really long time ago and you just won't let it go.'

'I'd find it a damn sight easier if anything had changed, but it hasn't. You'd react in exactly the same way.'

'I wouldn't,' Ruby said. 'I was frightened and I was angry.'

'What on earth did you have to be angry about? I was the one getting arrested.'

'I just wish you'd tried harder to, you know, not use it. If you'd just left well alone, the police wouldn't have questioned you.'

'Arrested me. Suspected me of murder.'

'Whatever,' Ruby said. 'Have you, though? Seriously. Have you ever really tried to be normal?'

'But I knew where that boy was. I just knew. You think I shouldn't have told the police? I mean, I didn't know he was already dead and it didn't matter anyway. You think I should've kept quiet even though there might've been a chance I could've saved him? And what about the closure for his family; did you even think about that?'

Gwen heard Ruby breathing. 'Okay, maybe not for that one. But I just mean usually. In like . . . everyday life.'

'It's not a bloody switch, Ruby. I don't get to choose. I've spent the last ten years trying really hard not to use it, to ignore every little sign, to pretend I don't know things that I shouldn't know, but it's impossible and I've been miserable.' As soon as Gwen said the words, she felt the truth of them. She'd been miserable. Really fucking miserable. 'It's like trying to wear shoes that are a size too tight. They pinch all the time and to begin with you think it'll be fine and you'll get used to it and the leather will give a little but, by the time you've walked around for an hour or two, every step is agony and all you can think about is ripping the bloody things off.'

'Please don't tell Katie,' Ruby said in a rush.

'I've already promised. I won't talk about finding stuff or—'

'No. I don't mean that. I mean the way I've been. I'm not proud of it.'

'That's okay,' Gwen said awkwardly.

'She hates me enough already without her finding out that I've been a total bitch to her new favourite person.'

'You've not been a total bitch,' Gwen said, smiling. 'You have to do me a favour in return, though. Come to the pub with me tonight.'

'In Pendleford?'

'I'm trying to settle in, meet people.'

'Did you hit your head? That doesn't sound like you.'

'Very funny.' Gwen tried to organise her thoughts. 'I'm probably just going stir crazy. I need to get out of the house for a bit.'

'You're just hoping to bump into Cameron Laing.' Ruby's tone was teasing, but Gwen felt like she'd been slapped.

'What?' Ruby said. 'What's happened?'

'Nothing.'

I used the Finding in front of him and he ran away and then I fed someone a de-hexing charm and he probably thinks I'm certifiable.'

'Fine. I'll come out. I'll meet you there. But no weird stuff, okay?'

The Red Lion was just as cosy as Gwen remembered. A fire was blazing in the hearth and there was a comforting murmur of conversation. Bob the barman was on his own and it was busy on both sides, so she hoisted herself onto one of the high stools to wait for Ruby. A couple were debating the merits of getting two glasses of wine or a whole bottle. A stocky man slid into the narrow gap between Gwen's stool and the couple. His tie was loose, the top button of his shirt undone and his face was red from either alcohol, excitement or from sitting too close to the fireplace. Gwen tucked her legs as close to the stool as she could, and fixed her gaze on the optics.

'Excuse me?'

With some reluctance Gwen turned to the man.

'I'm hoping you can settle a bet.' A gust of lager breath accompanied his words. 'Are you a model or an actress?'

'That's a terrible line. Very unoriginal,' Gwen said. 'In fact, it's so bad I'm guessing you don't even want it to work. Which is just bad manners.'

The man's goofy smile faded slightly. 'No. I'm serious.' He attempted a leer. 'Let me buy you a drink.'

'No, thank you. Why don't you head back to your friends now?'

Gwen had spotted the group of similarly clothed office boys. They were looking in her direction with absolutely no subtlety at all. A guy with a thick thatch of black hair and a purple shiny shirt nudged his friend and burst out laughing.

Unfortunately, her would-be-suitor was now looking at her with increased interest. Bollocks. She'd tried to be funny. That was never a good idea. Now he thought she was a challenge.

'At least talk to me for a bit.' He spread his hands wide. 'I mean, we're both human beings, right? Let's pass the time together.'

'I'm sorry,' Gwen said. 'I'm waiting for someone and I really don't feel like company.' She angled her body away and began fishing in her bag for her phone. If she pretended to write a text message, perhaps he would leave her alone.

A hand appeared in front of her face. 'Jason. Pleased to meet you.'

Gwen didn't take the hand. She pressed the middle button on her phone and pretended to read the screen.

'Don't I know you from somewhere?' Jason wasn't giving up.

'I don't think so,' Gwen said without looking up. There was a brief, blessed silence, but she could feel Jason staring at her.

'Gwen Harper,' Jason said. 'It is. It's Gwen Harper. Christ, I thought you looked familiar.'

Gwen looked at him. Pink cheeks, small beer gut straining the front of his tucked-in shirt, polyester suit trousers, sweaty forehead. 'How do you know—'

'God...' Jason was shaking his head. 'You've got balls.'

'Excuse me?' Gwen's stomach swooped.

Jason's voice seemed to have got much louder suddenly. 'Crazy Gwen. My God, I never thought you'd show up around here.'

Jason had not aged well, but she remembered him now. She had always thought he was decent enough, which just went to show that she didn't have her mother's intuition.

'Crazy Gwen Harper...' Jason was shaking his head as if she were some kind of mythical beast. 'Do you know what we used to call you?'

Gwen felt frozen and hot all at the same time. Her eyes pricked.

Jason started counting names off on his fingers. 'Freak show, Loony Tunes, Harptard. You know, as in re—'

'Hiya, Gwen, how are you?' Bob had appeared. Confusingly, he was leaning forward, his arms resting on the bar, smiling at Gwen like she was his long-lost sister.

'I'm fine, thanks,' Gwen managed.

'Pint of Fosters,' Jason said.

Bob's gaze flicked to Jason. 'You're barred. Get out.'

'What?'

Bob straightened up. 'You're not getting served here, mate. Get out.'

'Now,' Bob turned back to Gwen, 'what can I get you, my love?'

'Southern Comfort, please. Ice.'

'You can't do that,' Jason said, his pink face flushing deep red. 'I haven't done anything.'

'My pub, my rules,' Bob said. 'Either you go quietly or I call the police. Up to you.'

Jason mumbled something, but he must've seen something in Bob's expression because he retreated to his group.

Gwen tried to formulate a 'thank you' while Bob poured her drink.

'Here you go. Don't let idiots like that get to you.'

'Thanks,' Gwen said, confused.

'I knew your aunt,' Bob said, as if this explained everything.

'Great-aunt,' Gwen said automatically.

'Yeah, she was,' Bob said. 'She helped me out when my dad died. I took over this place from him, you know, and some big-shot on the council tried to stop the licence from being renewed. There's been a pub here for over a hundred years and then a committee decides it's not allowed. Anyway, Iris sorted it.'

'What did she do?' Gwen said.

Bob shrugged. 'Sorted it. I didn't ask questions.' He smiled, flashing white teeth against his sun-tanned skin. 'And now we've got Iris Mark Two. That's good news.'

'I'm not like Iris,' Gwen said quickly.

'Give it time,' Bob said.

'No. I'm really not.'

Bob held his hands up. 'Whatever you say. That drink's on the house, anyway. Just in case.' He flashed her a final bright smile and moved down the bar to serve somebody else.

Gwen had just bagged a table when Ruby arrived.

Ruby didn't look convinced. 'Well, this is colourful,' she said, making a show of dusting off the bench before sitting down.

'You're funny,' Gwen said. 'And you're buying.'

'I suppose you're broke,' Ruby said.

Gwen declined to answer. She pointed to the bar. 'Quick. Bob is round our side.'

Ruby went to get the drinks and Gwen leaned back, enjoying the smell of beer and woodsmoke and the pleasant anticipation of a glass of red wine. Then she heard a familiar voice and she straightened up. She glanced casually in the direction of the back room and, sure enough, caught sight of Harry. He had a pint glass in each hand and a packet of crisps between his teeth.

'Cam's here,' Ruby said, plonking down their drinks.

'Is he?' Gwen said in her most casual voice.

'Ha,' Ruby said. She took an appreciative sip of wine while eyeballing Gwen.

'What?'

'Ha,' Ruby said again.

'Would you please stop saying that?'

'I give you two five minutes, tops.'

'You're clearly delusional.'

'Five minutes and you'll be canoodling in a dark corner.'

'I don't canoodle. I'm a grown-up.' Gwen said as primly as she could manage.

Ruby opened her mouth.

'Don't say "ha".'

'I'm thinking it, though,' Ruby said.

Gwen decided to take the moral high ground but, before she could think of something clever and cutting to say, she caught sight of Cam. He was walking up the passageway, heading for the gents, no doubt. That's right. Keep on walking; ignore your old friends. Bastard.

'Good evening, ladies.' Cam paused at their table. 'Hello, Ruby. It's been a while.'

'Hello, Cam. Long time, no see.' Ruby grinned at Gwen and looked meaningfully at her watch.

Gwen ignored her. 'Don't let us keep you.'

'Right.' Cam looked surprised. If she didn't know better, she'd say that was a flash of hurt she'd seen cross his face.

'It was nice to see you again, Ruby.'

And he was gone.

'Well, that wasn't very friendly,' Ruby said.

'You're just pissed off because you were wrong.'

'I wouldn't say that; you've still got another two and a half minutes.'

'Drop it,' Gwen said.

'You're very touchy today. I'm just remembering the way you two used to be. Joined at the hip. And the lips. And everywhere else—'

Gwen glared at her.

'Fine, fine.' Ruby grinned, then said with exaggerated politeness, 'What would you like to talk about, then?'

An hour later, and Gwen was feeling very proud of herself. She had hardly thought about Cam at all. Well, she'd certainly done an excellent job of pretending not to think about him. And she'd hardly glanced in his direction. Okay, so there was a wall in the way and she couldn't see him anyway, but it was good going, she thought.

Harry appeared at their table. 'It doesn't seem right.'

'What doesn't?' Gwen said.

'You through here, us back there. It isn't very friendly.' Harry stuck out his hand to Ruby. 'I'm Harry.'

'Cam's friend,' Gwen supplied.

Harry smiled easily. 'For my sins.'

Gwen opened her mouth to say *we're fine*, but Ruby was already getting up, gathering her coat and drink.

Gwen glared at her behind Harry's back. Ruby shrugged and mouthed *what?*

'Hello, again,' Cam said.

Gwen sat down reluctantly.

'I don't think I ever met you, Harry,' Ruby was saying. 'Back in the day.'

'These two didn't do much socialising,' Harry said. 'By all accounts, they were permanently attached to one another.'

'Don't I know it,' Ruby said, rolling her eyes. Which was very unfair considering she had been exactly the same with David.

Gwen started to peel the label from her lager bottle.

'Oh, they were completely crazed,' Ruby said to Harry. 'They used to snog for hours and hours,' she said, warming to her theme. 'I thought they must've developed a way of breathing through their ears.'

Gwen aimed a kick at Ruby under the table.

'Ouch,' Harry said.

'Harry was after Gwen's time,' Cam said. 'We met housebreaking.'

Gwen raised her eyebrows and Harry said, 'Not breaking. House borrowing. It was strictly temporary.'

Ruby frowned. 'And then you became lawyers? Just like that?'

'Hey, hey.' Harry put his hands in the air. 'I'm no lawyer.'

'He's worse,' Cam said, smiling. 'Police.'

'You wish. The ladies love the uniform,' Harry said in a cheesy voice.

'That a fact?' Gwen said, extremely grateful they were no longer reminiscing about her and Cam's sex life. Actually, she could see Harry being a hit with or without a uniform. There was something incredibly sure and solid about him. Something unruffled. Something that said: *Hey, everything's going to be okay. Let's have a beer in the sunshine.* Cam, on the other hand, broadcast something like: *Everybody is up to something and I'm going to find out what it is.* Come to think of it, they were clearly in the wrong jobs.

'I'm a solicitor, to be strictly accurate,' Gwen tuned back into the conversation to hear Cam saying.

'Which is like a lawyer, only more boring,' Harry supplied.

'Thanks for that,' Cam said, 'but, essentially, yes.'

'So you don't do all that exciting courtroom stuff?' Ruby sounded disappointed.

'Barristers do the big-ticket stuff. They go to High Court and argue criminal cases. Solicitors deal with the big three.' Cam ticked them off his fingers. 'Divorce, death and The Council.'

'That sounds depressing,' Gwen said.

Cam shrugged. 'Pays the bills.'

'Divorce, though. Must be full of people arguing.' Gwen shook her head. 'Sounds like a nightmare.'

'Put it this way, I'm not exactly desperate to get married. I've seen how people behave to each other. And that's people who once loved each other enough to say "I do".' He shuddered.

Harry clapped him on the back. 'Ignore Mr Grim, Gwen. I'm sure he's got a sensitive, romantic heart underneath his hard exterior. I bet he's like a caramel. All gooey inside.'

'I am not gooey,' Cam said, looking disgusted.

'Sure you are,' Harry said, smiling as if Cam wasn't about to hack him to little pieces with a letter-opener.

'I just can't imagine you having the patience . . .' Gwen trailed off as she realised Cam was glowering at her. 'Sorry,' she said hastily.

'It's definitely one of the skills you've learned,' Harry said. 'When I met you, you were more likely to deck someone that annoyed you.'

'I tried that.' Cam managed a sort-of smile. 'But it turns out it's frowned on by the Law Society.'

'Spoilsports.'

Cam brightened. 'Now I just hit 'em in the wallet.'

Later on, Ruby was deep in conversation with a friend of Harry's and Gwen was waiting at the bar, admiring the different colours that alcohol came in. She was just planning a rainbow-themed drinking game, when she felt Cam next to her. Without turning, she knew it was him. Great. She had Cam-sense. That was a helpful power. Not.

'Can I talk to you about something?'

Gwen closed her eyes. His voice really was gorgeous. It made something thrum deep inside her, like she was attuned to its frequency.

Bob appeared and she gave him her order, changing her mind from red wine to Southern Comfort at the last moment. She needed a stiff . . . drink. She needed a stiff drink.

'What's up?' she asked, finally looking at Cam.

He paused while Bob placed a Southern Comfort on the bar.

'I've been thinking about us.'

'I'm sorry about Ruby,' Gwen said. 'She's got no tact.'

'That's okay.' Cam was smiling at her. He looked like his old self: that gorgeous lopsided smile, the devil's touch in his eyes. 'I don't know if you've noticed, but I'm having trouble keeping away from you.'

'Really?' Gwen said, brilliantly. She concentrated on staying upright.

'I was so angry with you for so long, but now you're here it's not my primary emotion.'

'Your primary emotion?' He was using his calm tone again. The one that made him sound like a particularly suave robot. Gwen grabbed the Southern Comfort and drank.

'I think we should have sex.'

Gwen choked, alcohol burning the back of her nose and throat. She coughed and snorted and had to get a tissue to wipe her streaming eyes. Finally, she managed, 'Pardon?'

'It'd clear the air.'

'Yeah, that's romantic,' Gwen said. She blew her nose and pocketed the tissue.

'I'm not talking romance. I'm talking closure.'

'Closure,' Gwen echoed.

Bob returned, uncorking a bottle of red wine with a pop.

'Yes,' Cam said easily. 'Then we can move on. As friends. As adults.' He looked he was discussing the weather.

'Wow,' Gwen managed.

'You don't have to decide right now,' Cam said.

'That's generous of you.' Gwen was torn between wanting to slap his smug face and wanting to tackle him to the floor and—

'Get me some nuts! Dry roasted!' Harry yelled across the pub.

'Gwen?' Cam said. 'Have you finished ordering?'

Gwen blinked. Bob was standing in front of her. His face was perfectly impassive. 'Right. Yes. Thanks.' Gwen was determined not to look at Cam, knew that she was blushing furiously. She scooped up her change and stuffed it into her jeans pocket, then picked up the drinks. Then she looked at him. He was looking cool and collected as always. And he was smirking slightly which, unfortunately, didn't make him any less desirable. Bastard.

CHAPTER 11

When Gwen woke up the next day, it was snowing and she thanked the sainted boiler man for fixing her heating. By lunchtime the flakes had stopped falling and she went outside to marvel at the fresh white blanket, the world made clean and new. She almost tripped over a lump on her back door step and made a mental note to always check before striding out. It was a package of silver foil topped with a layer of snow an inch thick. The path was pristine, any footprints masked by the new snow.

The air was still and cold, the world muffled. A magpie flew down from a nearby tree and Gwen automatically greeted it. It perched on the garden wall and screeched, a sound that was so exactly the sound of the front gate opening that Gwen did a double-take. A moment later, Amanda appeared from the side path and Gwen laughed at herself: it had been the gate.

'Is this a good time?' Amanda said. 'For tea?'

'Certainly.' Gwen scooped up the parcel, the foil freezing to the touch, and brushed the snow off the top. 'Come on in.'

'What's that?' Amanda nodded at the parcel.

'I've no idea. Someone left a ginger cake on my step the other day, though.' Gwen watched Amanda's expression. There was something tense behind her grey eyes. A wariness that stayed even as they exchanged pleasantries.

The warmth of the kitchen made the tips of Gwen's fingers and ears tingle. 'It's proper cold today,' she said, flicking the switch on the kettle.

'My car says it's minus six,' Amanda said. She was looking around as if she'd never seen a kitchen before. She turned suddenly. 'Can we have our tea in the other room?'

'The living room?'

'Any other room. Iris only ever showed me the kitchen. I'd love to see the rest of the house.'

'Sure.' Gwen found Amanda's enthusiasm oddly touching. 'Help yourself. Coffee or tea?'

'Is that real coffee? Yes, please,' Amanda said, already halfway out of the door to the hallway.

Gwen pottered between the kettle and the fridge, trying to ignore the magpie, which was on the kitchen windowsill, its long tail feathers half-crushed against the glass. She wanted to open the window and shoo it away; it was bad luck for a magpie – with its drop of devil's blood hidden under its tongue – to be near a window. Gloria had always said that it meant a death in the household, but that was ridiculous. Superstition. Still, Gwen tried to keep her eyes averted. If she didn't see the bird, maybe she could pretend it wasn't there.

With the tea brewed and the silver foil parcel unwrapped to reveal an iced Christmas cake, complete with a red frill and a snowman on the top, Amanda still hadn't reappeared. Gwen wrapped her fingers around her mug and wandered through the downstairs. In the living room, Amanda was on her knees in front of the writing bureau. The top was open, revealing a clean and empty interior and Amanda was busy opening the drawers underneath. She straightened up when Gwen walked in, bashing her head on the open lid.

'Oh. Hi.' Amanda was striving for casual, but couldn't stop herself from rubbing her forehead.

'Looking for something?'

Amanda flushed. 'I'm sorry. I just had to check something. I needed . . . to check.'

Gwen was alarmed to see tears in her eyes. 'Hey, it's all right,' she said, stepping forward. 'Can I help?'

'No, no. I was just . . . looking. Being nosey, I suppose.' Amanda forced a laugh.

'Were you looking for something in particular?'

Amanda took a deep breath. 'I'd love that cup of coffee,' she said brightly and marched past Gwen.

'Okay then,' Gwen said to the empty room.

Amanda was in the kitchen and she turned and gave Gwen a bright smile. 'The garden will be lovely in the spring. Iris had green fingers.'

So they were pretending nothing had happened. 'Take a seat.' Gwen gestured, sitting down herself. 'You seem upset. Is there anything I can do?'

Amanda shook her head. 'It's probably nothing. Just something Lily said, and she was probably just being mean. You know what she's like.'

'Not really,' Gwen said.

'Of course, you missed all of that.' Amanda sat forward, her face animated. 'She's bad news. You can't trust her.'

Gwen was tempted to point out that she'd just caught Amanda investigating her furniture.

'Seriously. You need to watch out for that one.'

'Why do you say that?' Gwen hated herself for asking. She felt like she was taking part in a bitchy conversation, the kind of nasty gossip that had made her own life so miserable.

'You know that house she lives in?'

Gwen nodded. She took a sip of tea and tried to pretend that she wasn't a big, fat hypocrite.

'Well, she inherited it from her parents. Her mum went into a nursing home ages ago. Early dementia or something, but her dad was still living there when he got sick. Lily moved in to look after him and not long after he died.' Amanda sat back, her eyebrows raised. 'So, there you go.'

Gwen frowned. 'I don't quite—'

'She killed him,' Amanda said. Her tone was matter of fact. 'Everyone knows it, but the police inquiry didn't find enough evidence to convict her.'

'That's a very serious thing to say. How on earth does everyone "know" it? Why would she even do that?' Gwen felt sick. She knew exactly what it felt like to be falsely accused of something so awful.

Amanda shrugged. 'Money? The house? She can't earn much from her job and you know what prices are like around here. Extortionate.'

'But to hurt her own father—'

'I heard that she didn't get on with him. He was a bit of tyrant by all accounts.'

'Poor Lily.' Pendleford was even more judgemental than Gwen had remembered. What was the phrase? Tried by a jury of your own peers. Just cut out the trial bit.

Amanda snorted. 'Hardly. She murdered an old man. Shoved him down the stairs and left him to die.'

'But maybe she didn't,' Gwen said reasonably. 'If the police investigated it, then why should we decide she's guilty? And if he was really ill, unsteady on his feet—'

'If you'd been living around here, you wouldn't be standing up for her. Trust me.'

Gwen decided to leave it. After all, she could look through Iris's journals and find out the truth. Or Iris's version of the truth, at any rate. She realised that she trusted Iris a great deal more than she trusted Amanda and that was a peculiar feeling.

As soon as Amanda left, the thoughts that Gwen had been avoiding came back with a vengeance. Cam leaning against the bar, looking like sex in a suit, and offering her one last bite of the apple. She paced through the house, looking for a distraction. Something to stop her from running to Cam's flat and stripping. As had become her habit, she settled down with one of Iris's journals.

Mr Byres is still feeling pain in his feet.

Excellent, Gwen thought. Reading about Fred Byres' chilblains ought to be the perfect anti-aphrodisiac.

He's convinced it's poor circulation and I'm sure that doesn't help, but he won't listen when I tell him what he really needs. He has to let his wife go. He's carrying her around and the strain is playing merry hell with his legs and feet. I can't tell him that though. He'd never visit again, and at least the salve gives him some relief.

Gwen scanned the recipe for the foot ointment and realised that she'd be able to make it easily. A practical project was just the ticket. If she was making ointment for Fred, then she couldn't be making mistakes with Cam. Sweaty, athletic, mind-blowing mistakes.

She stood up and gathered the ingredients. She measured olive oil into a pan, added dried marjoram and comfrey from Iris's stores, and put it on a low heat to infuse. The smell of the herbs as they warmed sent Gwen back in time. Suddenly she remembered Iris in this very kitchen. A tall woman with salt-and-pepper hair leaning back in one of the wooden chairs and smiling down at Gwen, holding out a sliver of apple. She turned to the table, half-expecting to find Iris there now. A prickling sensation on her neck made her turn back to the open book.

He has to let his wife go.

Poor Fred. No wonder he looked so hunched over, so defeated. Then it came to her; if the pain in his feet was emotional, a little heart's ease might be helpful. Iris was so certain that Fred needed to let go, but Gwen wasn't so sure. Why shouldn't Fred hold onto the memories and the love from his marriage? Why was starting over again supposed to be so brilliant?

Humming to herself, Gwen pulled on boots and a coat and went out into the garden to gather the heart's ease. The purple flowers were gamely struggling on despite the early frost, and she picked a healthy bunch. She crushed the petals in a pestle and mortar and grated beeswax on top. After she'd melted the wax with the oil and poured it into a glass jar to cool, she felt a lightening of the atmosphere, like after a summer storm.

At Millbank Comprehensive, Katie trailed out of double physics and thanked God it was lunchtime. Imogen was waiting in their designated spot next to the lockers. Katie dumped her bag and turned automatically towards the cafeteria, her stomach growling in anticipation.

'Not today!' Imogen's eyes were bright. 'Let's eat outside.'

'I haven't got anything,' Katie said, nonplussed. It was Thursday. The canteen had pizza on a Thursday.

'I've already got us stuff.' Imogen patted her coat.

Katie had been planning her meal for the last half an hour of double physics. She was going to have a slice of cheese, ham and tomato pizza and one of the chocolate flapjack things that you never saw outside of school.

Imogen had hold of Katie's arm and was marching through the corridor, a sea of smaller children parting in front of her.

'Why outside? It's freezing,' Katie said. 'Grey. Looks like rain. And I was going to have pizza and flapjack.'

'Consider your thighs saved then,' Imogen threw back, not slowing her speed.

'What's the rush?' Katie almost cannoned into a bench crammed with second years.

They pushed through the swing door and out into the open. Imogen let go of Katie's arm and stopped marching. She turned a vivacious smile in Katie's direction. 'We're going up the field today.'

'What?' This made absolutely no sense at all. Up the field was where the cool group hung out. They sat around on the cricket pitch, which was the furthest possible point from where the teachers patrolled the yard. The only more secluded place was behind the science blocks, behind a dip at the back of the grass, which was where the stoners smoked.

Katie stopped walking. 'What are you talking about?'

'We're going up the field. Exciting, no?' She gave Katie's arm another impatient little tug.

As they walked up the field, Katie slowed down again. She could see the group sitting ahead of them. The girls were sitting cross-legged, huddled together against the wind. The boys – so many boys – Katie felt her stomach flip in terror, were lounging about in their usual fashion. Some of them didn't even have coats on.

She reached for Imogen's arm. 'Let's not today. It's too cold.'

'We've been invited, Katie.' Imogen put extra emphasis on the word, dressed it in sparkling clothes and high heels.

'Still—'

'Come on.' Imogen moved ahead of her, was already smiling hello.

Katie followed, wishing she could tell Imogen not to smile as much. The cool group were a pack and they smelled weakness in an instant.

'Hi, guys,' Imogen said, plonking herself down in between Rachel Davis and Jessica Gibson. Katie stood for a moment, feeling awkward, not knowing where to sit. She wasn't going to force herself into the minuscule gap between Jessica and Imogen.

'Hey, Kitty Cat. Sit over here.' Will Jones patted the grass next to him and leered. He was a year older, had been held back earlier on in his school career. When Katie had first heard this, she'd been surprised. Now she knew that academic prowess had very little to do with social success; Will Jones was built like a brick wall and was a shit-hot forward for the school rugby team.

Katie forced herself to walk over. She sat on the edge of the boy's half, Will reclining on one side, Sasha Morgan a little further to the other. Sasha gave her a nasty look and turned away.

Imogen was giggling at something Rachel had said. She wasn't looking at Katie at all.

Katie felt her skin go into goosebumps; the hairs on the back of her neck stood up. Around her, people were talking and laughing; Gavin and Mark had got to their feet and were throwing a rugby ball back and forth; Imogen was showing off her earrings, but Katie felt an excruciating silence. *I'm sealed in a bubble*, she thought. Then, *Oh God, I've totally lost the power of speech.*

She felt a tap on her leg and looked in Will's direction. He was kneeling up, hands on his waistband. Then he unzipped his fly and out flopped a rubbery, flesh-coloured thing.

The boys burst out laughing. 'Will's got his tackle out again.'

'Jesus, man. You're so fucking proud of your dick,' someone said.

'Watch out, Katie, he'll have your eye out.'

Katie felt sick; she had looked away quickly, but the image was stuck. The incongruity of black school trousers and – that.

She felt her cheeks burning, a pounding in her ears. Then another voice broke in. 'Don't be such a twat, Will. Leave her alone.'

Katie looked up and straight into the eyes of Luke Taylor.

CHAPTER 12

Fiona Allen came today. I never thought she'd make it. I'd seen her at the church hall with those little heels named after an animal. What are they? Kitten heels? Those. Fussing with the floral displays and smiling all the time, smiling, smiling. When she knocked on the back door I don't know what I expected. That's a lie. I had seen some Love-Lies-Bleeding earlier in the week and seen her face amongst its drooping petals, so I had a strong suspicion she was running around behind Patrick's back. And good for her. I expected a gardener or handyman, something exotic for her well-bred tastes. A bit of rough. But people are constantly surprising. She's in love, of course, silly girl. Her paramour is Patrick's brother and he loves her back, apparently. Ardently, she said, as if her life had transformed to an Austen novel. Which, I suppose it has. If you discount the heavy-rutting that has put that pinkish bloom in her pallid cheeks.

Gwen shuddered. Well, that was a little too much information. Although, if Patrick Allen was going to oppose the local craft market, perhaps the insider information would come in handy. Knowledge was power and all that. Gwen immediately felt ashamed of the thought. She felt even worse about the little spark of excitement the secret gave her. Suddenly she could see why Gloria had liked reading tarot for people; she held all the cards. Still, this would be for the greater good. Plus, she could try to get a whiff of Patrick's aftershave; see if it was the same one she'd smelled after the break-in.

She fetched Patrick Allen's card and called him. He sounded fake-delighted to hear from her and suggested they go out for lunch. 'I'd rather just come to your office,' Gwen said, thinking of her flat-lining finances.

'My treat,' Patrick said jovially.

The bell rang, saving Gwen from throwing up. 'Sorry, I've got to go. Someone's at the door.'

Katie was illuminated by the porch light that was fighting the mid-afternoon gloom. Gwen had a moment to admire her youthful glow and the sparkling whiteness of her eyes before she blew into the hallway and began stripping off her outer layers. Her red gloves hit the floor, followed quickly by her bag, scarf and duffel coat. 'I'm starving.' She followed Gwen into the kitchen.

'You're always starving.' Gwen fetched the cake tins. 'Lemon drizzle or lime and pecan?'

Katie took a slice of lime and demolished it in short order.

'Are you on a tight schedule?'

'Huh?' Katie sprayed crumbs onto herself.

'You seem in kind of a hurry,' Gwen said.

'No. Just hungry.'

Gwen pushed the tin forwards.

'Thanks.' Katie took another slice of lime but, after the first couple of bites, she began to pick at it. The energy was fizzing off her.

Gwen waited.

'Aren't you going to ask about my day?'

'If you like.'

Katie pulled a face. 'Mum always asks. She wants, like, every detail.'

'Imagine that. The horror.'

'She wants to know what I learned, whether I got into trouble.'

'Is that likely?' Gwen looked at the angelic-looking girl rolling a ball of cake around her plate.

'No!' Katie pulled a dramatically injured face. 'I'm never in any trouble. I never do anything.'

'Ah.' Gwen sipped her coffee. It had almost gone cold, but she didn't want to get up and disturb the bubble of intimacy that seemed to envelop them. She had the feeling that Katie was working up to something. A question, perhaps.

'Was your mum like that? Gran, I mean.'

Mum. It was funny to think of her mother with that word. Gloria had never been 'Mum', always 'Gloria'. She'd been affectionate in a distracted way. Except when it came to training sessions. Then her attention had been intense. Uncomfortably so. 'Gloria wouldn't have asked you if you were hot if your hair was on fire.'

Katie thought for a moment. 'She wasn't very nice?'

'Not that so much. She's just in her own little world. Planet Gloria. Population one.'

'But when you were really little—'

'The same.'

'Oh.'

'I think Ruby is desperate not to be like her. Maybe she tries a bit too hard sometimes, but at least she's interested.'

Katie's face closed down.

Cat chose that moment to jump onto the outside windowsill, making Katie jump and then squeal. With remarkable energy, she was out of the chair and opening the window, letting in a stream of freezing air.

'Come on, pussycat. We've got cake.'

Katie held out a lump of cake and Cat sniffed it delicately. Gwen opened her mouth to say that lime cake probably wasn't very good for cats, when Cat jumped in a graceful arc from the sill to the floor, landing in an ungainly puddle and jumping up again to stalk towards the water dish, tail held high and an expression that said: *I totally meant to do that.*

Katie brushed her hands on her jeans. 'So, what are we doing today? More unpacking?'

'I think I'm pretty much done.' Gwen got up and shut the window. She turned to find Katie frowning at her.

'But where's all your stuff?'

'I don't really have anything. I rent furnished places, keep all my essentials in the van.'

'But what about books, music, clothes? You know – stuff.'

'In the van. I travel light.'

'That's what Dad said.'

Gwen forced a smile. 'Well, he's right.'

'What about your stock, though? Mum said you sold stuff. At car boot sales.'

'Not exactly car boots.' Gwen kept her voice light. 'More like antique fairs, craft markets, that kind of thing.'

Katie pulled a face. 'Sounds boring.'

'It can be.'

'So where is it?'

'What?'

Katie sighed. 'Your stock. Your business stuff.'

'I used to use a storage facility in Birmingham.'

'More renting?'

Gwen crossed her arms. 'It makes sense; I can move it if I want to, although Birmingham is quite handy. Kind of in the middle of the country.'

'But you don't use it any more?'

'No. I've downsized. I just keep my stock in Nanette now.'

'It's not a big business then.'

'Not any more. No.'

'Why not?'

Gwen, who had once withstood four hours of police questioning, gave in. 'Things haven't been going so well. Between you and me, the business is pretty much washed-up.'

'Oh.' Katie paused. 'What are you going to do?'

'I have no idea,' Gwen said. She felt a loosening in her chest as soon as the words were out. It didn't seem as awful to admit as she'd thought.

'What do you want to do?'

Gwen forced a smile. 'Now that's a difficult question.' *I want to run my business and make enough money so that I don't keep waking up in the night in a panic. I don't want to have the Finding. I want to live a quiet, normal life.*

'You should move your business stuff into the house. Then you can work on it properly.' Katie threw her arms wide. 'You've got this whole place.'

'Well—'

'But you're not staying?' Katie let her arms drop.

Gwen was stung by how hurt Katie looked. She took a step towards her. 'I don't have any plans—'

'When are you selling this place? Just give me some warning, okay? I don't want to come by after school and get slapped in the face by a For Sale sign in your front garden.'

'I don't have any plans to sell this house, Katie,' Gwen said as gently as she could. 'I can't for a while, anyway, and I might stay. I like it—'

'But not enough to move your stock in. Or your stuff from the van. Yeah, you're not staying.' Katie flung open the back door and headed into the garden, throwing over her shoulder, 'Mum was right.'

'Hey.' Gwen caught up with her halfway down the lawn. 'I might stay. I've never had a proper home before, so I don't really know how I'm supposed to feel.'

Katie rubbed her arms. Her nose was already pink from the cold. 'Whatever. You've gotta do what you've gotta do.' She pointed at the outbuilding. 'That would make a good stockroom, though. You could make it into an office. For your computer, packaging stuff, all that.'

'I don't use a computer.'

Katie looked at her pityingly. 'You should. Take a class or something.'

'Why?' Gwen said, ready to hear the joys of BookFace or VidTube.

'Sell your stuff online. Much better than hanging around crusty old fairs.'

'Crusty?'

'Probably. And wet. I bet you get rained on all the time.'

'Sometimes,' Gwen said, feeling a little faint.

'Let's look.' Katie crossed to the building and pushed at the door.

'It's locked.' Gwen got the key and opened it. Katie was right. The space was perfect. Before, she'd been distracted by mysteries and magic and silly superstition, but she could see the shelves full of stationery and mailing supplies, and a computer desk on the far wall. She could store things up above in the half-boarded loft, use the table in the middle for packing.

'What's it called? Your shop.'

'Curious Notions.'

Katie wrinkled her nose. 'Could be worse.'

'Thanks,' Gwen said dryly. 'Haberdashery like bobbins, needles and buttons is called "notions" and I just liked the way it sounded.'

'Well, you probably need to stick with it. You've already got customers; you want them to be able to find you.'

'They can always find me; I do the same shows every year.'

'But you won't have to,' Katie said, clearly exasperated. 'That's the whole point. You won't have to trail around the place any more. You can stay here.'

Gwen smiled at her. 'Do you want me to stay here?'

Katie gave her a superior look. 'I don't care one way or the other.'

'Right.' Gwen's smile widened. 'I love you too, honeybunch.'

The next day, Gwen crossed the town bridge, leaving the jumbled cottages and cobbled streets for the grander town houses on the other side of the river. Cameron Laing territory. She started scouting the pavements, as if her desire to see him would make him magically appear. The houses climbed the hill, creamy sandstone peeking from behind evergreens and the bare branches of oak and elm.

The Greenhouse restaurant was a monstrosity of modernism and glass awkwardly tacked onto a town house in what could only be described as a travesty of planning permission.

Patrick was already seated and he rose to meet her. 'I ordered you a gin and tonic, but I can get you something else if that's wrong.'

Gwen had resolved to be as awkward as possible, but now found she didn't have the energy. 'That's fine,' she said, taking off her coat. A waiter materialised just as she did and tried to help her with it.

'You look lovely,' Patrick said dutifully.

Gwen smiled. 'Thank you.' She had refused to dress up and was wearing an ancient T-shirt that had once been black but was now a washed-out grey; it had a cartoon of a cow on the front and the words 'moo power'.

'This is one of mine.' Patrick waved a hand, encompassing the tables, the waiting staff in their over-sized white aprons and, presumably, the kitchen area and toilets, too.

'Very nice,' Gwen said politely.

Patrick laid a hand on top of the menu, very obviously not bothering to look inside. 'I recommend the lobster.'

Gwen shook her head. 'I had seafood once. It gave me a funny tummy.'

Patrick's face wrinkled in disgust. A waiter appeared, hovering, and he smoothed it out. 'White wine to start, I think. Don't you?' He didn't wait for Gwen to answer, so she sat back a little in her chair and looked around while he displayed his intimate knowledge of the menu. The restaurant was about half full and Gwen counted three tables of older ladies. Groups of friends who had probably been meeting for lunches for years, sharing troubles and good times, going home knowing that, whatever happened, they had people on their side. In the far corner, at a small table, Gwen saw a familiar face. A face she had been expecting to see ever since blowing back into town. A face that she sometimes saw before she fell asleep at night. A face that represented every hateful attitude, every disapproving look and whispered comment.

Elaine Laing looked the same. The neatly styled hair was streaked with silver and white and the neckline a little softer, but otherwise it was undoubtedly the same woman. Perfect posture, a teeny-tiny padded handbag and pearl earrings. Gwen straightened her spine. Elaine's companion looked familiar, too. When she turned her head slightly, Gwen caught sight of Lily's profile.

'I didn't know they knew each other.'

'Everyone knows everyone around here.' Patrick glanced back. 'Do you mean Elaine Laing?'

Gwen nodded. 'That's my neighbour, Lily. I didn't know they were friends.'

'Colleagues, really. They're both on the community council. And I think Lily got involved with Elaine's pet charity, too.'

'Charity?'

'Feline Leukaemia, I believe. Yes. Lily has done very well, really. You don't often see her sort getting involved at that level.'

'Her sort?' Gwen said. 'Do you mean because she was brought up in a council house?'

'No, no.' Patrick waved a hand,.'I just meant that she's made something of herself. It's admirable.'

'Right.' Gwen folded her hands carefully in her lap to stop herself from stabbing Patrick with a fork.

The waiter reappeared with a half bottle of chilled Sancerre. It was delicious and Gwen had to grudgingly admit that Patrick had good taste. In some areas, at any rate.

'I actually invited you for a reason,' Patrick said. He paused while another waiter placed rolls onto their side plates with tongs.

'Well, I figured you weren't trying to get into my pants,' Gwen said cheerfully. The bread roll slipped and she caught it and set it on her plate. She smiled reassuringly at the blushing waiter, who looked all of sixteen. He hurried away.

'Um…' Patrick said.

'Anyway, I called you. I wanted to talk to you about having a regular craft market in the town,' Gwen said. She buttered her roll and took a large bite.

Patrick frowned. 'We can get to that later.' His crushing tone signalled that 'later' meant 'never'. 'I actually wanted to ask you for a favour.'

'You and the rest of the world,' Gwen said, slightly muffled. 'This bread is amazing.'

'Really?' Patrick frowned. 'Has Ed been to see you?'

'Ed?'

'He manages the Travelodge. I say "manages", but that's something of a matter of opinion.'

'Never met him.'

'Well, that's a relief.' Patrick cleared his throat again. 'As a new resident in the town, I was wondering how you felt about progress.'

'Are you a politician?'

'No. Not yet, anyway.' Patrick gave a little laugh. 'I own some businesses in Pendleford and I take a keen interest in the future of the town.'

'And what can I do for you?'

'It's just a small thing,' Patrick said.

'What?' Gwen tried to keep the impatience out of her voice, but her social skills, rusty at best, were stretched to breaking point.

'Did Ms Harper leave you anything?'

'She left me End House,' Gwen said. 'As you are already aware.'

Patrick poked the asparagus on his plate. 'Did you inherit the contents, too?'

'You know I did. You've seen the furniture.' Gwen had a horrible feeling she knew what Patrick was going to say next.

'Right. Well. Did she leave papers of some kind? Diaries. That kind of thing.'

And there it was. Gwen thought about the sacks of paper: the notebooks, the receipts, the used envelopes with lists of numbers scrawled in biro. 'She left me everything and I haven't had a chance to go through it all yet.' Of course, she had a pretty good idea of which papers Patrick was particularly interested in. Iris's diaries.

'Completely understandable,' Patrick said.

'Did you know my great-aunt well?' Gwen said. She wondered whether Patrick knew about his unfaithful wife, and a very evil part of her imagined his face if she *were* to let him read that particular entry.

'Not well, no. We didn't move in the same circles.'

'So, you're interested in her diaries because—'

'May I be frank?' Patrick leaned forwards and, without giving Gwen time to say 'no', he continued. 'A lot of people visited your aunt. A lot of people had faith in her... um... abilities. It was a load of nonsense, of course – forgive me – but harmless nonsense, I'm sure.'

Gwen nodded. 'No worse than aromatherapy.'

'Exactly,' Patrick said, visibly annoyed at the interruption.

'And a damn sight less dangerous than organised religion.'

'Pardon?'

'I'm pretty sure Iris never started a war or burned anyone at the stake.'

Patrick faltered, then rallied. 'Well, yes. I suppose that's true.'

'And you're interested in taking a peek in her diary in case there's some juicy gossip about your colleagues, employees, whatever.'

'No!'

'What, then?'

'As a businessman, sometimes I make investments, back community projects, that kind of thing. It's sound practice to research people who I may be entrusting with considerable sums of money.'

Gwen nodded. 'And you wondered whether any of these potential business associates had visited Iris and told her all about the time they lost a ton of cash or built a housing estate on marshland or—'

'Nothing salacious. Just anything that might be pertinent to my business interests. I wouldn't expect you to show me things that weren't of my concern. You could vet the information first.'

'I don't believe this,' Gwen began. 'If you think I'm going to show you my aunt's private papers—' She broke off as she realised that Elaine had stood up and was walking purposefully towards her table.

'I can see I'm wasting my time,' Patrick was saying.

'Hello, Gwen. You haven't changed a bit.' Elaine's cut-glass tone was as terrifying as it had been back when she was a teenager.

Patrick stood up quickly. 'Elaine! You look radiant as always.'

'Don't talk drivel, Patrick,' Elaine said, looking pleased. 'I'm simply haggard at the moment. Too much to do, too little time.'

'Would you care to join us?' Patrick looked around for a waiter.

'No, thank you. I just had to take a closer look at Gwen here. I didn't know whether to believe the rumours.'

'Believe them,' Gwen said. 'I'm back.'

'Not for long, I hope.'

Gwen was staggered by her open hostility. Patrick didn't seem sure what to say, either.

'I don't see what business it is of yours,' Gwen managed.

'We were just having a spot of lunch,' Patrick said, indicating the plates of food unnecessarily.

'Well,' Elaine said. She gave Gwen a swooping look up and down. 'I hope you manage to conclude whatever business you believe you have here.'

After she'd walked away, Patrick gave Gwen a questioning look. 'I didn't know you knew Elaine Laing.'

Gwen shrugged. 'I don't. Not really.'

'Well, I hope you'll think about my request. I might be able to help you settle into Pendleford, if that's what you decide you want. Smooth the way.' Patrick nodded in the direction of Elaine's retreating figure.

'I wouldn't let you look at my great-aunt's private material if it would make the entire community council prostrate themselves in front of me.'

'There's no need to be vulgar,' Patrick said. 'I can see this is a waste of everybody's time.'

'Not at all,' Gwen said, getting up to leave. 'It's been very eye-opening.' The only question in Gwen's mind now was: how badly did Patrick Allen want the information in Iris's diaries? Enough to have broken into End House? Gwen hadn't got enough of a sniff to know whether his aftershave matched the one she'd smelled before. She tried to picture Patrick Allen breaking into her house and smashing up her boiler, but it was difficult. He didn't seem the type with his manicured hands and cut-glass accent . . . But appearances could be so deceptive.

CHAPTER 13

After another broken night, turning over and over in her bed, unable to get comfortable, unable to switch off the 'Cam and Gwen' show in her mind, Gwen was half-mad with exhaustion. She put on her headphones and turned the music up to wake herself up, but clashing guitars just reminded her of Cam. She pressed shuffle on her iPod until an acoustic track came on, but that was worse. A song that she'd avoided for the last decade because it reminded her of Cam started playing, as if to taunt her. Dave Grohl's gravelly voice over a driving chord pattern. He breathed directly into Gwen's ears, wondering if *'anything could feel this real forever'*. She tried to work on her shadow boxes, but made mistake after mistake until the frustration became unbearable.

At six o'clock, she trailed into the kitchen, but was too jumpy to cook. At seven o'clock, she realised she felt achingly empty, so she ate a bowl of cereal and two slices of cake. It didn't help.

At eight o'clock, she gave in. She called Cam and said, 'Okay.'

'Okay?'

Instantly, her nerve fled. 'Forget it. I'll see you—'

'No. Give me five minutes.'

His urgency made Gwen smile. The wild feeling was back. One night with Cam. She shivered.

The next ten minutes passed in a whirlwind of activity. Gwen sprayed perfume on her wrists and neck, threw stray clothes into the laundry basket and lit candles in the bedroom. She closed the curtains and surveyed the effect. It looked nice. Seductive. Terror clenched her insides. This was crazy. She blew out the candles.

As if on cue, the doorbell rang. Gwen ran downstairs, then paused to comb her hair away from her face with her fingers, and opened the door.

'I drove as fast as was legal.'

Gwen was breathless. 'I was just . . . I don't know. I was just thinking about you. About us. And that thing you said.'

Cam smiled his crooked smile and stepped towards her.

The jolt of recognition as his lips touched hers threw Gwen hurtling back in time. He smelled the same, tasted the same, and his arms around her felt the same. She leaned into the kiss, her lust going from nought-to-sixty in an instant.

'Upstairs?' Cam broke the kiss to ask. Gwen squashed the tiny feeling of disappointment. Thirteen years ago, he would've had her naked on the hall floor. Then he kissed her again and all other feelings fled. It was Cam.

Gwen took his hand and led the way upstairs, feeling wild and excited and powerful. As soon as they got to the bedroom, though, everything changed. Gwen kicked off her slippers, feeling suddenly nervous. Now that they weren't actually kissing, the whole thing seemed a little ridiculous. What was the saying? *You can never go back.*

Cam paused. A strange expression ghosted across his face. 'I don't know about this.'

'Oh for Christ's sake,' Gwen said. It was one thing for her to feel unsure, but it was insulting for him to have second thoughts. She was a definite thing, for goodness' sake. Weren't men supposed to be driven by lust alone? 'Are you always this indecisive? Must really impress them in court.'

He was still looking at her with that weird expression. 'It's you, but it's not you.'

What on earth did he expect? 'It's been thirteen years. I've grown up.'

Cam shook his head, studying her like she was a piece of algebra. 'This isn't maturity. What are you so afraid of?'

Well, she wasn't answering that.

He put his head on one side. 'This is so weird. I always thought you were going to do something amazing.'

'Sorry to disappoint you.' Gwen felt like she'd been slapped.

'I'm not disappointed. But you seem to be. I think that's why you're so angry with me.'

'I thought we'd established that you were the angry one?'

'See?' He looked maddeningly smug. 'Uptight.'

'You can talk. You're the one in a suit.'

'It's just clothes.' Cam reached up and pulled the neck of his buttoned shirt over his head and dropped it on the floor.

Gwen took a sharp breath in. His chest was wider, his shape altogether more solid, but it was also unmistakably the same body. The muscles in his arms and chest still looked more like a man who spent his time playing in a rock band rather than pushing paper and, as Cam came towards her, she focused on the black tattoo on his right bicep and took an instinctive step backwards. 'What are you doing?'

He grinned. Lust had clearly won the internal struggle. The wide grin, slightly lopsided and very sexy. She remembered that all right. And what came afterwards. She swallowed. 'I thought we were going to discuss this a bit more.'

'Done talking,' Cam said. He took another step, raising his eyebrows questioningly.

Gwen held her breath. Inside her head, the argument was just getting going. Yes, it might give her closure. On the other hand, she might lose her mind and fall back into complete obsession. The kind of obsession that could break her heart. Getting over Cameron Laing had been the hardest thing she'd ever done. Was she really about to jump into bed with him again?

He paused. Looked at her with calm intensity that stopped her breath. 'You want me to go, say so right now.'

She managed to shake her head.

With that, he turned and kicked the door shut and crossed to her. 'I haven't been able to stop thinking about you. We used to be so good together.'

Gwen tried not to feel the cut of his words. The past tense that was like a knife.

'I want you to remember.' He took her wrist delicately, with his thumb resting on the underside like he was taking her pulse. She almost gasped at the electricity running in a current from the warmth of his fingers. She wanted those fingers, those hands, everywhere. He was crazy if he thought she'd forgotten him, but she was more than happy to pretend total amnesia if it meant he would touch her.

He didn't pull her forwards, but that was how it felt. An invisible force yanked her forwards and he caught her. His hands were on her, exactly as they should be, and the relief was immense. His hands were on her waist, her neck, her face. She closed her eyes, tipped her head back and waited for the kiss, to feel him like the old days. One moment of pleasure, one trip down memory lane. She deserved some fun. It had been a long time; one moment of fun and she'd be able to get her concentration back.

He kissed her and it was that strange mix of familiar and new. Her mouth, her tongue, her whole body said, *Hello again.* It was exciting and passionate and safe all at the same time. *Stop thinking,* she told herself. The words, *You can never go back,* popped into her mind. *Shut up. Stop thinking. Stupid brain.*

Cam pulled back and flipped open his belt buckle. Gwen smiled. This was more like it. This was the Cam she remembered. Wham bam. Fast and exciting. Not always entirely successful from her point of view, but always sexy, always fun. Sometimes, after he'd dropped her at home, she'd touch herself, reliving the evening in slow motion until she finished.

He walked her backwards until her legs bumped against the bed, then tipped her back onto it. He slid his belt from its loops and her eyes widened. That was new. What if he'd developed a kinky streak in the last decade? She wouldn't be surprised. Boy most likely to turn into deviant pervert. She opened her mouth to make a joke. 'No spanking' or 'steady on'. But he was there, kissing her deeply and she momentarily lost her mind. He was above her and she reached her arms up to pull his head closer, to keep his mouth on hers. After a moment he caught her hands and pulled them over her head, winding the belt around her wrists and then cinching it.

Her eyes flew open and she struggled to sit up. 'Cam.' The leather was smooth but unyielding. She pulled one arm and felt it dig into her wrists.

He pushed her back down and ran a hand up her leg, under her long skirt.

She wriggled further up the bed. 'I don't—'

'Yes you do.' Cam pushed her skirt up so that it bunched around her middle; the air felt unbearably cool and delicious on her legs.

'Cam—' she tried again.

'Busy.' He stopped kissing her inner thigh and grinned at her. 'Talk later, yeah?'

Gwen let her head fall back on the mattress. A moment later, she said, 'Oh my God.' And a few moments after that she realised that the person making the most obscene noises was her. Another minute and she wasn't cognisant of anything else at all.

'Oh my God.' Gwen felt as if every bone and muscle and sinew in her body had turned to liquid.

'You said that.' Cam appeared in front of her and she arched upwards to kiss him. Her arms physically ached from the need to touch him. She pulled at the belt, words no longer required.

She wrapped her arms around him, kissing him, pulling him closer. The weight of his body against her felt fantastic and started a low throbbing back in a place that had barely stopped shuddering.

'Oh God,' she said again, aware that she had lost her mind. She ran her hands over his chest and stomach, wanting him to be as incoherent as she was. He'd earned it after all.

He raised himself up, supporting his weight on his arms, kissing her jaw, her neck, dipping back to take her mouth. Gwen wrapped her legs around his body, pulling him close. 'Now…' she said against his mouth.

Cam rolled away, the suddenly cold air goosepimpling her skin, and she heard the rip of the condom packet. Then he was back and the heat Gwen thought would take ages to build again flared the instant he touched her. Her nerve endings remembered him, that was for sure.

He kneeled above her, looking at her with such naked longing that she forget to be self-conscious that her stomach and breasts were thirteen years older than the last time he'd seen them.

And then he was inside her, moving until the pressure built and she exploded all over again. She was shuddering, her insides contracting, her muscles quivering and Cam fell onto her, groaning as he let go.

Gwen buried her head in his neck, breathing deeply. 'Oh, fuck,' she thought. Then realised she'd said it out loud.

CHAPTER 14

Gwen woke up with Cam sprawled next to her, and felt cold air across her face. The cat was curled up at the foot of the bed, probably furious at having a strange man asleep in his rightful place, and the window was wide open. A few flakes of snow drifted over the sill and melted into the carpet.

Cat opened one yellow eye and then closed it again. No one in the house, Gwen thought, relieved. Then she thought: I have a guard cat. Couldn't Iris have left her an Alsatian, instead? Knowing Lily, however, even a big dog wouldn't be enough to dissuade her. She felt guilty at the thought. She was trying really hard not to listen to the gossip, to give Lily a fair go, but she couldn't help remembering the manic glint in her eyes. The way her smile always looked frozen in place.

She sat up slowly, trying not to disturb Cam, and looked around the room. The lumpy shapes of furniture, the curtains blowing in the night air. What was with the window? Was it Iris? But why would Iris want her to keep going to the window in the middle of the night? Unless she just wanted to annoy her. That might be right. Irritating her great-niece from beyond the grave.

Gwen sighed, admitting to herself that she was going to have to get out of the warm bed and shut the window. It was another cold night and a bright half moon floated in a sea of ink. The familiar elements of the garden – the wall, the shrubs, trees and paths – appeared ghostly in the moonlight. The hedge on the left of the gate was like a hunched animal, bulky and bulbous. Gwen couldn't see the lane from this angle, but the black expanse of the field stretched out, melting into the sky at the hidden horizon. 'What do you want?' Gwen was both surprised and pleased to hear the words out loud. Her voice was quiet and even; she sounded in control.

Out of the shadows, shapes formed. They became lumpy figures, lumbering from the gate and down the path towards the house. A parade of vaguely humanoid forms, heading for the back door.

Gwen felt the ice trickle of fear, but she made herself stare directly into the garden. They were the kind of thing that was terrifying when glimpsed out of the corner of your eye but when viewed head on revealed themselves to be illusion. The shapes continued forward, seeming to become more solid and threatening as the panic rose in her throat, choking her. Oddly, she heard her mother's voice. A memory of Gloria calmly explaining the charm for phantasms. She said that they increased in proportion to the victim's own fear and were dispelled by simple wishing.

The figure at the front of the pack was growing taller, lengthening and becoming more human. A ghostly light glowed from inside the shape, illuminating a face that had become the boy's. Puffy and white, the way it had looked when Gwen had found him. He opened his mouth wide and black water gushed out.

'No. Go away,' Gwen said aloud, not really expecting it to work. 'You are not real,' she added, wishing as hard as she could. The shapes dissolved.

Gwen took one last look at the now-empty path, closed the window and got back into bed. She was cold and shaking. Cat opened his eyes and let his disgust at being disturbed be known via the medium of unearthly screeching. Cam turned over and smiled at her sleepily in the half-dark. 'Hello,' he said. Then, 'Are you all right?'

'Fine,' Gwen said. 'Bad dream.' Someone was out there in the dark, casting a spell and sending phantasms to her house to frighten her. Maybe it was the man who'd broken into her house. Trying to frighten her out of the house, maybe even out of town. Or, more likely, it was the person who had helped Marilyn Dixon hex Brian. What had Iris written? *There's nothing worse than a frustrated witch?*

She decided to worry about it in the morning. In the daylight, when everything would seem more manageable. Besides, right at this moment, she had Cameron Laing in her bed. She stretched out alongside him, feeling all the places in which they fitted together.

He pulled her closer and, for a while, they didn't say anything else.

Gwen was too hot. Extraordinarily comfortable, yes, but definitely too hot. As her brain woke up, she realised that Cameron Laing was wrapped around her in the soft bed under approximately a thousand blankets. She shifted slightly and watched Cam wake up to the same realisation. She watched his expression turn from sleepy to alarmed and sat up first so that she wouldn't have to feel him pulling his arm out from underneath her.

Cam stumbled out of bed, pulling on his trousers before facing Gwen. 'Bathroom,' he said and Gwen nodded. She tried to adjust her expression to something relaxed and unconcerned, but she had the words, *Don't run away,* on a loop and didn't want to blurt them out.

Gwen listened to the water running in the bathroom next door and then a light thumping sound. Perhaps Cam was banging his head against the wall. Gwen tried to smile, but it wasn't at all funny.

After a couple of minutes he sidled back into the bedroom. He located his shirt and socks and, without looking directly at Gwen, said, 'I'd better get to the office.'

'It's seven o'clock.' Gwen kept her voice neutral.

He gave an unconvincing laugh. 'No rest for the wicked.'

'Okay,' Gwen said. 'Would you like breakfast before you go?'

'No. No, thanks. I'll get something on my way to the office.'

'Okay,' Gwen said again.

Cam was halfway out of the door when he paused. 'I'll call you.'

'Don't say that,' Gwen said.

'What?'

'Don't say "I'll call you" like that. Like I'm a one-night stand.'

'What do you want me to say?' Cam turned back, the frown that she was so used to seeing now back with a vengeance. 'Forget the past; we hardly know each other now. What do you expect me to say? Let's get back together. Let's pretend the last thirteen years didn't happen? Let's pretend you didn't run away from me the moment things got tricky?'

'Goodbye,' Gwen said. 'You're supposed to say "goodbye". Closure, remember?'

He swallowed. 'Goodbye, Gwen Harper.'

'Goodbye, Cameron Laing.'

Katie stuffed her hated backpack into the metal box and closed the locker door. When she turned around, she very nearly fell over. Luke Taylor was leaning up against the lockers a few feet away, and he was looking straight at her. Was he waiting for someone? Was he really looking at her? Or perhaps he was in a daydream and doing that looking-but-not-seeing thing. Should she say 'hi'? If he blanked her, she would die. It was better not to risk it. She turned to walk in the other direction. The wrong way from the dinner hall, but never mind.

'Hey.'

His voice was just behind her, and with two long strides he was alongside her.

'Don't run away.'

She glanced up, hardly believing her eyes. 'I wasn't. I was just—'

'Look. I didn't have anything to do with . . . the other day.'

Katie hesitated, trying to work out what he meant. Will Jones. 'Oh, I know. It's fine.' She paused, knowing she was blushing. She forced an unconcerned, hard voice. 'He's a twat, though.'

Luke shrugged. A few more steps and Luke stopped. 'Aren't you going to eat?'

Katie did her best coolly disinterested look. One she'd practiced. As if eating was vulgar and for lesser beings than herself. Imogen was always saying that boys liked girls who didn't eat.

Luke just looked confused. 'Oh. Okay.'

'You go on, though.' Like she was giving him permission. She wanted to punch herself in the face.

His lips quirked up. 'Thanks. I will.' He hit himself in the chest. 'Growing boy, you know. Need to keep my strength up.'

Katie nodded. Tried a smile. 'Well, see ya.'

'Later.' And he was gone, loping down the corridor.

At End House, Gwen was sitting up in bed, trying not to mind that Cam had bolted. She stroked the back of Cat's head, setting up a whole-body purring that sounded like a Boeing 747 taking off. She flipped through Iris's notebook, wondering if Iris had some excellent remedy for the pain in her heart. She read random entries, wondering what she should do with them all. There was a wealth of information and, although she would let Patrick Allen see them over her dead body, it seemed somehow wrong to let them just gather dust.

Thursday 24th March. Saw L again today. His pneumonia is no better and he still refuses to go into hospital. Mrs L distraught in that peculiarly constipated way she has.

Well, perhaps that entry wasn't worth saving for posterity. Gwen stopped reading and half-threw the book, sending it skidding across the splintered surface of the quilt. The journal was floppy with age and use, its pages splaying out where it came to rest. Gwen couldn't stand to see it like that, spread open uncomfortably. Almost naked. She shifted forwards and reached out. Then stopped. What had looked like a doodle and a load of nonsensical symbols – what Gwen had taken as a private shorthand – resolved itself into readable English. She leaned over and retrieved the book, her eyes scanning the words quickly.

The slugs are coming in under the door, coming right into my kitchen. When even the invertebrates are ignoring your authority, you know you're in trouble. I'm in trouble. I'm frightened, but mainly I'm just so tired. I think I might be leaving sooner than I expected. I've left some insurance – more for Gwen than myself – but it all depends on the perception of the thing. If people think you're powerful, then you usually are. Perhaps that's where I'm going wrong with the slugs. They don't think enough to be frightened of me.

And a picture of a rabbit wearing a striped beanie hat that would not resolve itself into anything else, no matter how hard Gwen squinted at it. She stopped squinting and closed her eyes. She felt cold all over. Poor Iris. It was a complicated kind of sympathy, though. The journals and messages were a window into the past and she couldn't deny that they made her feel special, wanted, but windows were a two-way deal. She felt hemmed in. Watched. The phone rang, making her jump.

'What on earth are you doing?'

'Hello, Ruby,' Gwen said. 'How are you?'

'How could you?' Ruby's voice was tight.

'How could I what?'

'The paper. Have you seen it yet?'

'What? No. I just got out of bed.'

'Well, go and get a copy. I hope you'll be very happy.'

'Ruby...' Gwen started, but Ruby had already hung up. Marvellous.

Gwen got dressed in warm clothes and walked to the corner shop. John was leaning on the counter, engrossed in a hardback book. He looked up and smiled at Gwen.

'Just this, thanks.' Gwen scooped *The Chronicle* off the stand.

'Good publicity for you in there.' John nodded at the paper.

'Oh Christ,' Gwen said.

'You show those snotty bastards on the other side of the river,' John said. 'I think it's a cracking idea.'

Gwen said goodbye and began flicking through the paper on the way back to the house. She found it on page six. A discussion of the proposed folk festival, very much from Patrick Allen's point of view.

A photograph of a tatty-looking market stall in the middle of the article had the caption: '*Threatening local businesses and lowering the tone?*'. Subtle.

Back at the house, Gwen made herself a strong cup of coffee and read the entire article. She was featured as: '*the latest in a long line of "alternatives" who have chosen Pendleford as their base of operations. While having an "art" community in the town is welcomed by a minority, there are many who feel Pendleford should be dragged into the twenty-first century, and those of the so-called sub-culture are counterproductive to this aim.*'

Well, Patrick Allen didn't waste time. Gwen was annoyed to find she was upset; not about the article, but Ruby's reaction. She grabbed Iris's journal again, feeling the comforting weight of the paper in her hand. Iris had opinions on everything; surely she had something to say about dealing with sibling lunacy. Or... the thought crept in. Perhaps she had a spell that would change Ruby's mind. Make her accept Gwen. Be a better sister. She flipped the book open.

A change of heart. To ease a confession, add thyme to well-brewed tea and wait quarter of an hour. Changing long held opinions is surprisingly easy. Wrap a single hair around a pebble and concentrate on the desired option. Place under the person's bed and after three nights they will hold the thought as their own.

Iris had scored out a few lines after this and then added in tiny, scrunched-up writing that Gwen almost couldn't read:

NB: Changing behaviour is not same thing as changing heart. When you pull the strings, does the puppet want to dance?

Gwen placed the book down carefully. She laced her fingers in her lap and tried to pretend that her insides weren't fizzing. She hated to admit it, but being the puppet master had a certain attraction. She'd never do anything malicious, of course. She could get people to always be polite, though. She hated it when people pushed ahead in queues or didn't say please and thank you. She could make sure Katie never got on a motorbike or into a car with a drunk seventeen-year-old or took Ketamine in a dodgy club.

She could make Ruby embrace magic. Accept her. Make her see how wrong she'd been. Maybe make her a little bit sorry.

CHAPTER 15

Six years of running Curious Notions, and Gwen still couldn't predict whether she would have a good day or not. Places that seemed to tick all the boxes – arty communities, plenty of money – could be quiet as the grave, and community centre craft drives sometimes surprised you. At the latter, it only took one or two customers to fall in love with the stall and they'd buy up half the stock. That was the curse and the blessing of her 'quirky' USP. If you liked it, you loved it, and if you didn't, well . . . Like the man who had paused by the stall, now. Gwen carried on fixing her Chinese lantern fairy lights to the top bar and ignored his expression of abject horror. Finally it morphed into confused amusement. He pointed at Hetty, a bit of taxidermy which Gwen had accessorised with a feather boa and fascinator. 'That's disrespectful.'

'Each to their own,' Gwen said. She gave him a big smile. 'Personally, I think it's jaunty.'

The man shook his head and continued to the next stall. Luckily, Gwen was next to a farmhouse produce stand filled with jams, preserves and chutneys and the man proceeded to salve his wounded sensibilities with some free samples.

Once he'd moved on, Gwen took the opportunity to catch the jam-stand-owner's eye and smile. It was always good to make friends with your neighbours. They could be an extra pair of eyes when watching out for thieves and might, if you were lucky, offer to watch your stall while you took a loo break.

'Are you open?'

Gwen turned to find a guy in his early twenties staring intently at his shoes. She looked around and, not seeing anyone else, assumed it was the greasy-haired shoe fetishist that had spoken. She put down the tangle of yet-to-be-fixed lights. 'Sure am. Can I help at all?'

'I want to get something for my girlfriend.'

'Okay.' Gwen nodded encouragingly and was rewarded with a darting look from beneath a fringe of lank black hair. 'What sort of stuff does she like?'

The man shrugged. He reached out a finger towards a blue-striped teapot, but stopped just short of touching it and snatched his hand back.

'Pick up anything you like,' Gwen said. 'Take a closer look.' It was a fact that people were more likely to buy once they'd held something. The balance of energy shifted, or something. Iris would've known.

'Does she like china?'

He shook his head.

'How about jewellery? Or an accessory? I've got some beautiful scarves at the moment.' She picked up a silk Liberty print and held it out.

Out came the finger again, he reached it out and touched the fabric once, then withdrew. And cleared his throat. 'She's not exactly my girlfriend yet.'

'Right.'

'I need something that'll make her like me.'

'Well, a gift is always nice. And well done for not going for something generic.'

He frowned. 'Huh?'

'You know. Red roses. Box of chocolates. It's good you're going for something individual. Shows imagination.'

'I already gave her flowers.' The man looked wounded. 'I think the florist put in some chocolates.'

'And I'm sure she loved them,' Gwen said robustly. She scanned the gathering crowd for punters. This guy didn't seem like a buyer. 'Can you see anything that reminds you of her?'

'Is that important?'

'For a really great gift? Yeah.'

'I don't know.' He picked up a yellow crochet beret. 'How about this?'

'Does she like yellow?' Gwen held up a hand. 'Don't say you don't know. Think. Have you ever seen her wearing yellow?'

He paused, the gears of thought clearing turning behind slightly glazed eyes. It took a while. Finally, he shook his head.

'What colours does she wear?'

His eyes almost crossed with the effort.

Gwen couldn't stand it any longer. 'Does she have a hobby? Does she like films? Music? Modern dance?'

His eyes widened. 'She likes dancing. How did you know?'

Gwen frowned. 'I didn't; I said—'

'Salsa!'

Gwen dropped her pen. 'Pardon?'

'She likes salsa dancing. She told me.' A fine mist of spittle accompanied his excitement.

'Perfect,' Gwen said, leaning back a little. 'What colour's her hair?'

'Black. Like mine.'

Gwen privately hoped, for the mystery girl's sake, that it wasn't too much like his. She selected a 1950s hair slide, jewelled with shiny black stones and sprouting a vibrant red flower and a bow of black and white polka-dot ribbon. She held it up. 'For when she's dancing.'

'Can you wrap it?'

'Sure.' Gwen folded the turquoise tissue paper, slipping in her 'thank you for your purchase' card amongst the layers, and tying the parcel with silver twine.

The guy had his parcel and he had his change, but still he hesitated.

'Was there something else?'

'Will it work?' he said in a rush. 'Will it make her like me?'

'It's a nice gift. I'm sure she'll like it.'

'I need her to start liking me really, really quick. That's why I came to you.'

'It's just a hair slide,' Gwen said slowly. 'It's not magic.'

'Okay.' He was nodding fast now, and starting to look a little crazy. 'You can't talk about it. That's cool. I get it.'

'Excuse me?' A woman in a green raincoat was pointing at a cake stand made out of vintage crockery and glassware. 'Can I buy that plate?'

'Not just the plate, I'm afraid; it's all stuck together. It's a cake stand.'

'Oh.' The woman looked inordinately pissed off.

'I have other plates,' Gwen began, but the woman had already gone.

Gwen sold a clown figurine that she'd been wishing she'd never picked up and a watercolour snow scene in a blue frame, then a girl and her mother paused to browse. The girl had a sheet of fine light brown hair that fell in a curtain, obscuring her face. Her mother was berating her in a carrying whisper. 'Where's your scrunchie? You look like a retard.'

The girl jerked as if an electric current had passed through her, then her shoulders hunched.

'How much is this?' The mother picked up an onyx paperweight, hefting it in one hand, as if considering it as a weapon.

'Five pounds,' Gwen said, resisting the urge to disarm the woman.

'And what does it do?'

Gwen blinked. 'It's a paperweight.' Saturday in Pendleford was obviously the day for double-dose crazy.

'Yes, but—' the woman leaned across the trestle table and lowered her voice 'what does it do?'

Gwen leaned forward and lowered her voice to match. 'It. Weighs. Paper. Down.'

The woman straightened, but kept up eye contact in a disturbingly focused way. 'I need something that will give her—' she jerked her head in her daughter's direction 'confidence. She's too shy. She'll never get on in life if she doesn't snap out of it.'

'I'm not sure that a paperweight is going to do the trick.'

'Okay. What then? I thought I had to pick up the first thing that caught my eye.'

'I'm sorry?'

'That's what I heard. Am I wrong? Do you choose? Or are certain things good for particular problems? Like, I don't know, earrings for better hearing.'

'I'm sorry,' Gwen managed. 'I'm really not sure—'

'It's for my daughter.' The woman had lost patience now, and was looking increasingly angry.

Struggling for safer ground, Gwen addressed the girl. 'Do you want to choose something, honey?'

'That makes sense,' the woman said, making none herself. She prodded the girl. 'Abigail, do as the lady says.'

A sliver of pink face appeared from behind the hair curtain and Gwen gave it an encouraging smile. 'What kind of thing would you like? Something to wear? Something for your room?'

Abigail opened her mouth, but her mother was already speaking. 'There's no point asking her. She's too shy to speak to strangers.'

The girl's head was turned to the left and Gwen looked too, trying to guess what she was after. There was a 1920s necklace tree, draped with costume jewellery, a pile of silk scarves and handkerchiefs, and a variety of flowery china. 'Do you like bright colours?'

The girl shrugged, but her hand had reached out and was touching a long necklace of multi-coloured glass beads. 'You can try that on, if you like. I've got a mirror.' She reached down and picked up the looking glass she kept for just such occasions.

'She won't wear that. She only likes black and grey. Drab things so she won't get noticed.' Gwen was royally fed up with the mother's voice and she'd only been enduring it for five minutes. God alone knew how Abigail coped. 'Like it would kill her to wear something light for once. Maybe a pastel blue or a nice lemon.'

Gwen saw Abigail's eyes close and her heart went out to her. 'How about something for your room? No one has to see it unless you want them to, then.'

Abigail nodded, so tightly and quickly Gwen almost didn't catch it. 'May I look at that?' The girl's voice was quiet but steady. It was lower than Gwen expected too, and she reassessed the girl's age. Abigail was pointing to a stripy crochet blanket Gwen had finished only the night before. 'It's handmade, but it's not vintage,' she said, handing it over. Abigail all but snatched the blanket and held it close.

'A blanket? How old are you?'

'It's a throw,' Abigail said. 'For my bed. I like it.'

'Fine.' Her mother expelled a big sigh, as if the girl had demanded crack cocaine. 'On your own head be it.' She turned to Gwen. 'This had better work.'

Gwen took the money, wrapped the blanket and said goodbye, all the while trying to decide if she was morally obligated to explain to the woman that the blanket wasn't magical; it didn't fly or anything.

By half three, the crowd had thinned considerably. The clouds had lowered, bringing a premature twilight and layer of damp to the proceedings. No one browsed in bad weather and she'd had a good day, so Gwen began to pack up.

'Quitting?' Mary-Anne from next door raised her eyebrows. 'I never leave early. I always convince myself that I'll miss the biggest sale of the day. Are you coming next month?'

'Yes.' Gwen realised that the word made her happy. She was coming to the same spot next month. An easy commute from her home, not miles and miles in Nanette, swearing over her road map and promising herself that she would splash out on a satnav for the next trip.

'See you in December.'

Mary-Anne gave her a thumbs-up, then turned back to a customer.

Katie was sick of people keeping secrets from her. She watched her mother tuck the copy of *The Chronicle* underneath a pile of magazines and asked her what was wrong. Her mother just said, 'Nothing,' which was clearly a lie.

'Was it something in the paper? Or are you still arguing with Auntie Gwen?'

'It's nothing,' her mother said again. 'And we're not arguing.'

Still lying.

'I'm going to fix dinner,' her mother said, getting up from the sofa. 'Can you set the table, please?'

Katie followed her mum into the kitchen to get the cutlery. She wished she'd stop pretending that she wasn't still fighting with Auntie Gwen. She was going to drive her away, just like last time. Katie curled her fingers over and dug them into her palms.

Her mother refused to talk about the weird stuff that happened in their family. Gwen was her only chance. Her mother was determined to pretend that nothing out of the ordinary ever happened to the Harpers, like it was a *bad* thing.

She'd heard her mother and Auntie Gwen arguing about it often enough. Before Gwen had disappeared, she remembered the big fight they'd had, but her mum refused to discuss it. Katie wanted to tell her that she knew that Gwen could find lost things and that Gran told fortunes – real ones – and that Gran's mother had been able to talk to the dead. She wanted to tell Ruby that she was young, not stupid. Or deaf.

Katie laid out the cutlery and placemats and filled water glasses.

'How was school?' Ruby asked, scraping chopped onions into a pan.

'Fine,' Katie said automatically. She needed to make things more welcoming for Gwen. Maybe if her and Ruby got on better, she'd stay.

'Can we invite Auntie Gwen for dinner?'

Her mother's head jerked up. She looked at Katie for a moment, then said, 'Sure.'

Katie thought about Luke Taylor. Gwen would definitely stay if she fell in love.

'Do you know any cute single guys?'

'I beg your pardon?' Ruby stopped stirring onions and looked at Katie.

'Not for me,' she said. 'For Auntie Gwen. You should set her up on a blind date. It's sad that she's on her own.'

Katie opened her eyes as wide as possible, aiming for an innocent look.

'I'm not sure she is,' Ruby said. 'There might be something going on with Cameron Laing. He was her boyfriend a long time ago.'

'Perfect. Invite him, then.'

'Why are you so interested?' Ruby said.

'She's family. It's nice to look after your family, isn't it?'

'I guess,' Ruby said, the frown still in place.

'That's settled, then,' Katie said, and left the room before her mother could change her mind.

CHAPTER 16

Gwen realised that she was truly powerless to say no to her niece when she found herself agreeing to a dinner date with Cameron Laing.

'I'm not sure he'll want to come,' she said when Katie rang.

'Mum's already invited him and he said yes,' Katie said. 'He's picking you up at six.'

Gwen wanted to explain that she and Cameron were not together and had, in fact, celebrated that fact with an official Goodbye Shag, but that seemed indiscreet. Besides, he was clearly comfortable with the idea. He'd probably tucked her neatly in the box marked 'just friends'.

Gwen spent the next day emptying Nanette and arranging boxes on the shelves in the garden room. As she carried and sorted, she pushed Cameron Laing firmly to the back of her mind. Eventually, her mind stopped torturing her for long enough to have an idea for a new shadow box. It had been months since she'd felt excited about making something, so she got to work straight away.

A sound broke her concentration and she looked up from gluing doll's house wallpaper. She'd been working so intently that she hadn't noticed the day disappear. Full dark had arrived and Gwen looked through the window into the pitch-black of the garden. The lights in the house weren't on and Gwen's vision was attuned to her anglepoise craft light. She couldn't see a thing.

A loud knocking made her heart leap painfully.

Cat brushed against her legs and Gwen patted his head a little before opening the door. She hadn't closed her curtains, so whoever was outside knew she was there.

It was Cam and he smiled as soon as he saw her. 'Were you thinking about hiding under the table?'

'Thank God it's you,' Gwen said, forcing a jokey tone. 'I never know which of my friendly neighbours is going to visit next.'

'It's nice that they're welcoming.' Cam ducked through the low doorway.

'I suppose.' Gwen had lost her breath at the sight of Cam. He looked completely at ease, as if nothing at all had happened. As if he truly had moved on. *Crap.*

'You're working?' Cam said.

Gwen glanced back at the table. 'I'm booked into a couple of markets. I could do with some bumper days, so if you could send all your rich friends shopping, that would be handy.'

'What makes you think I have rich friends?'

'Oh come on. You're a lawyer. You must have some.'

'It's not going that brilliantly, actually. I lost another client today.'

'Oh.' Gwen felt like hell. 'Sorry. What's going on?'

'My mother and my grandfather think I should join the Rotary, start making nice with Patrick Allen and his lot.'

'Well, that sucks.'

Cam shrugged. 'I'm good at my job. I'm just going to carry on being good at my job and the local politicians can go fuck themselves.'

'You're completely calm about it, then,' Gwen said, smiling.

'Completely and utterly.' Cam smiled back at her with real warmth. Gwen swallowed, trying to ignore the sense memories of their night together. Her whole body was leaning towards the man, hoping for a rerun. Oh Christ.

'You've been busy.' Cam was looking at her work table, at the half-assembled shadow box.

'Got to get my stock levels up. I'm famous now.' Gwen grabbed a copy of *The Chronicle* and handed it to Cam. 'Page six.'

She pressed air bubbles out of the wallpaper, smoothing it down carefully, while Cam read. Finally he looked up. 'At least it's positive.'

'Only if you ignore the sarcastic quote marks.' Gwen shook her head. 'I bet Patrick Allen has something to do with this.'

Cam looked surprised. 'You're probably right. He basically runs this town. Still, at least it's publicity.'

Gwen sat down. 'I guess. I've had a couple of enquiries today already.'

'That's good, right? You said you needed the business.'

Gwen was staring at a tiny paintbrush, turning it over in her hands. 'I just wish I could be sure people really like them. I worry that they're only interested because they saw my name in the paper.'

'You don't get to choose who enjoys art or how.'

'I'm not talking legally,' Gwen said. 'Although a law against keeping great works in the private collections of rich idiots would be good.'

'New from Mattel, Socialist Gwen.'

'Worst. Action figure. Ever.'

Cam laughed. He looked around the room. 'I didn't know about this place.'

'I think it was Iris's work room. I've been clearing it out.' Gwen pointed to a cardboard box filled with glass jars. 'Don't know what to do with that lot. Feels wrong to throw them away.'

'What about the boxes?' Cam indicated the shoe boxes lining the shelves.

'They're mine. I moved them in yesterday.'

'Oh. Right.'

'Don't look so shocked,' Gwen said. 'It's not that big a deal.'

'You're moving in,' he said.

'This is a really nice house.' Gwen looked away so that she didn't have to watch Cam's expression. If he looked as horrified as Ruby had, she didn't want to know. Instead, she concentrated on her shadow box. It lay on its back, the inside papered with to-scale striped wallpaper, the bottom edge carpeted in tiny burgundy pile. To one side sat a miniature armchair upholstered in dusky green velvet and a two-inch-tall reproduction of Van Gogh's *Sunflowers* that she was rather pleased with. Cam pointed at it. 'Did you paint that?'

'Yes.'

'It's really good.'

'Thank you.'

'I'm sorry, though,' he added. 'The colours are wrong.'

Gwen laughed. 'That depends on your perspective.'

'I don't get it.'

'They're little jokes. I put stuff in for people to find.'

'Like Easter eggs?'

'Sorry?'

'In computer games. They put in hidden stuff for people to find—' Cam broke off. 'Never mind.'

Gwen lifted another box from the shelf. 'Like in this one. Look.'

The box was one of Gwen's favourites. It looked like a jumble of sewing supplies: cotton reels, scissors, a thimble, but hidden amongst them were tiny figures. A dark-haired girl with red lips peeping out from inside a cotton reel, a boy in yellow dungarees hanging from a scissor handle, a messy-looking dog trapped inside a box of pins, his paws scraping at the clear plastic. There was a minuscule bone on the 'floor' just outside.

'Huh.' Cam seemed at a momentary loss for words. He straightened up. 'Are you ready to go, or do you need to get changed?'

Gwen looked down at her jeans. *Good thing this isn't a proper date.* 'I'm ready,' she said.

Outside Ruby's four-bedroom house in a pleasant street on the outskirts of Bath, Gwen remembered how she and Ruby had spent Saturdays in the city, walking around with linked arms. They'd been merciless in their opinions of the well-to-do Bathonians. The ladies-who-lunched and the men with cravats and Barbour wax jackets. Now Ruby opened the door wearing tailored black trousers and a black-and-white striped top, a silk scarf knotted neatly around her throat, and Gwen wondered when the hell everybody had become so grown up.

'Cam! Lovely of you to come.' Ruby leaned in so that he could kiss her cheek, diamond earrings twinkling in the porch light.

'Nice that you made an effort, Gwen,' Ruby said, her eyes sliding down Gwen's body, pausing significantly at her blue Converse One Stars. 'Come on through. David's just getting ready. He's only just finished work. You'll know what that's like, Cam.'

Gwen rolled her eyes, then realised that Cam had caught her doing it and was smiling in an annoying way. 'Shut up,' she whispered.

They were sitting in the cream-and-gold living room sipping gin and tonics when David came in. He had always been a restrained kind of guy, but Gwen could tell he was pleased to see her by the way he briefly patted her arm. However he didn't look quite so thrilled that Cam was back in their lives. 'You want a beer?'

'I'm fine with this.' Cam held up the hi-ball Ruby had thrust into his hand seconds before.

'No. You want to come and get a beer,' David said heavily. 'Now.'

'Okey-doke.' Cam stood up, put his glass on one of the slate coasters on the polished-glass side table and followed David.

Ruby watched him go, then said, 'Now that's a keeper.'

Gwen's heart leaped and she thought *I know*. She aimed for casual. 'What makes you say that? His steady income?'

'He used a coaster. It took me five years to train David.'

Gwen laughed. A joke. Of course Ruby was joking. For a moment, there, she had looked so much like Gloria, it'd confused her.

'You okay?' Ruby frowned. 'You're a little pale.'

'I'm fine.' Gwen took a hefty swallow of her drink, forgetting that she didn't really like gin. She was still coughing when David and Cam walked back in.

'Where's Katie?' Gwen asked, once she'd cleared her lungs.

'Upstairs preening,' Ruby said. As she spoke, the door opened and Katie bounced in.

'Say hello to Gwen and Cam,' Ruby said before Katie had a chance to open her mouth.

'Hey, Auntie Gwen.' She nodded at Cam, looking uncharacteristically nervous.

'Give me a hand?' David said, and Katie followed him into the kitchen.

Ruby stood up. 'You two go through to the dining room; I'm going to check Katie doesn't set fire to the starter.'

Once they were sitting in the immaculate dining room, Gwen asked Cam what David had wanted with him.

'Just to ask about my intentions.'

'Oh God.' Gwen put her hands over her face. 'I'm sorry. I'm thirty-one, for crying out loud.' She really wanted to ask him what he'd said. Like it mattered.

'I told him that I'd already had my wicked way with you, so my intentions were entirely honourable.'

'Oh. That's good.' Gwen could feel herself going bright red.

'I'm joking,' Cam said, looking adorably worried. 'I think David might've killed me. He seems to take the big brother role very seriously.'

'Oh.' Gwen laughed awkwardly. 'I knew that. Back in the day, he was always worried about you and me. He didn't trust you at all.'

'He was quite right,' Cam whispered. He smiled filthily and Gwen felt her heart rate kick up.

Thankfully, David and Katie arrived with food and saved her from having to say anything.

'So,' Katie said, once they'd all exclaimed over the perfectly presented scallops, 'are you going to be my new uncle?' She batted her eyelashes at Cam, while Gwen almost choked for the second time.

'Cam is an old friend of ours,' Ruby said. 'I told you that.'

'I promise we won't sit here telling boring stories about the past,' Cam said, patting Gwen on the back as she spluttered. 'What would you like to talk about, Katie?'

'Bad idea,' Ruby said.

'You're a lawyer, right?' Katie said. 'Does that mean you defend people even when they're guilty?'

'I don't really handle criminal cases,' Cam said, 'but that's the general idea. Everyone deserves to be represented, otherwise the trial system wouldn't work.'

'But what if you know the person is guilty, like one hundred per cent, isn't it unethical to defend them?'

'Yep, it's a genuine dilemma and one of the many reasons I don't do criminal law. But the lawyers defending criminals are doing a really important job. They're making sure that, beyond all reasonable doubt, that person is truly guilty. You don't want innocent people to be punished, do you?'

Katie shook her head. 'That's what Officer Friendly said.'

'Officer Friendly?'

'DCI Collins. He came to our school to give a talk.'

Cam laughed. 'Harry gave a talk? And you guys named him Officer Friendly?' He turned to Gwen. 'I can't wait to tell him that.'

Talk turned to David's latest work project and Gwen got up to help Ruby bring in the main course.

In the kitchen, Ruby nudged Gwen with her hip. 'Katie likes Cam.'

She's not the only one, Gwen thought.

'It'd be so great if you two could get it together.'

'Keep your voice down,' Gwen said.

'I mean, it'd be really good for your reputation. Give you a bit of respectability, you know?'

Gwen carried the plates through before she gave into the temptation to slap Ruby with a piece of herb-encrusted salmon.

After miniature cups of chocolate with homemade ginger biscuits and coffee made in the kind of machine usually seen in upmarket cafés, Ruby stood up. 'You guys take a drink through. I need to borrow Gwen for a minute.'

In the hallway, Gwen raised her eyebrows. 'What?'

'I want to show you something.' Ruby pulled Gwen upstairs. She stopped outside a door with a pink plaque that said 'Katie's crib' in glitter paint.

'In there?'

'Don't worry. We won't be long.'

'Isn't it—' Gwen had been going to say 'breach of privacy', but Ruby had already opened the door and walked in.

'Come on,' she said. 'It's nothing hidden. It's not like snooping.'

'It is a little.'

'Go and get some clean laundry to bring in and put away, if it'll make you feel better.'

Gwen sat on the bed. It was covered with a lilac duvet sprinkled with tiny embroidered silver stars. 'What are you worried about?'

Ruby crossed to a desk, overflowing with papers, pens, notebooks and hair accessories. She picked up a red exercise book.

'I'm not reading her diary,' Gwen said.

'Relax. Look.' She held it closer so that Gwen could read the writing in black felt-tip on the front cover. 'Spells.'

'And?'

'What do you mean "and"? Doesn't this worry you?'

'What's inside? A love spell? Something she copied from a fortune cookie?'

'Nothing. She hasn't used it yet,' Ruby said, putting the book back on top of the pile. 'But there are these, too.' She pointed upwards and for a moment Gwen expected to see cobwebs or stuffed animals hanging from the ceiling. Instead she saw the usual mix of colourful mobiles, crystals, dream-catchers and scarves she'd expect to find in any teenage girl's room. Not that she knew any, apart from Katie. 'And this.' Ruby opened the wardrobe doors and took something down from the top shelf.

'If you go through her stuff, you're bound to find something you don't like.'

'Can you stop being holier than thou for just one second? Look.' She thrust the object at Gwen. It was a crystal ball – the kind sold by The Crystal Cave. Made of glass and about as occult as an elastic band.

'So she's showing an interest in the spooky and Gothic; I'm sure kids her age are all about Ouija boards and all that. It's harmless. Just be glad she hasn't got a tattoo.'

Ruby let out a breath, like she was trying not to scream. 'Why can't you be on my side, just once?'

Gwen was shocked. 'I am on your side. I'm being comforting.'

'You're not. You're telling me I don't know what I'm talking about, that I'm overreacting, that I'm just a silly—' Ruby paused, struggling for the right word '... Muggle!' she finished.

Gwen swallowed a smile. 'I don't think you're a Muggle.'

Ruby teetered on the edge, her mood ready to go either way. Finally her lips twitched upwards. 'You know what I mean. You and Mum were always shut away talking about this stuff; I never had a look in.'

'We didn't talk about crystal balls.' Gwen paused. 'I actually don't remember Mum talking to me about anything very much. She watched me. She asked me to find things. As soon as I stopped doing that particular party trick, she lost all interest.' Gwen was surprised at how hurt she still felt by that. Larkin had been right: *They fuck you up. . .*

'Can I trust you not to tell Katie?'

'About this? Of course.'

'I don't want you to talk to her about powers or finding lost things or tarot cards. Any of it.'

'You know, you've made this pretty clear before.'

'I have worked too hard for this life. For Katie. I will not have it messed up.'

Gwen was shocked to see tears in Ruby's eyes. She put a hand on her arm. 'I promise.'

Back downstairs, Cam and David were sitting in uneasy silence, while Katie had her headphones on and a laptop open on the sofa. David jumped up and began clearing away the cups and Gwen looked at Cam in a way that he read instantly. *Get me out of here.* He stood up and took Gwen's hand. 'We'd better head off. Thank you for a lovely evening.'

'You don't have to go. It's not late,' Ruby said.

'I'm sorry, I'm really tired,' Gwen said. She hugged Ruby and David fetched their coats.

Gwen waved a hand in front of Katie to get her attention and then waved goodbye. Katie nodded briefly and went back to her web surfing.

After saying goodnight and thank you, Cam kissed Ruby on the cheek and held the door open for Gwen. Gwen tried to ignore the fluttering in her chest.

The night had got even colder and Cam turned the heater up full blast and drove carefully back to Pendleford. It was nice that it wasn't a date and neither of them felt under obligation to make conversation. Gwen leaned her head on the window and looked at the stars.

'Are you okay?'

Gwen roused herself. 'Just thinking about Ruby and Katie and David and us. It's funny how life turns out.' She paused. 'And I was thinking about Archie. Helen's dog? You haven't asked me about finding him. I was wondering what you thought about it.'

'That was a good guess,' Cam said.

'It was more than that.' Gwen's voice was flat.

'Uh-huh.'

Cam made the sharp turning into Gwen's road. His Lexus bumped over the rough ground. 'You need to resurface this.'

'When I win the Lottery,' Gwen said, more sharply than she intended. 'Sorry. Nanette doesn't like it much, either. Not doing her suspension any good.'

'Nanette?'

'My van. Nissan Vanette. Nanette. Obviously.'

'Obviously,' Cam said.

He parked outside End House. The light in the hall was on and it glowed through the stained glass above the front door, casting colours onto the overgrown path.

'Thank you for tonight,' he said.

'You're welcome,' Gwen said stiffly. 'Thank you for the lift.'

Gwen got out of the car and her heart began thudding when she heard him switch off the engine and follow her. *Just being a gentleman. He's just being nice.*

Gwen fumbled with her keys, trying to unlock the door. Cam's hand closed over hers and she turned to find him barely an inch away.

'Can I come in?'

'I thought we were just friends now?' Gwen said.

'Closure's overrated.' Cam smiled crookedly. And then he kissed her.

She kissed him back, feeling nothing but relief that he was holding her again. 'I don't want to do this if you're not sure.'

'I've tried keeping away from you, Gwen Harper. Doesn't seem to be working.'

In the hall, Gwen's bag hit the floor and their coats followed a moment later. Cam was walking Gwen backwards towards the stairs when he suddenly stopped short and groaned.

'Cat!' Gwen said.

Cat removed his claws from Cam's leg and began winding around his ankles.

'I'd better feed him,' Gwen said.

Cam had rolled up his trouser leg and was investigating the claw marks.

In the kitchen, Gwen tried to regain some sanity. One night was a one-night. Doing it again the following night was – what?

She was distracted by Cat. He was standing by the back door, fur on end and tail swishing angrily.

'What now?' Gwen opened the door.

'What's wrong?' Cam put his hands on her shoulders and she realised she must've cried out.

'Sorry. Just got a shock.'

There was a furry mound on the back step. It wasn't moving. 'What is it?'

'It's too big to be one of Cat's gifts. I hope.'

Gwen crouched down, peering through the half-light. It was a large rabbit. Grey fur, streaked with dried blood. Spread around it on the step was what could be more blood if it weren't so crumbly. Soil.

'It's okay,' Cam said. 'It was probably very old. Had a good life, ate lots of dandelion leaves.'

'Blood and bone and earth.' Gwen's voice was hollow. She moved away from Cam. 'I've got to bury it.'

'Now?' Cam said, but Gwen had already stepped over the body and into the gloom of the garden.

She was vaguely aware of Cam saying, 'Right, then.'

Gwen was shivering. She should've picked up her coat. Probably should've told Cam to leave, too. Now he would think she was truly mental. She felt sick, though. Sick with the need to bury that creature, to try and neutralise whatever bad magic had been raised by its murder.

'You don't have to do that now, Gwen. Gwen…'

Cam's voice seemed to be coming from very far away. What had her mother always said? *Blood and bone and earth.* Blood magic was ancient and powerful and really, really scary. Oh, crap.

With a heavy heart, Gwen went to the shed at the side of the house. She found an iron coal shovel and used that to scoop the rabbit into a bin bag. After digging a shallow grave at the end of the garden, marked with a lump of granite taken from the overgrown rockery, Gwen was sweating inside her top. She pushed her hair out of her eyes and discovered it was crispy with frost.

She was breathing heavily and became aware that Cam stood watching her. He had his woollen overcoat back on and his expression was unreadable.

'That's better,' Gwen said brightly.

'I did offer to help,' Cam said. 'I don't think you heard me.'

Gwen walked past him, trying not to think how messy she must look. 'Let's go back inside. Have a drink.'

Cam didn't answer, but he followed her.

As soon as Gwen's foot touched the tile of the kitchen floor, she could feel the wrongness. It flooded her. Bad mojo.

'What now?' Cam's voice was on the edge of exasperation, but Gwen couldn't worry about that now. She paused, one foot held up in the air. She forced herself to put it down, to feel the vibrations that were pulsing through the ground. She took a breath. 'Somebody killed that rabbit and left it for me. It's really bad—'

'No.' Cam closed the door and locked the new bolts. 'That's crazy.'

'It's bad magic,' Gwen said. She was shaking and couldn't stop. Shuddering. 'It doesn't feel right in here. I think the house is angry. Or something in the house. Something isn't right and I don't know how to make it better.'

Cam turned slowly. 'You've had a shock,' he began.

'Can we go to your house? Please? I think I need to give this place time to calm down.'

The drive to Cam's flat was quiet. Gwen didn't speak again until they got there and she was grateful that Cam didn't try to make conversation. He drove carefully and her tension eased with every mile that sprouted between her and End House.

At the flat, Gwen shucked off her hooded fleece and tossed her bobble hat onto a perspex Philippe Starck-style chair.

'Drink?'

'No. Yes, go on then.' Gwen looked around. 'Nothing that'll stain if I drop it, though.'

'Why would you drop it?' Cam looked perplexed.

'This place.' Gwen waved a hand. 'It's an invitation for mess. It's a question waiting to be answered. A glass of red wine waiting to be splattered across the rug.'

Cam frowned at his pale beige carpet. 'I don't have a rug.'

'The sofa, then.' Gwen gestured to the white couch.

'Please don't. That's quite new.'

Gwen sat on it, slipped forward, said, 'Whoops,' and hastily straightened up.

'Yes, there's a bit of a knack to that. I think the leather is polished or something,' Cam said. He disappeared for a moment, then returned with a glass of white wine and a bottle of lager.

He passed her the glass. 'You seem calmer, anyway. What was all that about?'

'I feel much better for getting away,' Gwen said. 'I think the house was angry, even though I buried the rabbit. I'm just going to give it time to calm down and then I'll be out of your hair.'

Cam took a swig of his beer. 'You are aware that you sound a little nutty right now?'

'I'm not crazy,' Gwen said. 'Someone wishes me harm. I don't know what I've done, but somebody really hates me. And whoever it is knows their stuff, because that rabbit was no accident. Blood magic.' Which, Gwen realised, put Patrick Allen out of the frame. Gwen could imagine him paying somebody to break into her house and sabotage her boiler, but she couldn't see him anywhere near something like this. Blood magic wasn't just the darkest magic or the most powerful, it was the ickiest, too.

'So you think someone killed a rabbit and left it for you?' Cam said.

Gwen took a swallow of her wine. 'Could you stop avoiding the subject, please? You were there when I found that dog, when I cured Brian, I've told you about finding things for my business, knowing things about objects that I couldn't possibly—'

'The dog was a fluke.'

Gwen stopped speaking, her expression carefully blank. After a moment she said, 'No, it wasn't.'

'Look, I know you had an…um, alternative… upbringing, but you don't really believe this stuff.'

'Unfortunately, I don't have much of a choice. I know you think I'm unhinged.'

'No, I don't,' Cam said. 'I think you were brought up believing certain things and that's very powerful.'

'You knew about Mum?'

'I heard the rumours.' Cam looked uncomfortable and Gwen felt a familiar sinking in her stomach.

'You never said anything.'

Cam gave a gallant attempt at a smile. 'I was trying to get you naked.'

'Oh.'

Gwen saw a wave of irritation pass across his face. 'Magic powers don't exist. You can't believe that you have them. Not really.'

Gwen gave a small laugh. 'Look, what about cooking? That's a kind of magic. You take eggs and flour and butter and produce something that doesn't look like any of them.'

'That's called chemistry, Gwen.'

'Now, yes, because we know about it. In the future, science will probably explain why I can find things, too.'

Cam shook his head. 'I don't want to talk about this. You're better than this. Magic is a word used by children and by adults as a way to scam the vulnerable and stupid.'

'You think I'm faking this to make money?' Gwen's face was white, her lips a narrow line. She placed her wine glass on the coffee table with exaggerated care.

'I don't know. I hope so, because the alternative is that you're a gullible half-wit—' Cam stopped. 'Sorry. I didn't mean that.'

'Yeah. You did.' Gwen picked up her fleece and made for the door.

Cam caught her arm. 'Don't go. I'm sorry.'

'It's fine.' Gwen avoided his eye. 'I'm fine. Thank you for the drink.'

'Look. It's a touchy subject for me. I don't like people being taken advantage of and you have to admit there are a lot of charlatans out there.'

'I'm not one of them,' Gwen said tightly. 'I'm going home now. Thank you for the drink.' She shoved her arms into her fleece.

'Let me drive you back at least,' Cam said.

'No. The walk will do me good. I need to cool off. Let the house cool off, too,' Gwen added and opened the door.

'I'm really sorry.' Cam had crossed the room. 'I believe you.'

Gwen blinked. 'Do you?'

'I believe that you believe it. Yes.'

'Well, that's not the same thing at all,' she said bleakly.

'It's the best I can do,' Cam said, looking wretched.

She knew how he felt.

'Please let me drive you back,' Cam said after a pause.

'I'm sure it's perfectly safe. As everyone keeps telling me, this is a *nice* town.'

Cam frowned. 'Why do you sound so bitter about that?'

'You wouldn't understand.' *You belong here*.

Cam looked at her with total frustration. 'Why do you keep doing that?'

'What?'

'You go quiet. Or you give a bit of an answer. Or you evade the question. Or you change the subject. You used to do it all the time, too. I'd forgotten because I think I'd idealised everything about you. About us. But it's really fucking annoying. Why can't you just talk to me?'

Gwen realised she was pausing again. Going silent. Whatever. 'You don't want to hear about what I'm going through,' Gwen said. 'It's difficult to talk when I know you think half the things I say are insane.'

'What about other stuff? Real stuff?'

'But that stuff is real. I know you don't believe it. I know you think—'

'I think you use it to hide behind,' Cam said. 'Like when you left. You couldn't handle things so you just ran away.'

'You have no idea what you're talking about.'

'Probably not. That's exactly my point.'

'Do you remember your dad's fiftieth birthday party?'

Cam frowned. 'What's that got to do with anything?'

'You told me about it, but I didn't know if I was going or whether your father even knew I existed or what.'

'I don't see—'

'Your mother called me beforehand. To make sure I wasn't attending. She also told me I was no good for you.'

Cam smiled a little. 'That sounds like her. She didn't mean it; she's just very—'

'She said that I was holding you back, that if I cared for you even a little bit, I should leave.'

Cam stopped smiling.

'She said I was going to ruin your career and your life.'

'And you just left.' Cam's face was hard, his expression a closed door.

'I was eighteen. She's pretty scary.' Gwen knew that was a cop out. She'd been eighteen years old, not eight.

'But you didn't say anything.'

Gwen chose her words carefully. 'Things weren't brilliant with you and your parents. I didn't want to make things worse and, besides, I thought she was probably right.'

'What are you talking about?'

'I was never going to fit into that world.'

'I didn't ask you to.' Cam ran his hands through his hair, visibly annoyed.

'No.'

There was a pause that lengthened into a silence. Gwen waited, hoping he would say something else. Something about how he'd been wrong, how he should've formally introduced her to his parents, how he should've shown her that he was proud to be with her. That he hadn't been ashamed of dating that 'crazy Harper girl'.

They looked at each other for a beat longer, then Gwen left. She closed the door carefully behind her, making sure it didn't slam, and made it out to the pavement before the tears spilled onto her cheeks.

CHAPTER 17

I'm so angry with her. How can she lie to people? Telling them what they want to hear and charging them for the privilege. It's immoral. I raised her better than that. She's changed. She says she has no choice and it's for the sake of the girls, but she's doing no better than I did there. Ruby's expecting. It's not common knowledge, but it will be soon. If only she'd come to me, I could've given her something to take care of that little situation. Too late now. I had one of my urges. I had to give her a nail, probably because of the iron. Couldn't do anything else until I'd delivered it. I left it for her outside the house because I'm not allowed in.

Gwen felt grateful for the first time in her life that her gift was finding lost things and not something else. Iris's compulsion to give people what they needed sounded awful. Especially when she wasn't even allowed to see the person to explain. Gwen knew what the ache of finding was like; it consumed her until it was done. What if Ruby had never found that nail lying outside her house; what if Iris had always felt that incompleted task, like something sharp digging into her skin?

Gwen stared at the open journal and, on a whim, ripped out the page with that entry. It was about Ruby, not her. If she could persuade Ruby to read it, maybe she'd feel a little differently about Iris. After all, it showed that she'd cared. She'd known that Ruby had pregnancy-related anaemia and, in her own slightly nutty way, had tried to help.

The next page in the journal had a recipe for fruit cake. She ripped that out too, and tucked it into one of the blank notebooks that Iris seemed to have bought in bulk. Then she started to go through the rest of the journal systematically, clipping out anything that featured Ruby and adding it to the pile. She wasn't Iris. She wasn't going to hex Ruby into changing her opinions, but perhaps she could open her mind with a little family history.

The phone beeped as she began sticking the fragments into a new notebook. She held her breath until she saw that it wasn't from Cam. It was Katie. She swallowed her disappointment and replied that Katie was very welcome to visit after school. She put the phone down and carried on sticking. There was a peculiar thickness in the air around her. 'You left everything to me, Iris,' she said out loud. 'This feels like the right thing to do.' Feeling only marginally foolish, she turned up the volume on the stereo and wrote 'Ruby' on the front of the notebook in different coloured pens.

Gwen was just sticking the last entry down when a sound in the hallway almost gave her heart failure. 'You've got to be kidding me,' Gwen said when Marilyn Dixon walked in.

'The door was open.' Marilyn didn't look even slightly abashed.

'No, it wasn't,' Gwen said. 'I bet you wouldn't have just walked in on Iris.'

Marilyn wrinkled her nose. 'It smells of glue in here. And isn't it a bit early for Christmas music?'

'That's The Supremes,' Gwen said. She flipped the notebook shut.

'Brian's gone,' Marilyn said, sinking onto the floor. 'He says he doesn't love me any more.'

'Oh, Christ. I'm sorry.' Gwen wiped the glue on her hands onto her jeans.

Marilyn looked up at Gwen. 'Please help me.'

'I don't think there's anything—'

'I know you sorted him out before. You can do it again.'

Gwen sat cross-legged next to Marilyn. 'Brian was acting under the influence of some bad advice. Some advice that was very compelling and I broke the . . . Well, it was like he was hypnotized . . .' Gwen trailed off.

'That witch put him under some kind of spell, I know,' Marilyn said.

'Who do you mean? Who did you go and see?'

Marilyn looked defensive. 'Well, you wouldn't help.'

Gwen closed her eyes. *The frustrated witch. The phantasms. Her interest in Iris's notebooks. Lily Thomas.*

'Lily Thomas,' Marilyn said, confirming Gwen's thoughts. 'And you stopped it.' She grabbed Gwen's knee and squeezed it hard. 'I want you to do the same again. Please. He says he's leaving everything behind. He's handed in his notice and bought a round-the-world ticket. He says he's going backpacking.'

'I'm sorry,' Gwen said again.

'Backpacking! He complained about carrying the shopping.'

'I don't think there's anything I can do.'

'But you can't just meddle in people's lives, you know.' Marilyn balled her hands into fists. 'It isn't fair.'

'Isn't that what you're asking me to do now?'

'I'm asking you to fix it. I want things back the way they were.'

'Do you?' Gwen said. Iris had been quite eloquent on the subject of Marilyn and Brian's marriage.

Marilyn hesitated. 'I made a promise on my wedding day.'

'As did he, presumably,' Gwen said, as gently as she could manage.

'I'm not just going to throw it away. All those years. Oh God.' Marilyn put her hands over her face. 'I'm too old. I can't start again. I can't.'

'Just imagine for a second that you could. What would you do? Where would you live?'

'I'd stay here; my mother's nearby. My friends.'

'Okay,' Gwen said, trying to be encouraging. 'And what would you do? What do you enjoy doing or wish you did more of?'

Marilyn took her hands away from her face and looked at Gwen. 'I'd like to learn about plants and stuff.'

'Gardening?'

'No, like Iris.'

Gwen got to her feet. 'Well, I can help you there.' She went to the bookcase and pulled out Iris's volumes on herbalism. 'Take these.'

'I was going to do a course in aromatherapy once. At the college. But Brian said it was a waste of time.'

'There you go, then,' Gwen said. 'Now's your chance.'

Marilyn pulled out a tissue from her sleeve and blew her nose. 'You really think I can do this?'

'Yes,' Gwen said with more conviction than she felt. 'You can do anything you want.'

Marilyn got up to leave. 'You're being very nice today.'

'I'm always nice,' Gwen said. 'I'm a nice person.'

'Mmm. This was on your mat.' She pulled an envelope from her coat pocket. 'Doesn't look like it's been posted.'

Gwen glanced at the plain white envelope, then hustled Marilyn out of the house.

Once she was alone, Gwen slit the envelope. *Please be from Cam. Please be from Cam.*

It wasn't.

Gwen read the contents with a sense of disbelief. She paced the room a few times, weighing up her options. Then read the letter again. She could either apply for legal aid and hope it came through some time in the next six months, conjure some cash out of thin air to pay somebody, or she could ask Cam. Her stomach swooped as she pictured his horrified expression. He thought she was a lunatic.

Gwen paced through the downstairs of the house, going round in circles in her mind. So, he'd never want a relationship, that didn't mean he couldn't be a friend. She knew that she couldn't feel any worse about him than she already did. She was at rock bottom. She picked up the phone to make an appointment with Cam.

At two o'clock the next afternoon, Gwen arrived at Laing & Sons. He'd squeezed her in on short notice, so she ought to be grateful, but looking around at the oak panelling, the leather desk chair and the tastefully worn oriental rug, she felt nauseous instead. It was the mirror image of his grandfather's office; the one she'd sat in on her last visit to the firm. It smelled of cigar smoke, leather and paper, and looked like it had been outfitted by a set designer with no imagination. And it still had more warmth than Cam's flat.

'Drink?' Cam opened a cabinet and revealed an impressive range of bottles.

'Um...' Gwen hesitated. Mixing proximity to Cameron Laing with hard alcohol might have disastrous consequences. She needed to keep a clear head. And control the wild hope that had begun fluttering the moment she'd seen his face. The hope that maybe he'd come to terms with magic. Her magic.

He leaned down and opened another anonymous wooden door. There was a small fridge and ice compartment. Gwen glimpsed juice, cola and bottled water.

'Water, please.'

Cam passed her a bottle with a professional smile and Gwen felt it like a slap.

The light brush of his fingers as she took the water still sent a bolt of electricity up her arm though.

Stupid hope.

He retreated back to his chair, looking instantly more serious behind the imposing desk. She guessed that was the idea.

'I brought the letter. Hang on.' She dug in her messenger bag and retrieved the evil A4 envelope, pushing it across the smooth surface of the desk like it was radioactive.

'I've got five minutes.' Cam opened out the paperwork and began reading.

Gwen unscrewed the water bottle and wandered around the room, sipping from it and trying not to look impatient. The pictures on the walls were dark oil paintings. They were traditional, representative work – the kind of thing that couldn't offend anybody, but still exuded a certain strength.

'Right,' Cam said after a surprisingly short length of time. 'This is fine. Nothing to worry about.'

'Really?' Gwen crossed the room to Cam's chair and perched on the desk. She didn't feel that Christopher Brewer threatening to sue her for defamation of character was 'nothing to worry about'. Especially when she'd only told Helen the truth. Christopher had terrorised the family dog, and he deserved whatever consequences his mother had dished out.

'Yes. It's a nuisance suit.'

'That's easy for you to say. It's not like he took my parking space.'

Cam smiled briefly. 'That would be far worse in this town. This is the kind of thing that is meant to annoy. The solicitor who drafted this letter knows it, but—' He broke off. 'Could you not do that?'

'What?'

'Sit on my desk. It's antique.'

'Right.' Gwen stood up and circled back to the client side of the desk. 'Is this better?'

'Thank you.' Cam looked marginally happier now that a tree's-worth of wood was separating them. 'I'm sorry to be uptight, but it's my dad's desk.'

'No worries. This is better anyway,' Gwen lied, sitting in the client chair a long, long away from Cam.

'Right.' He still looked distracted for a moment, but then snapped back to the matter in hand. 'The complaint is slander and the witness to the slander is a family member of the plaintiff.'

'But slander is if you say something that isn't true. I didn't do that.'

'That's a matter of opinion.'

'Isn't everything?'

'It's immaterial here. The point is that he would have to prove that what you said wasn't true and I don't see how he can prove what a dog did or didn't think.' Cam laughed without humour. 'Like I said, nuisance suit.' He shoved the papers back into the envelope with brisk efficiency. Gwen felt like a real client, being hustled out of the door as her time ran out. She realised a moment after she'd done it that she was standing.

The door swung open. 'Your one o'clock is here.' The trim secretary made no attempt to hide her curiosity as she looked at Gwen. 'Shall I tell them you're running late?'

'No, we're done here, thank you,' Cam said. He was opening a new folder and didn't look up.

'Right,' Gwen said. 'Bye, then.'

'I'll call you,' he said.

'Fine,' Gwen said, suddenly furious. It was probably irrational, but she couldn't help herself. 'Don't go to any trouble.' She marched out of the office, unable to slam the door in a satisfying manner because his secretary was standing in the way.

Gwen went straight from Cam's office to the Red Lion. She had never been so happy to see Bob. 'I need a drink.'

'Care to be specific?' Bob paused in the act of wiping down the bar with a cloth.

'Sorry. Yes. Beer. No, lager. No, wine.'

'I'll get you a Becks. It's on offer.'

Gwen picked up the frosty green bottle and took a long drink.

Bob eyed her. 'You want something to eat with that?'

'No. Yes. Maybe.'

Bob heaved a put-upon sigh. 'I'll get you a sandwich. Don't want you keeling over.'

'It's one beer, Bob. I'm not a child.' Or a teenager, she thought, the crossness back in force.

Bob shrugged. 'You look tired, that's all.'

'I'm sorry.' Gwen put out a hand, touched Bob's arm before he could walk away. 'I'm being grumpy. I'm really sorry.' And then, to her complete mortification, she felt tears in her eyes.

'I'll get you a cheese and ham toastie,' Bob said quickly and beat a hasty retreat.

'Damn it,' Gwen said, feeling like an idiot.

'You think you've got problems,' said a familiar voice.

Gwen swivelled on the bar stool and came face-to-face with Harry. She addressed his forehead, willing herself not to get tearful again: 'I'm not having the best day, no.'

'Bob! I'm getting a beer.' Harry lifted the hatch and walked behind the bar. 'This whole town's gone mental. I've had Marilyn Dixon asking me to handcuff her husband, the ice cream people are having an out-and-out war and it's five months before the season even starts, and then Christopher Brewer tried to—' He broke off abruptly and suddenly became very busy with pulling his pint.

'Christopher Brewer wanted you to arrest me,' Gwen said flatly. 'It figures.'

Harry shrugged. 'I'm not going to, if that's any consolation.'

'I'll drink to that,' Gwen said, clinking her bottle against his glass. 'He's suing me, too. Covering all bases.'

Harry ducked back to the punters' side of the bar and leaned on it, next to Gwen. Despite slumping and Gwen's high stool, he was still taller than her. If you didn't know what a sweetheart he was, he'd be imposing. Probably came in handy in his line of work.

'So, what's up with you?' Harry said.

'You mean apart from my position as most hated person in Pendleford?'

Harry grinned. 'It's not that bad.'

'Want to bet?' Gwen paused. She wanted to say: *and Cam is being an uptight arsehole and he really hurt my feelings and I'm frightened that he is never going to remember how to be a human being,* but Harry was Cam's best friend. It would be indiscreet.

As if reading her mind, Harry said, 'And how's Mr Stiff Upper Lip?'

'Cam? He's fine.' Gwen tried to make her voice sound normal.

'That bad, huh? Oh, man.' Harry took another long drink. 'He's under a lot of pressure at the moment. Try to cut him a bit of slack.'

'What sort of pressure?'

Harry took a long drink and wiped his mouth. 'The firm's been losing clients. Something to do with his grandfather passing cases onto Cam and the old crusty types in the town not trusting a young whippersnapper to do the old man's job.'

'Cam's a good lawyer, though, isn't he?'

Harry nodded. 'Don't ever tell him I said so, but, yeah. He is.'

'Is the firm in money trouble?'

'I don't think it's anywhere near that bad, but his mother . . .You know. She's a little uptight and Cam gets the full force of it 'cause she's on her own.'

'Since his dad died.'

'He came back to look after her, you know. She fell apart after he died. Cam did a law degree just so that he could take his father's place. It's a lot of pressure.'

'He seems to like it, now.'

'Yeah,' Harry said. 'But it wasn't the way he planned his life. He put his family first and I kind of admire that, you know? Not sure I would've done it.'

Gwen thought about her own reaction to family obligations: heading very fast in the opposite direction. 'It can't have been easy.'

Harry nodded. 'Just do me a favour, okay?'

'What?'

'Don't run away this time.'

'Hey!' Gwen felt the anger clench her stomach. 'I'm staying. He's the one who wants to keep everything separate, everything in his precious neat little boxes.

He's the one who acts like a complete stranger one moment and the next—' She broke off. *The next he's pulling my clothes off. Which I actually really like.*

Harry shrugged. 'You've lost me there.'

'I'm not leaving,' she said, realising that every time she said the words it strengthened her resolve. 'Whatever happens with Cam, I'm staying.' Gwen felt the truth of the words and waited for the accompanying terror. It didn't come. End House seemed to have amplified her powers so that she didn't even know if she'd be able to turn them off again, but Gwen realised that she felt remarkably calm about that.

'Good,' Harry said mildly. 'Now eat your sandwich. You look knackered.'

Gwen passed a familiar figure on the way home. Katie was wearing a black hooded top and jeans and had her hands stuffed into her pockets. She looked half-frozen. Gwen pulled over opposite the bus stop and wound down her window. 'Want a lift?'

Katie crossed the road and climbed into Nanette. She pulled headphones out of her ears and gave Gwen a quick smile. 'Thanks. I think I missed my bus.'

'Home?'

Katie nodded, not looking overjoyed at the prospect.

'No problem.' Gwen turned around at the next junction and pointed Nanette towards Bath. She glanced at Katie. She was staring out of the window, her face blank.

'Bad day?'

Katie shrugged. 'Not the best.'

'Do you want to talk about it?'

'Not really,' Katie said. 'If that's okay.'

Gwen drove a little further. 'You want to take a detour? We could go and throw rocks at something.'

Katie snorted. 'What?'

'Throwing things is very good for the soul.'

'You're mental,' Katie said, but in a tone which made it sound like a good thing.

'You're afraid I'll win. I can understand that. I have an excellent throwing arm.'

'Maybe—' Katie stopped speaking abruptly. Her neck twisted as she peered behind her seat, into the back of the van. She paused as if listening and then said, 'Is there someone back there?'

'No,' Gwen said, a little spooked.

'I thought I heard something. Well, not really heard.' Katie hesitated, then rushed on. 'You know that feeling you get that someone's looking at you and you turn and they totally are?'

'Yes,' Gwen said.

'I just had the weirdest feeling.' She looked around again a couple more times. Abruptly, she leaned forward and began patting the footwell. 'What's this?'

Gwen glanced across and saw that Katie had one of Iris's books in her hand. She didn't even remember putting it in the car.

'You can't read that,' she said.

Katie was already flicking through it. 'God, I know. The writing's terrible.'

'No, I mean you shouldn't. Your mum will have kittens.'

'Good,' Katie said. She began reading out loud. '"To forget old lovers; burn oregano. For enhanced fertility; place mandrake root under the mattress". What's mandrake root?'

'A plant,' Gwen said.

'Sounds made up,' Katie said, still flipping pages. '"To make a new friend or increase loving feelings, give biscuits or cakes baked with caraway seeds".'

'Please don't,' Gwen said. The traffic was building up as they approached Bath and she could only shoot tiny glances at Katie. 'I'm sorry. I promise you're not missing much. Iris was a bit eccentric.'

'Like you,' Katie said.

'Maybe,' Gwen said. She slowed Nanette for a queue, the red lights of the car in front reflecting on the wet road. 'Can I have that back, please?' She held out a hand for the book.

'I'm so sick of people keeping secrets from me. I'm not a little kid.'

'I know that,' Gwen said.

'Fine,' Katie said angrily. Then she turned her face to the window and refused to speak again.

Katie's stubborn silence upset Gwen more than she thought possible. She realised how much she had been enjoying being the cool aunt. And she was sick of tiptoeing around Ruby. It wasn't as if she even agreed with her sister. Ruby thought that protecting Katie meant stifling her, lying to her. She glanced at Katie. She was a good kid. Trustworthy.

'There are some things I could show you,' Gwen said.

Katie looked up. Her smile was pure sunshine. 'Can you show me how to hurt someone?'

'What? Katie!'

'Not hurt, then. Upset? Annoy? Embarrass.'

'Is someone at school bothering you?'

Katie shrugged.

'This isn't going to work if you're not going to be honest with me. I'm not your mum; you can talk to me.'

'Will Jones flashed me.'

'What? Hang on.' Gwen pointed Nanette in the direction of the nearest parking space. She couldn't concentrate on driving and wanted to look into Katie's eyes.

'Right.' She pulled over. 'Let's get into the back.'

'Okay.' Katie unclicked her seat belt and climbed between the seats.

There was a single mattress piled with a duvet and cushions and Gwen arranged them into a kind of sofa. She switched on the wind-up camping lantern and closed all the curtains.

'Cosy,' Katie said, looking around approvingly. 'I can't believe you lived in here for a week, though.'

'I don't recommend it,' Gwen said. 'And it doesn't exactly scream "excellent life choices".'

Katie giggled. 'I think it's cool.'

Gwen resisted the urge to say, *That's because you're fourteen.*

'So. Was it an old guy in a raincoat?'

Katie leaned back. 'No. Will Jones is in my year. He was just trying to embarrass me in front of everyone by waving his you-know-what in my face. It was horrible.'

Little git. Gwen fetched her tin of supplies from her handbag. 'How would you like to give him an itch in his you-know-what?'

Katie sat forward. 'You can do that?'

'Just for a little while. Maybe during assembly or, even better, does he play football?'

'Rugby.'

'Perfect. Next big match, I predict Will Jones won't be able to stop scratching his balls.'

Katie laughed. 'That's disgusting. But I don't know if anyone will notice.'

'They will,' Gwen said. 'I'm talking really itchy. Rolling around on the ground with both hands down his shorts itchy.' She hesitated. 'It's something I'd better do, though. I think you need to start with something a little simpler. Safer. I don't like Will Jones, but I don't want him permanently disfigured.'

Katie's eyes were wide. 'Is that possible?'

'The thing you need to remember about magic is that there are always consequences. It's like scales, if one side goes up, then the other goes down.' Gwen leaned forward a little. Katie was going to grow into a Harper woman; it wasn't fair to keep her in the dark. 'Look, before I opted out of the training, my mother taught me all kinds of spells and hexes. She showed me how to pay attention to things, to use my intuition like another sense, and she was completely obsessed with the Finding. She wanted me to practice it all the time. What she didn't tell me was that you start to feel hollowed out. That if you do a spell that's a bit too strong for you, you can zone out for days afterwards. You feel sick. You can't think straight.'

Gwen hesitated. 'Once, your mum tried something.'

Katie's eyes went wide. 'No way.'

Gwen nodded. 'She didn't inherit any special ability. I don't know why. But Ruby was still raised by Gloria; she couldn't help but pick up a few things here and there. Anyway, when I was really little, like five or six, I remember her landing up in bed for three weeks. She was really, really sick. Gloria told everyone it was flu, but it wasn't. Ruby had wanted a Lego set that was too expensive. A castle, I think. She did a spell to make Gloria buy it for her and the after-effects damn-near killed her.'

'Oh,' Katie said, her face pale.

'Do you see why she doesn't want you to know about this stuff?'

'I guess.' Katie swallowed visibly. She was subdued for a moment and then she rallied. 'Can you teach me to read cards?'

Gwen stopped herself from groaning out loud. Of course it had to be cards. 'No problem,' she said. 'It's not a game, though. You have to be careful with it. And you can't tell anyone else. And you definitely can't tell your mum.' Gwen didn't think she'd ever seen Katie so happy. It was like when she was petting Cat, times a hundred.

'Cross my heart and hope to—'

'Don't say that,' Gwen said quickly.

After a quick lesson in fortune-telling and a couple of friendship spells, Gwen drove Katie home.

She was rewarded with a quick strawberry-scented hug. 'Bye, honeybunch.'

Katie paused, her hand on the door. 'I asked my mum why you haven't been around.'

'It's complicated,' Gwen said.

'She says that you found a boy who'd committed suicide. Found his body, I mean.'

Gwen nodded. She didn't trust herself to speak.

'I know that must've been horrible and I can totally see why it messed you up and everything, but I don't understand why you would run away.'

'I didn't run away,' Gwen lied. 'I like moving around and I've just never really found somewhere I've felt comfortable.'

'You like it here now, though, don't you?'

'Yes.' Gwen smiled. 'I actually kind of do. If I can just keep a lid on all the crazy stuff and keep Iris's books away from you and the rest of the town and convince everyone that I'm not like Iris and that I'm completely normal, then I might really like it.'

Katie gave her a quick smile. 'Thank you.'

'You're welcome. And, for the record, I know you're not an idiot or a little kid. I'm just trying to stay on the right side of your mum. She's scary when she's protective. She's like a lioness.'

Katie shrugged, her face closed again. Gwen felt a stab of sympathy for Ruby.

'Goodbye, Auntie Gwen.' Katie got out of the van, a couple of snowflakes swirling inside when she opened the door. She paused. 'I don't know why you want to be normal, though. What's so brilliant about that? You've got a power, a purpose in life. Do you know how rare that is?'

Katie slammed the door and made her way up to the front door. Gwen let out a breath. 'Bloody hell,' she said quietly.

CHAPTER 18

Gwen let herself into End House and hung her coat and hat on the hooks in the hall. She flicked the switch on the kettle – as if a cup of tea was going to settle the tingling in her skin – and began to tidy up the worktops in a half-hearted fashion. There was something in the back of her mind that was nagging at her. Like a word teetering on the tip of your tongue or an itch that seems to move as soon as you scratch it.

She filled the sink with hot water and began methodically washing up, staring out into the dark of the garden. A movement on the grass near the hedge startled her. A flash of fur, low to the ground. A fox?

And that did it. The niggling thought leaped to the foreground, fully formed and shaped like a rabbit. Gwen dried her hands on her jeans as she went back into the hallway. When she'd found the rabbit, she'd been so intent on burying it, so embarrassed at freaking out in front of Cam and so shaken that she'd picked up the button and pocketed it on autopilot. Some part of her had assumed it had laid in the garden for years, but it had been worrying away at her subconscious. What if the rabbit-killer had dropped it?

It was a clear blue plastic button. About half a centimetre across and with two holes. It looked brand new. Gwen placed it into her right palm and closed her eyes. The nausea had got so much better and the

Finding seemed to come more quickly and clearly, too. Gwen couldn't help but feel a tiny stab of pride as the images slotted neatly into place. It was nice to be good at something. *And Katie was right; who else could do this?*

A pale blue shirt tucked into beige chinos, a braided leather belt. A black wool coat being pulled over the shirt, snagging on a button. Hands obscured by a bin liner, the plastic half-wrapped around a dead rabbit. The images flipped past fast, like a flick book, but Gwen held onto the last one, checking it carefully before she opened her eyes. It was a face in profile. Blond hair and a soft jawline, with a single cold blue eye visible. The journalist that she'd met at Lily's house. Ryan.

If she'd been in any doubt before, that clinched it. She hauled the crate of notebooks upstairs and now, propped up against several pillows, with Cat draped across her lap and purring like a buzz saw, she began to look through them in earnest.

16ᵗʰ June 2009. Number 12 having difficulty in the bedroom. Gave 3x prep. HWS, MF, CF. If that doesn't make him go the distance, nothing will. NB. Render on outhouse needs repair.

She flipped the page, looking for references to 'Lily'. For some clue as to why Lily had been terrorising Iris and had transferred that animosity – like an unwanted heirloom – to Gwen.

After months of tip-toeing around, Lily came right out and asked me today. She wants to be my acolyte. That's actually the word she used. Silly woman. I've told her 'no' in a hundred different ways, but she still forced me to say it outright. I caught her looking through one of my books, too. I'll have to keep them locked in the outhouse from now on. Be more careful. I've nailed bunches of broom above the doorways, but I know that won't be enough. If I could, I'd ask Gloria to look at my cards. I have a very bad feeling about that woman.

Gwen felt sick. It was one thing to suspect that somebody was stalking you, but quite another to have it confirmed.

That bloody woman was here again today. In truth I grow afraid of her. There is something desperate in her eyes. At the moment she fears me more than I fear her, but I can feel that balance shifting. The scales are tipping in her favour. I have a confession to make: I've resorted to untruths to keep her in line. I've told her that I have evidence that would convict her of her father's murder and that if anything unnatural happens to me, it will come to light. I didn't realise, until that moment, that she was guilty. She was spitting and hissing like a cornered cat. I know that this won't count as evidence, not the kind I'm pretending to hold, but I feel better writing it down anyway. She killed her own father to get his house.

I need to be more careful.

Gwen picked up the phone and dialled Gloria's number. When her mother answered, she launched straight in, before she could lose her nerve. 'Why did you abandon Iris? She was an old lady living on her own and we were the only family she had left.'

'You don't know what you're talking about.'

'I know she took you in when Annie died. She didn't have to do that.'

'Iris was very dutiful,' Gloria said, her voice several degrees below icy.

'Well, what was so terrible? What did she do to deserve being cast out?' Gwen felt sick; Iris alone, frightened. A murderer on her doorstep.

'I didn't cast her anywhere,' Gloria said. 'She didn't want anything to do with me, either. With any of us.'

'I don't believe you. Why would she leave me her house if she didn't care for me at all?'

'You think that's a blessing? You need to stay away from that place.'

'I'm calling from that place; I've got nowhere else to live.' Gwen closed her eyes and waited for the bolt of lightning to strike her down. After a moment she realised that she was still alive and that there was an ominous silence on the line. 'Gloria?' Gwen said, gripping the phone tightly. 'Mum?'

'When I came back to Pendleford, I thought it would be a new start. For all of us. I tried to tell people what they wanted to hear, instead of what the cards were really telling me, and I was good at it. I thought it would make things easier for you and Ruby.'

Gwen was stunned. 'Did you ever think about not reading the cards at all? That would've made life easier.'

'It's not that simple, Gwen. You, of all people, should know that. Anyway, Iris didn't approve. Said it was against the ancient code or something equally daft. We fought. We said nasty things that can't be unsaid. It happens.' There was the sound of a deep breath being taken. 'I can't believe you're back in Pendleford. What about that nice man you were seeing; is he still around?'

'Cam?'

'Mmm. I liked him.'

Gwen was momentarily speechless. 'I don't remember that.' She remembered Gloria telling her effectively the same as Elaine Laing; that she and Cam were from different worlds and had no future together.

She'd dropped it in, casually, while reading the cards for something else entirely. Completely oblivious to the effect she was having, as usual.

'Well, I didn't give you any hassle over boys, did I?' Gloria was saying. 'I let you make your own mistakes. That's called being a supportive mother and I can tell you I didn't learn it from your great-aunt.'

'There's a difference between giving supportive freedom and simply not being interested.'

'And there's a difference between being a teenager and having the right to blame your mother for everything and being thirty-one and responsible for yourself.'

'Wow, Gloria. You sound almost angry there. Better be careful; you're in danger of actually having an emotion.'

'I'm full of emotion, darling. Full of positivity and happy feelings; that's probably why you don't recognise them. You always were a glass half-empty kind of child.'

'I'm going now,' Gwen said. 'Phone Ruby some time, will you?'

Gwen tried not to feel the emptiness of the house, but it pressed upon her. She pulled on a thick cardigan and hurried out to Nanette, rubbing her arms. She got in automatically, not letting herself think about it. Inside, it was only sensible to start the engine so that the heater would wake up. Then it seemed only natural to buckle her seat belt and reverse out of the drive.

She took the track to the main road slowly, wincing at the pot holes. If she stayed, she should really do something about those. The roads were quiet and she took turnings aimlessly, following small lanes through the countryside around the town. She'd always found driving good for thinking, but now her mind was blank.

The motion soothed her, though. The mechanics of clutch-gear-shift, the ticking of the indicators. Darkness came in quickly and she flipped on her lights.

She'd made the decision unconsciously, but soon found herself on the main road towards Bath. She realised that she was heading towards her sister; that she was actually craving her company. She wasn't going to examine the impulse any further. She wasn't running away, she told herself. Just taking a break from being alone. Just for a little while.

David answered the door in a red-striped apron and reading glasses. 'She's having her hair done. Not sure when she'll be back, I'm afraid.'

'Which salon? I'll go and keep her company under the drier.'

Gwen drove into the centre of Bath, thanking the parking gods when she found a free space in a side street.

The salon was sleek but inviting and, looking through the big front window, Gwen could see Ruby was the last customer. She was talking animatedly with a teeny-tiny woman wearing black.

She pushed the door open before either woman could look up and catch her gawping at them like Charlie Bucket through the chocolate factory gates.

'Gwen?' Ruby's immaculate eyebrows drew together. 'You're here.'

'I came to see you. David told me about your appointment.'

'This is my friend Kim's place.' Ruby indicated the tiny woman who, Gwen couldn't help but notice, was taking a professionally dispassionate inventory of Gwen's appearance. 'Gwen's my sister,' Ruby said.

'Very nice.' Gwen looked around at the work stations with modern leather chairs, the gleaming display of hair products, and the space-age light fittings that cast a pleasant, flattering light.

'Kim's finished with me.' Ruby picked up her bag. 'Do you want to go?' She paused. 'Unless you want to get your hair done.'

It was an old joke.

'I'd love to cut your hair,' Kim said earnestly. She reached out and ran a lock through her fingers.

'Don't even bother trying,' Ruby said. 'She won't let you.'

Gwen was going to say something else, but she was caught by her refection in one of the many mirrors. All the flattering light in the world couldn't disguise the horror. Her usually pale skin was greenish, and the dark shadows underneath her eyes stood out, which didn't help, but her hair sat lank against her head. The natural wave just made it look messy and the centre parting she'd been sporting since primary school looked old-fashioned and middle-aged. 'Why didn't you tell me?'

'What?' Ruby said.

'That I look like crap.'

'I always tell you that,' Ruby said.

'I'm serious.' Gwen took a step towards the mirror. And jeans. When was the last time she'd worn anything except jeans? 'I look knackered and my clothes are boring and my hair is awful.'

Ruby came and stood next to her. 'Your hair isn't that bad. It's in beautiful condition.'

'Cam said I look the same and I thought he was being flattering. I mean, no one looks the same at eighteen and thirty-one, but he was right. I look the same, only older.'

'And that's bad why?'

Gwen thought about the forwards-backwards dance she and Cam had been executing and said, 'It can't be helping.'

'I could tidy up the ends for you.' Kim had her head on one side, considering. 'But a short cut would look really good. You've got the face shape for it.' Kim turned to Ruby. 'Hasn't she, Rubes?'

'I can't afford it,' Gwen said. 'Sorry.'

Ruby said, 'I'll pay.'

At the same time, Kim said, 'On the house.'

They looked at each other and laughed.

'That's very kind,' Gwen said, liking the feeling that it was a foregone conclusion. That a decision had been taken out of her hands.

She took a deep breath and sat down in the nearest chair. 'I want a total change.'

'Are you sure?' Kim said, combing and beginning to section her hair.

'I want a fresh start.'

Ruby rolled her eyes. 'It's only hair.'

Gwen fixed Ruby's eye in the mirror. 'Stop acting cool. I know you've been dying for me to beautify.'

Ruby flashed her a wide grin. 'This is true. Next we can do make-up.'

'No, thank you,' Gwen said. She closed her eyes and tried not to think about the dancing scissors and falling hair.

Kim asked her questions about her life and Gwen answered. It would've seemed ungrateful not to and Kim had clearly slipped into professional small talk out of habit. Ruby sat on a leather sofa with a magazine and Gwen could hear the pages flipping, so she told Kim about Curious Notions and her shadow boxes and tried not to put herself down. By the time Kim told her to open her eyes, she felt as if knots of tension had slipped undone. Maybe there was something in this pampering lark, after all.

She looked in the mirror. 'Bloody hell.'

'Don't you like it?' Kim looked anxious. Ruby appeared in the mirror and gave her a thumbs-up.

Gwen put her hand to her neck and touched the bare skin. She turned her head to the side. 'It's great,' Gwen said automatically. It was definitely *different*.

'You'll need to blow-dry it to make it sit like this,' Kim said.

'Uh-huh.' Gwen wasn't even sure she owned a hairdryer.

'But if you don't, it'll still look good. Just softer and your curls will come back.'

'I like my curls,' Gwen said.

'I know.' Ruby was smiling at her in the mirror. 'Me, too.'

'Thank you,' Gwen said, squinting at the new, sleek Gwen in mirror. 'I feel sick, but in a good way.'

'Lovely,' Kim said. 'I could put that on my next advert.'

Gwen drove the long way back to End House, taking the road through the centre of Pendleford. The street lights were on and flood lamps lit the beautiful architecture of the church and the town bridge. She watched people on the pavements, bundled up in coats against the cold, and the stone fish poised on top of the round house. Its mouth was open, as if it were about to speak to her.

Still feeling the same kind of dreaminess she'd felt all day, Gwen followed the road back to End House. As she crested the rise, the house came into view. She'd left the lights on in the hallway and the kitchen, and the stained glass above the front door was illuminated. The green checked curtains at the kitchen window weren't shut properly and a vertical slice of electric light shone out into the darkness.

Gwen pulled into the driveway and sat for a moment, looking at the stone building with its messy and forbidding garden and missing roof tiles and felt an ache in her solar plexus so strong it made her double over, her head brushing the steering wheel. She felt as if she'd just come home.

Ruby called on Friday to say that she'd spoken to someone at Bath's craft market and there had been a late cancellation. 'It's a really good one. Loads of rich people in Bath. More money than sense; I bet you'd sell a ton.'

'Thank you,' Gwen said.

'I didn't mean it that way,' Ruby said quickly.

'No, that's fine. Thank you. Really.' Gwen put the phone down, feeling slightly dazed at the interest Ruby was taking.

She was even more surprised on Saturday morning, when Ruby and Katie arrived at the house before the Pendleford craft market. Katie was fizzing with excitement. 'We brought you something. A present.'

'It's for work,' Ruby said, 'don't get too excited.'

'I've got to go soon,' Gwen said. She'd packed Nanette and was just filling a flask with coffee.

'We decided you need a new look.' Katie thrust a carrier bag across. 'To go with your stall.'

'No one is looking at me,' Gwen said, more crossly than she had intended.

'You're a one-woman company. You're part of the brand,' Ruby said. 'It's like…you wouldn't go to a hairdresser who had rubbish hair.'

'Mum's right,' Katie said, earning a stunned look from Ruby. 'You don't look right at the moment.' She held her hands up as if framing a photograph. 'It jars.'

'Thank you, oh, favourite niece of mine. Remind me not to bake you any more cupcakes.'

'I'm not being mean. You look fine for everyday stuff like going to the supermarket or whatever.'

'Not helping,' Gwen said.

'But you've got to look like you wear this stuff. Like it's part of your life,' Katie said, her brow crinkled.

'It is part of my life,' Gwen said.

'Exactly.' Katie's frown cleared as if she'd won the argument. Her forehead smoothed out like plasticine. *Youth*.

'Don't even try and argue with her. She's stubborn,' Ruby said.

'Well, I wonder where she gets that from,' Gwen muttered.

'Dad,' Katie said.

At the same time, Ruby said, 'Her father.' And then they laughed.

Which would've been a beautiful family moment if they weren't conspiring to get her out of her beloved jeans. Gwen opened the bag and looked inside. Something very red and floral was inside. Her heart sank.

'It's a dress. I wanted to get a prom dress but Mum said you'd never wear it.'

'She was dead right.'

'So it's a tea dress. Look, it's perfect.' Katie said with all the certainty of a fourteen- year-old.

Gwen pulled it from the bag and held it up. 'Is it made from a pair of curtains?'

'No. It's beautiful,' Katie said severely. 'It's made from angel's hair and butterfly wings and . . . and . . . beauty!'

Gwen laughed despite herself. 'Fine, fine. I'll try on the damn dress.' She made a show of stomping upstairs, making Katie and Ruby tut .

The dress was a bit long, but it fitted well on the bust and cinched in her waist. She had a quick look in the full length mirror in Iris's wardrobe and tried not to wince. At least the sleeves were long.

Back downstairs, Ruby and Katie considered her. Ruby tipped her head to one side and put a finger to her lips. 'Not bad at all.'

'It's an improvement,' Katie said. 'You'll need some heels, though.'

'I'm not standing in heels all day,' Gwen said.

'No pain, no gain,' Ruby said. She produced a pair of red shoes from her handbag.

'Oh, Christ,' Gwen said and squeezed them on.

'You know, it didn't strike me as weird until Katie said something, but don't you think it's odd?'

The seams of the dress were cutting into Gwen's side and the shoes pinched. She felt hot and bothered and slightly ridiculous. 'What?'

'You sell all that gorgeous stuff,' Ruby said, 'and none of it's for you.'

Gwen stared dumbly at her sister. It wasn't just that she was right or that Gwen had no idea why that was. *Do I think so little of myself?* But it was that Ruby had called something of hers 'gorgeous'.

'Have you started using eBay yet?' Katie asked. She had a vintage feather boa draped around her neck and was twirling one end.

'It's on my list,' Gwen assured her. 'Thanks for the dress and the shoes and the…you know…assassination of my fashion sense, but I'm afraid I have to go.'

'Can I help you today?' Katie said, the words coming out in a rush.

'Really?' Gwen said. 'I mean, of course you can if you want to. As long as your mum says it's okay.'

Ruby shrugged. 'Fine with me. You need the help.'

Katie was a trouper, helping Gwen unpack Nanette and set up the stall.

'That's everything,' Gwen said. 'Now we put our feet up and wait for the punters.' She realised that she should've brought another folding chair. 'You can have first go in the chair.'

'What about these?' Katie climbed out of the van with a Clarks shoe box.

'They're spare bits waiting for homes in my boxes.'

'You have a lot of bits.' Katie lifted the lid and raked through. 'How many guns do you need? Or anchors?'

Gwen shrugged. 'I've been collecting for a while.'

'You don't say.' Katie held up a small apple charm on a silver jump ring with a couple of silver leaves attached. 'I like this.'

'You have a good eye. That's Murano glass. Hold it up to the light.'

Katie did so and the swirls of red and green glowed. 'Pretty.'

'It's been too big for my boxes so far, wrong scale, but I'm glad I picked it up. Apart from anything else, the guy didn't know what it was. He had it in with a load of plastic bracelets and a Sindy doll.' Gwen shook her head at the memory. 'I mean, it's Murano glass.'

Katie squinched her face. 'Is it valuable?'

'Oh, yeah, but more than that it's beautiful. And unusual.' Gwen stared at the apple, remembering vividly the day she'd found it. It was like that with all her best finds: the feeling tingling, the moment caught in Technicolor, surround-sound detail. Caught and filed.

'What are you going to do with it, then?' Katie was asking.

Gwen blinked and looked at her niece. 'Give it to you.'

'Cool.' Katie held up the apple to the light. 'Can I put it on a leather thong or a ribbon or something?'

Gwen suppressed a shudder. 'I'll get you a silver chain. Hang on.' A few minutes' work with a pair of needle-nose pliers and a jump ring and the apple was a pendant.

'Can I make something else?' Katie said. 'With this.' She held up a dark grey charm in the shape of a revolver.

'If you like,' Gwen said. 'Have whatever you fancy.'

Katie took her time, selecting a tiny white bone die, a dark blue crystal and a silver feather to go with the gun. Gwen showed her how to attach jump rings to make a cluster and how to attach the whole lot to another length of silver chain. By the time they'd finished, the market had opened and was getting busy.

Two hours later, Gwen sat on her folding chair and watched Katie. She was a natural. She smiled hello, but then faded unobtrusively into the background, rearranging part of the display in a relaxed way while the punter browsed. She sensed when they were looking for her to interact too, and made eye contact, offering help or encouragement or making a joke to put them at their ease.

A girl not much older than Katie leaned over to look at a bracelet that was draped over a statue of Dionysus. Without the slightest prompting, Katie plucked it off the bronze and put it straight into the girl's hands and said, 'Try it on if you like. And then, in a voice so completely genuine Gwen could hardly believe she'd heard the same line, delivered the same way to the previous twenty customers, Katie said, 'It looks so good on you.'

'You should have a break. You must be knackered,' Gwen said when Katie turned to give her a victorious smile.

'I sold it! That last one wasn't going to buy anything, I could tell, but then she saw that bracelet and it was just perfect for her and she bought it!'

'I know,' Gwen said, smiling at her enthusiasm. 'You're my ace sales assistant, but you still need to take a break. I think this counts as slave labour otherwise.'

Katie's face fell. 'I hope she likes it.'

'What?'

'The bracelet.' Then, just as quickly, her expression cleared. 'Of course she likes it. She definitely did.'

Gwen could vaguely remember what she'd been like at Katie's age: her moods changing at the speed of light and energy and enthusiasm set at either zero or one hundred million billion and nothing in between. She smiled. Cam would probably say that was still the case. 'And you sold all your necklaces,' she said to Katie. 'You're really onto something with those.'

'I need to pay you for the materials, though; I used your stuff.'

'That's okay. Take it as part-payment for helping me out today.'

Katie brightened even further as she calculated her profits.

Gwen smiled, allowing herself to imagine Katie helping her out regularly. She'd always thought that she preferred to run the stall on her own, but now she wasn't so sure. It was nice to be part of a team for once.

It wasn't until she was at home, making a well-earned cup of coffee when she realised something: Katie had been *too* good on the stall.

CHAPTER 19

Back at End House, the air was still and a crow sat on the wall watching her calmly. Lily was at the back door.

'I had the locks changed,' Gwen said, by way of greeting.

'I brought you something,' Lily said. 'Thought you might be interested.' She looked altogether too cheerful for Gwen's liking.

'Come in,' Gwen said. She flipped on the lights. 'Would you like to sit down?' She was determined to be polite, to show Lily that she wasn't frightened by her.

'You're a dark horse,' Lily said.

'What do you mean?'

'This.' Lily reached into her handbag and put a stack of papers onto the table. Clippings. 'I had Ryan do a little bit of research for me.'

Gwen touched the topmost paper. A grainy black and white picture of a smiling boy. Sixteen years old, his whole life ahead of him. She still felt guilty that she didn't remember him from school. Whatever the papers had said, she hadn't known him at all. He'd been two years below her and that was like another species at that age, but still, she would've felt better if she could've pictured him alive. Or perhaps not.

'That was very sad,' Gwen said, pleased with how steady her voice sounded.

Lily smiled widely and Gwen suddenly realised why her teeth looked so oddly childlike. There were tiny gaps between her front teeth.

'This is my favourite bit.' Lily spread out the clippings and pointed to a piece that Gwen didn't remember seeing before. Despite herself, she leaned in for a closer look. *Schoolgirl held in connection with river boy death.*

She straightened up quickly. 'What do you want, Lily?'

'I want everyone in this town to know exactly who you are.'

'What have I ever done to you?'

Lily's smile faltered and something altogether more frightening bubbled up in its place. 'You think you're so clever, but you're not. I belong here and these are my people, my town. I look after them. They need me in the same way they needed Iris.'

'Fine.' Gwen waved her hands. 'You carry on. I'm not stopping you.'

'It's the Harper name. It confuses them. I want you gone.'

'I've got every right to live here.' *And nowhere else to go.*

'And I want Iris's journals. All of them. I need them.'

'I can't give you those; I'm sorry,' Gwen said. 'They're private.'

Lily shook her head. 'You think I'm so stupid.'

'Look. You can't threaten me with this. I didn't do anything wrong then, and I'm not doing anything wrong now. Stephen Knight killed himself thirteen years ago. It's very sad, but it had nothing to do with me.'

'No smoke without fire,' Lily said. 'People in this town love that expression. They'll hang you with it.'

'I haven't done anything wrong,' Gwen said.

'We'll see. Happy reading.' Lily gave a final, chilling look and left.

At Imogen's house on the outskirts of Bath, Katie was wishing that Imogen would take a breath. She hadn't stopped talking since Katie had arrived at three o'clock that afternoon, and she was exhausted.

'I know what we could do,' Imogen said. They'd painted their toenails peacock-blue, dissected the dress sense of every girl at school and played 'would you rather' until they were down to the super-obvious choices like: 'Would you rather snog Mr Wheaton (physics and chemistry) or dry kiss a dog'?

'What?' Katie was cosy under a double duvet on the blow-up mattress and was half-asleep. She kept her voice quiet and dreamy and added a fake yawn, hoping Imogen would take the hint.

'We should do a spell,' Imogen said.

Suddenly Katie was wide awake. She stayed silent.

Imogen's head bent over the side of the bed and she reached out an arm to poke Katie.

'Come on,' Imogen said. 'You must know loads.'

'No.' Katie had been going to say *I'm not allowed*, but she stopped herself in time. Nothing would fix Imogen on the idea faster.

'Nothing bad.' Imogen giggled. 'We could do a love spell on Luke Taylor.'

Katie felt herself blush and was glad it was dark. 'I don't know any love spells.' She felt the tugging sensation behind her left ear and ignored it.

'You must know something.'

Katie sat up, wrapping her arms around her knees. She was torn between wanting to tell Imogen as much as she could – to show off a little – and hearing her aunt's voice: *'It's not a game, this stuff. It's serious.'* She'd trusted Katie. Not like her mum. 'I don't. It's my aunt. And my gran. She reads tarot cards.'

'Fortune-telling. That's a good idea.' Imogen slid out of the end of her bed and began rummaging underneath. 'I've got ordinary playing cards.' Imogen held up a pack. 'They're Annabel's Disney Princess ones. Does that matter?'

'I don't think you can use playing cards. I think you need special ones.' Katie wasn't about to repeat what her aunt had told her. Anything worked, if you knew how to read it. And if you had the power of intention, whatever that was. Personally, Katie had intended to do things many times and nothing had happened, least of all any magic.

Imogen clicked on her lamp. It had a blue shade and cast a ghostly glow around the room. 'Come on; it's just a laugh. Don't be so boring.'

'Okay,' Katie said. If she didn't tell Imogen anything, and didn't really try, then she wasn't breaking any promises. Not really. She climbed out of her sleeping bag and joined Imogen on the bed. She was shuffling the cards inexpertly, her eyes lit up with excitement.

'What do you want to find out, anyway?'

'My future, dummy.'

'Yes, but specifically what? We'll be here all night otherwise.'

'Let's ask if Dan fancies me.' Imogen was going out with Matthew from their chemistry class, but had her eye on a year eleven.

'Okay,' Katie said. 'Think really hard about your question and then deal out three cards face down.'

Imogen shuffled a bit more, then dealt the cards. One of them was dog-eared at the corner, as if a toddler had chewed it.

'What now?'

Katie kind of liked the way Imogen was hanging on her every word. It made her feel powerful. 'You turn

over the first card,' she tapped the card on the left, 'and
it tells you what's behind you.'

Imogen flipped the card and they both leaned
forwards. It was the nine of clubs. In this deck, the clubs
were represented by little apple trees. Imogen looked
disappointed.

Katie had read her tarot book back to front several
times, but was still vaguely surprised to hear herself
saying, 'Clubs are like wands in the tarot, so I think this
is about beginnings, change, maybe creativity.'

Imogen perked up. 'And that's my past, right?'

'Yeah. But it's specific to your question. Not, like,
your general past. Not everything.'

'This one next?' Imogen flipped the middle card
before Katie had a chance to agree.

'Queen of Hearts.' Princess Jasmine gazed coyly up
from behind her sweep of black hair.

Imogen was staring open-mouthed. 'Hearts. I can't
believe it. I asked about love and the card is a heart.'

'A quarter of the pack is hearts. One in four chance,'
Katie said.

'But the queen. That's so weird.' Imogen looked
thrilled. 'What does it mean?'

Katie felt a cold breeze and she looked instinctively
to the window. It was still shut tightly. Her hair lifted
from her cheeks – the draught was very real. She
shivered.

'What?' Imogen was frowning, her face pale in the
half-light.

'I'm not sure…' Katie started. The breeze grew
stronger, her hair was flying now and she was amazed
that Imogen hadn't noticed. Her eyes began to water,
her ears were numb. 'I don't—'

'Come on.' Imogen tapped the Queen of Hearts. 'I
want to know whether Dan is in love with me. Whether

he dreams about me every night. Whether he's going to ask me out.'

Katie stood up, letting the pack of cards in her lap scatter over the floor. 'I'm starving. Let's raid the kitchen.' She looked at Imogen and, trying to mean her words with every fibre of her being, trying to make them perfectly and utterly true, said, 'You look really pale, Imogen. You must be very hungry.'

Imogen got to her feet so quickly that Katie had to step back to avoid a collision.

Imogen's eyes looked unfocused and she said, 'God, I really want some salt and vinegar crisps.'

Well, that was interesting, Katie thought.

CHAPTER 20

The next day, Katie went to her favourite shop, hoping to find answers. Was it possible that she had made Imogen feel hungry? If she was able to control the way people felt, she'd have a much easier time in school, that was for sure.

The Crystal Cave was filled with slices of marbled agate, packs of tarot cards nestled in carved wooden boxes, paper packages of incense, and books on everything from fortune-telling to Buddhism. The man who ran the place had white hair and a neatly clipped beard. He wore a braided leather belt and looked like a refugee from seventies San Francisco. He was also exceedingly suspicious of Katie, evading her questions regarding his stock, but she didn't care.

After sniffing all the scented candles, studying the most expensive crystals in the locked glass cabinet, and handling a stone statue of an Indian goddess until Mr Seventies felt the need to inform her that all breakages had to be paid for, Katie was none the wiser. She left the warm embrace of the shop for the sharp winter air of the street and was immediately stopped by a man in a suit.

'Could you tell me what you just bought in there?'

'Sorry?' For a moment, Katie panicked that she'd accidentally shoplifted something. Imogen was always nicking make-up in Superdrug and perhaps she'd picked up the tendency without even realising it.

The man stood a little too close and was staring at her in quite a disturbing way. He dug a gadget out from his pocket and held it in front of her face. 'I'm from *The Chronicle*. Can I have a word?'

Katie stared at the Dictaphone for a moment, trying to make sense of the situation. 'What? Why?' she said.

'Are you a Satanist? Did you buy chicken blood? A voodoo doll?'

'Sorry?'

'Hey!' A woman crossed the road. 'Stop harassing that girl.'

'We're just having a chat.' He looked at Katie. 'Right?'

'I don't want to talk to you,' Katie said, suddenly feeling as if she might cry.

'You heard her.' The woman was furious. 'Get out of here before I call the police.'

'All right, all right.' The man clicked a button on his Dictaphone and slipped it back into his coat pocket.

Katie watched, relieved, as he walked away. He got into an old navy BMW that was parked on double yellows. 'Thanks,' Katie said.

'No problem.' The woman flicked perfectly highlighted hair out from her eyes. 'People like us have got to stick together.'

'So he was a reporter or something. I don't understand why—' Katie stopped. 'What do you mean, "people like us"?'

'He wanted to talk to you because he saw you coming out of there.' The woman indicated The Crystal Cave.

'I don't understand.'

'His name's Ryan. He's been trying to work up a story on Satanism in Pendleford for a while now. He's really scraping the barrel if he's accosting school kids on the street. No offence.'

'How do you know?'

'Look, you've just had a bit of a shock,' the blonde woman said. 'Can I give you a lift anywhere?'

'I'm getting the bus to Bath,' Katie said, then realised that she probably shouldn't be telling this woman anything. Stranger danger and all that.

'I'll walk with you to the stop. I feel like I should check you're okay. And apologise.'

'What for?' Katie fell into step with the woman. She was tiny, shorter than Katie by an inch or two, and very skinny. She wasn't exactly threatening.

'He's been after a story for a while, but I won't give him one. If I had, he probably wouldn't have spoken to you. I feel responsible.'

Well, that was stupid. 'It's not your fault.'

'Well. Anyway.' The woman took a business card out of her handbag and passed it across. 'Take my number.'

Katie took the card. It had a mobile number underneath the word 'fixer' and had yellow daisies printed around edges that were raised slightly. Katie ran her thumb over them.

'What do you fix?'

'All kinds of things.' The woman smiled.

'Isn't that a Mafia thing? From the movies?'

Her smile got even bigger. 'That's where I got it from. You like it?'

'Yeah. It's cool.' Katie laughed. 'But I still don't know what you mean. Do you do home repairs or what?'

'Gutters and leaky roofs? Hardly,' the woman said. 'More like marriages.'

'So you're a kind of therapist.'

'Oh, come on.' The woman's tone was vaguely chiding. 'You know exactly what I am.' She smiled and Katie noticed how incredibly white her teeth were.

At the bus stop, the blonde woman patted Katie on the shoulder. 'It was very nice to meet you. Do call me if you need anything at all.' She smiled again and Katie wondered what toothpaste she used. 'I'm always available for you, Katie Harper.'

'I'm not Harper,' Katie said. 'I'm Katie Moore.' But the woman was already walking away.

Gwen walked past Cam's secretary and she jumped up. 'He's fully booked today—'

'It's fine, Melissa. I've got an appointment.'

'I make the appointments,' Melissa said.

Gwen was too keyed up to stop and argue about it. She opened Cam's door. 'Is now a good time?'

Cam stood up when he saw her. 'Um. Yes. It's fine.'

'I'm sorry,' Melissa said over Gwen's shoulder. 'I tried to stop her.'

'It's fine. Thank you.'

Gwen sat on the edge of the desk and then stood up again quickly. 'Sorry, I forgot.'

But Cam wasn't looking cross. He was looking slightly stunned. 'That's okay,' he said, 'it's a comfy desk. You look different.'

Gwen reached up and felt the back of her neck. 'I got a haircut.'

'It's different.'

'You called.' Gwen smoothed down the skirt of her dress, the material settling silkily around her hips. 'I wasn't sure if you meant to come down right away or later.'

'Now's good,' Cam said.

'I think I just made an enemy out there.' Gwen nodded to the door, behind which she imagined Melissa was fashioning weaponry from the stationery supplies.

'Oh, don't worry; she's a bit over-zealous sometimes,' Cam said, still staring.

Gwen nodded. 'So, where's the fire? I'm not being sued again, am I?'

'No. But there is something I need to tell you about.' Cam seemed to be finding it difficult to talk to her face; his gaze kept ranging lower to the dipping neckline of her dress.

'Okay.' Gwen smiled at him encouragingly. If she'd known it would have this effect on him, she'd have put on a frock ages ago.

'An article in the *Guardian*.' He took a deep breath. 'I'll sue them for defamation if you like.'

'Hang on. *What* article?'

Cam opened the weekend edition and slid it across the desk. Gwen scanned the text, trying to ignore the photograph of Stephen Knight as a slightly spotty kid scowling for his school picture.

'It's in the magazine bit. I don't think anyone from around here is going to read it. I wouldn't even have seen it if—' He broke off.

'Your mother gave it to you,' Gwen said. 'She's determined, gotta give her that.'

'She's just being protective. She's worried about anything that might reflect badly on the firm. It's common knowledge that we're acquainted.'

'Acquainted?' Gwen repeated.

'I didn't mean it like that,' Cam said. 'I just mean that's the bit that's public knowledge. There's nothing wrong with keeping your private life private. Speaking of which . . . Did you speak to this journalist?'

'No,' Gwen said, furious that he felt the need to ask. 'Surely you know this is the last thing I want?'

Cam shrugged. 'Publicity can be good. For your business. And I don't know what other services you provide . . .' He trailed off when he saw her expression. 'Sorry. So you didn't, then?'

Gwen ignored him and concentrated on scanning the article. She finished and sank into the nearest chair. 'I feel sick.'

'No one round here will have even read this.'

'It says Pendleford in the headline; I think they will.'

'Yeah, but most of the people around here don't read the nationals.'

Gwen wanted to be comforted by Cam's intellectual snobbery, but she'd met enough of the locals not to be convinced. 'We're in Wiltshire, not on Mars. Plenty of people commute to London, for crying out loud.' Gwen felt another lurch in her stomach. 'Oh, Christ; everyone is going read it.'

'So what?' Cam said. 'You haven't done anything wrong. And I bet there's loads of stuff in there that isn't even true. Let me send them a scary letter, get them to print a retraction.'

Gwen shook her head. 'It's pretty accurate, actually.'

Cam looked sceptical. 'What, about the witchcraft bit? That's clearly nonsense.'

'People did accuse me and my family. That's all it says and that definitely happened.'

'Well, they're clearly crazy. No one with any sense will give that credence.'

'You don't understand. People will think the worst, anyway. No smoke without fire and all that bollocks. It was like that last time. This is just going to stir it all up.'

'What happened?' Cam's forehead creased. 'Did you know the kid? He was at your school?'

'I didn't hurt him. I didn't even know him. Some kids came forward at the time and said I was secretly in love with him, saying I was a crazy rejected girl. I didn't put a spell on him or hypnotise him into killing himself or any of that. But I did use the Finding when he went missing. That's how I knew where his body was. I didn't push him in the river—'

'Of course you didn't,' Cam said, shocked.

'But I did use magic – or whatever you want to call it – to find him. I just didn't know I was going to be finding his body. I thought I might be able to help.' Gwen realised she was crying.

Cam came out from behind his desk and wrapped his arms around her. 'I'm sorry. I didn't know this was going to upset you. '

Gwen sniffed. 'I never talked about it at the time. I was too frightened to speak to you about it.'

'Wait.' Cam pulled back to look at her face. 'You were frightened of me?' He looked horrified.

'Not of you. Of your reaction.' She pulled a face. 'I thought it would be the same as your mother's is now.'

'She's just being protective of me. Well, the firm. She's obsessed with how many clients we have. We've lost a few recently and she thinks it's to do with a loss of confidence. You can't really blame her for worrying. The firm means everything to her.'

'But this is nothing to do with the firm.'

'If people know we're together . . .'

'We're not together. We're just friends.'

'I don't think you and I will ever be just friends,' Cam said. He didn't look thrilled about it.

At once Gwen felt angry. 'I loved you, but I couldn't be honest with you. I was so ashamed of my family and my powers and what had happened. I was frightened of the way you'd look at me, that you wouldn't love me any more, so I left.'

'You said you left because of my mother.'

'She was the icing on the cake,' Gwen said. She took a deep breath. 'It was complicated and, let's be honest, it's not much better now.'

The intercom buzzed. 'Mr Laing? Mr and Mrs Shaw have arrived.'

Cam pressed the button. 'Ten minutes.' He put a hand on her arm.

She felt the heat through the thin material of her dress and looked up into his eyes. 'I don't want trouble. I want to stay here. Live a quiet life.'

'Tomorrow's chip wrappings. Nothing to worry about,' Cam said. 'I'm going to put the word out that there's a journalist sniffing about. I don't think the council will want any more publicity like this and they're pretty influential.'

'I don't know. Lily's on the community council and she's the one who started this. She's friends with the journalist and brought me a load of old cuttings about the original case. I didn't realise what she was threatening at the time . . .'

'That sounds like harassment. Do you want me to apply for a restraining order?'

'Against an upstanding member of the community? Do you think that's a good idea?'

'Lawyer, remember. Any excuse for some paperwork.' Cam smiled.

Gwen felt weak with gratitude for his logical, egotistical definiteness. 'Thanks for the offer. I'll keep it in mind.' Without thinking, she went on tiptoe, intending to kiss him chastely on the cheek. He moved at the last moment and kissed her fully.

They stumbled backwards, Cam lowering Gwen onto the desk and stretching out on top of her. Gwen pulled her legs up and around him, pulling him close. The intercom was buzzing and Gwen pushed Cam away.

He looked a little dazed. 'I don't think this friendship thing is working out,' he said, reaching for her again.

'No.' Gwen sat up.

Cam helped her off the desk, smoothing down her skirt like the gentleman he was. Cool air rushed into the widening gap between them. *Come back.* 'I can't keep doing this,' Gwen said. Trying to stay rational.

'But we're good together,' Cam said. 'I'm tired of fighting that fact.'

'But the next moment you'll be running away from me. What do you really want?'

Cam frowned slightly. 'I think it's a bit early for the big relationship talk, don't you?'

'But is this a relationship at all?' Gwen said. 'Because, if so, I need to be able to be honest with you. About everything.'

'Absolutely,' Cam said.

His habitual closed expression was back in place and Gwen felt cold inside. 'I think you're wanted.' Gwen nodded to the intercom, which still sounded like an angry fly.

'I hope so,' Cam said, looking at her.

'That information is classified,' Gwen said. *Say you want all of it. Me, the Finding, everything. Say you don't care what anybody else thinks.*

Cam reached out and pulled her close. He kissed her thoroughly, which was very enjoyable but not the same thing as a declaration.

'Later?'

She smiled, even though her heart was squeezing painfully. 'Later.'

'Shall I come to you?'

Melissa popped her head around the door. 'The Shaws are getting restless, sir.'

'Send them in,' Cam said, frowning at the floor. Gwen realised that his papers were lying in drifts around the office.

Mr Shaw walked in, shooting Gwen a look that could've felled an elephant. He paused and looked at the chaos. 'What on earth?'

'Spring cleaning,' Cam said smoothly. 'Please take a seat.'

Gwen raised a hand in goodbye, then slipped away.

By eleven-thirty on Friday, Gwen had had four visitors to her back door. Amanda had come round for a cup of tea and spent half an hour wandering around the house, pointing out building jobs that needed doing. A woman Gwen vaguely recognised from the post office dropped off a gardenia in a zinc pot as an early Christmas gift. There was a brown luggage label attached which said: 'In loving memory of Iris and everything she did for my family'. Fred Byres wanted to know if Gwen had baked any more fruit cake, because it had done his chilblains 'the power of good'. Gwen gave him the salve she'd made the week before, feeling guilty that she'd forgotten about it. He squinted at the small jar, looking less than thrilled. 'Are you going to make some more of that cake, though?'

'Sure,' Gwen said, trying not to be offended. She'd looked up that bloody ointment recipe for him, spent time making it. Okay, so then she'd forgotten all about him when her own problems stepped in, but still.

'Just what's needed in this weather,' Fred was saying. 'I like to have it with hot tea. Is that right, do you think?'

It occurred to her that the actual item she gave Fred might not make any difference. The act of being cared for — even in this tiny way — was enough of a balm. In an instant she saw how alone he was, how lost without his wife.

'I'll drop one round,' she said, and was rewarded with a brief smile.

Finally, Marilyn Dixon blew into the kitchen like a force of nature. 'I can't stop, just came to see if you've got any old glass jars.'

'I do, actually. Iris left boxes of the things,' Gwen said.

'Wonderful! I'm making pickles.'

'What happened to the aromatherapy?'

'That...' Marilyn waved a hand dismissively. 'You can't eat smells. I'm making pickles, chutneys and relishes.'

Marilyn did look a little less angular than before. Healthier. It suited her.

'I've brought you some tomato, lime and chilli jam. To say thank you.'

'There was no need—'

'And I wanted to make sure we were square. No debts. No favours.'

'Of course!'

'Good,' Marilyn said robustly. 'Brian hates spicy food, you know. Said it made him feel odd.' Marilyn's face clouded for a moment.

'How are you doing?' Gwen said. It was hard not to notice that Marilyn seemed edgy. Wary. In fact, she was practically backing towards the door.

'Fine, fine.' Marilyn shrugged. 'I don't really like sleeping alone, but no doubt I'll get used to that.'

'I heard Brian moved into a flat in Trowbridge.'

Marilyn was at the door, but she hesitated. 'It's horrible. I looked it up online. It says it's got one bedroom, but it's barely more than a studio. All he can afford on his salary.' Marilyn leaned forward. 'He hadn't had a pay rise in five years, you know.'

Her tone was so spiteful that Gwen felt a spark of sympathy for Brian. She went to fetch a box of jars and loaded them into the back of Marilyn's car.

'I saw that piece in the paper,' Marilyn said. She reached into the front seat of the car and produced Iris's herbalism book. 'I've brought the plant book back. I don't want anything to do with that kind of thing.'

'Probably for the best,' Gwen said weakly, taking the book from her. 'I've never hurt anyone, you know,' Gwen said. 'No matter what you might hear.'

'Got to run,' Marilyn said. 'I'm going to yoga at one.'

'Not you, too,' Gwen said.

'Pardon?'

'Nothing.' Gwen waved her on. 'Enjoy!'

Gwen decided to get out of the house before she could have any more visitors. She walked to the Red Lion for lunch. Bob would calm her down; he was always reassuringly prosaic. And there was nothing like a man who fed you.

The fires were lit at the pub and the murmur of chat and clink of glasses instantly made Gwen feel happier. She headed for the bar to wait for Bob, then glanced through to the back room and froze. Cam and Harry were sitting at a table and they weren't alone. Two women, with identical honey-coloured hair and expensive soft-looking leather bags at their feet, were with them.

Was he on a date? Gwen felt sick.

'All right, Gwennie.' Bob appeared in front of her. 'I've been on my feet all day. All these bloody punters.'

Gwen smiled at Bob and ordered a drink. She pretended that she hadn't noticed Cam and Harry. It was none of her business. *He's free to have lunch with whoever he likes.* Her stomach swooped even lower.

Bob moved, mercifully blocking her view. 'Did you see my camper?'

Gwen shook her head.

'I got a respray. Blue.'

'Nice,' Gwen said, not paying attention.

'With flames going up the sides.'

'Cool,' Gwen said. Bob was leaning on the bar and she caught a glimpse of one of the women. She had a good profile. And she probably had normality stamped all the way through her, like a stick of rock. Gwen tried hard not to hate her.

'And I've mounted a live crocodile on the front as a peasant-clearer.'

'Nice,' Gwen said.

'You're not really interested, are you?' The hurt in Bob's tone snapped Gwen to attention. 'Crocodile?' She peered at Bob's wide sun-tanned face.

'Cam's in the back if you'd rather talk to him.' Bob smiled to soften his huffiness. 'He's prettier than me.'

'Sorry.' Gwen put a hand on his arm. 'I'm distracted.'

'I'll say.' Bob leaned over and whispered in her ear, 'If it helps, he looks fucking miserable.'

Gwen smiled. 'It really does. Thanks.'

Bob moved back. 'Now, you coming to look at my van, or not?'

'Lead the way.' Bob lifted the hatch and Gwen ducked through.

'Louise!' Bob called to the back, where his part-time staff member was clearing tables. 'I'm going out back with Gwen.'

Gwen saw Cam's head jerk up. He twisted in his seat and Gwen waved before following Bob. Cam's expression had been the Master of the Universe one, but she thought she'd seen momentary concern in his eyes and she felt incredibly cheered.

After admiring Bob's van, Gwen walked back through the pub, determined to say a cheery 'hello' to Cam and Harry and then get the hell out of there.

'Join us.' Cam stood up. He'd already pulled up another chair ready.

'Hey, Gwen,' Harry said, smiling. 'Have you met Felicity and Jemima?'

'No. Hi,' Gwen said. 'I don't want to intrude.'

'Don't be daft,' Harry said. 'You can help settle a debate. Is sushi disgusting or delicious?'

'Veggie sushi is delicious. I haven't tried the other kind.' Gwen sat down, stuffing her bag under the table.

'You can't have vegetarian sushi,' Jemima said. 'That defeats the entire purpose.'

'Well, the sushi bit only refers to the rice,' Cam said. 'So—'

'Cameron,' Felicity was looking at him with an irritated expression, 'we were talking about Christmas Eve.'

'I like salmon rolls,' Cam said. 'What about you, Harry?'

Felicity sighed. 'Can you tell your mother that I won't be able to make her bash this year?'

'Of course, no problem.' Cam seemed determined not to look at Gwen.

'Alex and I are going away for Christmas,' Felicity said. 'Skiing.'

'It won't be the same without you,' Jemima said. 'I'll be so bored. No offence,' she said to Cam.

'None taken,' he said.

'Did I see you at last year's?' Felicity asked Gwen. 'You look familiar.' She was smiling warmly and obviously trying to include Gwen in the conversation. Gwen tried to smile back. 'No. I've never been.' *I've never been invited.*

'You're not missing much,' Felicity said. 'Honestly, Cam, do you remember that one when we were ten or something? And my uncle hadn't realised you can't mix certain antibiotics with alcohol? My God, he puked everywhere. All over the buffet table, in the punch bowl, everywhere. I've never seen your mother go so white.'

Cam smiled. 'As I remember it, she was waving a ladle. I thought she was going to hit him over the head with it.'

Harry stood up and drained the last of his pint.

'You're not leaving already?' Cam said, looking up.

'I'm a very busy man.'

'No, you're not. What is it this time? *Assassin's Creed*?' Cam addressed the others. 'Harry develops regular crushes on computer games.'

'I couldn't possibly say.' Harry raised a hand. 'See you later.'

'I can't believe you're blowing me off for a game,' Cam said.

'There's more to life than sitting in the pub with you,' Harry said, grabbing his jacket from the back of the chair.

'Take that back,' Cam said.

'We'd better get going, too,' Jemima said. 'It was lovely to catch up, Cameron. You work too hard.' She gave Gwen a thin smile without any warmth. 'Nice to meet you, Jane.'

Felicity nudged her. 'Don't be a bitch.' She leaned over and kissed Cam on the cheek. 'She's always like this around you. Can't get over us not getting married.'

'You two were engaged?' Gwen felt as if the air in the room had suddenly disappeared.

'Back in primary school, perhaps.' Felicity laughed. 'But now I'm going to marry lovely, lovely Alex. He's a city boy, but he's a total sweetheart. Not a dickhead at all.'

Jemima was gathering her bag and coat. 'Your poor mother won't take that very well, will she, Cam? She's always adored Flick, hasn't she?'

'She'll survive,' Cam said, giving Jemima a cold stare.

Katie watched her dad scrape the windscreen of the car while her mum sat in the front seat, her mobile held up to her ear. It took them a couple of attempts to get out of the driveway, the wheels spinning on the icy ground, and Katie watched until the car was out of sight before collecting her supplies. In the past she would've loved her mum or dad to walk in and find her sprinkling herbs into bowls and lighting candles, but that was back then, back in what she now considered to be her childish phase. Back when she thought it was all a joke, something to wind her mum up. She'd enjoyed hiding stuff around her room, like her notebook with 'spells' written on the front, so that her mum would have a nasty shock if she went snooping. It would serve her right.

Katie wasn't playing any more.

After she'd read Imogen's cards, it was like a tap had been turned on; power just seemed to be running through her. She'd been sitting in geography, staring at the back of Luke's head, willing him to turn around *and he had*. It was like Gwen said: intention was everything. Intention had power.

Katie got down onto the floor and pulled out the bottom drawer of her bedside chest. There was a space on the floor at the back and she retrieved the Hello Kitty tin which contained her supplies. Nothing very incriminating, unless you knew what you were looking for and Katie was pretty certain that her mother knew nothing at all.

Getting Luke's hair had been the most difficult part. She'd walked past him so many times, trying to get up the nerve, had even pretended to pluck fluff off his jumper when she thought she saw a hair, but it turned out to be a long blonde one and definitely not his. In the end, she'd enlisted Imogen's help. She'd come up with a crappy story about wanting to put it into a silver locket to wear 'close to her heart'. Vomit. Imogen had accepted it, though, and in her confident, pretty way had simply tousled his hair as she'd walked past at lunchtime that same day, pretending that her hand was stuck in his hair gel and making everyone laugh.

Now she had a couple of brown hairs, a couple of inches long and the exact shade of Luke Taylor's beautiful fringe. At least she hoped so; she didn't want to end up with some random guy in love with her. Although that wouldn't be so bad. Any guy in love with her would be a huge step forward.

She dropped the hair into the mixing bowl, added the dried sage she'd got from the kitchen, and picked up the darning needle. This was it. The sticking point. Katie was not a fan of needles or blood. Or pain, for that matter. She told herself it was a test of her feelings. If she was willing to do this for Luke, then she would deserve him. Be worthy. And didn't they always go on about love and suffering in English class? Maybe there was something in it.

After a couple of false attempts, where she succeeded in first lightly denting her finger pad and then scraping the first couple of layers of skin, Katie struck gold. Well, blood. Squeezing the drops out hurt more than she expected, the end of her finger throbbing, but then it was done. She sat back on her heels and lit a match, watching it burn towards her fingertips before dropping it into the bowl. Blood, hair and herbs sizzled instantly, a rank smell escaping. Katie breathed it in, working on instinct and repeating her request over and over in her mind.

Katie was rinsing the bowl in the sink when her phone beeped. A text message from an unknown number.

hi k luke here. U ok?

Katie let out a whoop. Magic was awesome.

CHAPTER 21

20th August
Money truly means nothing when you don't have your health. I visited Robert Laing today at his request. We've never moved in the same circles, but that doesn't mean anything at a time like this. The cancer is in his stomach. I said I'd visit him every week – every day at the end. There isn't much I can do, but sometimes just being there is all that is left. Someone has to bear witness and it's often too hard on those closest to the patient. Of course, Robert Laing has the misfortune to be married to a human icicle. No doubt his soul isn't exactly clean, but that is harsh punishment enough without filling his belly with vile shadow too.

14th September
The days with Robert are mixed. He has lost his awkwardness with me and talks and talks. He's weak, but restless. He's an intelligent man and has lived an interesting life. Morally ambiguous, true, but interesting. I'm learning all kinds of new things. He insists on maintaining a façade in front of his son, which I quite understand, and in front of his wife, which seems almost sad. It's a good thing I am not a sentimental woman. He told me today that he wished he'd worked less, enjoyed the small things more. Not a startlingly original deathbed realisation, I grant you, but that doesn't make it any less true.

7th October

If there is one thing you can say about Robert Laing, he has been remarkably efficient. Or, at least, his illness has. He's into his final twenty-four hours of life and when I told him, he smiled for the first time in ten days. The pain is intolerable, and beyond anything I can do. I tried to tell Elaine that the end was near, but she took against me. I don't blame her. The woman was born with too little sense to balance her lack of humanity and, truly, this is a test that even the finest people fail. I take what pain I can and come home exhausted, but I know I leave far too much behind. My toenails are falling off in protest; every step hurts and, I will admit it here where no one can hear me, tonight I cursed Robert Laing's name. Selfish, but there it is.

I'll soak my feet for a little while, and drink some whisky before I go back. I can help so I must.

Katie stood in the doorway to the lounge, not sure whether to go in or not.Ruby was lying on the sofa with a box of tissues balanced on her stomach and tears streaming down her face. Katie glanced at the television, expecting a Meg Ryan film to be playing. It was off.

'Are you okay?'

Ruby nodded, swiping at her cheeks with her hands. 'Just thinking.'

'About what?' Katie perched on the arm of the sofa beside her mother's feet and waited to be fobbed off with a non-reply.

'Just thinking about your gran.' Ruby blew her nose into a tissue and folded it up neatly as she spoke. 'And your grandad. And your father and what might've happened if he hadn't been so brilliant.'

'When you got up the duff with me?'

Ruby gave a watery smile. 'What a lovely way of putting it. Yes. That.'

'But why are you crying? Aren't you happy that you got married?' Katie was going to say *and had me*, but she chickened out.

'I'm really happy…' Her voice caught and she tried again. 'I'm so happy with your father and with you, I'm very lucky and it's just hit me that Gloria – your gran – wasn't so lucky.'

Katie frowned. 'But she had you and Auntie Gwen.'

'But she had to bring us up on her own. I've been pretty hard on her, that's all. I feel a bit bad.'

'I don't remember her very well,' Katie said. 'I know you didn't get on. And that she drove your dad away. Made it so he couldn't visit. Never told him where you were and moved around loads.'

'What?' Ruby looked surprised.

Katie looked at her hands. 'I heard you say that to Dad once.'

Ruby sat up, dislodging the box of tissues. She reached out as if she was going to take Katie's hand, but then moved it back, taking a Kleenex instead and blowing her nose.

'I shouldn't have said that.'

'If it's true—'

'I have no idea,' Ruby said shortly. 'And I can't exactly call Gloria up and ask her.'

'Why not?'

'We don't have that kind of relationship,' Ruby said. 'Anyway, I don't think I should let my dad off the hook so easily. He was a grown man. He could've stayed or visited or written to me.'

'Maybe we could go and visit Gran. In Oz.'

Her mother looked suddenly very tense and Katie wished she could reach out and take the words back.

Instead she said, 'It's a long way, though. Expensive.'
Katie stood up. 'Do you want a cup of tea?'

Her mother raised her eyebrows, looking more like
herself.

'What?' Katie said, putting a hand on her hip. 'I make
tea.'

'This I have to see.'

Katie walked to the kitchen with her mother trailing
behind. At the door, Ruby grabbed her suddenly in an
unexpected hug. Katie stiffened for a moment and then
hugged her back.

Gwen stood between twin stone lions and rang the
doorbell, fighting the overwhelming sensation of being
eighteen all over again.

Elaine Laing's maid answered the door and led the way
through a tiled hall and into a pale and elegant sitting room.
Elaine, looking identically pale and elegant, rose from
her perch on a delicate green chair, and greeted Gwen.

'Please, sit.'

Gwen had heard warmer tones from the self-service
tills in Tesco, but she chose the sturdiest-looking chair
and sat down.

'Would you like some tea?'

'No, thank you, I'm fine.'

Gwen swallowed, trying to formulate the right words.
Elaine saved her the trouble by launching in. 'I'm glad
you've come, actually. There's something I've been
meaning to speak to you about.'

'Okay,' Gwen said. She had a feeling she knew where
this was going.

'It's a little delicate,' Elaine said.

'You want me to stop seeing Cam.' Gwen decided to
cut to the chase. This visit was going to be hard enough
without dragging things out.

Elaine's lips twitched. 'Precisely.'

'I think we've been here before.'

'I'm not saying you have to leave town this time.' Elaine paused. 'Unless you wanted to, that is.'

'I'm very happy here,' Gwen said stiffly. 'It feels like home.'

'Of course it does,' Elaine said. 'It would be expensive to move, too, I'm sure. I'd be happy to help with the costs.'

'You want to give me money for moving?'

Elaine shrugged imperceptibly. 'Or not. It's your choice.'

'I can't believe this.' Gwen sat back in her chair. She'd been prepared for a chilly welcome, but this was ridiculous.

'Don't take it personally.' Elaine leaned forward and, for a moment, Gwen thought she was going to reach out and pat her hand. 'This is just business.'

'It's kind of hard not to take it personally.'

'I'm sorry,' Elaine said, not sounding it. 'But, really, it's not as if you two are serious.'

'I remember that line from last time. You might want to get some new material.'

'This isn't a joke.' Elaine pursed her lips. 'I am aware that I am interfering and I'm also aware that my son will not be pleased that I am interfering. I know that my actions might seem extreme or overly controlling—'

'Now, who could possibly think that?'

'But they come from the heart. I want the best for him.'

'And I'm not the best thing for him?'

'It's not personal, dear. It's not about your qualities as an individual.' Elaine looked distinctly unsure about this. 'Cam wants the firm to be a success and I'm sure you want that too. For him.'

'I want Cam to be happy,' Gwen said.

'Wonderful. Then you agree. A fresh start. You'll like that.'

'I don't see what is so bad about Cam being with me. Why would that affect the business? And don't say reputation—'

'But that's what it comes down to. People might find your work – diverting – some people might even want to avail themselves of your services, but don't ever mistake that for liking you.'

Gwen wasn't going to get into a discussion about services she might or might not be providing to people. It was none of Elaine Laing's business and countering 'making potions' with 'finding lost things' probably wasn't going to be very convincing. Instead she said, 'What has liking got to do with providing legal services? If you want people to like you, I've got to say being a lawyer is not the way forward.'

'People trust us, though. You can dislike your lawyer, but you've got to trust him.'

Gwen shook her head. 'I still don't see what this has to do with Cam's private relationship with me. It's not like I'm a criminal.'

Elaine folded her hands neatly in her lap. 'I am not going to discuss your merits as a person. This is not about you; this is about your family's unfortunate reputation which, sadly, you are clothed in.'

'So this isn't because you hate me, but because you hated my aunt.'

Elaine stiffened. 'I didn't even know your aunt.'

'That's a lie.'

'I beg your pardon?'

'It's okay. I understand, but it's a lie and we both know it's a lie, so can we move on?'

Elaine's face twisted, and Gwen caught a glimpse of the anger and pain contained within Elaine's pastel twin-set. It wasn't pretty. 'Iris was a witch,' Elaine said. 'She was an embarrassment to the community, a liability to the firm.'

'So you've decided that I can't live in End House. Because I'm related to her.'

'You can live wherever you choose.' Elaine's eyes darted left as she spoke. 'I just thought you might be more comfortable in a less quiet town. Somewhere more bohemian.'

'But you want me out of my aunt's house?' The flicker of guilt behind Elaine's eyes made Gwen realise something: Elaine had stolen the title deeds to End House. Right from the beginning, she'd wanted to get rid of her. She'd taken out insurance in case she couldn't simply order her away like last time. Gwen hadn't even been given a chance. 'I know you took the title deeds,' she said, letting the anger show in her voice.

Elaine froze, her tea cup suspended halfway to her mouth.

'They weren't in the file when I picked up the keys, but I didn't really think about it until now.'

Elaine replaced the cup onto the saucer. The gentle chime of china on china rang in the sudden silence. 'That is a very serious allegation.'

Elaine had gone very pale, and a part of Gwen almost felt sorry for her. Almost. 'I understand that you don't want me around and I understand that you're desperate to protect Cam.' Gwen took a deep breath. 'I want to clear the air between us and, to be honest, I've got enough problems without worrying about you and whatever you're planning.'

Elaine licked her lips. 'I'm sure that we can come to some kind of arrangement. There must be something you want.'

'I'm not leaving this time. I love it here and I love your son.' Gwen swallowed the lump that had formed in her throat. 'I'm not running away and I'm not Iris. I don't know why you hated her so much, but I'm not my great-aunt. I'm not your enemy.'

Elaine looked at the floor. She was silent for so long that Gwen was beginning to wonder if this was Elaine's way of dismissing her from the room.

Finally, she looked up. 'It was her fault.' Elaine was squeezing words out from behind clenched teeth. Her face was a horror mask. 'It was her fault he died.'

'Who? Mr Laing?'

'Cameron's father,' Elaine said. 'It was Iris Harper's fault.' She reached into the pocket of her cardigan and produced a handkerchief.

'What happened?' Gwen said. 'I know he was very ill.'

'Stomach cancer.' Elaine dabbed at her eyes.

'And Iris visited him, didn't she?'

'She said she could help. He trusted her.'

'Did she say she could cure him?'

Elaine's face twisted again. 'No.'

'And what did your husband say?' Gwen felt it was important, suddenly, to make Elaine understand; Iris hadn't done anything wrong. She'd done her best to help.

'He was desperate. He was in so much pain. Even the morphine didn't take it away.'

'But what did he say?'

Elaine was far away now; she was looking in Gwen's direction, but seeing something else entirely. 'He said that she comforted him.'

Gwen flinched at the raw pain in her voice and, feeling like the worst kind of bully, she said: 'You're angry because he turned to someone else.'

'I was his wife,' Elaine said. She sounded like a lost child and Gwen felt awful. Then she added, 'Imagine how it *looked*,' and Gwen felt a little better.

'This is not the same, and I'm not Iris,' Gwen said. 'You can't push me out of town. Not this time. And I won't let you steal my house.'

'I haven't the faintest idea what you are talking about.' Elaine was trying to claw back her composure, but her face was flushed and her voice shook.

'I don't think Cam would be very pleased to hear that you stole documents from the firm, but I'm willing to keep quiet about that if you stop trying to break us up.'

Elaine's eyes flashed. 'He won't believe you.'

'Maybe not,' Gwen said. 'You want to risk it?'

After a moment of seething thought, Elaine said, 'Fine.'

'You have to stop pressuring Cam to break things off. And let Lily know that she has to drop this legal case against me. If the title deeds to the house appear back in the folder – which I will leave on my kitchen table for the next few days – then I will simply assume they got there by magic.'

'I agree to your terms.' Elaine spoke as if every word was an effort.

Gwen thought about Felicity and the Christmas Eve parties. She imagined Elaine pushing suitable young women at Cam, like a linen-wearing pimp. 'You have to invite me to the house and make me welcome.'

Elaine opened her mouth to argue, but Gwen pressed on. 'If you don't, I will not only tell Cam everything, but I will also give Ryan a juicy story for the paper. Insider theft within Laing and Sons; it won't look good.'

Elaine closed her mouth with a snap. Her eyes looked murderous. 'You wouldn't do that. It would hurt Cameron, too.'

'You hurt him all the time by trying to control him.'

'I only do what's best for him.'

'You're lucky his teenage rebellion involved sleeping with an unsuitable girlfriend. It could've been spectacular. Do we have a deal?'

Elaine inclined her head.

'Excellent.' Gwen stood up. 'I brought you something.' She unzipped her bag and pulled out the notebook. 'Iris kept a journal. This one has a few entries about Mr Laing. She wasn't very nice about you, I'm afraid, but I thought you might've been wondering about what they talked about.'

'I didn't enquire about my husband's private business,' Elaine said stiffly.

'Well, you should have.' Gwen put the book down on a side table. 'I'll see myself out.'

Elaine didn't say anything and Gwen made her way through the echoing hall to the front door. She didn't know if she had just left a comfort blanket or a bomb, but it seemed as if that journal belonged more to the Laings than it did to her. And you didn't get to choose your inheritance.

Within minutes of leaving Elaine's house, Gwen's bravado fled. Her hands shook and she felt prickles of sweat on her neck. In her anxiety, she felt as if every second person was looking at her sideways. As if they distrusted her. Disliked her. Elaine's attitude hit her all over again and her eyes prickled. *Freak. Not good enough. Weirdo. Odd one out.*

A woman tightened her grip on her toddler's hand as she passed Gwen. Perhaps she was simply preparing to cross the road, but Gwen felt it as another slap in the face. She decided to go to the pub. At least she could be sure of a welcome there.

Bob was out from behind the bar, wiping down tables and laying out cruet sets for the lunch crowd. Gwen threw her bag down on the table nearest the fire and herself into a comfy chair.

'All right, Gwennie?' Bob said. 'How's tricks?'

'Is that supposed to be funny?'

Bob grinned. 'Just an expression.'

Gwen shoved her bag out of the way and laid her head dramatically on the scarred surface of the table. 'Everyone hates me. I'm a disaster. I should just leave. Oh, no. I forgot, I can't because I've got no money. No career.' She was about to add *no boyfriend*, but was beginning to sound pathetic even to herself.

'From what I hear, you're the hero of the hour,' Bob said.

Gwen lifted her head to look at him. 'What?'

Bob swiped his cloth around. 'Oh, yes, Fred says his chilblains have never felt better. Isn't that right, Jack?' Bob called out to an old man in a tired brown suit. Gwen had seen him before and he always seemed to be seated in exactly the same place, wearing the same suit. Perhaps he had a whole wardrobe of identical outfits, but Gwen doubted it. Jack raised rheumy eyes from the newspaper that he held close to his face. 'What's right?'

'Our Gwennie is a regular hero.'

'She's a good girl.' Jack nodded. He gave Gwen a rare smile, showing uneven teeth, then disappeared behind his paper.

'You keep up like this, they'll build you a bloody statue,' Bob said.

'No, thank you,' Gwen said, trying not to think about the little memorial to Jane Morely on the wall of the pub.

'Suit yourself.' He shrugged. 'Half the town thinks you're some kind of guardian angel, anyway.'

Bob's friendly smile wasn't enough to make Gwen ignore the flaw in his sentence. 'What about the other half, though?' she said. 'What have they been saying?'

Bob looked away. 'You don't want to worry about that.'

'They think I'm a fraud. That I'm playing some long con. That one day, they'll wake up and I'll be gone with the town's riches in my back pocket, or that I'm corrupting the town's youth, or bringing shame onto Pendleford and ruining its reputation and its chance for development grants or tourism or whatever.'

'Whoa, there, Gwennie.' Bob waved his bottle of cleaner. 'Not so dramatic. I don't think most people have thought about it that much.'

'Some have,' Gwen said, 'and, unfortunately, they tend to be pretty vocal.'

'Have you thought about answering back?' Bob said.

'That doesn't usually work out that well for me,' Gwen said, thinking of Ruby.

'Maybe you need to raise your voice,' Jack said unexpectedly. He didn't look up from his paper or speak again so Gwen looked at Bob. He raised his eyebrows and shrugged, as if to say: *the octogenarian with alcohol-dependency issues has a point.*

Gwen shook her head. 'Haven't you heard that phrase "the lady doth protest too much"? Who on earth is going to believe a word I say, however loudly I say it?'

Bob retreated behind the bar. 'You're the one with all the brains, Gwennie, but if I were you, I'd think about something concrete. Evidence for the defence kind of thing.'

Gwen closed her eyes. Even vaguely legal jargon made her think about Cam. Made her feel a little bit turned on, truth be told. She blinked quickly and got the hell out of the pub before she embarrassed herself in front of Bob and the town's oldest barfly.

I wish Gloria would let me see the girls or, at least, give them the choice. I'm old enough to know that life isn't

*fair, but I've spent the last fifty years giving people what
they need, whether I've wanted to do it or not, even when
it's made people hate or fear me; it doesn't seem right.
And not just for myself. Poor Gwen will be coming into
her gift all alone. She only has Gloria to guide her and
that's worse than nothing. Gloria will teach her that you
help only when you see benefit to yourself and that is not
a good path to walk. It leads to some very dark places.*

Gwen clipped the entry out and added it to the pile
that she counted as 'hers'. She had several piles, now,
each with a Post-it note stuck on the top and a person
or family's name, as well as a non-magical recipes pile,
one full of herbalist cures, and the notebook for Ruby.
She looked at the few sheets which bore Helen Brewer's
name and wondered if she was being punished for
taking money for finding Archie. If she was completely
honest, she'd felt a creeping guilt about that ever since.
The letter from Christopher's solicitor had been almost
a relief. As if her comeuppance had finally arrived and
she could deal with it. Being sued for defamation of
character wasn't top of her bucket list, but it could be
worse. And Cam had said that Christopher didn't have a
snowball's chance in hell anyway.

Across town, Gwen parked her car in Helen Brewer's
quiet cul-de-sac and rang the doorbell before she could
think about it too much.

'What do you want?' Helen didn't take the security
chain off, but she didn't slam the door shut either. Gwen
tried to feel cheered by this.

'May I come in?'

'Christopher isn't here.'

The tip of Helen's nose was bright red. Whether from
cold or crying, Gwen couldn't tell. 'I wanted to talk to
you, actually. Five minutes?'

Helen shook her head violently. 'It won't do any good. I can't control Christopher.'

'That's okay. It's not about that.'

Helen shut the door and Gwen heard the chain jangle. It opened again and Helen stepped backwards. 'Five minutes.'

The house was just as Gwen remembered it; unnaturally tidy and filled with more pastel colours than seemed sensible with a dog. She perched on the pale pink sofa. 'How's Archie?'

'Fine,' Helen said. 'Thank you,' she added, looking embarrassed.

'I just came to bring you something.' Gwen wished she'd planned something to say. It suddenly seemed unbelievably awkward. 'I've been going through my great-aunt's papers.'

Helen went very still.

'And I feel a bit weird about it, really. She kept lots of notes, like diaries, but not really about her own life.'

'Stuff about other people.' Helen's voice was barely a whisper.

Gwen stood up to pull the folded sheets of paper from her back pocket. She passed it across. 'I don't know what to do. I don't want to know this stuff, so I was just going to burn the lot, but it doesn't really feel like my property.'

Helen read the notes quickly, blushing. 'You could use this against Christopher. Get him to drop the stupid legal thing. I told him not to sue you. I told him—'

'That would be blackmail,' Gwen said. 'I wish I hadn't read this and I'd rather just forget that I did. It's none of my business.'

Helen gave her a long look. 'You're very different to Iris.'

'Good,' Gwen said. 'I think.'

Helen folded the pages. 'I'm sorry about Christopher. It turned out you were right about him. I saw him kick Archie. On Monday night, when he thought I was at bridge.'

'I'm sorry,' Gwen said.

Helen shook her head. 'I thought I'd raised him better than that.'

Gwen stood up. 'Well, thank you for seeing me.'

Helen rose and walked her to the door. The wind had picked up and was howling outside, a cold draught flowing in from the badly fitted letterbox.

'I'll see what I can do,' Helen said suddenly. 'I'm sure Christopher will drop this nonsense when he realises I won't back him up.'

'I really appreciate it,' Gwen said carefully.

'He kicked my dog,' Helen snapped. 'It's nothing to do with you.'

'Right. Bye, then.' Gwen was halfway down the path when Helen called out, 'You should burn it all. But make sure everyone knows you've done it.' Then she raised her hand in a half-wave and shut the door.

Gwen got into Nanette and turned the heater up full. It wasn't a bad idea, actually. Holding a public bonfire might make her look like a lunatic, but appearing normal didn't seem to be on the cards any more. *In for a penny . . .*

Back at home, Gwen looked up the number for *The Chronicle* on Ruby's second-best laptop and dialled. The helpful woman who answered the phone explained that Ryan was on his lunch break and, with minimal prompting, that he was taking it at The Red Lion.

Twenty minutes later, Gwen walked into the pub. Both fires were blazing and Gwen, already warm from her speed-walk into town, pulled off her coat and scarf.

'All right, Gwennie?' Bob hailed her, then turned his attention back to the pint he was pulling. The place was packed and Gwen was surprised at just how many people she recognised. Stranger yet were the number of nods, smiles and greetings as she made her way to the back room.

Ryan was sitting on his own, his back to Gwen. She had no trouble recognising him, though, and complimented herself for her restraint in not slapping the back of his rosy-red neck. There was a spare chair at the little table and she sat down. Ryan looked up and did a double-take. 'Um—' he began, less than brilliantly.

'I'll be honest with you,' Gwen said, stealing one of Ryan's chips and pointing it at his chest. 'You're not my favourite person at the moment.'

'What?' Ryan seemed mesmerised by the chip, but he managed to drag his attention to Gwen's face. 'What do you want?'

'I want to put an advert in the paper but I'm broke, so I want you to write an article instead so it doesn't cost me anything.'

'And why would I do that?' Ryan said.

'Why wouldn't you? I thought this town was all about being neighbourly.' Gwen bit the chip. It was cold so she put the other half onto the edge of Ryan's plate. His gaze followed it and she said, 'Don't worry; I haven't got a cold or anything.'

Ryan looked her in the eye with what appeared to be some effort. 'I don't owe you any favours.'

'I was thinking more from the goodness of your heart,' Gwen said. 'Or, perhaps, to cleanse your soul a little after that unfortunate rabbit incident.' Suddenly the hurt and anger of that moment flooded back and Gwen leaned forward. 'My niece could've found that poor creature. Did you even think of that?'

'I didn't have anything to do with—' Ryan said quickly. Then he caught himself. 'I don't know what you're talking about.'

'Nice save.' Gwen selected a slice of cucumber from Ryan's side salad and gestured with it. 'Just run the piece.'

'Or what?' Ryan said, lifting his chin and trying to look tough.

Gwen fixed him with her best steely stare. 'Use your imagination,' she said, and popped the cucumber slice into her mouth.

'This is insane,' Ryan said. 'What did you want me to write about, anyway? The paper won't publish it if it isn't in the public interest.'

'It's as much in the public interest as that fascinating piece on Martin Bower's prize-winning cabbage.'

'Small town news, what do you expect?'

'It was on the front page, Ryan. Really.' Gwen shook her head. 'I'd say you should be thanking me for filling some column inches.'

'So, what is it? What's the big story?'

'I'm holding a bonfire.'

'You're a bit late for Guy Fawkes.'

Gwen ignored him. 'On the green outside here on Saturday night.'

'You can't do that,' Ryan said. 'There are rules, by-laws, all kinds of permits.'

'I've cleared it with the council and the community council and with Bob in the pub. When I say bonfire, I'm being symbolic, really. It's more of a brazier.'

'A brazier.' Ryan frowned. 'What the hell?'

'Bob is lending it to me. He uses it in the garden.'

'I don't really understand—'

'That's okay. Here are all the details.' Gwen put the article she'd carefully typed up that morning. 'I'd like it in Thursday's edition.' She pushed back her chair, the legs scraping on the stone floor.

'You can't just expect—' Ryan said and Gwen lost it. She leaned over the table, her face close to his and said, very quietly, 'Don't fuck with me, Ryan. I'm not known for my patience and I reached the bottom of the barrel a long time ago. *I know you broke into my house.*' Gwen was only guessing on that last point, but she figured that Lily didn't have too many friends to call on. Ryan swallowed and then nodded.

Gwen straightened up. 'Excellent. Thank you.'

CHAPTER 22

Gwen was investigating the overgrown herbs in the garden when she heard the telephone. It was Harry, sounding less calm than usual. 'Are you busy? Can you get down to Cam's office?'

'What's wrong?' If another person was taking legal action . . .

'It's Cam. Do you know about his granddad?'

Gwen went cold. 'What's happened?'

'He died last night. Cam found him.'

'Oh no.'

'Can you come?'

'Why don't you call Felicity?'

Harry didn't say anything. He just stayed silent long enough for Gwen to feel petty and stupid. 'Fine,' she said. 'I'll be there in ten minutes.'

'Thank you,' Harry said politely.

'Do you think he'll want me there?' Gwen asked quickly before Harry could hang up.

'Christ, Gwen. I don't know what he wants. He's trying to take out all the furniture in his office. It's built-in, though, so it's—' Harry broke off and Gwen heard a muffled struggle. Harry came back on the line slightly out of breath. 'He's going to rupture something.'

Gwen got to the firm in time to see Elaine Laing putting on her coat in the reception area.

'I've sent Melissa home and I advise you to do the same. This is a family matter.'

'Where are you going?' Gwen said.

Elaine coloured slightly. 'There's no reasoning with him right now. It's best to just let him cool off.'

A crash sounded and Harry's face appeared in the doorway. 'Gwen! Hi-ya. Come and join the party.'

Elaine leaned in close, startling Gwen. 'If you breathe a word of this—' she began.

Gwen faced her. 'If you took the time to get to know me, you'd know how insulting that was. I'm just like my great-aunt and I'll take your secrets to the grave.'

Elaine took a step back as if Gwen had slapped her. 'You can't talk to me like—'

Gwen ignored her and went into Cam's office.

Cam was wearing a black T-shirt and smart trousers. His dark blue shirt and suit jacket were laid neatly over the back of his chair. He was unscrewing the hinges from a cabinet hidden amongst the wood panelling.

'Hello,' Gwen said. 'Have you been to bed yet?'

Cam glanced over his shoulder, then began pulling at the door. 'He died in his office, you know. I found him in his office. At his *fucking* desk.'

'I heard.' Gwen glanced at Harry, who made a face.

'My dad was buried with his whisky glass in one hand.' Cam heaved and the door popped free. 'That's what I used to say. It was a joke, but it wasn't very funny. I can't picture him without it. Sitting here, behind this desk, that bloody glass in his hand.'

'All right, mate,' Harry said. 'You want to put the door down?'

Cam looked at the piece of wood in his hand as if surprised to find it there. 'I just thought it was time for a change.'

'Have you slept yet?' Cam had found his grandfather just before midnight. He must've been up for over thirty-six hours and it showed.

'Too much to do,' Cam said. 'Busy.'

'Melissa called all your clients,' Harry said. 'You should go home and get some rest.'

'Can't.' Cam waved the cabinet door for emphasis. 'We're in trouble, you know. Got to show a united front. Got to show that Laing and Sons is strong and that we can provide a continued, unbroken service. Any sign of weakness not allowed. You know how it is.'

'Come back to mine,' Gwen said. 'I'll make you some food and you can take a nap. You can come back to work later, if you want.'

Cam turned his bloodshot eyes onto Gwen and seemed to see her properly for the first time.

She smiled encouragingly, gently. 'Come and rest. Regain your strength and you can get straight back to whatever it is you're doing.'

'I'm taking this out.' Cam gestured to the bottles and glasses arranged on shelves. 'Gotta move with the times. Be a dynamic, forward-thinking firm.' A look of anguish crossed his face.

'Absolutely.' Gwen nodded. 'Tell me about it on the way, okay?'

Harry was parked right outside in an unmarked car. He drove them to End House, Cam staring and silent.

Later, after Gwen had convinced Cam to eat some buttered toast and drink a mug of tea, he asked if he could stay.

'Of course.'

'This is so stupid,' he said finally. 'I wasn't like this when my dad died.' Gwen turned her back while he shed some clothes and got into bed.

Gwen sat on the edge of the bed. 'What was your dad like? You never talk about him.'

'When he died I was so angry.' Cam closed his eyes. 'So fucking angry. I don't even remember feeling sad. That's not good, is it? That's not right.'

'I don't—'

'I mean, I was sad, but it was just overlaid with all the other stuff. I knew that it was the end of my life. Him dying.' Cam gave a short laugh. 'That sounds a bit dramatic, but I knew that was it. No more choices. No more music. No more London.'

'Is that when you decided to study law?'

'Decided isn't the word.' Cam gave her a wry smile. 'That's when I felt the heavy sword of family obligation fall squarely on my head. I knew I had to take up Dad's place. I'd always known it would happen eventually, but I thought I'd have more time or that something would happen to change things. I don't know.'

'It's understandable that you were angry. You felt trapped.'

Cam looked at her. 'I was trapped. And I hated him for it.'

Gwen reached for his hand, squeezed tightly. She knew how it felt to inherit stuff you didn't ask for or want. She knew that trapped feeling all too well. 'You should be proud of yourself. You stepped up and looked after your family. And if you hate it now, perhaps…'

Cam blinked. 'Thank you for this,' he said. He ran his hand over his face and looked at his wet hand with surprise. 'I don't know why I'm crying. I didn't even like my grandfather very much. And he was so old. It's not exactly a tragedy.'

'I don't think that's how grief works.'

'But I shouldn't be grieving at all, that's my point.'

Gwen shrugged. 'That's emotion for you, refuses to follow logic.'

Cam blew his nose, then laid his head back on the pillow. 'I'm actually really tired. Is it okay if I go to sleep? Just a quick nap.'

'Of course.' Gwen stood up to leave.

'Will you stay with me? Lie down here.' He lifted the quilt and patted the mattress next to him. 'I promise to keep my hands to myself.' A faint smile, the ghost of the normal Cam.

'Sure.' Gwen took off her cardigan and jeans and got into the bed. She lay in the half-dark and listened to Cam's breathing. Just when she thought he'd gone off, he rolled over on his side, facing her. 'I don't know what my dad was like. I didn't really know him.'

Gwen didn't know what to say to that. *Sorry*? 'Go to sleep; you'll feel better tomorrow.'

Gwen turned on her side and, a moment later, felt Cam's arm across her body.

Cam was his usual capable self in the morning. Over the next couple of days, he kept Gwen up to date with the ongoing nightmare of funeral arrangements and work and his mother's unceasing devotion to outward appearances. He arrived at End House late every night, worn out from soothing concerned clients and organising a hundred tiny details. 'Thank God you're here,' he said into her hair as they lay together. She knew that it was vaguely inappropriate, but a wild bubble of happiness accompanied her every move. She knew that they'd turned a corner. Cam had come to her for comfort. That had to mean something.

Gwen pushed the hair from out of her eyes and leaned over the baking dish once again. She felt like she'd been filling cannelloni for ever. The first three batches had mysteriously burned, while remaining uncooked on the inside. This one, the fourth attempt, was going to cook perfectly. Gwen didn't care if she had to open the oven every two minutes; they were not going to burn. She eyeballed the cannelloni and told them sternly, 'Not on my watch. Not again.'

'Knock knock.' Cam pushed open the door. 'Is this a bad time?'

'Not at all.' Gwen tried not to show how pleased she was to see him. The last thing Cam needed was more pressure in his life. 'Did you hear me talking to the cannelloni?'

'Little bit.'

Gwen hoped the fact that she was already flushed from cooking would hide her embarrassment. 'Come on in.'

Cam unlaced his boots before stepping out of them. He wrinkled his nose as the smell of burnt pasta hit.

'I know, I know.' She frowned. 'Nothing is coming out right any more. I used to be such a good cook.' *I think my oven has been hexed.*

'What's going on?'

Gwen looked away. 'I'm just distracted.' Like she could tell Cam about phantasms and cursed appliances. He'd have her sectioned.

'Nothing to do with your weird witchy powers, then?'

'The weird powers that you don't believe in?'

'The very same.'

Gwen paused. 'No.'

'You're lying,' Cam said mildly. He crossed the room, stepping over Cat until he was very close to Gwen. She tried to take a step back, but felt the counter edge on her back.

'Gwen Harper. Tell me what is going on.' He ducked his head to look into her eyes. 'Please?'

It was the please that did it. Gwen side-stepped neatly away. 'I need to get back to my cannelloni.' She wasn't going to bring up Lily Thomas or Iris's journals or the people that still kept turning up at her back door asking for help she couldn't give or any of it. She wasn't going to be another burden, another problem for Cam to solve. His face was lined with fatigue and worry and grief. She put her hand out and touched his cheek. 'Was there something you needed?'

Cam shot out an arm and grabbed Gwen around the waist. 'You are leaving me with no choice.'

Gwen started to speak, but found herself unable to finish. Cam's lips were soft upon hers and her thought processes were momentarily derailed. She wanted, more than anything, to sink into him. The solid, reassuring, wonderful-smelling bulk of him. Instead, she pulled herself together and pulled away. Cam's arms tightened around her, hauling her back. He kissed her again.

'No,' she said. 'I need to finish the pasta.'

'Sod the pasta.'

Gwen laughed and kissed him back.

'So, here's what's going to happen.' Cam tightened his arms around her. 'We're going to go upstairs and get naked and horizontal and very, very happy.'

Gwen felt the blush increase in intensity. In fact, she thought, her head was going to catch on fire any second.

'And, after that, when I've got you nice and relaxed, you're going to talk to me. You're going to tell me what is going on and I'm going to help you.'

Gwen opened her mouth to speak, realised she had no idea what to say, and closed it again.

Later, Gwen snuggled in close to Cam, breathing in the smell of him and enjoying the sensation as he stroked her hair.

'Shouldn't we have "the talk"?'

'I already know about the birds and bees.' She heard the smile in his voice.

'Don't I know it,' Gwen said, snuggling closer. 'No. The one about our exes. Past relationships.'

'No thanks.'

She lifted her head to look at him. 'I don't mean we have to have a blow-by-blow account.'

'Well, that's a relief,' Cam said, cocking an eyebrow.

Gwen bit him gently. 'I'm serious. Don't you think we should talk about the important events from the last thirteen years? The people who have been important to us.'

'No.'

'Really?' She struggled to a sitting position.

'I will answer any questions you have about my past loves. . .'

Gwen winced on the word 'loves'.

'But I have no desire to know about yours.'

'Oh.' Gwen tried not to be offended. 'Aren't you even a tiny bit curious?'

'No.' He paused. 'That's not entirely true. But here's the thing. I intellectually accept that we have been apart for a long time and that you will have had relationships with other men. I accept that as a logical fact. I don't need details.'

Gwen was quiet, marvelling at his self-control. His self-possession. It was scary.

'I will say this, though.' Cam reached up and cupped her cheek with his palm. 'I've been living my life, thinking I'm reasonably happy and that this is as good as it gets, but now you're back I realise how wrong I was. It was a pale imitation of happiness. I haven't felt like this about anybody or anything else. Ever.'

'Oh.'

'Does that cover it?'

Gwen nodded, unable to speak.

'Good.' He patted the mattress. 'Now come here.'

Much later, after Gwen had dozed off and woken up
and found Cam's arms still tightly wrapped around her
and he'd moved and they'd begun all over again, Gwen
stretched and climbed out of bed.

'Don't go.' Cam reached for her.

'I won't be long,' Gwen said. 'I really have to finish
that cannelloni. If you're very good, I'll bring you a cup
of tea in bed.'

Cam lay back. 'Okay. I should probably rehydrate
after all that exercise.'

'Exactly.'

She felt him watching her as she pulled on her
underwear. Her bra had made it all the way underneath
the window and her socks were on top of the dressing
table. *Good throwing arm.*

'So, what's the pasta-obsession, anyway?' Cam said.

Gwen pulled her T-shirt over her head. 'It's for
the wake. For your granddad. I know your mum will
probably pay for outside catering, but it wouldn't feel
right to go empty-handed.' She did up her jeans. 'You'll
have to tell me what sort of flowers to order, too. Unless
he wanted donations to charity.' Cam's face had gone
weirdly frozen. 'What?'

'The funeral was today.'

'Oh.' For a moment, Gwen felt cold, too. Then the
numbness gave way to a single, crystal-clear thought:
he still won't ask me to be part of his world.

Cam was struggling out of bed, fighting with the
quilt. 'I didn't mention it because I didn't think you'd
want to come.'

'Right,' Gwen said. She blinked. 'Right.' The man
was bereaved. This was not the time to pick a fight.

He grabbed his shirt and began putting it on. His
startled look settled into one of certainty. 'I didn't want
you to feel obliged.'

That did it. 'Bollocks,' Gwen said. 'You didn't invite me because you're embarrassed to be seen with me. I don't belong.' *I've never belonged.*

'For Christ's sake. It was a funeral, not a party.' Cam was being defensive.

'Stop doing your Master of the Universe look,' Gwen snapped. 'Can't you just say "sorry" like a normal human being? You don't have to be right all the time.'

'But I am right. It was a family occasion. A funeral. It wasn't anything to do with you—' Cam stopped. 'I just mean—'

'I know exactly what you mean,' Gwen snapped. 'You don't think I'm good enough to be part of your life. Not properly. You're happy to sneak over here at night, but you're never going to take me out to dinner in town, be happy to be seen with me. I'm never going to be invited to your mother's fancy bloody Christmas Eve party.'

'What are you talking about?'

'I'm not Felicity, am I?'

'No.' Cam looked annoyed. 'I'm not with Felicity. I don't want Felicity. I want you.'

'Well, you don't get me,' Gwen said, feeling tears spill down her face. 'I deserve to be with someone who isn't embarrassed to be with me. I deserve someone who accepts who I am and what I do.' Gwen's voice had gone hoarse with the effort of not sobbing. Cam was staring at her as if she'd lost her mind and she realised that she didn't care. Last time she'd left Cam without a goodbye because she'd been too scared to be honest with him. She wasn't going to make the same mistake twice. 'I deserve to be with someone who is on my side. I don't care that you don't believe in magic, but I do care that you don't believe in me.'

'We'll talk about this later, when you've calmed down.' Cam laced up his shoes, grabbed his jacket.

'No.' Gwen shook her head. 'This. Us. Whatever it is. It's over.'

His face went closed, angry. 'Fine. If that's what you want.'

Gwen felt her throat close up. She thought of Elaine Laing and the triumph she'd feel. She'd thought that without Elaine dripping poison in Cam's ear, things would be different. 'I don't want a half-relationship,' she said. 'I don't want to be your dirty little secret.'

Cam shook his head. 'I've got to be practical. I've got to be sensible. People are relying on me. You have no idea how that feels.'

Gwen managed a grim smile. 'Right.'

'Especially now, with my grandfather gone. I can't afford any scandal. Any disruption.'

'I understand,' Gwen said, her insides hollowing out with misery. 'I do understand that.'

'And I can't stand that you still believe the nonsense you were fed as a child. I hate it.'

'Oh,' Gwen said, feeling sick at the coldness in his tone. 'It's good we're being honest now.'

'Did I tell you where my family's money went? Why it was so important that the firm didn't fail after my dad died?' Cam said.

'No. I assumed—'

'The firm had been doing well and Dad had made plenty of good investments. Mum should've been fine when he died. I would probably still have needed to train and take his place in the firm, but the money situation would've been okay.' Cam's voice went very quiet.

'While he was dying, my mother tried all kinds of things to make him better. Every charlatan on the block took her for a ride. Aromatherapy. Electrolyte baths. Every crackpot theory, every alternative therapy. She spent thousands.'

'I didn't know,' Gwen said.

'It wasn't like her,' Cam said. 'She's always been very logical, very intellectual. She was just so desperate.'

'My great-aunt Iris visited your dad,' Gwen said. 'But she never took his money.'

Cam hesitated, halfway out of the door. 'Well, that's something I suppose.'

'And she really helped him. Whatever she did, it helped take away some of his pain.'

'Don't,' Cam said, holding up one hand as if he could physically block her words, more angry than Gwen had ever seen him. 'Just don't.'

Gwen stood alone in the bedroom and listened to the slam of the front door.

CHAPTER 23

At Millbank, Katie stood outside the science block staring at her mobile until the tiny black characters of the text message blurred. She, quite literally, couldn't believe her luck. Of all the girls in school, of all the girls he probably knew out of school while hanging out with the cool crowd and doing daring things like going to the pubs in town or hanging out at the folly, he had chosen her. Katie Moore. She read the three texts for the thousandth time and hugged the phone to her chest.

Finally, after composing and discarding several versions in her head, she spelled out:

ok c u 2nite x

The kiss. She'd put it in, she'd taken it out. He'd used one on his last text and she didn't want him to feel stupid for doing so and she wanted to show she felt the same way but, and this was so important, not in a way that said she felt more than he did. If Katie had learned anything from films and TV, it was that no boy liked a desperate girl. Or even a keen one.

That evening, she feigned period cramps. She made a hot water bottle and, clutching it to her middle, cried off dinner.

'Are you sure?' Her mum was shredding celeriac and radishes for a Jamie Oliver recipe, the small TV on the counter showing the very same man, bish-bashing garlic and assuring the viewers that everything was 'beautiful'.

'I think I'll just go to bed. Maybe watch a movie on my laptop.'

Ruby was already looking back at her vegetables, the giant Sabatier knife flashing.

'Use your headphones if you're going to have the volume high,' she said absently.

Katie escaped upstairs. First she ate the sandwich, apple and packet of crisps she'd stashed in her room earlier. She didn't feel hungry, but the last thing she wanted was her stomach making embarrassing gurgling noises when she and Luke were alone. She felt a swirly, stabbing sensation in her midriff and wondered whether eating was going to solve the problem. Then, she began preparations. She painted her nails electric-blue and tried to read while they dried. The text kept jumping around, though, reforming into Luke's face. She put the book down and got into bed. Lying on her back and staring at the snowy peaks of the Artexed ceiling, Katie ran through every encounter of the last few weeks. Their exchanges had been short and she'd memorised them almost word for word. If she closed her eyes, she could watch them again and again, like skipping back on a DVD. When she tried to imagine what might happen tonight, what it would be like to be with him, alone and out of school, her entire body went into tingling overdrive and her mind raced so fast, it all became a blur.

Time seemed to skip. One moment, she was looking at the clock and wishing the long hours away and the next, she was creeping to her dressing table to apply eyeliner and mascara and wondering if she had enough time to change her clothes. Again.

Katie took the flask that the fixer had given her and unscrewed the top. It was white with daisies around the base, just like the woman's business card. Katie hesitated, but couldn't make herself believe that there would be anything dangerous inside a flask that cute. It was probably Vimto or something. The woman had said that she had to drink the lot in one go while thinking about what she called the 'object of her desire'. Katie closed her eyes and pictured Luke. Luke smiling at her. Then she drank. The woman had warned her that it was a herbal potion and an acquired taste. That was putting it mildly, Katie thought, as she drank the disgusting fluid. Once the flask was empty, Katie took several deep breaths, trying to stop herself from throwing it back up. It was only the thought of ruining the spell that stopped the churning in her stomach from becoming disastrous.

It was almost ten. Katie zipped up her black hoodie and pulled on her favourite blue gloves. They were fingerless and showed her newly painted fingernails perfectly. She added another silver ring to her left hand, twisting it the right way so that the moonstone faced outwards and checked the clasp on her apple necklace. She looked in the mirror and the girl looked back. She didn't look like herself. The black eyeliner and dark red lipstick made her look older, harder. Was it too much? She rubbed most of the red off with a tissue and looked again. Her cheeks were flushed and her eyes were sparkling and she thought – surprised – that she actually looked okay. It was now or never. Laughter from the TV was almost dulled by the closed living room door and Katie pictured her parents inside, cuddled up on the sofa. Her dad was probably lying with his head in her mum's lap and she'd be stroking his hair. It wasn't even that she thought it was gross. Although part of her did, a little bit. But it was more that it made her kind of ache inside. Like something was missing.

Her dad always locked the doors, even when they were all home. He said he'd seen a news story once that had made a lasting impression. She'd asked him for details, but his lips had pressed together so hard they'd gone white. Katie unlocked the back door and slipped out, locking it again behind her and pocketing the key.

She wasn't supposed to be in town at night at all, let alone on her own and without her parents' knowledge. The delicious thrill of leaving the house quickly morphed into fear as she passed a pub and the door swung open, releasing a gust of warm, stinky air, and a burst of noise. The voices sounded adult and manly, almost violent.

Katie increased her pace so that she was speed-walking along the side street. She felt both better and worse as she crossed Milsom Street. There were more people around, which felt safer, but the huddle of smokers outside the Wetherspoons seemed rough and frightening.

The crowds petered out as she crossed from one side street to another, working away from the centre and towards the leafy residential area of Bathwick. Lots of people had left their curtains open and rooms were lit up like stages. Katie saw bookcases and armchairs, fireplaces and tasteful wallpaper. Bath was so very civilised. Dead, she called it. Perfectly preserved, but soulless. She was itching for something new, something modern, something unequivocally alive. Something young. Okay, she admitted, she didn't really *know* what she wanted, but she trusted she'd recognise it when she found it.

Starting on Bathwick Hill, Katie steadfastly ignored her misgivings. Yes, it was dark and quiet and the trees were casting eerie shadows, but she wasn't going to turn back now. She'd come this far and Luke Taylor was waiting for her. She hoped he was waiting outside. She'd never been invited to one of Will Jones's house

parties before. His parents went away fairly regularly
and he and his big brother had become legendary for
throwing wild events. Gossip was often flying around
about the police being called or so-and-so being sick in
the street or such-and-such losing their virginity under
a pile of coats. Katie's mind refused to follow that line
of thought any further. Luke was going to be waiting
outside. He was going to hold her hand and walk her
home afterwards. And then he'd kiss her. It was going to
be magical.

Will's house was halfway up Bathwick Hill. It was
massive, set back from the road, and part of a row of
similarly enormous properties. Katie had passed curving
driveways and high walls and, on the other side of the
road, parkland and trees stretched out into the darkness.

Luke was standing at the bottom of the driveway and
Katie's heart made a break for freedom via her throat.

'You made it,' Luke said. He had his hands in his
pockets and his shoulders were hunched against the cold.
'Shall we?' And they walked up to the house together.

Katie felt a tingle that started at her toes and went all
the way through her body. He'd been waiting for her.
For her. It was like something from a film. It was way
better than John Cusack standing on top of his car with
his tragic eighties boom-box in her mother's favourite
film. It was even better than Edward Cullen telling Bella
Swan that she was his own brand of heroin. Or as good
as, anyway. It was certainly the single most exciting
thing that had ever happened in her life.

Inside the house, a wall of noise and heat hit her.
Bodies were crushed in every room and on every
available surface. Three girls Katie recognised from
the year above were perched on a coffee table watching
Will rolling a cigarette on top of a table mat on his lap.
She hoped he had his fly zipped.

'Drink?' Luke made a gesture with his hand at the same time and Katie nodded.

He leaned down and yelled into her ear, 'Back in a minute.'

As soon as Luke's broad back disappeared into the press of people, Katie felt her confidence drain away. She fought her way to the nearest wall and stood against it, pretending that she came to parties all the time and *chose* to stand on her own. She tried not to be jealous of the couples dancing and kissing, the friends shrieking at each other. She tried to think aloof thoughts.

Five minutes felt like an hour, and Katie's skin was prickling with embarrassment and the heat so she was actually relieved when Freya Hallett threw sweaty arms around her and screamed an enthusiastic hello. 'Isn't this awesome?' Freya's face was bright red and shiny and her breath one hundred per cent proof.

Katie smiled and nodded.

'Have a WKD!' Freya shoved a bottle of blue liquid into Katie's hand. 'I've had four.' She stuck out a very blue tongue and collapsed into giggles.

Katie had first met Freya at Saturday morning orchestra practice when they were at primary school. She'd played the viola and had carried a leather case for her sheet music which Katie had coveted. Now Freya was leaning her face on a patch of wall next to Katie, her cheek smashed into the patterned wallpaper. 'So. Hot.' Freya closed her eyes and didn't say another word.

Katie took a tentative sip from the bottle. It tasted like radioactive squash. At least she could pretend to be talking to the halfway-comatose Freya now, and Luke would be back any second. Surely. She sipped some more.

Katie was surprised to discover that she'd reached the bottom of the bottle. She was also quite pleased with herself. Apart from an inch of (disgusting) wine in her glass on birthdays and Christmas, she hadn't drunk alcohol before but she didn't feel at all intoxicated. Although she did feel slightly more affectionate towards Freya, who had slumped to the floor and was sporting a lovely pattern of indentations on her face from the textured wallpaper.

Katie decided it was time to find Luke. She ventured away from the solid safety of the wall and moved from one packed room into another. She was just beginning to wonder whether the house had any end when she found it. A big kitchen fitted with modern appliances and shiny granite worktops. French doors led out onto the garden and one was wide open and swaying in the wind. Katie went to close it before the wind decided to slam it and smash the glass. She stood, her fingers on the chrome door handle, when she heard a familiar laugh. A deep voice joined the laugh, soft and throaty and undeniably boy-like. The hairs on her body raised as her mind caught up with her vision. Illuminated by the lights from the house, Imogen was entangled with a boy. A tall boy with floppy brown hair. A tall boy with floppy brown hair and the delicious throaty voice.

Luke.

Katie didn't know if she'd made an involuntary noise, but at that moment Luke looked over Imogen's shoulder and into her eyes. Katie knew she must be framed by the door, lit up by the light of the kitchen like a television screen. She tried to force her face into an unconcerned expression, but that wasn't happening. Every muscle was frozen in misery.

'Hey,' Luke said. Unconcerned. As if it'd slipped his mind that his hands were all over her best friend.

Imogen turned and, seeing Katie, did a full double-take. It would've been funny in any other circumstance. 'I didn't know you were coming.' Imogen's voice was squeaky.

Katie turned and fled the scene with one thought: she was going to find another of those bottles of tasty blue. Another couple of those and perhaps she wouldn't care any more.

CHAPTER 24

Gwen let herself in through her back door and dumped her bags onto the table. Cat appeared in the doorway, glaring at her with undisguised fury. He let out one of his God-awful screeches.

'In a minute, you impatient beast.'

Then she took a second look. Cat looked unhappy. His fur, which usually stuck up in random tufts around his face and neck, was standing to attention all over his body, like someone had just connected a wire and plugged it in.

Coldness dripped down her spine. What if someone was in the house? A knocking at the door almost made her cry out.

She wrenched it open, determined to be angry, not frightened. For a long moment, she stood on the doorstep looking out into the black and white garden. A flurry of snow whirled out of nowhere, obscuring her vision and the wind scraped across the skin on her face like razor blades. Gwen stayed motionless, squinting out into the blurry white, trying to see if there was someone there. 'Hello?' Her voice was a weak thread, whisked away instantly by the gale. Another second and her hands began to burn from the icy cold. She stepped back inside, shut the door and locked it.

'I'm not scared.' She looked around the kitchen. 'I'm not leaving, so you might as well stop it.' Feeling bolstered, she went into each room of the house and repeated her mantra. 'I'm not scared. I'm not leaving.'

Gwen had almost convinced herself that she wasn't frightened any more when the phone rang. She jumped, then laughed at herself. *So much for the mantra.* It was Ruby, sounding as breathless and stressed as Gwen felt. 'Is Katie there?'

'No. Why?'

'She's not in her room. Her bed hasn't been slept in.'

Gwen looked at the clock. It was half past seven. 'Could she have left for school already? Made her bed?'

Ruby snorted. 'Get up early for school? Not likely.'

'Have you tried her mobile?'

'Only about a thousand times.'

'I haven't seen her; I'm sorry.'

'I'm going to call the police.' Ruby's tone was challenging.

'Okay, if you think—'

Ruby took a deep breath. 'If this is some kind of joke you two are playing on me, you'd better stop it now.'

Gwen was stunned. Just how irresponsible did Ruby think she was? How cruel? 'What on earth are you talking about?'

'I know you've been planning something. I'm not stupid. I know you want to take her away from me.'

'Hang on—'

'I won't let you. She's my daughter.' Then the awful sound of Ruby crying and the phone went dead. She'd hung up.

Gwen redialled and spoke the moment it connected. 'I haven't planned anything. I don't know where Katie is.'

There was a short silence then Ruby said, 'Oh God,' very quietly.

'When did you last see her?'

'Last night. She went to bed early. She had a sore stomach.'

'Okay. Have you rung around her friends?'

'David's doing that now.'

'I'm sure she's just gone to someone's house. Let me know, won't you?'

'Okay.'

After hanging up, Gwen paced the floor. She put the kettle on to make tea, and then discovered a mug of hot water, no tea bag, ten minutes later. Finally, Ruby rang.

'Any joy?'

'No.' Ruby's voice was bleak. 'Her hoodie's gone and her trainers, but her uniform is all here. She's not gone to school. We've rung the police.'

'Oh, honey. It's going to be okay. I'm sure she's skiving with a friend.' Gwen wanted to ask about boyfriends, but was worried she'd send Ruby over the edge.

'Was she seeing anyone?' Ruby was already there.

'Not that I know of. But you'd know better than me.'

'I doubt it.' Ruby's voice was so quiet Gwen had to strain to hear. 'I've lost her.'

'No. She'll turn up. She'll be okay.'

'Where is she, Gwen? Why wouldn't she leave me a note? She knows the rule. If you go out, you leave a note. On the fridge. There's a pad there. And one by the phone in the hall.'

'I don't know. I'm sorry.'

'Okay.' Ruby sounded so worried, Gwen wished Katie was with her, wished she could produce her like a rabbit from a hat. Ta-da.

Gwen held the phone for a moment after Ruby had hung up. There was only one other person she wanted to speak to, but they were over. She wasn't with Cam, she had no right to call him and he had no responsibility to pick up. She tried to concentrate, to process the news: Katie was missing. Gwen's stomach swooped lower. The phone rang and she realised that she was still standing in the same position, gripping the plastic casing tightly.

'She was at a party,' Ruby said. 'David just spoke to Imogen. She said she saw Katie there, but only for a bit and she doesn't know when she left or where she went. We're going to go and start looking.'

'I'll come and help.'

'No,' Ruby said quickly. 'Thanks, but she might come to your house. To see you. I want you to be there if she does.'

'Okay,' Gwen said. 'Keep in touch.'

'I can't believe she went out without telling us. I never thought she'd do anything so stupid.'

Gwen made soothing noises and steadfastly didn't voice her own thoughts. Katie was probably somewhere in Bath. Maybe with a boyfriend. When Gwen was a teenager, the only truly stupid things she'd ever done had been over a boy.

She made a cup of tea and carried it with her as she paced the house. A while later she realised it was cold and poured it down the sink.

Gwen looked out of the window; the snow had started again. Innocuous swirling flakes giving way to a steady fall of thick white. Snow that meant business. And Katie could be out in it. She gave in and called Cam. The need to hear his voice was overwhelming. They might not be an item, but they had been once. That had to count for something.

He answered the phone sounding wary, but his tone changed as soon as Gwen explained what had happened and she drew a few moments' comfort from his voice. He was sympathetic and positive. 'I cut school all the time at her age. She'll be at a friend's house watching films and eating crisps.'

'Absolutely.' Gwen tried to believe him. 'I really hope so.'

'I'll call Harry, though. Just to be on the safe side.'

Gwen's breath came out in a whoosh. 'Thank you.'

'And I'll come round after work…' he hesitated and in that silence a thousand unsaid words hung in the air '…if you want me to.'

'I do,' Gwen said. 'Please.'

Less than an hour later, and Gwen couldn't stand being in the house any longer. She checked in with Ruby and then walked through the town. She checked the park and the shops that Katie liked. She called everyone she could think of, but nobody had seen Katie.

At eleven o'clock, Ruby rang. Gwen snatched up the phone. 'Is she home?'

'No.' Ruby paused. 'I want you to find her.'

'I've been all around the town. I checked Claire's and the park and—'

'No. I mean I want you to find her.' Ruby's voice was steady. 'Find her. Use the force or whatever you call it.'

Gwen was silent for a second, thinking, and Ruby misinterpreted.

'For God's sake, you're not going to hold a grudge now? You want me to apologise. I'm sorry, Gwen, I'm really sorry. I've been a shitty big sister. Now, please—'

Gwen cut across her. 'It's not that. It doesn't always work.'

'It's Katie. It's got to work,' Ruby said.

'I'm going to try,' Gwen said. 'Of course I'll try.'

'Thank you.' Ruby's voice cracked.

'Right. I'll do it now.'

'Okay.' Ruby paused.

When she didn't say goodbye, Gwen realised Ruby was waiting for her to do it there and then. 'I mean, I've got to go. I'm going to hang up. I can't do it with you watching.'

'I can't see you,' Ruby said.

'You know what I mean.'

'Fine.' Ruby sounded stronger. More like herself. 'Call me straight back.'

Gwen went into the kitchen: the safest, most soothing room in the house. She could see Katie everywhere. By the fridge, demanding cola, at the table scoffing white chocolate chunk cookies and leaning against the counter, drinking tea from the Snoopy mug and complaining about her teachers.

A sob escaped and Gwen clamped a hand over her mouth to stop any others following it. She wasn't going to cry. Crying suggested tragedy. There was nothing to cry about because she was going to focus and she was going to find Katie and there would be nothing left to do but give her an almighty bollocking for worrying them like this.

She sat at the table and took several deep breaths. She half-expected Katie's location to simply spring into her mind, she was thinking so feverishly, but it didn't. Instead the entirely prosaic list of possibilities looped round and round. It was agonising. God only knew how Ruby and David were feeling.

Okay, something of Katie's. The Snoopy mug might do. Katie had certainly adopted it. With it clasped in both hands, as if she were warming her fingers, Gwen closed her eyes. She fixed an image of Katie in her mind's eye and waited.

And waited a bit more.

Twenty minutes later, she was going cross-eyed from staring at the Snoopy mug and the panic had been almost entirely replaced with an awful calm. She couldn't do it. The one time in her life when she'd actually thanked her mother, the powers that be, Mother Nature, whoever, for her strange ability and it had deserted her.

The knocking made her jump. *Katie*. She crossed the room in giant steps and yanked open the door. It was Cam, looking tall and serious and grown-up in his dark suit and tie. 'No news,' he said immediately. 'Sorry.'

Disappointment and relief at seeing him vied for prime position. 'It's been too long, now,' she said. 'And it's freezing out there.'

'I know.' He stepped inside and, for a moment, she thought he was going to hug her, but then he moved back and folded his arms.

'Ruby called me,' he said. 'She wanted to know what Harry thought. And she asked me to bring you this.' He pulled a scarf from his jacket pocket and Gwen took it automatically. She gazed at the thin cotton in her hand and realised with a jolt that it was Katie's. It was a cheap light blue-grey scarf with translucent sequins and many loose threads and she'd seen it knotted artfully around Katie's neck many times. She swallowed. 'Thank you. I need a minute.'

'I'll wait in the other room.'

Gwen wondered how much Ruby had said to him. She thought about his face when she'd found Archie, his instant dismissal.

'I know you think this is crazy. A waste of time—'

'It's worth a try,' Cam said, his voice tight.

Gwen smiled weakly. 'I hope so.'

Cam hesitated. 'You know I don't believe in this stuff.'

'I know. You think Archie was a lucky guess.'

'Not a conscious one. I don't think you intentionally, um—'

'You don't think I'm a filthy, lying fraud,' Gwen supplied helpfully.

'Exactly.' Cam looked grateful. 'And I really hope it works. But if not, is it okay if I call Harry to offer my services? I want to go out and look.'

'Definitely. We should do everything. Thank you.'

'Good.' Cam's shoulders went down a notch.

Gwen waited until she was alone and then another minute to check Cam wasn't going to pop back to ask her something. Then she held the scarf up to her face, scrunching it up and inhaling the faint traces of Katie's scent. Nothing except a hit of Impulse body spray. She rubbed the material between her fingers, closed her eyes and tried to open her mind. She imagined a blank screen unrolling, ready for the image of Katie to appear. Of her surroundings. She forced the desperate mind-chatter to quiet and watched the blank screen as patiently as she could. Nothing.

Five minutes more – minutes that seemed to jerk past – and Gwen couldn't sit at the table, alone with her failure, any longer. She jumped up and went through to the living room. Cam sat on her sofa, a slice of black bisecting the riot of colour. She couldn't speak, only shake her head. Cam stood up and this time he did put his arms around her. Gwen was ashamed that she could think about how good it felt to have his arms around her, however briefly. They weren't together and it was ripping her apart inside but, for that one moment, she could hold onto him and gather a small measure of strength.

After a few minutes, Gwen took a deep breath and rang her sister. Ruby answered on the first ring. Gwen could hardly get the words out, the depression was pressing down on the top of her head and squeezing her from the sides. She wrapped her arms around her body and squeezed with her arms, too.

'I don't know why.' Gwen couldn't stop crying. 'I'm sorry, Ruby. I'm sorry.'

Ruby was crying, too. Gwen could hear her hiccupping and swallowing. 'Is it because I've been horrible?'

'No! Ruby, I swear I'm doing my best.'

'But what if it's like karma or something? That it won't work because of the way I was that time?'

Instantly, Gwen knew what she was talking about. The day Gwen had gone to hide from the journalists and the curious people and the kids from school who wanted to shout some more names at her. She'd gone to David's parents' house and Ruby had refused to let her in.

'I know it wasn't your fault, but I was really angry with you,' Ruby was saying. 'I thought we were going to have to move again and I'd finally got settled. I actually had friends and I had my life and I had David.'

'This isn't the time,' Gwen said, feeling awkward. 'But, you know, you were twenty. If Gloria did another flit, you didn't have to go with her.'

Ruby didn't seem to hear her. 'It wasn't all about you and magic and that poor kid who committed suicide. I was dealing with my own problems. I didn't need anything else right then.'

'I'm so sorry Stephen Knight's death was inconvenient to you,' Gwen said, the old anger bursting through. 'I'm sorry the worst days of my life gave you a headache. Did it spoil some of your dinner dates with David? Sour your skiing trips with his loaded family?'

'I'd just had a baby. Which, for the record, is fucking horrible. I was sore from the stitches and I'd never been so tired in my life. I was a new mother living in David's family's house being treated like the poor country cousin who didn't know to keep her legs together. David was studying all hours for his endless bloody exams, and I needed a mother, but all I had was Gloria waltzing in and out offering to read the baby's cards and I needed you but you were either shagging Cameron Laing or—'

Gwen felt terrible . 'Ruby. I'm sorry. I'd forgotten about all that.'

'Yeah, well,' Ruby heaved a big, shuddering sigh and then, sounding more like herself, she said, 'You were eighteen.'

'And you were only twenty,' Gwen said. She felt stunned by the realisation. She'd been angry with Ruby for so long she'd forgotten how young they'd both been.

Ruby sniffed. 'Can I come round? I can't be here any more. David is being all sensible. If he says "she's fine" one more time, I'm going to start throwing things.'

'Of course,' Gwen said. 'You can always come here.'

CHAPTER 25

Gwen surveyed her kitchen table and the assembled people with concern. She'd started the morning feeling like a fraud, and now she felt like a very public fraud. 'I don't know if this will help,' she said for the third time.

Ruby patted her shoulder. 'It will. Don't you remember? Gloria always said you could gather power from other people. Like a kind of circuit thing. Electricity.'

'I feel ridiculous.' David was scowling, his usually boyish features twisted and black. He shot an accusing look in Cam's direction. 'Why are you going along with this nonsense? It's a waste of time.'

Cam shrugged.

Gwen swallowed. Gloria had also said that non-believers sapped energy. Maybe this was just going to make it worse. But then, what could be worse than drawing a blank?

Cam was already holding her right hand, and she reached out her left and clasped Ruby's.

Ruby was staring intently at David. 'Please,' she said.

David exhaled. 'Fine.' He picked up Ruby and Cam's hands with an air of martyrdom. Gwen didn't blame him. She felt like she was pouring salt on their wounds. Giving false hope. Every bad thing she'd ever heard levelled at her mum or Iris.

She closed her eyes. The scarf was in the middle of the table, but she didn't need to see it. She had held it and stared at it for so long its image was burned into her brain.

Cam squeezed her hand lightly and she took the impulse and fed it through the rest of her body, squeezing and then relaxing, pushing the tension out through the soles of her feet. The blank screen in her mind flickered and she ignored it, concentrating on the tension flowing downwards and away. She pictured it moving through the carpet and the floorboards to the foundations of the house. The flickering screen was definitely an image and, gradually, the flickering slowed and the picture cleared.

It wasn't Katie. It was a stone wall. An old stone wall. It was like a photograph taken from the ground, the wall towered above Gwen. She concentrated, looking for clues. Snow thick on the ground, blinding white. The picture shifted so suddenly, Gwen thought she might be sick. Now there was the tip of a shoe. A red trainer. Katie's red trainer. The wall had shifted so that Gwen could see its ragged top and a slice of grey sky. Then the screen went blank. Gwen waited a moment to see if anything came back and then opened her eyes.

Three pairs of eyes stared back at her. Gwen became aware of her stance. She was leaning forward over the table towards the scarf and there was an aching pain in both hands. She was gripping Ruby and Cam so hard her muscles were complaining. She released them. 'Sorry.'

Ruby's face fell and she turned to David. He took her in his arms, gazing stoically at the wall behind.

'No. For hurting your hand,' she clarified hurriedly. 'I think it worked.'

Ruby turned back. 'Katie?'

'I think so. Yes. I saw her trainer. She's lying down next to a stone wall. Old, like a castle or something. Somewhere windy.'

'There aren't any castles around here. Where's the nearest?' Ruby looked around wildly. 'Dorset? Cornwall?'

'It might not be a—' Gwen said.

'I'll Google it.' David had his iPhone out of his pocket.

Cam's phone buzzed and he got up from the table to take it. He listened for a moment, then said, 'Okay, thanks.'

'Harry?' Gwen asked.

'Yep. He's been talking to Katie's friends. No one's seen her, no one had any plans with her.' He hesitated. 'A name came up, though. Luke Taylor.'

Everyone turned and looked at Ruby, who shook her head slowly.

'Apparently she and him have recently hooked up.' He looked at David and quickly amended. 'Become friendly. Friends, I mean. Just friends. People have seen them talking.'

David put his iPhone down. 'You lot go looking for castles. I'm going to have a word with Mr Taylor.'

'I don't think that's a good idea,' Cam began.

David stood up. 'When you've got a daughter, you come back and tell me that.'

Cam held his hands up. 'Harry is on his way. He's the police and he's also a friend. If the kid knows anything, Harry will find out.'

Ruby put a hand on David's arm. 'Cam's right. Let Harry talk to the boy. I want to go and look for her. I'm going insane just sitting around. I need to do something.'

'Will you tell Harry about what I saw?' Gwen watched Cam carefully, wondering whether he still thought she was delusional or a fraud.

He didn't hesitate. 'I'll text him now. Give me every detail.'

Ruby was still gazing imploringly at David, who was standing very still, a battle etched plainly across his face.

'Let's make a list of the nearest castles; we'll split up and start looking.'

'Sherbourne,' David said. 'That's got to be the nearest.'

'That's near Yeovil. How the hell would she have got down there? Why would she—'

'I don't know,' he snapped. 'You asked. I answered. I don't know.'

'What about Castle Combe?' Cam said.

'That's just a village, isn't it?' Ruby said.

'There's a little bit of the original castle left in the woods. Bit of a crumbling wall, basically.' He turned to Gwen. 'Could that be it?'

'We can check it.' Gwen bit her lip. 'It might not even be a castle. I just saw an old wall. It made me think "castle", but what if I'm sending you on a wild goose chase?'

Ruby shrugged. 'It's all we've got. And it's better than nothing. We've been door to door all around the party house and everywhere else we can think.'

'Old walls,' Cam said. 'What else has old walls?'

'Really old. And uneven on the top,' Gwen added.

'Bath has plenty of old walls, but they're not in ruins.' Ruby was already pulling on her coat.

'So does Pendleford. What if she's just lying in a field next to a dry stone and Gwen just got the perspective wrong?' David said.

'Hey,' Cam said.

'No, he's right. I don't know.' Gwen sank down onto a chair, put her head in her hands. 'I don't know,' she mumbled. 'I'm sorry. I'm so sorry.' She closed her eyes and reran the two images, trying to see them afresh but intact. What if her faulty memory or desperation added something that wasn't there? Her wild goose chase could spiral even further out of control.

There was the wall. Old. The stones near the ground were very rough-looking, but the ones further up were block work. A little yellowish lichen. The next image, with the top of the wall, the slice of sky. The uneven top was more regular than Gwen had first thought. Block work suggesting crenellations. Exactly why she had immediately thought 'castle'. So she wasn't leading them astray, but how on earth had Katie gone as far as Sherbourne?

In the car, Cam concentrated on the road while Gwen stared out of the window. Castle Combe was only five miles away so, even though she was almost positive it wasn't the right place, it made sense to double-check. Ruby and David had started towards Sherbourne, the more likely option.

Cam took one hand off the steering wheel and touched her knee. 'She'll be okay. It's been less than twenty-four hours.'

'That seems very long, suddenly.'

'I know. But Harry says that most missing people are found within the first day.'

Gwen didn't say anything, but she knew he meant most of the missing people who were found alive got found quickly. That didn't account for the ones that stayed missing. Her stomach clenched. It gurgled, too, and Gwen realised that she hadn't eaten since the night before.

The traffic was light, even approaching Bath, but as they skirted the east edge of the city, the cars in front slowed and soon they were snarled in one of the ever-present queues. Even the bad weather didn't seem to put a dent in Bath's traffic problem.

Gwen gazed out of the side window, seeing nothing. She had walled in the scary thoughts. The images of Katie lying alone and injured, or worse. The images of homeless kids. Lost kids. She went back over the two images for what felt like the millionth time. 'I'm sure it isn't a crumbled top; the more I think about it, the surer I am.'

'Don't worry. It won't take us long to check this, then we can rule it out. At least we're doing something.'

'I know.' Gwen lapsed into silence again.

They inched forwards, the familiar yellow stone buildings of Bath spread out before them. To the left rose Bathwick Hill and Gwen took in the familiar scene: the picturesque way the buildings rambled up its side. Even at this dead time of year, with a dark grey sky and bare trees, it was attractive.

The crenellations of Ralph Allen's folly were just visible. They inched forwards, turning a bend in the road, and Gwen gazed back at it. It was typical of a Bathonian. To build something just to improve the view from his own window. Showy, expensive, but oh-so-tastefully done. Ruby and Gwen had developed a shorthand when they'd gone to school here; they'd put on comedy-posh voices and trill 'this is *Bath*, darling'. Then it hit her.

Crenellations.

The folly was a mock front of a medieval castle. Made out of bath stone, it was fifteen feet high and had crenellations on the top of the walls, for battlements. From behind, the effect was lost. It was like a piece of scenery from a film set or a Lego model.

'The folly.'

'What?' Gwen pointed and Cam looked. 'The sham castle,' he said. Then a second later, louder. 'The sham *castle*.'

Gwen stared at him, stunned with the realisation. 'Katie's there.'

'Use my phone.' Cam plucked it from the side pocket and handed it across, just as traffic began to crawl forward again. 'Phone Harry. He might be able to get there quicker.'

'Right.' Gwen's head was frozen. She felt a rush of gratitude to Cam. He didn't believe her, but he was acting as if he did. Somehow she managed to find the address book and press the button for Harry. There were traffic sounds wherever he was and someone in their queue was beeping their horn, but she managed to get the essentials across.

'On it,' Harry said and cut the connection.

As Cam drove, Gwen leaned her head against the glass and thought about the last time she had visited the folly. She had been with Cam, and they'd walked up Bathwick Hill one clear moonlit night. They had a bottle of Jack Daniels and had made up shapes from the stars, admired the lights of Bath spread below them, talked and drank. It was too cold to lie on the ground, not that Gwen wouldn't have done so anyway, but Cam had held her up against the wall, her legs hooked around his waist. She felt a flush of guilt at thinking about sex at a time like this.

She blinked as the car stopped. 'This isn't it.'

'It's a golf course. I don't think I can get any closer.'

'Over there.' Gwen jumped out and almost skidded on the icy ground. She caught her balance and opened the gate. A sign said: Private. Staff only.

Cam took the service track too quickly, the back of the car fish-tailing as he took a corner. When they saw flashing lights up ahead, he went even faster, pulling to a long, sliding stop. 'Oh my God,' he said. 'You were right.'

Gwen already had her seat belt off and was out of the door, running, her feet crunching on the snow.

The doors to the ambulance were open and they were lifting a figure on a board inside. Two police in uniform came to meet her. She pushed past them. 'That's my niece.' She saw feet disappearing into the ambulance. One red trainer, one stripy sock. 'Oh God. Katie!'

Cam was with her now. He had his hand on her arm, was pulling her back. 'Let them look after her.'

'I just need to see her,' Gwen said, pulling against Cam.

'Come on. We'll follow them to the hospital.'

Gwen struggled forwards, but the doors slammed shut. 'Is she all right?' She turned to the police, trying to shut out images of Stephen Knight's lifeless body. That couldn't be Katie. It couldn't be. 'What's happened to her? Is she—'

'She's unconscious. They'll be able to tell you more at the hospital.' The man nodded at Cam. 'Mr Laing.'

'Oh God.' Gwen put her hands to her face. 'Oh God.'

'Is Harry here?' Cam said.

'Over there.' The second policeman jerked his head in the direction of the castle.

Cam set off and Gwen, holding onto him so that she didn't keel over, had no choice but to go with him.

As they got closer, Gwen saw the rough and ready back of the folly. Something she hadn't appreciated in the dead of night with her brains exploding with lust, was that the back was nowhere near as fancy as the front. It was almost slap-dash, in fact. They walked through the archway and there was the city, spread out below them, and there was Harry, crouched over by one of the fake towers.

He was poking through the snow with a pencil, but he straightened up as they approached. 'I've phoned Ruby. They're coming back.'

Cam nodded. 'What does it look like?'

Harry glanced at Gwen. 'No obvious injuries, no sign of a struggle. She's got hypothermia, though. Hopefully moderate rather than severe, but that can cause confusion, lapses in judgement. Her mobile phone was less than a metre from where she was lying, but she either lost it or forgot about it.'

'But why would she let herself get that cold? Why wouldn't she have come back, used her phone?' Gwen closed her eyes, felt herself swaying like a blade of grass.

Harry shrugged. 'Maybe the hypothermia set in quickly, made her thinking muddled. Maybe she was drunk.'

'What's that?' Cam was pointing at a plastic bag.

Harry held it up. An empty alcopop bottle, some bright blue liquid still in the bottom. 'Not much of a mystery.'

Gwen opened her eyes in time to see a look pass between the two men. She filed it under 'later' and said, 'We need to go to the hospital. Now.'

The drive to the hospital passed in a blur. Gwen felt feverish. She laid her head against the cool glass of the window and marvelled at the heat in her head. Her body was in overdrive, while her brain seemed to have shut down.

'You were right,' Cam kept saying. 'I can't believe it. How did you do that?'

Gwen was too overwhelmed to answer him. She shook her head. 'What the hell was she doing up there? And what if we were too late?' She thought about the hours that had passed. Katie lying outside, unconscious, in the cold. She wrapped her arms around her middle, as if she could physically hold herself together.

Miraculously, they found a place to park at the hospital. Even more amazingly, Gwen made it to the right department without fainting.

'She's not awake yet,' the nurse at the desk said. 'You can go in, but just for a minute.' The nurse had curly brown hair tied in a very high ponytail. It looked insultingly jaunty to Gwen but, at that moment, everything did. How could people be walking around, talking on their mobiles, eating chocolate bars, *breathing*, when Katie was critically ill? It wasn't right. Nothing about this was right.

Ruby and David looked up as they walked into the room and then looked straight back to Katie. Gwen thought she'd prepared herself for the sight of Katie in a hospital bed, but she was nowhere even close to ready. Katie looked so young. Just a little child again. She was lying unnaturally straight, her hands lying neatly at her sides on top of several layers of blankets.

'They warmed her up,' Ruby whispered. 'Her core temperature was really low. Hypothermia.'

'They said she was really lucky,' David was whispering, too. 'Another hour out there and—'

'Don't,' Ruby said. 'Don't say it.'

'Is she all right?' Gwen said, stepping closer to the bed. She reached out and touched Katie's hand. The one that didn't have tubes coming out of the back.

'They don't know. She hasn't woken up yet. They don't know how long it'll be.'

A nurse appeared, wheeling a portable blood pressure monitor. 'You'll have to go now. Only two at a time.'

'Call me later,' Gwen said.

Ruby didn't look up, and Gwen's last impression was of her sister's hunched form, bent over Katie's bedside.

CHAPTER 26

Back at End House, Cam went upstairs and ran a bath. He poured a glass of wine and pushed it into Gwen's hand. 'Drink this, then go and have a soak. It'll help.'

'Okay.' Gwen hadn't realised that she was shivering. The red wine slopped about in the glass until she held it with both hands.

Cam rubbed soothing circles on her lower back as she sipped her drink. 'You found her; she's safe.'

Gwen felt the tears well up again and she buried her head in Cam's shoulder, breathing in his scent and letting the pressure of his arms soothe her. 'What if she isn't okay, though? What if she doesn't wake up?'

'She will,' Cam said.

Gwen thought that if she voiced her worst fear, perhaps she'd feel better. She didn't. The tears kept falling until they were dripping off her chin. She scrubbed at her face with her sleeve.

'Are you hungry? Shall I order a takeaway?'

'Not for me,' Gwen said.

'You need to eat something.'

'Okay,' Gwen said. She realised that she hadn't eaten that day. She took another hit of wine, willing it to undo the knot in her stomach.

'Right.' Cam started hunting around the kitchen. 'Do you have any menus?'

'Just put the cannelloni in the oven. It'll be ready in forty minutes.' Gwen hesitated as Cam looked at her, suddenly wary. The cannelloni. Their big argument. It seemed to belong to a different time.

'About that...' he began.

Gwen shook her head. There was no room for anything else right now. She went upstairs to the bathroom before he could say anything else.

She soaked in the bath and tried to stop crying. Every time she thought she was getting a handle on the situation, she would think about how Ruby must be feeling or about how pale and young Katie had looked, and she started sobbing again.

She had just got into some clean clothes and into the living room, when the doorbell rang. Cam jumped up from the sofa. 'I'll tell them to sod off,' he said.

But he didn't come back through. After a couple of minutes, Gwen followed him and found an uncomfortable-looking Harry in her hallway with an older man in a police uniform.

'Katie's fine,' Cam said immediately. 'No change.' He put an arm around her shoulder.

'I'm sorry,' Harry said. 'I need to ask you a few questions.' He gestured to the uniform. 'This is PC Albion.' PC Albion was gazing around as if he'd never been inside a house before. 'We can do it here, though,' Harry added.

'What the bloody hell is going on? Harry? Is this an official visit?' Cam looked tense, Gwen realised with a jolt of fear.

She moved out from under his arm. 'I'll make tea. Make yourselves at home.' She escaped to the kitchen to do some deep breathing. The penny dropped. Harry meant questions here, rather than at the police station. Something was very wrong. *No, no, no. Not again.*

She flicked the switch on the kettle and got out mugs. The kitchen looked the same. The dresser looked the same. The cupboards were still perky lemon and the mugs were still aqua polka dot, but there was something wrong with the picture. Oh yes, the police were sitting on her sofa waiting to question her.

She carried a tray into the living room and PC Albion jumped up to help her with it. Everything was surreally polite and calm.

'Okay, Gwen. First off, I need to ask where you were last night. It's routine.'

'I was here.' Gwen sat in the armchair by the door.

'Alone?'

'Yes.'

Harry looked questioningly at Cam. 'You weren't with her?'

Cam shook his head, looking furious. 'Don't say anything else, Gwen.'

Harry met his stare without flinching. 'Gwen has agreed to answer a few routine questions. It would be better if she does so.'

'In her home, Harry?'

'Not if you prefer we relocate to the station.' Harry's voice was even and toneless. Then he said in his normal voice, 'Come on, man, don't make this harder than it already is.'

'Make what harder?' Gwen said.

Harry was still looking at Cam. 'If I don't follow procedure, I could make things worse.'

'Make what worse? Katie's definitely okay, isn't she?' Her heart clenched. 'What are you not telling me?'

'Nothing.' Harry looked uncomfortable, and Gwen would've felt sorry for him, but there wasn't any room in her mind for it. This whole thing was so weird and she was exhausted from not sleeping the night before,;the adrenaline that had kept her going while they were looking for Katie had ebbed away, leaving her shaky and tearful. She blinked. Harry was speaking and she needed to concentrate.

'So, you say you were here last night,' Harry said. 'Did you see anyone at all? Speak to anyone on the telephone?'

'No, I don't think so.'

'Can you remember the last time you saw Katie?'

'At the hospital.'

'And before that?'

'I'm not sure. A few days ago.' Gwen closed her eyes to force her brain into proper activity. 'She came round after school on Monday. We made cakes.'

Harry nodded. PC Albion wrote something down in his notebook.

Gwen waited.

'And how would you characterise your relationship?'

'She's my niece,' Gwen said.

'Do you get on well?' Harry said.

'I think so. Yes.'

'How would you characterise her mood?'

'In general?' Gwen said.

'The last time you saw her.'

'On Monday?'

He nodded.

'She was fine,' Gwen said. 'A bit wound up from school, I suppose, but fine.'

'Has she seemed depressed lately?'

'No.'

'Angry?'

Gwen shrugged. 'She's fourteen.'

Harry gave a small smile. 'I'm trying to ascertain her state of mind last night.'

'Why not ask her?' Too late, Gwen realised that he couldn't. She felt her throat close up.

'Once Katie's awake, I'm sure we'll be able to clear all of this up,' Harry said, 'but, in the meantime, I've got to write a report.'

'I don't know why you're asking about her state of mind. Why does it matter?'

'What do you mean?' Harry said.

'She went missing. That's not like her. She's a really good kid. And she was found unconscious. Clearly something happened to her.'

'Clearly.' Harry paused. 'What we don't know is how she got to the folly and what she was doing there.'

'What if she was taken there? She could've been abducted.' Gwen shook her head in frustration. 'Why are you asking me? Isn't it your job to figure out what happened?'

'Oh, we will, Ms Harper,' PC Albion said and Harry shot him a filthy look.

'The thing is,' Harry said, 'there's some question as to how you found Katie. If you weren't involved with her, um, mishap, how did you know where to look?'

Gwen felt sick.

'And you do have a history. Of this kind of thing, I mean. The Stephen Knight case.' Harry looked uncomfortable.

Gwen felt the room swoop to the left. 'I had nothing to do with his accident. Or suicide. Whichever you people decided it was.' Gwen's hands were curled into fists and she dug her nails into her palms.

'Gwen has a supernatural ability to find things that are lost,' Cam said calmly and Gwen almost fell off her chair.

PC Albion's head shot up, while Harry just gazed steadily at Cam.

'I don't understand it,' Cam said. 'I don't know whether it's a special kind of intuition or what, but Gwen can find things. That's how she knew where Katie was.'

'You want that on record?' Harry said.

'I am willing to swear to it in court,' Cam said. 'However, this interview is at an end. If you want to charge Gwen, charge her. Otherwise you're going to have to leave.'

'It would be best if she cooperated. Certain allegations have been made, and we have to investigate those allegations fully.'

'I'll cooperate. I want to help,' Gwen said, standing up. Harry shot her such a look of sweet exasperation that she felt her knees buckle. She sat down again.

Cam didn't turn around. 'Harry is doing his job, but he wants you to listen to me. Can you do that? Please?'

'Okay,' Gwen said, giving up on understanding what the hell was going on.

Cam followed Harry and PC Albion to the door. When he came back into the living room, his expression was grim. 'They're coming back with a warrant. Apparently they received some kind of tip-off.'

'But I haven't done anything.'

'I know. But we need to prepare.'

Gwen stood up. 'But—'

'Trust me.' Cam tried to smile. 'I'm your lawyer.'

'Lily Thomas,' Gwen said. 'She wants me out of here, she wants to get into the house and steal Iris's journals. I bet she's the one who's made allegations. I think she left me that rabbit.' Gwen swallowed. 'I know you think I'm crazy—'

'I don't,' Cam said. 'Didn't you hear what I said?' He shook his head. 'I don't understand it, but I believe you. This unusual ability is real and it probably saved Katie's life today. I'm not going to be the one to argue with that.'

'What about Lily?' Gwen was half out of her chair again. God knew what else that woman had planned, what she'd planted in the house before calling the police. Taking advantage of her opportunity. Gwen felt a bitter taste in her mouth and forced herself to swallow before she threw up.

'Sit down,' Cam said. 'Breathe. I'm going to call Harry. And Elaine.'

Gwen launched upright, the blood rushing to her head and making her giddy. 'Your mother?'

Cam looked uncomfortable. 'She came to see me yesterday. Said that Lily had come to her for advice on contesting Iris's will. She said that Lily had some idea of getting you out of the house permanently.'

'What?'

'I was going to tell you, but when Katie went missing it got pushed out of my head.'

'What else did she say?'

'Just that the title deeds for the house were in the safe in my grandfather's office. I don't know why I didn't look there before. I'm sorry.'

'You've had a lot on your plate,' Gwen said faintly, trying to process the information.

'If we have evidence that Lily has been executing a campaign of harassment, that'll weaken any case she's trying to make against you.'

'Right.' Gwen's legs went liquid and she sat down.

'Go to bed,' Cam said. 'Get some rest, I'll be up in a little while.'

Upstairs, underneath the covers in her brass bed, Gwen listened to the sound of Cam pacing downstairs, the rumble of his voice as he made call after call. There was something to be said for not being alone, she thought. Cat curled up next to her stomach, a giant furry hot water bottle and, without intending to, Gwen slipped into sleep.

CHAPTER 27

The next day, Gwen expected Cam to go into work, but he didn't. He drove to the hospital and sat outside in the corridor while Gwen sat with Katie. Ruby was hollow-eyed and exhausted.

'Have you slept?' Gwen said.

'I don't feel like it, but I must've dozed off at some point. I dreamed that Katie woke up.' Ruby's voice broke and Gwen reached out to take her hand.

Katie was pale and too still for Gwen to kid herself that she was just sleeping. 'Do they know anything else? Have they said—'

Ruby shook her head. 'David's gone home to get some stuff for Katie. No one will tell me how long she'll be like this. They say we've got to wait and see.'

Wait and see. Gwen squeezed Ruby's hand. 'She's going to be okay. She's going to wake up.'

'They said there might be brain damage. From the hypothermia. They won't know until she wakes up.'

'Oh Christ.'

Tears squeezed out from under Ruby's eyelids. 'I keep thinking I'll stop crying soon. That there won't be anything left. I keep waiting to go numb. I thought people went numb in situations like this. But I don't.'

'What can I do?' Gwen said.

'You found her,' Ruby said. She looked away from Katie, then straight into Gwen's eyes. 'I'll never forget that.'

Later, when Harry called Gwen and asked her to come down to the station to make an official statement, Cam insisted on coming with her. 'Don't you have to go to the office today?'

'Sod the office,' Cam said.

Walking back into Pendleford police station, Gwen was expecting to be hit by bad memories of Stephen Knight, but her system was overloaded by worry for Katie. Plus, this time she wasn't eighteen years old and it wasn't an unknown policeman but Harry on the other side of the desk. He kept apologising. 'Just got to follow the routine,' he said. 'Got to make sure I do my job. It's to protect you.'

Cam still looked like he wanted to punch something, but Gwen was glad he was there. He was infinitely gentle and calm with her. Fetching bottled water and putting his hand comfortingly on the middle of her back while she wrote her statement.

When PC Albion came in and asked whether Cam should be in the room, he said, 'I'm her lawyer.'

At the same time Harry said, 'Back off.'

She rang David and heard the report on Katie. No change. 'She should've woken up by now,' he said. 'The doctor doesn't know why she hasn't. He said there's no medical reason, but that sometimes people's bodies just react this way after a shock. They shut down for a while. Her system is just rebooting itself or something.'

David sounded determinedly calm and confident. Gwen knew he was reassuring himself with the words and she was quick to agree with him.

Hanging up in the empty house, Cat winding around her ankles, Gwen felt the false confidence evaporate.

The next day, Gwen woke up as Cam slipped out of bed. He was moving quietly, trying not to wake her, and Gwen kept her eyes shut. She wasn't ready to face the day. Not a day that included Katie being ill. The pain knifed through her and she curled around it. Another day in which Katie was lying in a hospital bed and people thought, actually believed, that she could've had something to do with it. Gwen squeezed her eyes shut.

'There's someone at the door,' Cam whispered. 'I'll get rid of them. You go back to sleep.'

He closed the door and Gwen sat up, imagining Ryan or some other journalist. *Just like last time.* She sat straighter, holding herself very still for a few moments before realising that she was trying to listen, that she couldn't just sit up here in the dark, wondering. She put on a dressing-gown and crept to the top of the stairs. Harry's voice floated up from the hallway and her shoulders went down a notch. At least the papers didn't have the story yet.

'There's good news and bad news,' Harry was saying, and Gwen went down a couple of steps to hear better.

'Are you going to arrest Gwen?' Cam said, his voice cold as stone and twice as unfriendly.

'No.'

'You may come inside then,' Cam said.

There was the sound of the front door closing and muffled shoes on tile. Gwen caught Cam saying, 'Give me the good news.'

'Gwen is no longer a suspect.'

She felt the tension in her body drain out and she sagged against the bannister.

'She shouldn't have been in the first place,' Cam said.

Gwen walked downstairs in time to see Harry holding up his hands. 'Just doing my job.'

'Yeah, well—'

'And you know I fucking hated it,' Harry said. He caught sight of Gwen and nodded. 'Morning. Sorry to wake you.'

'I'm happy to be woken up for news like that.'

Cam put his arm around Gwen's shoulders and pulled her close. 'What's the bad news?'

'After an illuminating chat with your mother, we had an official word in Lily Thomas's ear. However, that's about as far as I can go.' Harry nodded to Gwen. 'I know you told me before that you'd had unwanted attention, but the law isn't much good if someone is careful and determined.'

'Restraining order?' Cam said.

Harry shrugged. 'Can't hurt. And I'll keep an eye out. Unofficially.'

'Thank you,' Cam said. He looked at Gwen. 'I didn't believe you when you told me Lily was after you. Before, I mean. I thought you were being paranoid. I'm sorry.'

Gwen blinked. Cam was really taking this honesty thing to heart.

Harry rubbed his hand over his face. He hadn't shaved and his eyes were bloodshot. 'I'm sorry I can't do more. I've tried saying "it doesn't feel right" to my boss, but it's not an angle I can push.'

'Modern policemen aren't allowed hunches?' Cam said.

'Something like that.' Harry shrugged.

Cam let out a long breath. 'It's not what Morse led me to believe.'

'I'm sorry.' Harry said seriously.

The next day was the opening of the Bath Christmas market and Gwen was still booked in to run her stall. She showered and got her stock ready, working on autopilot and hoping that keeping busy would help. It didn't.

She went to the hospital on her way to the market. Katie was the same and Ruby looked worse. 'Shall I take over here for a while? Let you get some rest.'

Ruby shook her head wordlessly.

Gwen hated feeling so helpless. She held her hand against Katie's forehead and it was cool to the touch.

'She's not got a temperature,' Ruby said. 'They can't tell us anything new. They say we just have to wait.'

Gwen nodded, not trusting herself to speak. The last thing Ruby needed was for her to dissolve. 'I'm going to open my stall at the market for a couple of hours but I've got my mobile on me. Call if you need anything or if anything happens.'

'I will,' Ruby said.

Gwen kissed Katie, whispering into her hair, 'Wake up.'

The Bath Christmas market was held in the paved square in front of the Abbey. When Gwen had first seen the little wooden houses arranged around the edge, she'd thought she'd come to the wrong place and stumbled into a large garden centre by mistake. However, looking around now at the inviting displays and twinkling fairy lights, she had to admit it looked very, well, Christmassy. 'And very classy, darling,' Mary-Anne said. 'Nothing tacky in lovely Bath; the committee simply wouldn't allow it. They're even worse than Pendleford's lot.'

'Pendleford has a committee?' Gwen said, and then remembered. 'Oh. Patrick Allen's crew.'

'The very same.' Mary-Anne was dealing out soaps in rainbow colours with the speed of a croupier. 'Watch out for that one.' She winked at Gwen. 'He's got an eye for the ladies.'

'Right. Thanks.' Gwen didn't think Patrick Allen would ever be interested in her type. Thank God.

The display table was smaller than her usual one and it took longer than she expected to get her stock arranged. She nailed small pieces of wood to the back wall of the shed and rested a shadow box on each. By the time she'd finished, there were a good number of shoppers wandering past and the smell of roast chestnuts wafting through the air. A brass band began playing carols and Gwen felt her eyes pricking with tears. Again. What if Katie wasn't out of hospital in time for Christmas? She blinked and held up a mirror for a lady who was looking at a pair of earrings. *Get your mind on the job. Katie is going to wake up and want some presents on the 25th. It's not going to be very festive at End House if you don't make some bloody money.*

After an hour, the temperature had dropped further. The sky was clear – no cloud cover – but at least it was dry. Lots of the punters were carrying cardboard cups of mulled wine or hot chocolate and Gwen began to crave some. She rubbed her hands together and wished she were wearing big ski mittens rather than fingerless gloves. It would be harder to make change, but at least she wouldn't be worried about losing her fingertips to frostbite.

'Hello, Gwen.'

Gwen almost did a double-take. It was Elaine Laing, in the expensively coated flesh. 'Hello,' Gwen managed.

Elaine studied her stall and Gwen felt herself tense. *If she says something disparaging, I'm going to let her have it.*

'The market looks nice this year,' Elaine said. Her cheeks were pink from the cold, making her look more human than usual. 'A good variety of stalls.'

'Yes. The organisers did a good job,' Gwen said.

Elaine reached out a finger, clad in camel-coloured leather, and lightly touched a Liberty-print scarf. 'Is this genuine?'

'Of course,' Gwen said.

'I apologise,' Elaine said and Gwen almost fell over.

'What are those?' Elaine pointed at the shadow boxes.

'They're expensive,' Gwen warned automatically, as she always did. And then she felt stupid. She always felt diffident about the asking price, but they took so long to make, she really couldn't afford to price them lower. However, she knew that Elaine Laing probably considered seventy pounds pocket change.

She chose her favourite box and lifted it carefully down.

Elaine put her hands behind her back as if to stop herself from touching, and leaned forward to look.

Gwen steeled herself for the disparaging comments or stupid questions. It was the hardest thing about running the stall: the feeling of exposure.

'Why are you selling these here?' Elaine looked genuinely confused.

Gwen gritted her teeth and counted to ten, very fast. Then she said, 'I like them. I like making them and this is my stall. I decide what to sell.'

Elaine smiled thinly. 'I meant, why aren't you selling them through a gallery?'

'Sorry?'

'They're art pieces, correct?'

'Well. Craft or art. It's all a matter of opinion.'

Elaine straightened up. 'Is each piece one of a kind or created in strictly limited edition?'

'I never do the same piece twice. I couldn't; the components are all unique—'

'Are they all titled? Do they carry some kind of message or theme or mood?' Elaine was ticking points off on her fingers. 'Are they expressions of self?'

'Sorry?'

'I was just thinking that they should be in a gallery. Or a high-end gift shop at the very least. This—' she waved at the wooden huts, the fairy lights, the crowd of Christmas shoppers, 'is very pleasant, but I'm not sure you're reaching your audience.'

'My audience?'

'All art is performance,' Elaine said crisply. 'Surely you know that? I'll take this one.' She reached into her handbag and extracted a purse. 'Do you take credit cards?'

Gwen wrapped the shadow box carefully in tissue and put it into a cardboard box and then a bag. As she processed Elaine's card, she wondered whether either of them were going to mention their last conversation. Gwen decided just to be grateful for whatever had brought about the change from a spitting and furious Elaine to this terrifyingly efficient, art-spouting, shadow-box buying creature.

Abruptly, Elaine said, 'I was very sorry to hear about your niece.'

'Thank you,' Gwen said, concentrating very hard on the credit card machine.

'I know the head of paediatrics at Bath Royal and I've spoken to him about Katie's care.'

Gwen looked up, surprised that Elaine knew Katie's name.

'And I hear I'll be seeing you on Christmas Eve.'

'What?' Gwen said.

'I trust you'll wear something suitable? I'm sure you won't want to embarrass Cameron.'

'Thank you for your purchase,' Gwen said, as she always did.

Elaine gave her a patronising smile. 'I wouldn't want you to feel out of place.'

'Clearly,' Gwen said, keeping her expression neutral.

Elaine leaned in slightly. 'You wanted in, Gwen. You're going to have to live up to the Laing standards. That, as you would no doubt put it, is the deal.' She gave a final wintery smile and walked away. Gwen watched her march straight to the exit as if her mission had been accomplished. *Oh boy.*

Gwen was exhausted when she got back to End House. She trailed up her garden path and unlocked the front door. She hung up her coat and turned, almost tripping over Cat. 'Silly thing.' She bent down to stroke him, but he wouldn't stay still. He was winding round and round her ankles in a figure of eight. His mouth opened, showing pink gums and sharp teeth and gusting fish-breath into Gwen's face, but no sound came out. It was as if something had stolen his screech. Gwen's body tensed: something was very wrong.

She tried to pick Cat up, but he sprang away. Gwen moved to the kitchen doorway and that was when she saw Lily. She was standing at the kitchen sink, gazing out of the window into the garden. The light from the hallway illuminated the dark kitchen so that Lily's blonde hair seemed to glow. Her hands, gripping the edge of the counter, were strangely black. Gwen flipped the light switch and the blackness resolved into dirt. Lily's perfect pale pink fingernails were broken and encrusted with brown earth, as if she'd been digging with her bare hands.

'Hello, Lily,' Gwen said. Her throat clicked when she tried to swallow.

'Gwen!' Lily turned and smiled radiantly. 'I've been waiting for ever.'

'I was in Bath.'

Lily waved her hand. 'I brought you some carrots. From my garden.'

Gwen glanced at the pile of vegetables on the draining board. They were whiteish yellow, sickly-looking.

'How did you get in?'

'I told you.' Lily gave her strange tinkling laugh. It lifted the hairs on the back of Gwen's neck. 'Neighbours all look out for each other around here.'

Gwen edged backwards, thinking that if she could grab the phone in the hallway, she would call for help. Lily did not look at all well.

'I'd rather you stayed here. Rude to leave so quickly.' Lily's eyes were shining feverishly. 'We've got such a lot to talk about.'

Gwen looked at the pile of vegetation again. 'That's Wolfsbane.'

'Aconite, yes,' Lily said. 'I was wondering what to do with it. I've got such a lot.'

'It's poisonous,' Gwen said. 'You need to be careful.'

'Don't pretend to be concerned,' Lily snapped. 'You don't care about me. You've heard what everyone says. I'm evil.'

Gwen swallowed. 'Nobody's saying that.'

'Liar.' Lily spoke mildly, but her eyes hadn't lost their crazed glaze.

Gwen felt the counter behind her and realised that she'd been backing away.

Lily took a step forward. 'You're as bad as Iris, you know. I tried to be a friend, I welcomed you, but you've been keeping secrets. You're keeping what's mine. Just like Iris.'

'I don't know what you're talking about,' Gwen said. 'I don't have anything that belongs to you.'

'Stop playing games.' Lily's voice went up at least an octave. 'You know what I want. Iris must've written about it. She scribbled everything down in those little books. I know.'

'I know she was scared of you,' Gwen said. Her own fear was there now, unmistakable and pressing onto her chest.

Lily shook her head, smiling eerily. 'I can't live like this. The worry is too much. It's exhausting.' She smoothed a hand across her brow, as if erasing the lines there. 'All you have to do is give me the evidence and I'll leave you alone. I'll even let you stay here.'

'What evidence?'

'Iris called it her insurance. Evidence that put me in the house when my poor father had his accident. She said if anything happened to her, it would be found. Now I've gone over and over that day and I'm sure there isn't anything, but I can't help worrying.' Her mask had slipped. Lily was breathing heavily, her silk blouse stained with crescent moons of sweat under each arm. 'I'm not going to jail. He never wanted to be an invalid. He was in pain. I gave him peace, so it's only fair I got his house.'

'Did he want that kind of peace?' Gwen couldn't help thinking about an old man standing at the top of a staircase, feeling a shove in the small of his back and the sensation of falling, the lurching panic.

'What other kind is there?' Lily said. 'Besides, he knew I wasn't cut out to be a nursemaid. He *knew* that.'

Lily was between her and the doorway to the hall. The route to the back door was clear, but it was much further and Lily only had to take a couple of steps, lunge a bit, and she had it covered. 'I know what you can do. I know how you found your niece. And that dead boy. All you have to do is find Iris's evidence. It's not such a big ask. You've been doing favours for people all over town.'

'I can try,' Gwen said. 'But I can only find what actually exists.'

Lily's mouth twisted. 'How convenient.'

'It's the truth,' Gwen said. 'And I promise you that Iris didn't tell me about any evidence. I really don't think it's real. I think she made it up.'

Lily's smile fled. The expression that replaced it was so much worse. 'You're not leaving me much choice, Gwen. I've got to be certain no one knows. It's nothing personal, you understand?'

Gwen slid her hand behind her back and felt around on the counter for a weapon. 'Can't we talk about this?' Gwen said. 'Work something out?'

'Everyone around here knows you're unstable. Doesn't matter what the police say, half the town thinks you had something to do with your niece going missing. I made sure of that. And now she's so poorly, too.' Lily's mouth twisted. 'When she dies it won't take much to convince everyone that you killed yourself out of guilt.'

'Nobody will believe a word from you.' *Good job, Gwen. Insult the crazy woman.*

'But the herbs that Katie took are right here, in your kitchen.' Lily's blue eyes were like marbles. The whites showing all the way around. 'And the flask that Katie drank from belongs to you.'

'What are you talking about?'

'You really should have checked the contents list for the house when I told you to, Gwen. Iris had a pretty little flask and you inherited it along with the house. Such a shame you decided to brew such a nasty concoction to feed to poor little Katie.' Lily shook her head in mock sadness. 'It's truly tragic when someone turns on their own family like that. I tried to warn everyone that you were trouble and now they'll know how right I was.'

Gwen's insides were like ice. 'What did you give Katie? Tell me.'

Lily ignored her. 'I'm doing you a favour, really. You don't know what it's like in this place. You make one little mistake and they never forgive you. Never let you forget.' Lily produced a knife. 'You're the crazy one. Everyone knows it. And now you're suicidal, too.'

Gwen's fingers closed around the handle of something. She brought it out in one deft movement, hoping for a knife or the steak mallet. It was a spatula.

Lily laughed happily. 'What are you going to do? Spread me?'

Damn.

Lily was moving slowly to one side, stealthily. A look more dangerous than Gwen had ever seen crossed her face. Her voice was quiet, insidious. 'You'll never belong in Pendleford. You may as well give up. Give me the evidence and you can leave. I don't mean you any harm.'

Gwen forced herself to pause, to look as though she were seriously contemplating Lily's words. Then she ran for the doorway. She made it into the hallway, but could feel Lily right behind her. Everything seemed to have slowed down; she was hyper-aware of everything: the slippery tiles on the hall floor, the sound of her desperate breathing, the scent of oak and earth and, underneath those, something foul.

The knife slashed down to her left, slicing through her sleeve. She dived through the nearest open door in the hope she'd be able to shut it behind her.

She was too late. Lily was halfway through into the dining room. Her hand grasped the back of Gwen's shirt and she yanked, pulling Gwen backwards. She stumbled, almost toppling over.

Gwen managed to pull away in one panicked movement. She stumbled forwards, picking up the only portable item on the vast expanse of the unused dining table. A plant pot. She edged behind the table and hefted the ceramic in her hands, getting ready to throw it.

Lily was still talking, varying in volume like a radio being tuned in and out. 'I am never going to stop, you know. You may as well leave. I am never going to let you have End House. It's just not yours. Not by rights. And you're just like her. Sitting in your big house, laughing at me, thinking you're better than me.'

'I don't want to be like Iris. I don't want people to visit me; I want a quiet life.' Gwen tried to sound reasonable. Soothing.

Lily shook her head violently, the knife waving. 'It's all just words. You should know better. Action is what counts.'

Gwen thought about screaming, but knew no one was close enough to hear. Damn the stupid isolated house and damn her pathetic witchy powers. What good was the ability to 'find things' now? She needed super-strength or the ability to shoot lasers from her eyes.

Lily was creeping forwards, circling the table. 'I tried to tell your niece that. You've got to go after what you want in life. No one's going to hand you anything on a plate.'

Gwen felt sick. 'When did you speak to Katie? Tell me what you did to her. Please.'

Lily paused, looking outraged. 'I gave her what she wanted. I gave her power, which is more than you, her so-called aunt, did. You and Iris. You're selfish. You want to keep everything for yourselves.'

Oh God. Katie.

Lily started moving again, taking tiny steps and moving on the balls of her feet like a parody of a ballet dancer.

Gwen moved crab-wise in the other direction, but she knew it wasn't going to be much longer. She was trapped behind the table and as soon as Lily got close enough to use that knife, it was all over. She was unarmed and no match for the ball of insane fury advancing towards her.

Without warning, the crack in the ceiling wrenched apart. To Gwen, it looked as if invisible fingers had hooked themselves either side and pulled. But, of course, that wasn't possible.

A split second later, and a large chunk of plaster fell squarely onto the top of Lily's head. She went down in one movement, hard. Smaller pieces of plaster and an unholy amount of white dust rained down from the hole and within a split second Gwen couldn't see anything. The dust was in her eyes, up her nose, and in her throat. Then she heard it. Cam's voice.

'Help!' she yelled and coughed, her voice coming out thick and strange.

'Gwen?' Cam's voice and the sound of a door opening. Gwen almost wept with relief. Instead, she had a coughing fit.

The dust cleared, settling around the room like a sprinkling of fake snow and, suddenly, wonderfully, Cam appeared. He looked at Lily's crumpled form and sprang forward.

'Careful! She's got a knife.' Gwen made her way from behind the table.

'Christ. Are you all right?'

Gwen nodded. Her eyes were streaming and she pulled up the tail of her shirt to wipe them.

Cam bent over Lily, felt for a pulse in her neck. Her eyes were open, lips parted in an expression of furious surprise. She looked like a gargoyle and even before Cam said, 'Call an ambulance,' Gwen knew she was dead. He kicked out and something went skidding across the floor. The knife.

Gwen made it into the hall and called for an ambulance. Then Cam was there and she leaned into the solid weight of him, burying her face in his shirt and blocking everything out.

'What happened?' Cam was asking, his hands stroking her back rhythmically as if she were Cat.

'The ceiling came down,' Gwen said into his chest. 'It was so fast, she didn't have a chance to move.'

'It's okay,' Cam said. 'It wasn't your fault.'

She felt a weight bash into her calves and looked down. Cat stared plaintively up at her and let out an unearthly shriek. Gwen had never been so pleased to hear it. She bent down and stroked Cat, scratching him under his chin and feeling her heart swell with love and relief.

Katie. 'I need to go to the hospital,' Gwen said. 'Now.'

'Are you hurt?' Cam said quickly.

'No. It's Katie. I think I know what's wrong with her.'

Cam looked around. 'We should really wait for the ambulance. And I need to call Harry.'

'I think Lily might have hexed her. Or she told her to try a spell and it hurt her. It's dangerous if you're not strong enough. I swear it's true. I know you don't—'

Cam handed her his car keys. 'You go. I'll wait five minutes before I call Harry. And I won't tell him where you are.'

In the car, Gwen used Cam's fancy hands-free kit. 'Gloria?'

'Hello, sweetie.' Gloria's voice was sleepy. 'What time is it?'

'When Ruby got sick that time, how did you make her better?'

'What's happened?' Gloria's voice was instantly alert.

'It's Katie. I think she did some magic. Something big. Now she won't wake up.'

Gloria took a sharp breath in. Then she said, 'What kind of magic?'

'I don't know.' Gwen rubbed her face in frustration.

'When your sister got ill, she'd used one of my spells. Something she'd overheard me doing for a client. It took me a while to work it out, but I needed to give her something of mine. Everything has to be balanced, remember.'

'What did you give her?'

'It has to be something really personal. And something powerful.'

'What did you use?' Gwen was out of Pendleford and on the main road to Bath. She pressed the accelerator.

After a pause, Gloria said, 'Pain. Do you remember my broken thumb? I smashed it with a hammer to wake your sister up.'

'Oh.' Gwen swallowed. 'Thank you.'

Gwen rang End House and spoke to Cam. She knew that Lily was beyond feeling pain, but she wasn't about to give up. She told him what she needed and he agreed immediately. No argument. No horror. Gwen turned the car around at the first available place and headed back to Pendleford. Gwen saw strobing lights as she neared her road, but thankfully Cam was waiting. She pulled up beside him and wound down her window, but he was already crossing to the passenger side and opening the door.

'Aren't the police here? Don't you have to stay?'

'I don't care,' Cam said. 'Harry can arrest me later if he feels like it.'

'Did you—'

He held up a small bundle. 'Got it.'

Gwen concentrated on driving carefully all the way to Bath. The last thing they needed was to get stopped by a traffic cop.

'Thank you,' Gwen said. She knew Cam must be wondering what the hell was going on.

'No problem. Just to warn you, it's an offence to mess with a crime scene so it might be best you don't mention this to Harry.'

He was helping her; he deserved an explanation. Gwen took a deep breath. 'Lily gave Katie some magic. A spell or a potion, I don't know exactly, and she used it. If you use magic that's too strong then it can hurt you really badly.' She swallowed, waiting for Cam to argue, call her crazy, grab the steering wheel and attempt a citizen's arrest.

'And you need Lily's blood, why?'

'It's like there's an almighty fight going on inside Katie. Lily's magic wasn't balanced by Katie's, because Katie isn't strong enough. That's why she's knocked out. While there's an imbalance, while the fight is going on, she'll stay like that. I need something really personal to Lily to help even the odds a bit. And you can't get much more personal than blood.' Gwen didn't add that pain was even better. She wasn't sure how much of this information Cam was ready to hear.

'What happens if Lily's magic wins the fight?' Cam said.

Gwen didn't want to answer him, didn't want to say the words out loud. 'She'll die.'

At the hospital, Gwen asked Cam to distract Ruby and David. 'Get them out of the room, if you can.'

'I'll try,' he said.

David was asleep in a chair, his legs stretched out, a pillow tucked under his head and Ruby was in the same position Gwen had seen her every time; her chair pulled up to the bed and holding Katie's hand.

'Hi,' Ruby whispered, glancing at David. 'He's only just gone off.'

Gwen looked at Katie, so pale and still. Now that Lily had lifted the scales from her eyes, Katie looked exactly like Ruby all those years ago. Gwen couldn't believe she hadn't seen it before. She remembered how still Ruby had been. The long days and weeks while Gloria became increasingly frantic.

Gwen took the bundle from Cam and unfolded it. Cam had done a good job, soaking his handkerchief in the blood from Lily's head wound. It was dark red in the centre and already turning to brown at the edges, but Gwen did her best. She smeared some on Katie's forehead, whispering every anti-hex incantation she'd ever learned. Words came to her that she'd long forgotten, bubbling up from her subconscious. She rubbed the blood-soaked cloth across the back of each of Katie's hands and then, lifting the blankets, on the soles of her feet, too. The words were coming thick and fast now. She felt them flowing through her, from Gloria, from Iris, from generations of Harper women.

Gwen was vaguely aware, at the very periphery of her attention, that Ruby was speaking, David was awake and shouting, and Cam was trying to calm them both down. She felt hands on her arm, trying to pull her away from Katie, but she shrugged them off easily. She leaned in close and whispered the final words directly into Katie's right ear. Then she dabbed Lily's blood onto Katie's lips.

David succeeded in pulling her away then. He snatched the cloth from Gwen. 'Have you lost your fucking mind?' His face was white with anger, his eyes wet with tears.

'Wait a minute,' Cam said, stepping between them, his hands up.

'Daddy?'

Everyone looked at the bed.

Katie's eyes fluttered open. Ruby and David flew to her.

'Hey, baby,' David said, and the love and relief in his voice made Gwen's eyes prick.

Katie moved her head slowly, looking at the faces. She looked deathly serious and utterly unlike herself. Her eyes seemed almost blank and, for an awful moment, Gwen considered the possibility that she had some kind of brain damage.

'You gave us a scare, kiddo.' Ruby spoke so softly Gwen could hardly make out the words.

Tears leaked from Katie's eyes. 'I'm sorry, Mum,' she whispered, her voice cracked and even quieter than Ruby's. 'I'm so sorry.' At once she was enveloped by Ruby and they were both crying. Cam shot a horrified look at Gwen, who squeezed his hand. She grabbed a box of tissues and placed them on the bed next to the Ruby-and-Katie-and-David huddle.

'I'll call a nurse,' Gwen said and they backed out to the corridor.

Thirty minutes later, Katie had been checked by the doctor and the ponytailed nurse informed them that visiting hours were over. Cam had gone in search of hot drinks and Gwen went in to say goodbye. Ruby and David were back in their guard positions, sitting on either side of the bed. Katie was sitting up, sipping a cup of water.

'The nurse says we have to go,' Gwen said. She stepped closer to the bed, drinking in the sight of her niece. Alive. *Awake.*

'Okay,' Ruby said. She stood up suddenly and hugged Gwen. 'Thank you.'

Gwen didn't trust herself to answer, so she just squeezed Ruby back.

Back at End House, after the professionals had taken Lily's body away and Harry had come with another officer and taken photographs of the ceiling and the floor and the cracks in the walls, Gwen walked through the house. In each room she studied the ceiling for cracks and paused, listening, in case Iris had anything to tell her. She didn't care if she was acting like a lunatic. She didn't even care if Cam heard her muttering to herself. After completing the upstairs, the living room with its diseased walls and her beloved kitchen, she paused by the door to the dining room. She surveyed the mess of plaster dust and the hole in the ceiling that was like a gaping wound. Perhaps it was her imagination, but the whole place felt lighter. The room was a damn sight uglier, but the bad feeling, the slowness in the air that she'd only been vaguely aware of, had gone. She whispered goodbye to Iris and closed the door.

Cam was making tea in the kitchen. He handed her a mug and Gwen wrapped both hands around it, breathing in the steam. The adrenaline was ebbing out of her body, leaving her weak and slightly sick. Cam was watching her warily, and Gwen closed her eyes. *Here it comes,* she thought, *this is when he makes a graceful exit.*

'I don't know what to say,' Cam began. 'I was so sure—'

Gwen shook her head,;she didn't blame him. Magic had been hard for her to accept, and she'd grown up with it. 'It doesn't matter.' She was numb, but she knew that wouldn't last. Later, the pain would hit her. She had the childish sense that if she didn't open her eyes and look at Cam then he couldn't leave, couldn't say goodbye.

'I can't believe I got things so wrong,' Cam said. 'You told me but I wouldn't listen.'

Gwen opened her eyes.

'I'll make it up to you,' he said, looking wretched. 'Tell me what I can do.'

'You already have.' Gwen put her mug down, reached out for him. 'You helped me. You believed me. Or, if you didn't believe exactly—'

'I trust you.' Cam said. 'I don't understand what happened, but I know it's real. You were amazing.' He pulled her close and Gwen wrapped her arms around him, holding tightly, hardly believing the words she was hearing. 'This supernatural stuff is real. And you're like a superhero.'

Gwen pulled back slightly to smile at him. 'Is that a bid to make me wear a Wonder Woman costume? I always knew you were kinky.'

'I'm being serious. I was wrong. I've been holding you away, trying not to get too close. I'm a fucking idiot.'

The intensity of his voice made Gwen's throat close up. 'Well, it was a lot to take in. That's why I never told you about it before, when we were younger. I was frightened it would be too much, that you'd think I was crazy.

'And I did.' Cam gave her a rueful smile. 'Sorry. But that wasn't just it. I think I was using that as a bit of an excuse.' He took a deep breath. 'I didn't trust that you were going to stay this time.'

'Oh.' Gwen blinked.

They looked at each other in silence for a moment. Then Cam smiled, breaking the tension. 'So, what else is going to rock my world view? You don't have to hide anything from me any more. Are werewolves real? Unicorns?'

Gwen shuddered, thinking about Lily's house. 'Don't mention unicorns. They're evil.'

Cam hugged her again, speaking into her hair. 'Made-up evil, or really real evil?'

'You're taking this belief thing very seriously, aren't you?'

'Like I said…' Cam kissed her '…I've got a lot of making up to do.'

CHAPTER 28

Giving people what they need is not popular, but at least it's honest. And I've been fair. I've done the best with what I was given, too. There's nothing worse than a squandered talent.

Gwen spent the rest of the week running her stall at the Bath market and making new shadow boxes. Every spare moment was spent reading through Iris's journals. It felt important, like she was bearing witness to Iris's life. A life that seemed to grow increasingly small and frightened as the journal dates got closer to the present:

She keeps bringing me gifts. Like I don't know what she's up to. Never lets a truth out untwisted that one. I'm Iris Harper. She can't fool me. I'm Iris Harper and I mustn't forget it.

At eight o'clock every night, Cam would arrive, bearing dinner. On the Friday, it was Thai curry with hot and sour soup to start. Gwen washed the glue off her hands, while Cam plated up the food.

Afterwards, Gwen sat back, groaning. 'So. Full.'

Cam smiled at her with such fondness that Gwen thought she was going to start crying. Again. It was like a bloody dam had burst.

'I've been thinking,' Cam said, playing with the stem of his wine glass. 'Would you like to come to my mother's Christmas Eve party?'

The shock made Gwen blink. 'At your mother's house?'

He nodded. 'It tends to be pretty stuffy. It's mainly clients and whoever my mother is trying to set me up with.'

'Are you sure she'll let me across the threshold?' The words were out before Gwen could stop them. 'Sorry.'

'I know she's difficult,' Cam began. 'She's had a lot to cope with, though.'

'I know. I am sorry. She's just lost your granddad.'

'She really misses Dad, too. I think this has brought it all back. She's been talking about him quite a bit.' Cam looked up. 'So, what do you think? You on for the social event of the season?'

'I'm not sure,' Gwen said. 'It doesn't sound like my cup of tea.'

Cam's face fell and Gwen rushed to explain herself. 'I'm really happy to be invited. Thank you. I just think that maybe that's all I wanted.' She hesitated. 'For you to invite me. Does that make any sense?'

'Sort of.' Cam frowned. 'I still think you should come, though. My mum is expecting you, now. I kind of told her you were my date.'

'Oh, well then.' Gwen forced a smile. Her mother's voice sounded clear in her mind. Unhelpful as always. *Careful what you wish for.*

Gwen stretched. 'We can't go on eating takeaway every night. I'll be the size of a house in a month,' she said.

Cam held up the Styrofoam cups, an injured expression on his face. 'Soup's good for you. It's nourishing.'

Gwen laughed. 'I'm not sure the deep-fried dumplings are quite as healthy.'

'I'd love you if you were size of three houses,' Cam said. 'But if you're that concerned, I'm happy to help you work off some energy.'

'You're a true gent,' Gwen said, mind fizzing at his casual use of the 'l' word.

'Or we could work up an appetite.' Cam walked Gwen back towards the counter and boosted her up onto it. She wrapped her legs around his waist and gave in to the kiss.

Cam pulled at the tie at the waist of her wrap dress and it unravelled. He slid his hand inside the material, his fingers sending electricity across her skin. Gwen leaned forwards, kissing him harder.

'I like this dress,' Cam said against her mouth. 'Easy access.'

'Are you calling me easy?' Gwen said. Then she gasped as he ran his thumb across her nipple.

'I'll call you anything you like,' Cam said. He bent to kiss her neck and cupped the back of her head with his hand. 'Have I mentioned that I like the haircut?'

'I don't remember,' Gwen said, her mind clouded with wanting. She pulled his shirt out of his trousers and ran her hands up inside it. Cam sucked in his breath. Gwen felt a rush of power that was intoxicating. She was a mess, true, but uptight Cameron Laing looked punch-drunk, his eyes dark and focused on her.

'Well,' Cam said. 'I. Really. Like. It.' He punctuated each word with a kiss. Gwen kissed him back with everything she had. The past melted away and there was nothing but the moment. Her and Cam moving together, their breath mingling, and his voice in her ear whispering that he loved her. All of her.

By the following weekend, Katie had made a full recovery. She was out of hospital and, according to Ruby, showing no ill effects at all. 'She hasn't shut up,' Ruby said, and Gwen could hear the smile in her voice.

She went round to the house to visit; to hug Katie and, possibly, to throttle her for being so monumentally stupid.

Katie was on the sofa, covered in a duvet, a side table pulled up close and covered in magazines.

'Hot drink?' Ruby asked.

'I'm boiling,' Katie said. 'If I drink any more hot chocolate, I'm going to be sick.'

'It's a hard life,' Gwen said, smiling.

'Tea?' Ruby asked.

'Yes please.'

'It's not much of a thank you,' Ruby said. 'I looked, but Hallmark don't make a "thank-you-for-saving-my-baby" card, so tea will have to do.'

Gwen looked at the floor, stunned. Ruby had run out of the room, her face red, and mumbling something about getting a tissue.

Gwen looked at Katie, who looked as horrified as she felt.

'She'll calm down soon. Be back to normal before you know it,' Gwen said. 'Then we'll both be in trouble.'

'Thank God. I'm in danger of being fussed to death,' Katie said, clearly hoping for a laugh.

Gwen shook her head in mock-seriousness.

'Too soon?' Katie said. Her mobile phone buzzed and Katie launched herself off the sofa to grab it, the duvet slipping onto the floor.

Gwen rearranged it over her as Katie scrolled through her text message. She looked up and gave an unhappy smile. 'I've never been so popular.'

'They'll all be talking about something else next week. People are very self-obsessed, you know.'

Katie hesitated, looking properly sick for the first time since Gwen had arrived. Her heart lurched. 'What's—'

'I did a spell.' Katie spoke quietly, but Gwen still glanced reflexively towards the kitchen. She hoped Ruby wasn't listening. 'I know. What kind?'

'It was meant to make him fall in love with me, but it didn't work.' Katie's pale face coloured. 'I'm sorry. I know you warned me.'

'Come here.' Gwen pulled Katie in for a hug. 'You think I never made a mistake?'

Katie looked up at her, eyes shining with cautious gratitude. 'You're not angry?'

'No,' Gwen said. 'I have no room for angry. Nothing left. I'm a husk.'

Katie's face fell again. 'I'm so sorry, I never meant—'

'What in God's name were you doing up that hill, anyway?'

Katie looked down. 'I was upset and I had to get away from that house. It was all I could think about.'

'How much had you had to drink?'

Katie glanced to the kitchen. 'Just a couple. I swear I wasn't drunk, but I couldn't stop crying—'

'Over a boy?'

Katie glanced up. 'He was kissing my best friend.'

'Ouch,' Gwen said. 'Still. Going for a stroll in the middle of the night in winter. Not your smartest move.'

'It wasn't snowing when I started and I thought I was going to walk just a little way and they'd come looking for me to apologise and stuff, but they didn't so I kept walking and then I got lost. And I felt really weird. There was like a rushing sound in my ears, and I couldn't stop walking. I know that sounds stupid, but I really couldn't stop. It was like something was making me keep going.' Katie's eyes filled with tears. 'I was really scared.'

'Oh, baby.' Gwen put her arms around Katie. 'It's okay.'

'Then the rushing sound got really loud and I don't remember anything else. Not until I woke up in hospital. I'm so sorry.'

'Shush. It's all over. It worked out. You're fine.' Gwen hugged her harder.

'Why didn't it work?' Katie mumbled into Gwen's shoulder.

Gwen pulled away so that she could look into her niece's eyes.

'I'm not going to try it again,' Katie said hurriedly, 'but I really thought it had. I kind of felt something shift. I've thought about it and I didn't imagine it. I know it sounds mad—'

'Not as much as you might think,' Gwen said. She checked that Ruby was still in the kitchen. You couldn't pretend this stuff didn't exist. Not if it came a-calling for you. 'Bollocks,' Gwen said.

'Auntie Gwen!' Katie laughed, a hand over her mouth.

'Look. If you felt that spell work, then it probably did. Chances are, you phrased things a little sloppily.'

'I was really specific.' Katie was shaking her head. 'I know you have to be careful about that.'

'Okay; what did you say?'

'That I wanted Luke Taylor to fall in love with me,' Katie said promptly.

'Are you sure?' Gwen arched an eyebrow.

Katie nodded.

'But what did you think underneath your thoughts?'

'What do you mean?'

'Deep down, did you really think he could love you? Did you truly believe that a spell could make Luke Taylor actually fall deeply, madly, head over heels in love with you?'

Katie winced. 'Maybe not. Not like, completely and totally. But if I thought there was a real chance of it, then I wouldn't even need a spell, would I?'

Gwen grinned at her. 'Now you're getting it. So, what did you really think? What was that very last, heartfelt thought? The one that bubbled up, beyond your control, as you blew out the candle or finished the potion?'

'How did you...?' Katie began. Then she paused for a moment and said, 'I wanted him to notice me.'

'There you go,' Gwen said. 'And you got your wish.'

Katie whistled. 'Magic's a bit of a bitch.'

'Damn skippy,' Gwen said.

On the last day of the market, Gwen treated herself to a beautiful leather journal from one of the other traders. It was a cheerful red colour and had a flap that was held shut with an ornate brass latch. Gwen opened it flat and, taking a good writing pen, wrote the date on the first page. After a moment's hesitation, she wrote. 'For Katie'.

Later, she was half-heartedly cleaning the hall floor when her mobile rang. It was Bob from the Red Lion. 'That little crap-weasel came through,' he said without preamble. 'Have you seen it?'

'No. What?' Gwen was struggling to focus on Bob's voice. She stared at the yellow police tape that flapped in the entrance to her dining room, still trying to believe that Lily was truly gone. Amanda's husband was due that afternoon to quote for rebuilding the ceiling and redecorating the room.

'The local rag,' Bob said. 'Ryan put your announcement in. For the book burning.'

Gwen closed her eyes. She'd forgotten about that.

'They've got the time as five-thirty, so it'll be proper dark. We'll need plenty of torches and I'm going to do some snacks.'

'Don't call it a book burning; that sounds terrible—'

'Whatever you like,' Bob said patiently. 'It's on.'

'Thank you,' she managed. 'I'll come and help set up.'

'No need. You sound like you need a rest,' Bob said cheerfully. 'Just make sure you turn up. Don't leave me hanging, Gwennie.'

Gwen looked at the bags of Iris's books arranged in her hallway. Lily had done a pretty good job of collecting them together, but there were still more. Gwen lay on the carpet in the bedroom and hooked a couple out from under the brass bed. She fetched three from the under-the-sink cupboard in her workroom and flicked through to check that they were just recipes. She added those to her own pile, ready to read, test and transfer to her own book. She felt a burst of happiness at the thought.

The phone rang and she picked it up, expecting Cam.

'Are you all right?' Gwen had never heard her mother's voice sound so shaky.

'Katie's fine,' Gwen said with a rush of guilt. 'Sorry. I should've called.'

'Thank God.' Gloria let out a whoosh of breath. 'I read your cards. I'm sorry, I know you hate it when I do that, but I did and I wasn't sure—'

'It's fine. You helped,' she said, hating that it was still so hard to say that to Gloria.

'Katie's really okay?'

'She's fine. I mean, she's fourteen, so there are issues, but she's got Ruby and she's got me, so she's going to be okay.'

'That's good,' Gloria said. 'And I will send her something at Christmas.'

'Or you could visit,' Gwen said. She closed her mouth immediately afterwards, amazed and slightly horrified by the words.

There was a silence.

Gwen rushed to fill it. 'I know it's really expensive and you probably can't manage it, but I just wanted you to know that you're welcome. I've cleared your old bedroom and I'm going to paint it sky-blue. I've pulled up that horrible carpet. The floorboards are a bit of state, but once I've painted them white and got a rug, it'll be quite nice.'

'I don't know if we'll be able to leave the farm,' Gloria said, actually sounding a little wistful.

'I understand,' Gwen said.

'But I might be able to come on my own.'

Gwen sat down in shock. Ruby was going to kill her.

After saying goodbye, Gwen took several deep breaths. Her mother had taught her that you never look back, but Gwen had shown her that it was, at the very least, an option.

Cam arrived with a duffel bag filled with Maglites and packets of glow sticks. 'For the kids,' he said. 'I saw them in the shop and thought they might be a good idea.'

'It's not Bonfire Night,' Gwen said.

Cam shrugged. He was wearing a thick grey jumper and dark jeans and looked more relaxed than Gwen could remember.

Gwen wished she felt the same way. She frowned at the carrier bags filled with notebooks. 'I bet nobody even turns up.'

'It doesn't matter.' Cam put his arm around her shoulders. 'You'll still be getting rid of this lot.'

The cold snap was showing no signs of abating. The pavements were frosted and their footsteps crunched loudly in the quiet evening. As they hit the main road into town, the traffic streamed past. They passed a floodlit church and navigated the cobbled streets down towards the river. The gudgeon was still poised on top of the round house, its mouth wide open as if serenading the sky. 'Good evening,' Gwen said to it.

Cam looked sideways at her. 'Are you sure you're okay?'

'Bit nervous,' Gwen said. 'I'm making a statement. What if nobody likes it?'

'Ah, but you come with the Laing seal of approval. They wouldn't dare to not like it.' Cam pointed to his chest. 'Master of the Universe, remember?'

'How could I forget?' Gwen smiled, some of the tension leaching away. As they reached the beginning of the bridge, Cam veered off course. He tugged Gwen's hand gently and guided her down the slope towards the river.

'What are you doing?'

'Old time's sake. Humour me?' In the dark of the bridge, Cam leaned against the stonework and pulled Gwen close. He kissed her thoroughly until her breath was gone and her remaining nerves had been chased out by lust. She buried her head in his neck and breathed deeply. He smelled of Cam: soap and deodorant and warmly delicious man.

'I hope this fire thing isn't going to take long,' Cam said, his voice husky, and kissed her again.

'We could just go home?' Gwen managed, breathing heavily herself.

'Don't tempt me,' Cam said. 'Come on.' He helped her back up the hill to the street. 'Sooner we get there, sooner we can go home to bed.'

'That's the spirit,' Gwen said. Then she caught sight of the green. There were thirty or forty people already there. They were bundled up in coats and scarves, some holding cardboard coffee cups, some with torches. As they got closer, Gwen recognised faces and people waved and nodded to her.

Bob was in the middle, poking the glowing centre of a metal brazier with a stick. The firelight lit the underside of his chin, making him look demonic.

'All right, Gwennie.' Bob slung an arm around her shoulders. He nodded to Cam. 'Mate.'

'I didn't think anybody would come,' Gwen said, gazing at the green in wonder. She put down her carrier bags and rubbed her hands where the handles had cut into her palms.

Bob looked embarrassed. 'I put a sign up in the pub. Free hot dogs.'

'That was very kind of you,' Gwen said, not at all sure it was.

The crowd had fallen silent. There was a shuffling of feet and then a small child said, 'When are the fireworks?'

Gwen turned to face the group. She tried not to think about the green, the site of the murder of Jane Morely. This wasn't a witch trial. This was an exorcism.

'What's in the books?' a voice from the back shouted.

'Secrets,' Gwen said. Her voice sounded weak and she swallowed, trying to get some lubrication in her dry throat.

Cam squeezed her hand and she stepped forwards, straightening her back. 'Thank you all for coming. As many of you know, I am Iris Harper's great-niece. I inherited her house and everything inside it.' Gwen looked around, trying to speak to everyone. She gestured to the bags. 'These diaries and notebooks cover Iris's life in Pendleford. She wrote about the things she did, the people she helped and, sometimes, about the things that people told her.'

There was a murmuring in the crowd. Gwen caught sight of Patrick Allen, standing off to the right of the group, his arms tightly folded.

'I wanted to honour Iris's contribution to the community. I think that she was always here for the people of Pendleford. She wasn't always nice—'

The murmur turned to gentle laughter and someone called out, 'You got that right.'

Gwen smiled in the direction of the voice and continued, 'But she always helped if she could. She lived alone, but I like to think that she considered all of you – and your parents and grandparents – her family.'

Gwen ignored the sceptical faces. If Cam was right, everything could be spun. It was all in the way you presented the facts. 'When Iris left me her notebooks, I don't think she intended for me to read them. There are secrets in these books, confidences whispered to her in times of need. I think she intended me to protect them and, by extension, to protect all of you.' She took a deep breath. 'I've decided that the best way to do that is to destroy them.' Gwen motioned to Cam, who picked up a bag and tipped it directly into the brazier.

There was a communal intake of breath as the flames leaped and a shower of sparks flew up to the sky. Someone said, 'Ooh.'

'I think the best way to honour my aunt and everyone in Pendleford is by starting afresh,' Gwen said. 'Thank you.'

There was a moment of silence and then Helen Brewer stepped forward and began clapping. There was a smattering of applause which abruptly grew in size when Bob appeared with a tray of hot dogs.

Gwen stepped back towards Cam and helped him empty another bag of books onto the fire.

A figure shuffled over. 'I hope your fruit cake recipe isn't in that lot.' Fred Byres gestured mournfully to the remaining carrier bags.

'Wouldn't matter,' Gwen said cheerfully. 'I've committed it to memory. You won't go without while I'm around.'

Fred gave her a sweet, shy smile that made him look twenty years younger. 'You're a good girl. I'm going to tell everyone at the seniors club about you.'

Mercifully, Reg called Fred over for some food, so Gwen was saved from kicking him in the ankle.

Harry appeared. 'Evening, all.' He looked at Gwen nervously. 'Are you still speaking to me?'

'What's a little near-arrest between friends?' Gwen said. She gave Harry what she hoped was a reassuring smile.

Harry looked like he might cry, so Gwen quickly changed the subject. 'What do you think?' She gestured to the fire. 'Censorship is alive and well.'

Harry opened his mouth but Cam was back, stuffing empty carrier bags into his coat pocket.

'Where were you today?' Cam said. 'I missed you at lunch.'

'Um..' Harry looked embarrassed. 'Busy. You know. Work.'

'Do you want to come back to mine for dinner, Harry?' Gwen said. 'We've got plenty.' She looked at Cam, who nodded.

'Well—' Harry hesitated.

'And there's cake. And wine.'

Harry hesitated. 'I need to make a phone call.'

'Invite her, too.' Gwen smiled sweetly.

'What?' Harry said, his face suddenly wary.

'Your mystery friend. She's invited for dinner, too.' Gwen paused. 'Or he's invited. If it's a—'

'It's a woman.' Harry's face had gone pale, except for two bright spots of red on his cheeks.

'What mystery friend?' Cam said.

'Honestly,' Gwen said, enjoying herself enormously, 'I would've thought a lawyer would show better attention to detail. The woman Harry has been seeing. It's about time we met her, I think.'

'Since when?' Cam looked at Harry in amazement.

'I am allowed, you know,' Harry shot back. 'I'm police. It's not like the priesthood.'

Cam's mouth hung open. 'I know that,' he said finally. 'I just thought you would've mentioned it.'

'Oh, for goodness' sake,' Gwen said. 'You two are as bad as each other. Hug it out or something.'

Harry and Cam looked at Gwen with mutual confusion. 'How did you know?'

Gwen fixed them with a witchy smile and said, 'I know everything.'

'Gwen!' Ruby rushed across the grass, towing a pink-nosed Katie by the hand. David followed, looking bemused. Gwen pulled Katie in for a hug, not caring if she was offending her delicate teenage sensibilities. Katie whispered in her ear, 'Mum's never going to let me out of her sight, is she?'

Gwen pulled back and beamed at her. 'Not a chance.'

Katie rolled her eyes and Gwen hugged her again, just because she could.

'I didn't have you pegged as a book burner,' David said over Ruby's shoulder. He patted Gwen's shoulder awkwardly. 'I hope it works. Whatever it is you're doing.'

'Thank you,' Gwen said.

Ruby looked around. 'Pendleford looks quite pretty at night, doesn't it? All the lights.' She looked back towards the high street. 'Do you remember when we used to hang out at that bus shelter on the high street? Hoping to meet boys, but only ever looking at them walk past while we ate chips from Gino's?'

'Absolutely not,' Gwen said, smiling at Cam.

Gwen leaned closer in to him. She watched the orange sparks flying up, listened to the crackle of the fire and enjoyed the sensation of his arm around her waist.

'Honestly,' David muttered, looking around with something close to fear. The crowd had dispersed a little, but some had laid down coats and were lying on the frosted grass, looking at the stars. Children ran in and out, waving glow sticks and shouting. 'Haven't these people got Sky?' He shook his head. 'This is a weird little town.'

Gwen waved her arms in an expansive gesture. She encompassed the brazier, the crowd, the town and, right on the boundary where it bled into the countryside, End House. 'I know,' she smiled, happiness radiating out to the tips of her fingers, 'I fit right in.'

***

ACKNOWLEDGEMENTS

A book is not a solo effort and this novel would not exist without the support and guidance of the Best Agent in the World, Sallyanne Sweeney.

Huge thanks, also, to Sally and Victoria, and the rest of the team at Carina UK.

And, finally, thank you to my friends for believing in me, encouraging me and keeping me (mostly!) sane. Special thanks to the We Should Be Writing crew for their wise words, thoughtful critiques and boundless enthusiasm.

Also from

CARINA

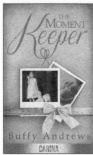

Your parents make you who you are.

But how much do you really know about them?

After her father's sudden death, Evie leaves her life in Dubai behind and returns to England.

Evie knew that coming home would be hard. But, whatever she expected, she's definitely not prepared for her whole life to unravel in front of her. And, as one secret after another is uncovered, she begins to realise that everything she thought she knew about her family has been one big lie…

Sometimes, one small mistake can have life-changing consequences...

One blistering summer's day, Ellen Moore takes
her eyes off her baby.

Not for very long, just for a few seconds. But this
simple moment of distraction has repercussions that
threaten to shatter everything Ellen holds dear.

Powerful and emotionally charged, *Little Mercies* is
about motherhood, justice and the fragility of
the things we love most.

'Totally gripping' —*Marie Claire*

'Her technique is faultless' —*Sunday Express*

www.mirabooks.co.uk